THINNER, BLONDER, WHITER

THINNER, BLONDER, WHITER

Elizabeth Maguire

CARROLL & GRAF PUBLISHERS • NEW YORK

THINNER, BLONDER, WHITER

Carroll & Graf Publishers
An Imprint of Avalon Publishing Group Inc.
161 William St., 16th Floor
New York, NY 10038

First Carroll & Graf edition 2002

Book design by Michael Walters

Library of Congress Cataloging-in-Publication Data is available.

ISBN: 0-7867-1019-5

Printed in the United States of America
Distributed by Publishers Group West

For Karen

THINNER,

BLONDER,

WHITER

THINNER

Who among my generation does not remember the days of Black Power with a smile? Who does not have at least one delicious memory of forbidden conquest? We believed that the spiritual and sexual seduction of the white female would cause the white male to implode, to turn in upon himself. With our hair free in Afros, we told those young white lovelies—would-be Freedom Riders, filled with moral indignation and good intentions—that failing to sleep with us constituted racism.

Thank god, those days are over. Now at least in the sexual arena we are free to love one another, black, brown, beige, white, yellow, without coercion or condescension. You could say that, in a sense, we have joined forces. After all, who has benefitted more from affirmative action than all those wonderful white women?

—Samuel Reid, from the preface to *A Native Son Bears Witness*

1

Sam always had a thing for white women. Ever since Annette Funicello had twinkled at him from the television screen, ears and breasts alert. But I was the first white woman he had ever truly loved, he said. His safe haven.

No one wants to hear what draws you to a married man. That never stopped me. Once I even tried to explain it to my brother Corky and his friend Fitz. We were sitting in the night auditor's office at the hotel where Corky worked, waiting for a wedding party to wind down. Back when I could still slake my thirst for scotch without throwing up blood. Back when Fitz's gentle presence could hold my brother on this side of the line between sanity and oblivion.

"So, tell me, Julia, is it true that black men won't go down on their women?" asked Corky, grabbing the bottle of Johnny Walker Black he'd lifted from one of the bar stations. He filled our plastic cups and threw the empty bottle in the metal bin beneath the desk. The clang of glass told me that it hit another bottle when it landed.

"Jeez, Christopher Moran, watch what you say to your sister, will you?" warned Fitz.

"I just want to know what it's like to ride the Soul Train," said Corky, rotating his hips so that the unsteady seat of his swivel chair spun around in a circle. "Tell us the truth, Jule. Is it really as big as they say?"

Fitz spit out his diet ginger ale. "What, are you drunk already?"

I let the smoky burn of the scotch warm my belly. I thought of Sam. The curved whites of his eyes, the indignant flare of his nostrils. The pale vein of a stretch mark etched into his honey skin just above the hip. Why did I think my brother could understand?

"I'm not even going to dignify that question with an answer," I said. "Though the answer would be: yes."

"That's my Julia!" laughed Corky, sliding wet lips across my cheek.

"I have to go check on the desserts. I'll be right back. Make yourself at home."

The labored beat of a wedding band thumped from another floor. Fitz left to give himself an insulin shot. I placed my plastic cup, now almost empty, on the desk and closed my eyes.

Naked, I was straddling Sam's lap, tracing the contours of his face with my sticky fingers, trying to see through him, into him, inside him. Licking the salt off his damp skin, tasting the oil that clung to the tight stubble of his beard. With a sigh he stroked my hair and lowered his mouth to meet my white flesh. "I've never seen such a pale shade of pink," he said, and then he swallowed me, a whole breast disappearing between his full lips. I moved in rhythm to our breathing, straining to get closer than skin and muscle would allow. "Without you, there would have been no book," he murmured, holding himself still inside me. When I cried out, he put his good hand over my mouth. "You'll never know," he whispered as he nuzzled the nape of my neck, "you can never ever know."

When my brother returned he found me asleep, my cheek pressed into a deep dent in the metal filing cabinet that was wedged between the wall and my chair. He shook my shoulder.

"Julia, you must be having some bad dreams. You were moaning in your sleep. Wait right here." He returned with a styrofoam cup of black coffee and a paper plate that sagged beneath the weight of a yellow square crusting with pink and purple rosettes. I looked at him, confused. "Wedding cake. Only the middle section left." He shrugged.

I poked the frosting and sucked the sugar off my finger. The margarined sweetness hurt my teeth. "Ouch, Corky. Time to look for a new baker," I said, gulping a large swallow of the coffee.

Fitz tipped two aspirins out of a plastic pillbox that he dug from the frayed pocket of his khakis. He handed them to me with a small bottle of water. "Come on," he said, taking my hand in his, "I'll walk you out." He led me through the lobby to the deserted taxi stand.

"I should know better than to try to talk to my brother about anything real," I said. The late-night traffic rushed by, ignoring us. "And you don't have to wait."

The light of an empty cab appeared at the corner, nearly hidden between a bus and a stretch limousine. Fitz jumped into the street and waved his arm at it, talking to me over his shoulder. “Don’t get so bent out of shape, Jule. He just worries about you.” The taxi slid into the hotel’s small circular driveway. Fitz ran behind it to open the door for me. “Besides, your brother’s curious. Who isn’t?” he asked.

I grazed his freckled ear with a kiss. “He should worry about his own love life. Curiosity killed the cat.”

“I’ll keep that in mind,” he said, with a tight laugh that sounded like a puppy sneezing.

William Fitzgerald, called Fitz by all who loved him, stood smiling on the steps of the hotel as my driver slipped into the stream of cars on Seventh Avenue. When I turned around to wave he was still shaking his head, his long red curls dancing above the heads of the two Colombian bellhops stuck with the night shift. He wiped his eyes on the sleeve of his blue shirt and patted the shoulder of the short man to his left as if they were cousins. It was the last time I ever saw him.

2

Death announced by answering machine should stop the tape. Erase the beeps with a screech of pain. But it doesn't. Instead, it lingers in the air while the machine moves on to credit card collectors and friends who wonder why they haven't seen you in a while.

So I found out about Fitz's death while I stood naked in the living room of my railroad apartment. I was drying myself in front of the fan, twisting around to see if power funk aerobics was having any effect on the round backside reflected in the mirror behind the sofa. The news deserved a more dignified hearing. As it was, I had to rewind the tape and play it again to be sure I'd heard my brother correctly.

His voice was small and tight, the way someone sounds after swallowing helium. "Julia, it's Corky. You won't believe what happened. Fitz is dead. I'm the one who found him. Here at the hotel. They just took him away. I don't know what to do. Call me. Please."

With the second hearing I lost my balance. The old wing chair caught me and I rested on its arm, trying to imagine my small universe of family and friends without Fitz. The terse patter of his Bronx Irish accent echoed in my ears. But I would never hear it again.

The fan caught me in the hum of its breeze and then turned its head away.

I dialed my brother's number at work, but a busy signal brayed back at me. Each time I pressed redial I met the same shrill sound. Finally, I pulled on jeans and a white T-shirt, slipped on sandals, and hurried down the stairs to search for a taxi in the swelter of the New York evening.

The Seventh Avenue entrance to the Pan American Hotel presented a steel and glass front that looked like it belonged in a suburban strip mall of an early and tired vintage. Tonight the lobby was crowded with busloads of women wearing tightly waved hair and crinkly warm-up suits. I pushed my way through the cloud of their berry-scented cologne, and marched down a hallway to an unmarked panel of buttons and a sliding door that warned "Employees Only." This was the elevator to the second floor bar and service kitchen, where my brother ruled as the Director of Food and Beverage for one of midtown's biggest convention hotels.

The secret life of the hotel took place in a netherworld that looked like the wings of an opera house. Tables on their sides. Gilt chairs with red plush seats folded against the wall. Tall stacked shelves on wheels huddled by the steel-topped wait stations. The smell of steamed food on the burners. Brown men speaking Spanish, running around in white coats.

And in a steel cage that doubled as a short-term liquor supply closet sat my brother, commander of all he could see. Above his head hung a crowded fly strip and a laminated three-month calendar thick with streaks, the new events marked in purple felt pen: "Rotary Club," "Brooklyn Democratic Club," "B'nai B'rith-Kosher." Boxes of scotch and vodka teetered in chin-high stacks. My brother was hunched over his gray metal desk, chopping lines of cocaine with a credit card. Tino the headwaiter stood by his side. He handed Corky a rolled twenty-dollar bill. My brother leaned over and snorted a line.

"Corky." I rattled the door of the cage. "I'm here."

He finished sliding the bill along the second line of white powder, and stared at the track he'd left behind. I shook the cage door again and called his name. He lifted his head and turned his swollen neck. The pretty face that had tormented my teens had disappeared. Now he looked as if someone had hooked a bicycle pump to his mouth and inflated him with air. Slowly, his eyes sought me out, as if in darkness.

"Julia?" he asked, his brow pinched tight. "At last." He pushed his chair into Tino's thigh and opened the door. "Julia. Fitz is dead," he whispered. His face collapsed like the brown paper lunch bags he used to fill with air and punch to scare me when we were kids.

"I came as soon as I got your message." I threw my arms around him and waved at Tino to leave us. Corky sank into his chair and let his head fall against my stomach.

I hugged my brother as I had hugged him a hundred times before, rocking him gently with my hands resting on his shoulders, while the sounds of the kitchen clattered behind us and the slightly sickening smell of overcooked chicken filled the air. Looking down at the top of his head, I realized with a pang that his hair was thinning. When we pulled apart, Corky grabbed a paper napkin from the desk and blew his nose. A spot of blood spread through the cheap paper.

"Is it really a good idea to be doing that right now?" I asked, looking at the desk.

"I need to pull it together for the Queens Baptist Fellowship. The Ne-gro reverends have a big dinner scheduled tonight." He took a gulp from a glass filled with brandy and pulled his lips back from his gums, just like the talking TV horse Mr. Ed used to do. He rolled the twenty tight again and held it out toward me. I shook my head no. With a finger pressed tight on one nostril he vacuumed up what was left on his desktop.

I grabbed the bill out of my brother's hand. "So what happened to Fitz? Was it the diabetes? Did he go into some kind of sugar shock?" I asked.

Corky blinked at me, confused. "Diabetes? What are you talking about?"

"I'm talking about: how did Fitz die?"

"I thought I said on your machine. He was murdered, Julia. I found him in the freezer. Lying on top of the ice."

"Murdered?" I reached for his glass and lifted it to my lips. I gulped too much and coughed most of it back through my nose. Corky handed me one of the paper napkins. "Where are the police? What did they say?" I asked, through the burn of the brandy.

"They were here all day. An army of them. The last two left just before you got here." He took the glass from me and wrapped his own trembling hand around it. "I didn't even call you until the ME gave the okay to take him away. They couldn't tell how long he'd been dead because of the cold. What it does to the body and stuff." His voice faded so that I could barely hear him. "I found him this afternoon when I opened the ice locker. Not the big walk-in one but the long chest inside that makes all those thousands of cubes for the banquet bar stations. Someone had dumped him in there. His eyes were open and rolled back in his head. Ice cubes everywhere." Perspiration dripped from his forehead to his ears and down into the tight fold of his collar. He shivered.

I did not want to know what all those freckles looked like dead and frozen. "But how did he die? Exposure to the ice?"

"No blood. No gun. That's all the cops can tell so far. I can't think about someone hurting him. He was the best. You know?"

"Has someone told his mother?"

"The detective said he would call. But I'm going to have to talk to her. And his sisters. Reg and Mary Ann and all the rest of them." A couple of fat tears slid down his cheek. "Julia, I'm scared."

"Of course you're scared, Corky. I'd be terrified if I found my best friend dead." I stroked his arm. "Do you have any idea why someone would do this?"

"No clue." He took a deep breath and squeezed his hands between his legs. "I've been so busy, for August. Canadian radiologists one night. Queens chamber of commerce the next. Weddings in between. What if the whole thing is my fault?"

"How could it be your fault, Corky?" I looked over his shoulder beyond the cage to make sure Tino and the other waiters were out of earshot. My brother stared at his hands. "Did he do as much of this shit as you do?" I pressed, sliding the credit card through the white streaks on the desk toward him.

"Not Fitz. You know he never touched the stuff. And I don't really do a lot myself, Jule. It's just a service to the night staff. . . . " He fought to keep the wobble out of his voice.

"Right. That's why you're sitting here with powder on your nose, two seconds after the cops leave. Did Fitz help you provide the service?"

"Never. It's just Lee and me. But we've got everything under control."

"You don't owe anybody any money?"

"Of course not. Sometimes we're a little behind, like a month ago, but not right now. Right now we're golden." He snorted, coughed, and swallowed the bitter postnasal cocaine drip with a grimace. I fought the urge to pour the contents of the ice bucket on his desk over his dumb head.

"Okay. Nobody needed to make an example out of him to scare you. Then how could it be your fault?"

He rubbed his eyes with the heel of his hand. I pinched the inside of my arm so that I wouldn't hit him.

"Corky, if you don't get to the point I'm going to scream."

"Okay, okay. We were supposed to have dinner last night after I got off work, but I blew him off," he said, looking at his feet. "The sous-chef and I were going off to score."

"So?"

"Look at this." On his desk sat a large date book with a cover that advertised Bartucci cocktail olives. He opened the book and pulled a square of yellow paper from its middle. Corky's name was written on the paper in block letters circled by little dashes. Slowly, he unfolded the paper, as if it took all his concentration to keep it from flying out of his hands. He smoothed the creases flat with his palm so I could read the message written in blue felt tip pen.

> Hey buddy—don't forget about dinner tonight. I stepped in shit and you're the only one I can talk to about it. I need to ask your advice before it's too late. See you at ten. Fitz.

I winced at the sight of the familiar handwriting, neat and slanted just like the nuns taught us to do. "Corky, this doesn't say anything. It could have been girl trouble, for chrissakes."

"No, it wasn't. I can feel it."

"You're driving me crazy here." I sighed.

"Then look." He opened one of the drawers on the side of his desk and slid the hanging folders to the front. From the back of the drawer he extracted a portfolio of imitation leather with a zipper that went around three sides. The peeling brown vinyl left smooth patches of polyester. Just like the pink blotches Fitz had on his nose after every summer sunburn flaked off.

"What is this?" I asked.

"Fitz wanted me to lock it up for him in the petty cash safe two days ago. I was supposed to bring it to dinner last night," he said. His arms hung limply by his side as if he were reciting the "Song of Hiawatha" in Sister Edith's third grade assembly. He stood, waiting.

I unzipped the folder and looked inside. It was filled with dog-eared standardized reading tests and the kind of multiple choice answer sheets that require a number two pencil. Patterns of lead circles danced on each page. Red corrections flared in abundance. An inside pocket of the case held some pens and a cassette tape and a small calculator.

"Corky, this looks like homework from his tutoring job. What's the big deal?"

"He asked me to hold it for him." He sniffed.

"That doesn't mean it has anything to do with his death. But if you think it does, why didn't you give it to the police?"

"And have them on my ass, thinking I did something wrong? No way. Then they'll start looking at my every move. Not right now, Julia. You know what I mean." He tapped his nose.

"Corky, you can't have it both ways. You have to tell them—"

"Not yet. Not until I figure out what was going on. All I know now is that if I'd been there for Fitz last night, maybe he'd be alive now." He started gasping in hard fast breaths. I thought he might be having an asthma attack. "Julia, you have to take this briefcase for me," he said.

"So I can be the one who's withholding evidence? No thank you."

"You're the one who says there's nothing important in there."

I opened the portfolio flat on the desk like a butterflied chicken breast and reached my fingers deep into the inner flap. What should I be looking for? I flipped through the answer sheets topped with names. "Shabil Hazaaz," "Maria Gonzales," "Murphy Jones." On the top was a handwritten list of scores by name, in alphabetical order. Tidy. Just like Fitz.

"Have you shown this to anyone else?" I asked.

"No," he insisted. "Fitz said I was the only one he could trust. And you're the only one I trust. You have to take it. Please." Wet streams dribbled from his nose. His hand gripped tightly around my arm. "I'm begging you. I can't look at it."

Something desperate in his voice cut through the cocaine and the grief and the familiar wheedling. Underneath it all sounded a note of terror. "Corky, what is it?"

"What if I do the wrong thing with it? Lose it or give it to someone or let someone take it? No one can fool you. But I'm the one who's worthless. Unreliable. Stupid and worthless and full of shit." He started kicking the cage, grunting and crying as the wire mesh shook beneath the force of his foot. "Maybe I should just blow my own brains out and make it easy for everyone," he shrieked. Two waiters carrying trays of salt and pepper shakers stopped and looked at him through the wire of the cage.

"Okay, Corky. Calm down!" I grabbed his shoulders. "No flip-outs at work. Remember to breathe." He stopped and tried to look at me, but his dilated pupils couldn't stay focused on any one point for very long. Rutting moans sounded from somewhere deep in his chest. "Touch metal," I said, just as I'd first done when he was twelve years old and I discovered him lying on the storage bin in our basement, his back pressed against the concrete wall behind him, his cheek against the cool surface of the metal storage chest. That had been the day he'd tripped and blown the relay in the state finals for his junior high track team. The day he began all the maneuveurs and tricks and disguises that led to the ribbon of cocaine in front of him now.

I pushed him into the chair and held him there with my hands on his shoulders. "Touch metal," I repeated. He nodded and placed his palms flat against the desk.

"Now, here's what we'll do," I said gently. "Tonight I'll take the briefcase home with me, and I'll keep it until we decide what else to do with it. But I think all that blow is making you paranoid, isn't it?"

He sniffled. "There's nothing in there." I found another paper napkin on the desk and started wiping the damp streaks off his upper lip and his cheeks. His soft face went limp as I cleaned it. His hands relaxed and slipped into his lap.

"You're probably right, Jule. It will turn out to be nothing. But it makes me too nervous. I can feel him looking at me with those blue eyes. You know?" He was still swallowing gasps of tears.

"I know, Corky. I know." I smoothed his hair. "You're in shock."

"Thanks, Jule. I'm so glad you came." Relief revived him, filled him with easy hope.

I folded Fitz's yellow note and slipped it inside the portfolio. I zippered the case and tucked it beneath my arm. "Be careful, Corky. Slow down on the blow. You're upset enough. It's going to make you crazy."

"Absolutely, sis, absolutely. Now I've gotta go to work." He opened the top drawer of the desk. A blue silk tie was neatly folded in one of the compartments designed to hold paper clips. Corky unrolled the tie and threaded it beneath his collar. He tied a perfect knot without glancing at the hand mirror that sat in another one of the drawer compartments. He stood up and lifted a navy blazer off a hook that was clipped to one of the links of the cage. "I have to make sure that the filet mignon is cooked enough for the ministers. These folks like their meat well done." He licked his middle finger, swiped it across the white smudge on his desk, and smeared the residue on his gums.

"Cut the crap, Corky."

"Sho' thing. And get me a cor-vwa-see-ay." He looked at me over his shoulder as we walked out of the cage, almost daring me to hurt him back. "Those reverends sure love their brandy, even though Baptists aren't supposed to drink. But you know all about that, don't you?"

"Yeah, well, maybe you should try it. The not-drinking part."

"Sista Julee is dry this week because of her tummy aches. But next week it will be back to Dewar's and soda, maybe just a little bitty bit of blow."

So already he was making his jabs, needing to equalize things between us now that I'd talked him down off the ceiling. I ducked to avoid three waiters carrying trays filled with plates of pale lettuce covered with shredded carrots. Corky picked some carrots off a plate with his fingers and popped them in his mouth. "Hey, Tino. Get this. My sister doesn't party anymore because her black, married, one-handed boyfriend is giving her an ulcer." The waiter, such a close friend of my brother's that he'd asked Corky to be godfather to his new baby girl, stopped and stared at him with implacable brown eyes. Like me, he'd seen these aftershocks of embarrassment and rage before.

"You asshole," I said, pushing to escape through the pack of white coats.

"Whoa, Jule, don't get mad. You're so uptight these days. I miss having fun together," he said, pulling at my shirt. He slipped a thick arm around my waist. "I don't know what I'd do without you."

"I can't do this anymore, Corky. Especially not now. Don't forget, Fitz was my friend, too."

"I know. I can't believe I won't hear his voice tomorrow. Scolding me." He cocked his index finger at me, and attempted a smile. "You better straighten up your act, Moran," he mimicked. His face looked like it might crumble again. I gave a reluctant peck to his sweaty cheek.

"I'll call you as soon as I find out anything, okay?" he said. Then he turned toward the steam tables and clapped his hands. "Okay, guys, let's get a move on with those salads. *Vamanos!*"

I left the kitchen through a swinging door and found myself in an empty ballroom, its sad walls covered with flocked red wallpaper. Through the ballroom door I entered a carpeted corridor that was filled with dignified black men in dark suits and stiff white shirts, strolling toward another ballroom down the hall.

Get every bottle of VSOP my brother has in stock, I thought as I watched them. That way there's less for him. From the broad stairway at the end of the hall, I ran down to the main lobby, desperate to shake off the acrid smell of the place. The hot cloud of the summer night enveloped me as soon as I was spit out of the revolving door. I headed east toward Sixth Avenue to find a taxi to take me back uptown. Fitz's relic, the sad vinyl briefcase, stuck to my skin where I held it tight under my arm.

It was hard to imagine anyone hurting William Fitzgerald. He had always been good without being a prig. Someone who could get through years of fraternity life without touching a beer, and still win the affection of everyone around him. Even my self-destructive brother had been devoted to him. When the Catholic school where Fitz worked burned down, Corky had given him a job in banquet sales so he could earn some money while training for the certification he needed to teach in public school. And now he was dead. Corky's best friend Fitz. Murdered in Corky's hotel.

The horn of a limousine howled at me. I ran to the planted divide in the middle of the avenue with the briefcase clutched to my chest. The black car sped away. I looked again, surprised by the greenery around me. St. Bartholomew's dome loomed before me, and the discrete deco facade of the Waldorf Hotel was on the corner to my right. Without realizing it, I had left Sixth Avenue far behind and come as far east as Park. On the wide sidewalks, normally deserted at night, small groups of tourists strolled in search of the slightest caress of a breeze. I decided to keep walking myself and catch a bus on First Avenue.

Without Fitz, Corky would be more in the thrall of Lee Cohen. The third of their college trio. The charmer who spent all his free time sitting around Corky's office, waiting for Fitz and Corky to be done with work. The idea of Lee and Corky dealing drugs and partying with the night staff, using curses and slang they'd never once heard over the family dinner table, was almost laughable. Old fraternity brothers inventing an imaginary wise-guy past. Where had it led them?

A bus groaned to a stop and opened its doors at 50th Street on First Avenue. I climbed up its steps into the chill of the air-conditioning. My shirt was wet with perspiration. It clung to my skin like the wet strips of newspaper I had failed to master the winter my mother was on a papier-mâché angel campaign. The doors of the near-empty bus closed behind me and we lurched forward. I slid into a seat and pressed my face against the window, watching the ugly commerce of First Avenue speed by.

Two teenage boys jumped on the bus, laughing, dragging oversized duffel bags behind them. Their cheeks were flushed with the rosy patches of exertion, and large felt numbers pulled at the thin fabric of their nylon athletic shirts. Corky had once looked like them. But sports had brought him none of the natural antidepressive properties now advocated by mental heath gurus and personal trainers. I remembered one particularly awful night at dinner his sophomore year of high school. Corky had been disqualified from the quarter-mile sprint for the third time in a row. Too many false starts. My father kept asking in his most outraged and rational voice how someone could have possibly, I mean possibly, been so stupid. Each time he'd asked the question, the sarcasm became more pointed, the voice louder, until finally he screamed, "If you're too much of a wimp to compete you don't have to humiliate yourself in public too, do you?" Corky had just disappeared into himself. He'd stopped eating, stopped breathing, even. Sat in his chair, still as a possum, until my father pushed away from the table in disgust. After that, every day when Corky came home from practice he'd tell my mother he was so tired from the workout he had to take a nap. She'd smile at his labors, but I knew better. Finally one afternoon I'd gone to his room and pulled the large foam earphones off his head. He opened his bloodshot eyes and smiled.

"You're stoned, Corky."

"I hate running," he'd whispered. "Round and round in a circle. It's sick."

"Then quit. Do something else. This is crazy."

"Dad would kill me. After all, I'll never get the grades my precious big sister gets." He'd put the headphones back on and rolled over, his back to me.

Now Corky was scared and angry, just as he'd been then. Did he know more than he'd told me about Fitz's death? That would explain why he was so frightened, so guilt-ridden. Or was he just suffering the easy remorse of a drunk who hadn't been clearheaded enough to notice what was going on? I squeezed the shabby briefcase and thought about Fitz. The gentle, sober one, racing from one job to another in his threadbare clothes. Looking for help, though no one knew why.

At last, I surrendered to a sob. As the bus rolled northward, I used the frayed paper napkin I found in a pocket to wipe away my tears.

3

And now, before we continue with our liturgy, some of those who loved William would like to remember him to us," said old Monsignor McGrath in his best navy chaplain voice. Slowly he made his way down the steps from the lectern that was raised high above the Bronx congregation like a kind of Gothic ladder and bucket, lifting his white robe in his thick fingers as he descended. He genuflected with some difficulty midway in his path across the altar, and lowered himself into one of the wooden chairs behind the small podium from which laypeople were allowed to do readings or make announcements.

The people on either side of me shifted in discomfort. Oh great, I thought. Whole point of a funeral mass is to postpone the private testimonials until the cocktail hour. Now we have to wail like Baptists.

A short woman in a suit that had fit her better three children ago climbed out of the second pew and walked around the coffin that filled the center aisle at the front of the church. She moved toward the podium with a bowlegged athletic stride that probably worked better with sneakers than pumps.

"I'm Regina Fitzpatrick O'Donnell. Most of you know me as Reg. I'm William's oldest sister." She adjusted the stem of the microphone so that she didn't have to stand on her toes to speak into it, and brushed a strand of died blond hair off her forehead. "I want to say something about William's special place in our family. Why we all thought of him as the littlest angel."

I turned away from the sight of her face, which was pulled so tight with sorrow that she looked as if she were squinting at a sign in the far distance. My eyes found the stained glass window of St. Francis that glowed above the Fifth Station of the Cross on the wall to my right. Veronica washes the face of Christ. It was late in the morning on a hot August day, and the sunlight that streamed through the small open window below Francis's feet painted Veronica's veil with an eerie brightness. Reg held it together for longer than I expected, like the tough girl she'd no doubt once been. It wasn't until she started talking about how her own kids would never know their uncle that she fell apart.

"Thank you, Regina," said the priest, putting his arm around her. She nodded, instinctively wiping the thick eyeliner that had begun to melt around her eyes. "Now William's close friend Christopher Moran would like to say a few words," he continued.

Reg made it down the steps from the podium. She stopped in front of the casket and made the sign of the cross before sinking into her pew, where family members threw many arms around her. A little girl with tight blond braids climbed onto her lap and wrapped herself around Reg's neck. They rocked together.

I twisted around to watch my brother approach the altar. No one stood up in the sea of dark suits.

"Christopher?" asked Monsignor McGrath, peering into the congregation.

A sandy-haired man in a navy blue blazer and khakis hurried up the side aisle. As he neared the front of the church, I gasped. It wasn't my brother. Instead, it was Lee Cohen.

He took the steps to the altar two at a time and slid behind the podium without missing a beat. "Corky, I mean Christopher, is too upset to address all of you today," he began. "My name is Lee Cohen, and the three of us were very tight in college. So tight that people called us the Three Musketeeers. So, I'm going to tell you a story about what William Fitzgerald meant to us."

Lee was completely at ease. The natural politician. The seducer. As I knew all too well. Wasn't that why I'd had that disastrous affair with him all those summers ago?

"Fitz was our fraternity brother in college, upstate. As you know, guys in a fraternity tend to do a little bit of partying in their free time," he said with a delicious, bad-boy shrug. The crowd actually chuckled. Like a pro, he waited just long enough for them to quiet down. "One day, Fitzgerald stood in our lounge and said to Corky and me, 'what if you took the time and money you spend on drinking just one Saturday a month, and used it to help someone in need? I know families right in this town who live in broken-down homes, without enough money to clothe their kids.' " Lee breathed deep and looked around the church, stopping to meet the eyes of the people he found there. The microphone could have been a daisy, for all he needed it. He gripped the front edge of the podium, and leaned forward. "The amazing thing is, Fitz had the power to rouse us, to get us to do something. Soon it wasn't just the Three Musketeers, but the entire fraternity. We called it the Fitzgerald fund. Once a month we took our booze money—which was embarrassingly high, I can tell you—and fixed somebody's broken boiler, or bought a kid a coat, or took an old lady to the doctor. Somehow Fitz always knew who was in trouble. When he got so sick"—he folded both hands before him—"before they figured out about the diabetes, we tried to give him the Fitzgerald fund to get home to New York. He looked at me from his hospital bed and handed the envelope back to me. Know what he said? 'No thanks, buddy. Give it to somebody who needs it.' "

The woman next to me choked in a sob. It felt as if the entire congregation began to cry at the same moment. Even Monsignor McGrath brushed his hand across his eyes. I fixed my gaze on Veronica's veil, again.

"William Fitzgerald was the finest man I've ever known. He will live with each of us every day of our lives. Thank you." Lee dipped his head and left the altar.

Monsignor McGrath lowered his mastiff-shaped head to the microphone. "With this mass we celebrate the passing of a soul to eternal life with Christ. And yet, it's hard to remember that we are supposed to be celebrating, when we are so saddened by our own loss. Like you, I am selfish. I don't want to say good-bye to someone who brought me as much joy as William did. It is the hardest farewell of all." He walked to the center of the altar and raised his round palms to the ceiling. "Let us pray."

I prayed and stood and knelt and prayed without having to think about my words or my movements, just as I'd done every Sunday of my life until I went away to college. During communion I squatted in my pew, eying the long lines for a glimpse of my brother. From the choir stall behind us the parish's best soprano sang a warbly "O, My Redeemer" to the overwrought chords of the Italian organist. Corky was nowhere in sight.

At the end of the mass the Monsignor approached the coffin, flanked by two younger priests, one Korean and one Indian, and four altar boys. I realized with a start that the freckled twelve-year-old gripping the crucifix so tight was Fitz's nephew Brian. A spicy, dry smell filled the air as the Monsignor waved the long chain that held the censer around the coffin. He intoned the familiar words about granting eternal rest unto him, oh Lord. I whispered the response, "And may perpetual light shine upon him," wanting the words to come true. The pallbearers—all of whom were Fitz's brothers and cousins—took their places around the coffin. When the six men, ranging from bald to gray-haired to blond, hoisted their load onto their shoulders, the finality of their task shook me. I too began to cry, along with the women who followed the coffin down the aisle.

It took a long time to inch my way out of the church, behind the crowd of cousins and friends and neighbors. At last, I found myself on the massive gray stone steps of St. Brendan's. Mrs. Fitzgerald stood on the sidewalk below like a stout pigeon, calmly instructing her distraught brood of daughters, as well-wishers gathered around her, trying to offer condolences. The men from the funeral home loaded flowers into the hearses with expert precision, as husbands shouted to their wives about who should follow whom to the cemetery, and in what order. I stood alone, watching, until Lee tapped my shoulder.

Without thinking, I threw my arms around him like I had not done for several years. The day's event had thawed the frost that usually chilled any exchange between us.

"Lovely talk, Lee."

"Meant every word of it, Jule," he mumbled.

I pulled away, smoothing my hair. "Where the hell is my brother?"

"He's here. He's just incapacitated. Emotionally, that is."

"Where?" I scanned the sidewalk. I saw only women in knit suits and men loosening their ties in the midday sun, thinking about the drinks that would come later. Two little boys in plaid jackets and clip-on bow ties jumped up and down the stairs. Then, in the doorway of the church, I saw him.

I ran up the steps. Corky withdrew behind the carved door. I followed, my eyes blinded for a moment as they readjusted to the darkness of the vestibule. My brother was holding on to the rack that displayed the weekly bulletin and the *Catholic News*. I was relieved to see that he was impeccably dressed in a black suit with a dark blue tie. A starched white collar pressed against his full, cleanly shaved neck.

"What's going on, Corky? Where have you been?" I put my hand on the fingers that were clenched tight around the thin wooden slat of the rack.

"I can't face the Fitzgeralds again, Julia."

"Face them? You're supposed to be grieving with them."

"I can't. I feel so ashamed," he blubbered. Tears streamed down his face. Lee coughed from the doorway a few feet away. Corky leaned toward me and put his finger to his lips as if to say, "Shh."

"Look," I said, "You have to go to the cemetery at least. You owe it to Fitz. You don't have to go to the lunch afterwards."

"Come on buddy," said Lee. "I've got my car. We'll go together. You and me and Julia."

"No. I can't," I said too quickly. "I mean, I don't feel comfortable. I'm not as close to them as you guys."

"Okay then, just Lee and me," said Corky, sniffling. He looked at me with injured eyes. "Unless the two of you were enjoying a little happy reunion?"

I handed him one of the tissues in my pocket, and pressed my mouth to his ear. "Don't start that crap now," I whispered. "Fitz deserves better than that."

"You're right." Corky blew his nose. "I'm sorry. Everything is screwed up today."

"Lee, somehow I just know that you have a cell phone I can

borrow for a second," I said. He pulled it from an inner pocket of his jacket and flipped it open. "I'll meet you guys outside in a minute," I said, giving my brother a shove. "Corky, tell Mrs. Fitzgerald you've been here. Go."

Lee put his arm around Corky's shoulder and led him down the steps. I punched in the number of my voice mail at work to see if Sam had called to confirm our dinner. Four messages, but none from him. I dialed his private office number, dragging my fingers through the slightly oily contents of the holy water font while I listened to the familiar litany of instructions. Callers interested in a speaking engagement should contact his lecture agent, graduate students should call his secretary. The rest of you, it better be important, and here's the beep.

"Sam, it's Julia. Since you haven't called to say otherwise, I'm still planning to meet you tonight at five o'clock. My place? It's been a terrible week. I need to see you. Bye."

I snapped the phone shut, and leaned against the stone arch of the doorway. Lee handed Corky a pill, which he swallowed. For once, I didn't mind.

Near the hearse stood a policeman in a blue uniform, talking to a tall man in a black suit who could have been one of the family, judging from his pink complexion and his thick auburn hair. The tall man crossed his arms and kept his sunglasses trained on my brother while they spoke. I didn't like the way he followed my brother's every move. He took a few steps toward Corky without seeming to lose the thread of his conversation with the cop.

I ran to my brother's side and put my arm through his.

"These Catholic funerals are a major production, huh?" asked Lee, lighting a cigarette with a slim silver lighter. "That wake last night. Yuck. Give me shiva any day. No dead bodies."

"My mother always said that wakes are important, because they give closure," I said. "But I've always thought they were morbid. You guys going to be okay?"

Lee nodded and patted my back a little too low down for comfort.

I kissed my brother on the cheek and began to make my way toward

Bainbridge Avenue, where the D Train began its route in the Bronx. At the corner I looked back and saw my brother collapse on the solid shoulder of Mrs. Fitzgerald. It was better than seeing him hide in the shadows. I kept walking, past the proud brick two-family houses, past Dempsey's Tavern and Grill, where according to family legend my father had once tried to court my elegant mother with a pitcher of beer. I'd actually eaten lunch there with my grandmother, on those rare occasions we went out together without benefit of my father's car or credit card. I stopped at the open door and stepped inside, breathing the thick sweet smell of beer and roasting lamb. All the tables had been pushed together in four long lines. Waitresses in black skirts were setting places, while a skinny teenage boy with a notepad walked up and down, counting chairs. It looked like the funeral lunch would be held here, just like my uncle's had been. The bartender looked up from the bottles he was arranging, squinted at my black dress, and called out, "They back already from Gate of Heaven?" I told him it would be at least an hour before they returned from the cemetery, and kept on walking.

There was always a train waiting with its doors open for the signal to leave the 205th Street station, as I knew from all the times I'd visited my grandfather at Montefiore Hospital around the corner. By habit, I looked for a car that already held other female passengers, and sat down across from two round nurses speaking Haitian French. I plopped my bag on my lap and hugged it, thinking about my brother. What had he done, to feel too ashamed to speak at or even attend his best friend's funeral?

Some nagging part of me knew that I should also feel ashamed to leave the funeral to do what I planned to do. Yet shame was the one emotion that had always been missing from my repertoire. I was actually desperate to escape the tears and the scotch and the overcooked lunch, to lose myself sliding on Sam's body in the heat. A bell dinged and the doors of the subway slid shut. As we pushed ahead I anticipated the taste of Sam, though in my heart I knew there was a very good chance I'd end up eating dinner alone that evening.

4

All week Fitz was with me. He seemed to be sitting in my ear, whispering stories of times gone by. But there was still no news from the police about what had happened to him.

I sat at my desk at Beckham & Coates, staring at our new catalog. Its cover announced in bright pink letters the slogan that someone in marketing had come up with to explain our identity as one of the last serious publishers not under the control of a TV or film company: "Extra-large ideas for medium-sized minds that want to grow." Attached to the catalog was a note from my assistant, Kit: "Sounds like we're selling elastic-waisted pants! Send to our standard agent list? Draft letter attached." I sighed. Fitz would have found Kit lacking in the virtue of modesty. I picked up a pen to cross out the ten glowing adjectives I knew I'd find strung like pearls in the first sentence of Kit's copy.

"Julia, listen to this. Your pal Mel dropped it off while you were at lunch." I looked up. Kit leaned in my doorway, holding the latest edition of the *Weekly Watch*. "Did you read Bob Cameron's publishing column? I quote, 'Beckham & Coates' Julia Moran is the race woman of the New York publishing scene. First Sam Reid's Pulitzer . . . next, who knows? Keep your eyes on this prize!' Way to go, Julia."

"Kit, Bob's just an old gossip looking for things to say about the Literacy Volunteers benefit."

"Who cares? There's no such thing as bad publicity, right?" Kit folded the newspaper in a neat square and lifted an eyebrow. "Nice flowers."

I smiled at him without acknowledging the pink-tipped cream roses that sat in a glass bowl on my desk. Kit knew he was not allowed to say who they were from.

"Several messages, too. The last was from an airplane," he said, handing me the afternoon's messages, neatly typed on a single sheet of paper. Never in my life had I encountered an assistant who raised efficiency to such a high art. I would have grinned, but three of the five calls on this list were from Sam.

"They're always from an airplane, Kit."

"Well, someone sounds very desperate to talk to you. Anyway—do you want to give me back the letter to send out with the catalog? I've done the labels," he added.

"First, I need to finish revising it." I waved my felt tip pen in the air. "Please close the door so I can concentrate, okay? Thanks." A small twitch of impatience tugged at the corner of his mouth. He shut the door without a word. I laid the pen on top of the catalog.

The race woman. It was true that I had a reputation for turning professors, politicians, and poets into commercial success stories. And after Samuel had made the best-seller list, I'd also become known as one of the premium editors of black books. "You think you would be 'queen of the Negro people' without me, white girl?" he had once asked with a laugh, before ripping a hole in my bra and pushing me to the floor of his hotel room. But long before he'd won the prize I had sought out the manuscripts, persuaded the writers, cajoled the agents. It was my chance to ride for freedom, thirty years later.

Now I sat surrounded by stacks of submissions, folders holding book proposals sliding like cards in a loose deck. I couldn't bring myself to look at them. In the shadow of Fitz's death, none of it mattered. I spun my chair around and tilted it back, resting my eyes on the stone curlicue that swept up from the cornice of the building across my gritty window. Still no word from Corky. And Sam was only frantic because he'd stood me up last week. What would be his excuse this time—the demands of the new post at City University, his lucrative lecture circuit, his wife? Or did he just want to be sure I'd still help his friend, the Reverend Vaughn, publish his memoir? The phone rang. I decided not to let it go to voice mail.

"Julia Moran."

"Hello, beautiful." The timbre of Samuel's deep voice always surprised me, pleased me. But I remembered that I was angry with him.

"Funny how you can always find time to call me when you really want to," I snapped.

"I always want to, baby. But last week I had to meet the governor. And the family came into town for the dinner."

"Well, I'm a busy person, too. You could at least respect me enough to let me know when plans change. I left a goddam funeral to see you."

"You're right. I need to be more considerate. I hate to make you unhappy." These conversations had taken on a ritual life all their own. I was almost bored hearing us recite our lines.

"It scares me that I don't even expect to count on you anymore, for even the smallest thing. Especially at a time like this," I said.

"Time like what, baby?"

"A close friend of the family was murdered. My brother's best friend. At the hotel where my brother works."

"Julia. Why didn't you say? Let me be with you, make you feel better."

I fought the flash of longing that shot through me. "It's a little late for sympathy."

"I can give you more than tea or sympathy, Julia. What do you think I want to do right now?"

A reluctant flicker moved between my legs. "What?"

"I want to arrive at your office, unannounced. You will look up from your desk to find me standing before you. Then I will close the door. And put a chair beneath the doorknob so that no one can come in."

"Why?" I breathed into the phone.

"You will be silent. You will rise from your chair but I will push you back on that desk, so that all those damn papers fly to the ground. I will hitch up your skirt around your waist, and rip those panty hose down around your knees."

A flush of wet dampened my underpants. "And?"

"I want to see that nice white ass of yours lifted in the air, baby, as you open yourself for me. And then I will fuck you like you've never been fucked before. Very slowly. Very sympathetically."

The only sound was my slow and heavy breathing. It echoed on the telephone line as if I had my mouth on a microphone.

"So, my lovely Jule, I'll meet you at your place in an hour?"

"I can't, Sam."

"Baby. . . ."

"I made other plans already."

"I'll cancel the dinner with Belafonte. For you."

"Sam, I—"

"Don't say no, Julia. I've been calling you all week. When you won't speak to me it's like a part of me is broken."

"Okay. Okay. I'll reschedule Gordon, but I want to go out. No Chinese food."

"I hear you, baby."

In three hours we were sitting on my lumpy sofa, eating eggplant with garlic sauce and prawns with black beans. We were both naked except for the cotton T-shirt that Sam never removed. I'd unfolded a small tray table in front of him, since it was difficult for him to hold a plate with the gray fiberglass claw that was strapped from above his elbow in place of a left hand. I'd seen him pass a tray, hold a glass of wine, and pick up a fork with that claw, but I knew it was a strain to balance anything for too long.

"I know you wanted to eat out, Julia. But I love being alone with you in this little room. It's my private port in a storm," said Sam, pressing my hand to his lips.

The CD player moved to the next disc. Slow piano, a hint of a drum, and a sad horn.

"So you found the Ellington-Coltrane recording I told you about. That's my girl. Always in a sentimental mood." I put down my plate and curled against him in his lap. He gently picked and pulled at strands of my hair. "Grief creeps up on you, doesn't it?" he said softly.

I nodded and pressed my wet eyes against his T-shirt. He raised me to him and I stayed there against his neck, holding on as tight as I could—partly for Fitz, partly for Sam and me. When I felt Sam's hand caressing my thigh I sat up and gave him a soft punch in the shoulder.

He smiled. "Forgive me for saying this when you are blue, Julia. But you are the sexiest woman I have ever known. Truly sensual." He lifted a bottle of beer to his lips, taking a long, gulping swallow. In bed, Samuel himself was fast and efficient, as if he were running a race without me. But the fierceness of his desire, his hunger, turned me inside out. I could spend hours exploring him. The patches of fuzz in secret places. The gray ash on his elbows when they were dry. The folds where his skin became inky black or the swells where he lightened to gold. My fingers slid under his T-shirt to the curve of his stomach. When I stretched my hand up toward his cheek he stopped it in midair, squeezing with the full force of his good hand.

He purred, "And, you are one of the truest friends I have ever had. I depend on your love. It sustains me."

Lately, Samuel's talk had been filled with these references to the power of our friendship. It had to be one of the reasons my stomach was starting to hurt all the time. Three years into the affair, I was beginning to suspect that couples therapy with his wife must be working. But we both knew that I could not bring myself to ask. Instead, I resorted to Samuel's favorite subject: himself.

"I hear that there was quite an uproar when you spoke at the Garvey projects in Brooklyn last week," I said. "When you were with the governor?"

"Those damn fools. They wouldn't recognize Martin if he came back from the grave and sat on their laps. It's as if their parents have taught them nothing. No self-reliance. No pride."

"Well, you can't always reach kids who are fourth-generation welfare with pride. The only pride they see wears a big gold chain and sells crack," I said.

"Don't lecture me about the 'hood,' girl. I snap shut the locks on my car doors just as fast as you would in that neighborhood. I hate that authentic ghetto crap." Frowning, he let the prosthesis fall onto the small table, rocking it dangerously.

"No kidding, Sam. I helped you write the book. Remember?"

He chuckled. "Indeed you did. Indeed you did. You are my partner in crime." He stood up and stretched his arms over his head. "You know how hard I've been fighting the university for another head for the Graduate Center? Well today, Alan Feiner, the CEO of Feincom, agreed to endow a full professorship! A chair in the 'history of African-American expression.' So I'm free to make it music, dance, art, literature—whatever I want. Now I can steal Brad Winston from Columbia."

I bounced on my haunches and clapped. "Sam, that's fantastic! That's a lot of money, isn't it?"

"Three million dollars, baby," he laughed, slapping his good hand against mine. He howled and did the dance steps he always described as the Funky Chicken, though they looked more like cheerleading to me. "I knew it was worth advising his son's undergraduate thesis myself, before I left Princeton. Can you imagine? Little Jacob Feiner on the history of Blue Note Records?"

"Sam, you didn't."

"I did. And I didn't give him the top grade either—that's how we got the money. He respected me for making it a 'magna minus.' Knew I couldn't be bought!"

I jumped up and held his face between my hands. "Samuel Reid, you're a genius."

"Damn right. Kid barely deserved a pass, let alone a 'magna minus.' And Dean Smithson will still owe me a slot. Ha!" He narrowed his eyes and gazed hard into mine. "Am I smarter than my friend Elijah Vaughn?"

"No contest."

"Has he called you yet? What a fantastic life story. I think you should let him dictate his memoir on tape and then transcribe it."

"Sam. I'm not in the mood to talk about work right now."

"You're right, baby. Come and kiss these African lips."

He pursed his full lips and slowly enveloped my mouth in his, chewing on my lips and my teeth and my tongue. I slid into the crook of his good arm as we both fell to the sofa. He held me there until I almost stopped breathing. When he stopped kissing me he pulled me up to sitting position. "Be a good girl."

"What?" I breathed.

He leaned back with his legs spread wide apart. "Suck my dick, sweetie. Tell me you love my black dick."

"I think I've already established that fact tonight, don't you?"

"Please? Pretty please?" He blinked in mock desperation until I laughed.

I slipped to my knees before him, adjusting myself on the rug so that the hard floor wouldn't distract me from my task. Holding a breast in each hand, I cupped them around his penis and began sliding them up and down. I looked up at him and smiled.

"I love your dick, but not because it's black." This was our oldest joke. From the early days together when I had been afraid to laugh about the obvious fact of our colors.

"Silly white girl. Tell me you love my black dick." He pulled my hair so that my head was tilted far back.

"Samuel Reid, I love your black dick." I did, too. It was a beautiful brown color, fading to a grayed black at its roots. Not all purple and angry-looking like so many others I'd seen. I bent my head and took the fullness of him in my mouth, running my tongue up and down as I sucked. I reached for his right hand and moved it beneath mine to help me finish him off. The whole time I could feel the weight of the fiberglass on my right shoulder. When he was done, I rested my head on his thigh, and wiped my mouth with the end of his T-shirt.

"Well, I have to get the last bus to Montclair, beautiful."

My stomach twisted. I struggled to say, "I thought you were staying in the city tonight."

"No, baby, I can't. Now don't ruin the whole evening by making a scene."

His nonchalance was brutal in a way that the accent acquired during those years at Princeton could not hide. But I knew from experience that a fight would not end well. Without a word I stood up and walked to my bedroom, where the sheets were still tangled in a ball at the end of the bed.

Fuming, I rummaged to find a T-shirt and shorts, while Sam showered in the bathroom on the other side of the kitchen. I pictured him standing in the ancient claw-footed tub, the vinyl curtain that hung from the overhead ring clinging to his legs like seaweed. At least he would hate the feel of the plastic against his body. When he emerged, a towel around his trim waist, he tiptoed through the kitchen as if he might step on a crab. As he pulled on his pants he looked up at the flakes of paint that had begun to curl in the corner of the ceiling.

"You should live in a more modern space, baby."

"This is a great apartment for Manhattan. If you don't like it, feel free to share some of those lecture fees with me, genius."

I watched him knot his sea green silk tie, amazed as always that he could actually do it. He tipped my chin up with the fingers of his good hand, whispered, "I love you. I'll call tomorrow," grabbed the jacket of his pearl gray suit from one of the brass hooks by the door, picked up his expensive leather overnight bag, and dashed out the door. His footsteps disappeared down the three flights of stairs. I kicked the Mexican rug in frustration.

Standing at the bedroom window, I saw two taxis refuse to pick up Sam before he grabbed the door of a third and jumped in. I walked back through the two narrow rooms of the apartment, opening the windows that dotted the outside wall to get rid of the smell of eggplant and sex. If only I could still drink, this would be the moment. But when I took a sip of the beer he'd left behind, all I could taste was sour soap.

When the phone rang an hour later, I thought it might be Samuel calling from his cell phone. Just before I leaned over to pick it up I heard the sound of my brother's drunken voice on the answering machine. "It's Corky. Jewel of the Morans. Where are you, diamond-head, sapphire-slut? Are you fucking that bastard?" He burped loudly. "Call me if you get home. Don't forget we have to go see Gramma tomorrow," he mumbled, and hung up the phone.

By the time Sam did call from what he said was the street approaching his driveway, I was in the bathroom throwing up the Chinese eggplant.

5

I sat on the stoop in front of my apartment building, waiting for my brother to pick me up for our monthly visit to our grandmother in the Bronx. It was a hot, still Saturday morning—so hot that anyone who could leave town already had. I sipped the iced coffee I'd bought at the deli on the corner and assessed the aspiring squalor of 89th Street between First and York. It was lined with tenements, anchored by a full-service high-rise at either end. My landlord had just installed two antique-looking lamps on either side of our front door, but the left one was already listing westward. It was another reminder that our building had never been elegant or refined. It was just old.

A stooped woman in a faded housedress and a wilted straw hat shuffled by, leaning forward on a two-wheeled shopping cart. She was the only other person on the street at ten-thirty in the morning. I could hear the hum of air conditioners and an angry siren in the distance. Corky was late, as usual. Maybe there was traffic from Long Island. For reasons that I didn't fully understand, he liked sharing half of a two-family house with Lee in a distant part of Queens. All I could figure was that it offered the illusion of suburban comfort.

A beat-up looking white Pinto stopped in front of my building. I didn't recognize the car, but I did know the man behind the wheel. It was Lee Cohen. The man I usually avoided, only inches away and for the second time this week.

"What's going on?" I asked, squeezing behind the bulk of my brother and sliding onto the turquoise vinyl.

"My car is unavailable," said Corky. "Lee's working at a Youth Job Corps office in the Bronx while he studies for the bar exam. He said he'd give us a ride."

Lee had put aside his Jewish heritage to graduate from St. John's

Law School, a Catholic institution that was supposed to be a seeding ground for the career in New York politics that he craved. Despite their ecumenical policy it had taken a substantial donation from his father to get him in, and probably more to keep him there.

"Lee, since when do you work on weekends?"

"Julia, hon, you should learn to be more trusting. Devoted public servants like myself work all the time." From the driver's seat Lee turned around to smile at me. The curve of his almond eyes and the perfect bow of his full lips were as disarming as ever. They hinted at depths that weren't, in fact, there. But they were one of the reasons I, and so many others, had surrendered to his charms.

"What's the deal with this tin can? Where's the ancestral Saab?" I responded, looking away.

"You can't park the Saab among the afflicted, my dear. It's too much of a temptation for them. On the other hand, no one wants this piece of shit. Even its parts have low market value."

"Parts is parts," chuckled my brother to himself as we turned up First Avenue.

"Why aren't we going to the FDR Drive?" I asked.

"Your brother has an errand to run," replied Lee as he swerved to avoid hitting a group of children dancing in the spray of a fire hydrant. "It's a short stop in Spanish Harlem. You know—where the rose grows." He turned onto 128th Street and stopped in front of a string of burned-out buildings.

"What the hell is this?" No one answered me as Corky struggled out of the car. In his long-tailed pink shirt, khaki shorts, and gold-rimmed sunglasses, he looked ridiculously out of place. Two black boys in baggy pants, looking no more than eleven or twelve years old, stared at him without moving from their spot in the rubble as he nodded and walked up the steps. I didn't want him to disappear inside that building.

"Should someone who works for the city be doing this?" I asked.

"Doing what, Julia? I'm just sitting in a car, minding my business."

"Then what about my brother? He's in enough trouble already. You're not helping."

He answered me with one eye on the street, one eye on the rearview mirror. "Yes, I am helping."

"No, you are a couple of asshole white boys in way over your heads."

"Jule, I am recouping an investment and helping to get your brother out of debt."

"My brother needs rehab, not another drug deal."

"Well, as the saying goes, I believe that he needs to figure that out for himself. Sort of like Dorothy and the ruby slippers, huh?" He winked at me in the mirror.

"I don't want to see him ending up like Fitz."

"Fitzgerald was a man who did not know how to handle life's shades of gray. For him, the world was black or white. Right or wrong. Your brother, on the other hand, understands gray very well. Gray is where he lives." He drummed his fingers on the steering wheel.

"My brother lives under a fluorescent bulb, in a twenty-four-hour-a-day world that's white all the time. Not gray. And how can you be so matter-of-fact about Fitz? What about all for one and one for all and all that other male-bonding fraternity brother crap?"

"You know that I'm heartbroken about what happened to William Fitzgerald. He was one of the best people I ever knew. A piece of me is gone." He tapped his chest above his heart with his fist. "I would have helped him if he had asked me. But he didn't. And I can't do anything to change that now, you know?"

"Helped him with what?"

"Whatever it was that got him killed, Jule."

Corky emerged from the building with a folded newspaper under his arm. Once he was sitting in the passenger seat he nodded at Lee, who slapped his thigh.

"Good. All set. Now to the Bronx. Land of our fathers," said Lee.

We left the island of Manhattan by the grimy Willis Avenue Bridge, the route taught to each of us by our parents because it was one of the only approaches to the mainland that didn't charge a toll. We sped past the watermelons that were stacked by the road at the Bronx end of the bridge; past the auto parts dealerships that baked in the sun; past the twenty-four-hour McDonald's that no one we knew had ever entered. Lee made a set of turns on streets I didn't recognize, until we were heading northward on the Grand Concourse.

I looked out the window at the empty stores. Colored plastic banners hung limp in front of dirty windows. Plantains, flowered dresses, and tube socks for sale.

"When Grandma was young the Concourse was elegant—designed to be a boulevard in the European tradition. She could rent a horse and ride all the way to Yonkers," I said. We stopped at a light in front of Borough Hall.

Lee looked out the window. "The Yankees must be playing at home today. Too many niggers on the street for a Saturday, when the courts are closed."

"If the two of you start this I'm getting out of the car," I snarled. "Since when did you decide it was funny to talk this way? You only sound like idiots."

Corky laughed and said, "You can't say the n-word in front of Julia. She loves the Negro people."

"That's right. And I'm sure they love her."

"Meaning what, asshole?" I asked.

"Meaning you're oh so kind and full of understanding," said Lee. "Write my book for me, Sista Julee." He caught my eye in the rearview mirror. "I heard your man Samuel speak on behalf of this Reverend Vaughn who's challenging the mayor in the primary. He's quite a performer. I'll bet he would have a future in politics if it weren't for that hand, huh?"

"What's the hand got to do with his future in politics?"

"Well, I don't think the general public would embrace it, do you? Black *and* differently abled? It's a little too PC for prime-time TV."

We circled around beneath the Concourse onto Kingsbridge Road. Lee stopped the car across the street from the small white clapboard house that was once Edgar Allan Poe's cottage and was still proudly pointed to by Bronx grandparents as a testament to their borough's lost cultural standing. Now, standing amid the shabby apartment buildings, it looked like a modest suburban house that had woken up in the wrong neighborhood. Lee pointed to a small storefront in the bland redbrick building to our right. A tall black woman in a pantsuit the shade of canteloupe stood in the doorway talking to a cop. "That's my Job Corps development office. Right below the headquarters of the local community board. Paid for with your tax dollars." He honked twice. "See that woman? She runs the office. Absolutely gorgeous. But all she cares about are these stupid pregnant teenagers. I can't get her to give me the time of day. Yet." He waved to her, and rounded the corner. He pulled the car into an alley and said, "Be right back."

He grabbed the newspaper from Corky before jumping out of the car.

"I can't believe we're with this jerk. What is he, your new babysitter?" I said from the backseat. My brother didn't speak or move. I wondered if he was still breathing.

"What's he doing? Moving dope out of this office?" I asked. Corky didn't answer.

Over the door frame someone had painted a circle with crossed lines that broke it into quadrants. I pointed it out to Corky and told him about a book I'd published on Southern folk art that cataloged all the signs of protection that were painted on shacks and barns to signal safe haven to runaway slaves. My brother said nothing. Lee appeared in the door beneath the painted circle, and threw his newspaper into the green dumpster that sat against the side of the building. He slid into the driver's seat and pulled out of the alley without a word and sped back up a street crowded with parked cars to the Concourse.

At the light he called out in Spanish to a young boy and girl who were trying to open a fire hydrant. They replied, laughing, and he answered them before giving a honk. I fought a glimmer of admiration for his command of another language.

"So how'd you get this job, Lee?" I asked.

"Short answer is: my dad. Same as last summer. The local Democratic Club handpicks the paid staff for this office, so they can make sure that the kids who get jobs through the program don't step on any union toes."

Corky woke up: "Remember the summer after sophomore year when your dad got both of us jobs working for the Morris Park Democratic Club? They sent us to deliver subpoenas to invalidate the signatures on that Puerto Rican guy's nomination?"

Lee howled. "Oh man, those bastards met us with shotguns at the door. Wooo! We ran out of there. . . . "

"Jule, you wouldn't believe how much time those local clubs spend invalidating each other's petitions," Corky continued.

"I guess I wouldn't," I mumbled.

"Politics is dirty business. I guess that's why I love it so much," laughed Lee. "But what goes around comes around. Now that same guy is a friend of my dad's. His son even works as an assistant to the education deputy for the mayor. A *colega muy ambisioso*." I stared out the window as we passed block after block of apartment buildings in the yellowish brick of the 1930s and the Bronx. Lee made a U-turn and stopped in front of one that looked pretty much like all the others. He jabbed his thumb at the broken fountain that sat neglected in the courtyard of the building. "Next stop, Bedford Park. Tell me the Grand Concourse is still grand, Jule."

"Thanks for the ride, Lee."

"I'm going to stop by my dad's office. I'll be back in a few hours to pick you kids up, okay?"

"Make it no more than two," said Corky, as he slammed the car door.

Silently, Corky and I walked through the crumpled papers and empty cans that filled the courtyard of the apartment building where my grandmother had lived for almost forty years. Corky pressed the buzzer. Nothing happened. I pulled the spare key out of my bag, though we didn't need it. The heavy brass door opened to our touch. We ignored the elevator and made our way up the stairway, careful not to touch the old stucco walls thick with grime. I smelled the good, pungent scent of Puerto Rican *soffrito*. Someone was sautéeing the garlic and cilantro for rice and beans.

My grandmother's dark apartment reeked, as always, of boiled potatoes, though I'd never seen her boil any. "Hello, dears. Come in.

How nice to see you." One leg had been shorter than the other since she broke her hip, so she favored that side, wearing an orthopedic shoe and throwing herself against the wall as she walked. Pictures of grandchildren filled the top of the baby grand piano that hadn't been played since my grandfather died.

"Have a drink?" she asked.

Corky took off his sunglasses and I saw that his eyes had almost disappeared into his face. "No thanks, Gramma. Just a Coke."

Relieved, I said, "Me too."

She returned with a tray that swayed precariously. I took it from her and said, "What do you need us to do?"

"Oh, just change the filter on the air conditioner in the bedroom. The super don't care that it's so choked up with dust it don't work." Corky went down the hallway to the bedroom. "And your mother bought me new white sheer curtains before they went to—where'd they go?"

"Sante Fe, New Mexcio."

"Yeah, that's right. Santa Fe. Your grandfather was there before we were married—when he sold silver. Before the depression."

"Yes, that was before you met him."

"When I met him he was still traveling. Me, I stayed put. I was born on 203rd Street and I'll die on 204th Street. I haven't gone very far in my life, have I?"

I stood on a chair near the window and began pulling the old thin curtains, dark with soot, off the rod.

She continued, "Then your grandfather lost his job and we had nothing. Your father didn't grow up lavish like you kids. But we had some good times." Her hands were fluttering in her lap. She heaved herself out of the chair. "I think I'll cut that nut ring," she said, and swayed out of the room.

Corky came in sucking on ice cubes. "The filter's all done."

"Come here then and help me do these curtains," I said.

He stood obediently, sliding the dirty white fabric off the end of the rod.

"Lee shouldn't be in that job, Corky. He hates the people he's supposed to be helping."

"Naw, he doesn't. He loves the work. He grew up on it. His father's an old friend of the mayor's. They were old Bronx Democratic Club stooges in college, before Manny Cohen went into the family business and the mayor became an assistant DA. Even now Manny spends half his time brokering deals for city contracts. He's an incredibly connected guy in the Democratic party."

"So is Lee's father going to take the bar exam for him, too?"

"Come on, Jule. You just don't want to believe the guy has any strengths." I aimed my foot at his thigh, but he blocked the kick with the curtain rod. "The bottom line about Lee is that he just loves old-time city politics. He's the only Jew I know who wishes he were Irish, or even Italian."

His hands were shaking so hard that he had to rest the naked rod against the window. He dug into the pocket of his shorts and found a lint-dotted handkerchief that he wiped across his damp forehead.

"Corky, where is your car?" I asked, still standing on the chair. He looked up at me. Finally, I could see his eyes, and I found only terror and confusion there.

"I don't know."

"What do you mean, you don't know?"

"I don't remember," he hissed, and picked up the rod again.

My eyes were burning with dust and tears. "This has to stop."

"You're telling me," he grunted.

"When did you lose it?"

"Last night. I got really fucked up because I was upset."

"About Fitz?" I shook out the new curtain and starting inching it onto the rod.

"Sort of. Yesterday morning I came into work and someone had broken into my office. Used a crowbar to open the drawer I keep locked."

"Did you tell the police?"

"Naw. Just hotel security. The general manager is afraid we're going to get a bad reputation if we keep going to the cops. Insurance might go up, too."

"Maybe one of your staff just wanted to see if there were any goodies hidden. Grab a bottle of scotch to take home for the family."

"Not my guys. I give them anything they want. They don't have to steal it. Besides, no one went near the liquor that was there. All of the cases are unopened. VSOP brandy, Absolut, Johnny Walker. Untouched."

"Then maybe someone was looking for petty cash?"

"Everyone knows I don't keep cash in the second floor bar office. But someone threw my files around. My menus, my calendars, my budgets. Someone was looking for something, Jule. I think someone was looking for Fitz's briefcase."

"Why? Has someone left a threatening message that says, give me the briefcase or else—?"

"No."

"People steal things in hotels all the time, Corky."

"I know. That's what Lee said."

"Well for once Lee and I agree about something."

"Yeah, maybe you're right. But Lee doesn't know about the briefcase part."

"I didn't know you could keep anything secret from him."

He turned his head away from me. "That's what Fitz wanted," he said.

"Okay then. If you're really that worried, you have to call the cops."

"Not now," said Corky. He shook out the second panel of new curtains. "Quiet."

My grandmother rolled back into the room and threw a plate of coffee cake on the low table in front of the sofa. "So, what's new with you two? Keeping busy? Remember, you have to keep busy. Sit down and tell me what's happening."

Corky told my grandmother stories about the weddings in the hotel while I put new cedar blocks in her dresser drawers. The idea of someone breaking into my brother's desk scared me, though I didn't want to admit it to him. He was already more unhinged than I had ever seen him.

"You don't look too good, Christopher. Burning the candle at both ends?"

"No, Gramma. Just working hard."

She looked at him with a squint that warned she was no fool. "Your uncle Stephen used to look like you do. Shaking, sweating, jumping at the sound of a mouse. And I lost him. Everyone says he was an alcoholic. Your father says your grandfather and I should have kicked him out of the house. But your grandfather wouldn't do it."

"Well, how would putting Stephen on the street have helped him?" asked Corky, picking one of the sugared walnuts off the top of the coffee cake.

"It would have helped him see he couldn't go on the way he was. He had more than the others, but nothing suited. He was always miserable." She shook her head, still hurt. "You look like you're headed for the same thing, Christopher. Your parents gave you everything but nothing suits. Remember, if you decide you need help, you can always come here. I'm always ready to help you out of any trouble if I can."

"Thanks, Gramma. I'll keep that in mind." Corky got up to go to the bathroom and rolled his eyes at me behind her back.

A loud knock at the door announced the return of Lee. He presented my grandmother with a box of chocolates and a bottle of Irish Mist. She pulled him to sit by her side on the slipcovered sofa, happily holding his smooth hand between her two bent arthritic ones.

"Typical Lee to make us look bad," muttered Corky to me as we finished putting down the new Roach Motels in the kitchen.

"He's a man for women of all ages," I answered. We returned to the living room and sat down to eat a piece of the coffee cake while Lee made my grandmother laugh. He put her in such a good mood that she didn't seem upset when we said we had to go.

"You give that lovely William Fitzgerald a big hug for me, you hear?" said my grandmother, patting my brother on the shoulder. "I'd love to see that boy again."

"Will do, Gramma," said Corky, slipping out of her reach and ignoring my startled expression as he headed for the stairs.

Lee had parked the Pinto next to the fire hydrant in front of my grandmother's building. Of course, there was no ticket waiting for him beneath the windshield wiper. He held the door open while I climbed into the backseat. Corky slurped from a Dixie cup filled with ice cubes.

Lee slid into the driver's seat and pressed the cigarette lighter into the dashboard. "Best thing about these old cars," he chuckled. Without looking at the traffic he pulled out from the curb. "I've gotta tell you guys. Your grandmother is a pisser."

"Same as ever," said Corky, tilting his seat backward so the turquoise vinyl almost reached my nose.

"What was all that about Fitz when we left?" I asked, pressing back against the seat with my knees.

"Okay, Julia, I get the message, stop kicking me," said Corky. He played with the knob by his side and yanked his seat forward. "I didn't tell her about Fitz because I didn't want to upset her. You know how much she loved him."

"So you're going to let her keep asking? For the rest of her life?" I asked, slapping at the back of his neck. "What if she hears about it from someone who knows the Fitzgeralds?"

"I dunno, Jule. I didn't really think about it."

Lee touched the glowing red tube of the car lighter to the cigarette in his mouth and sucked. He slipped the lighter back into its hole, took a drag of the cigarette, and rested his left elbow in the open window. "So what's up with the cops, anyway? They say anything about what happened to Fitz?" he asked, shooting a look at my brother.

"The detective says he was dead before he was put on the ice. There was a major blow to his head. He had a small skull fracture, internal bleeding in the brain." I could hear my brother swallow, as if just saying the words made him sick.

"Jeez, Cork. That's awful." Lee paled. "They say who did it?"

"Nothing new about who, or why. This cop's been going through Fitz's address book. Contacting all his friends and family."

"Yeah. I talked to him last week. He didn't seem too sharp," said

Lee. We stopped at a red light. Lee tugged gold-rimmed sunglasses out of his shirt pocket and adjusted them on the bridge of his nose while looking in the rearview mirror. "Too weird if they never find out why it happened, huh? Why someone would leave him there on ice for everyone to see? It's freaking strange."

"So weird you have to figure it was done on purpose, right?" I asked. "Like it was supposed to scare someone?"

"Well, if that's what they were aiming for, it worked. I'm freaked out by the whole thing. Aren't you, Cork?"

My brother grunted.

"But you never know. Maybe it's just some nut job. We're talking about Fitzgerald, for chrissakes. The friggin' Boy Scout," said Lee. He flicked his cigarette between his thumb and middle finger and sent a small arc of sparks flying across the street. When the light changed, he switched into the fast central lane of the Concourse and made all the green lights until we reached the small battered sign marking the turnoff for the Third Avenue Bridge.

Corky just stared out the window, saying nothing.

6

"Come on, Mel," I pressed, "I don't want to go alone tonight."

"I hear you complain about him all the time. Do I really have to sit there and look at him, too?" said my best friend at work, crossing her long legs.

"Excuse us, Kit," I said, to the noble assistant who was sorting the contents of my outbox. He left my office with a loud sigh of frustration. I pushed the Metro section of the *Times* across the desk toward her. "See, Sam's one of the hottest items in town. His secretary sent me two tickets, complimentary." I didn't say, which isn't much compared to the old days, when he used to pick me up in chauffeured cars to ensure I'd be there, adoring, in the front row.

She scanned the column and handed the paper back to me. "Give me a break, Jule. Haven't you seen this show often enough? Seems to me you'd be better off keeping your distance."

"I have to go," I admitted. "Pat wants me to make sure that the head of that Sugar Hill imprint isn't there, trying to steal him. And I even have to write a puff piece about him for her monthly highlight report to Bob in corporate."

"You poor thing. I'm so glad that two of my girl power paperbacks are on the list this month," she said, wavering. "Keeps me off her radar."

"When you don't have a best-seller and it's your turn, I'll owe you, Mel. Big time."

It was true that Sam's first brushes with politics had been a wild success, despite Lee's doubts about how a prosthesis would play with crowds. His move from the ivied walls of Princeton to the grit of City University, where he now headed the program in African-American studies, was one step in a calculated drive to raise his visibility on the political landscape. And Sam's support of Reverend Elijah Vaughn's run for mayor had charmed the entire city of New York. Vaughn was an old-fashioned church man who had banished crack and gangs from his South Bronx neighborhood, attracting devoted followers, both black and white. Sam loved his role as the intellectual heavyweight who lent the reverend credibility. The *Daily News* had recently dubbed him, "the Brains behind the Baptist," and Sam pulled the clipping from his wallet with delight whenever he had the chance to show it to someone who might not have seen it yet.

But tonight was Sam's first solo appearance in months. His return to the redemptive act of public speaking. Lectures like these gave him an audience for the legendary Reid charm, a forum for flexing the famous Reid muscles of indignation. They also paid fees so high that they added up to more than half of his substantial income. The best perk, Sam liked to say, were the hotel rooms. Paid for by someone else, and almost always luxury, at his insistence. I had to agree, as I'd been inside many of them with him—late at night after the celebratory dinners were finished or early in the morning before he'd caught the next plane out of town.

So Sam was now a local New York sensation. And whether I wanted to or not, it was part of my job description as his devoted editor to bear witness to his events, and fend off the competition.

The determined line for Symphony Space stretched a full block down Broadway. Beneath our feet, the sidewalk still pulsed with the heat of the August day. I noticed the requisite middle-aged radical ladies in caftans, beads, and sneakers, and a few earnest lefty journalists I knew from what remained of the downtown alternative papers. But mostly we were surrounded by Sam's varied black fans: serious young men wearing pillbox-shaped African caps of orange, black, and green; thick fifty-something women with straightened hair and sensible pumps; laughing girls with enormous gold earrings; tired men in work shirts that had their names stitched on the pocket. Lions' manes of braids hung everywhere around us. By comparison, I felt distinctly plain and pale.

A caramel spaniel off its leash trotted to us and sniffed my calf. I smiled and offered my hand for more smelling. The dog embraced my leg, moaning with joy.

"You and dogs," said Mel. "I don't know what it is." A bearded man in a T-shirt whistled and the dog ran off with a yelp.

"I know. I keep telling myself that when I get my life together I can finally have one."

"Well, it's the last thing you need right now," she answered, lifting her sunglasses to rest on her head.

Mel stood like a blond giraffe above the beads and hair extensions. She'd just had a haircut and I had to resist the impulse to run my fingers up the razored ruff at the back of her neck, like I'd done to Corky when he was little. There was a row of small silver rings along the rim of her left ear, and she wore no makeup except for the plum gloss that made her full lips look constantly wet. I wiggled my toes in my sandals, already slick with perspiration, and shifted the enormous satchel I always carried to my other shoulder. My self-inflicted albatross, it hit my thigh with the dead weight of three unread manuscripts.

"Heard anything from Sandra?" I asked.

"Nah. The girlfriend is gone for good. After four years—can you believe it? One last terrible fight and she refuses to speak to me." A shadow of hurt passed across her green eyes. "She always was one for dyke drama." She shook her head at the bag digging into my shoulder and calmly untwisted its strap. "How is your brother doing, by the way?" she asked.

"Awful. I've never seen him so screwed up." The thought of him made me restless, impatient to move. I grabbed Mel's arm and pushed our way through the crowd in the lobby.

We found our seats near a side aisle in the back of the old auditorium. The air-conditioning was barely working, and despite the frantic whir of several old standing fans at the rear of the theater, our thighs wouldn't slide across the hot, tired nap of the frayed velvet seat cushions. Undaunted by the heat, people shouted and laughed and hugged as they scrambled up the stairways to the upper boxes. I felt as if I were only an office friend of the groom's mother at a large family wedding.

No one paid attention to the white man perspiring in his three-piece suit at the microphone, reading a list of Sam's achievements. "Great energy here, Jule," said Mel with a smile when he left the stage and the lights dimmed. "Looks like the stage is set for your man."

The crowd shifted in its collective seat before settling into quiet anticipation. In the darkness, one circle of light burned around the podium on stage. Samuel emerged from the wings and crossed the stage like an astronaut just before liftoff: a long-legged stride, arms swinging, square head held high. The high cheekbones were set off by the short hair that made him look young and clean-cut. My vintage Sidney Poitier integration look, he'd once said as we lay in bed. Guess which film? *To Sir with Love*? I'd asked, playing my fingers over the soft nap of his newly cut hair. No, he'd laughed, every black boy's favorite is, Mr. Spencer Tracy, may I have permission to fuck your daughter, please, sir? Then he'd put his good hand to work until he released himself on my tummy, saying, "*Guess Who's Coming to Dinner?*"

Now he walked to the podium and took a sip of water. He began to speak with slow, deliberate words. The man I knew best without his clothes stood alone in a navy pinstripe suit beneath the peeling ornamentation of the Symphony Space proscenium.

He began as he usually did, thanking the audience, the sponsors, his friends in New York. Then he widened the circle of his words to the familiar yet horrifying statistics about black men. More black men in jail than in college.

Oh Lord, said a man from the balcony.

More black boys dead before twenty-five than ever before in our history.

Lord, help us, shouted another man.

Leaning back from the podium, Samuel asked, "Confronted with such brutality, how do we love ourselves?"

He rested his fiberglass claw on the stand before him with a low thump that shook the glass of water. The crowd whimpered as one.

"How can we love our black bodies?"

Moans and cries shot out from different corners of the theater. The woman sitting in front of us called, "Amen."

"How can we cope when the world despises us, hurts us, scars us?" He waved the claw.

Mel leaned toward me while keeping her eyes fixed on the stage. "Did he lose the hand in a lynching or something?" she whispered.

"Nah. Accident with a power saw at his grandmother's house," I answered.

She hunched forward with her chin on her hand. I willed her to feel the spell Sam cast.

"Those of us whose parents educated us, expected the best for us, who felt that there was nothing we could not accomplish, must expect the same of our children. We must stop feeling guilty about our success. Didn't Du Bois speak of the 'talented tenth,' with his genius and his prescience?" In the rows closest to the stage, several older men in dark suits rocked back and forth, calling, "Say it, brother."

Sam was pacing back and forth now, his good hand clenched in front of his chest.

"There have always been poor black people. There have always been middle-class black people. There have always been rich black people. We are not a homogeneous entity. We are not defined by the most unfortunate among us."

Like a pot simmering, the crowd bubbled with splutters of applause and shouts. "They all love him," murmured Mel.

"Of course they love him," I said.

In the seat to my right, a man with a delicate mustache and goatee shook his head. "Not everyone," he observed. I followed the finger he pointed and saw half a dozen homeboys of varying heights and sizes assembling in the far aisle by the microphone stand that had been placed there for the question period. He clucked his tongue in disapproval. "Even if they disagree, they should show the brother respect. It's an enormous help to Reverend Vaughn to have the attention of the white media that Professor Reid guarantees. That should not be put at risk."

"Do you work for Reverend Vaughn?" I asked, ignoring Sam's baritone and the louder shouts from the crowd.

"I've been his right hand for many years. Now I'm in charge of the platform for his campaign." He dipped his head in a nod, "My name is Isaac Lord."

"I'm Julia Moran from Beckham & Coates. I'm a great fan of your candidate. In fact, I'm talking to him about publishing his memoir."

"I know of Miss Julia's reputation." He offered me his hand and I took the long dry fingers in my own. With his narrow eyes beneath round wire frame glasses, his long, flat nose, and his golden skin, he looked a little like a street-smart Mr. Peanut. We smiled at each other just as a thundering, earsplitting kaboom from the other side of the theater made us jump.

Several women screamed. Then the entire theatre went silent. Mel grabbed my hand, as the pulse in my neck jumped hard and fast. On the stage, Samuel had stopped dead in his tracks. He looked down at his torso as if checking for bullets before squinting out into the audience. From his expression you could see that he was confused, until his gaze fixed on the microphone stand in the audience. He planted his feet far apart, and faced his challenger.

A thick-chested teenager in baggy pants, a loose leather jacket, and a red scarf tied around his head stood with the microphone dangling from the cord in his hand. His other arm was extended forward, his middle fingers curled downward in rap artist style. He had swung the microphone against the wall, and the air still vibrated with the sound. Around him gathered friends in oversized clothing, folding and un-folding their arms, shifting from one foot to another. Isaac Lord touched a finger to my knee, and rose from his seat. He walked around the back of the theater and appeared in the other side aisle behind the boys lined up there.

The boy in the red scarf held the microphone to his mouth, and shouted, "You an Uncle Tom, man."

Samuel ruled from the stage, pointing his good hand at the boy.

"There is nothing white about excellence, young man. My mama would have tanned my behind for saying what you just said."

The crowd exploded in laughter and applause.

Isaac Lord whispered in the ears of the two boys closest to him. One of them pulled on the sleeve of the teenager in the red scarf.

With a scowl he slipped the microphone back in its holder on the stand. The teenagers marched out of the theater single file, arms by their sides like prizefighters. Isaac followed them, looking like a hip guidance counselor in his knit shirt and pleated pants.

"There was a time when any adult in a black neighborhood could discipline any woman's son. Perhaps we need to return to our sense of community, and take care of our children," bellowed Sam. The crowd exploded. Whistles. Shouts.

"Now," Sam asked almost primly, walking away from the podium, "Shall we continue?"

He proceeded with his usual pantheon of black excellence, concluding with the requisite favorite quotes from James Baldwin and Ralph Ellison. The nervous introducer, who had removed his jacket and vest, returned to moderate the thirty-minute question period. The aisle that had been vacated by the teenage boys was now filled with a queue of modest-looking older people, most of whom clutched a piece of paper on which I knew was scribbled the Question.

"Professor Reid, I am a great admirer of your work. I love my black family and my black church, but I am homosexual and so I feel I do not have a true place at the Lord's table. How can I love myself when my minister preaches against people like me, even as we sing in his choir?" asked a man with a gleaming shaved head. His muscles flexed with tension beneath his tight T-shirt.

"My son, you ask a profound and painful question. Of course your minister needs to embrace you and your gay brothers and sisters. Our people have a long tradition of tolerating our homosexual brothers at home—saying, well, you know, he's just that way—while criticizing them in public. But do not abandon hope. NO! I say, you must struggle to educate your church, your people. We love you, son. Yes, we do love you!"

The crowd shouted in affirmation. The gay man wiped his eyes and backed away down the aisle. Mel rocked forward in her seat.

"Professor Reid, I come to bear witness to hope. Two years ago, I was addicted to crack cocaine, living on the street. I had abandoned my children. All was lost." A thin woman wearing a blue hat with a fluttering net clutched a Hallmark gift bag to her chest. As she pressed her mouth to the microphone, her voice shook.

"I found hope. Through God and the teachers at my clinic. And reading your books helped me to hope. So I want to thank you, Professor Reid. I have made a tape of gospel songs inspired by the six lessons in your book *A Native Son Bears Witness*. I offer this to you as a gift, to thank you for helping me to heal."

"Bless you, my dear, bless you. You testify to us that any adversity can be overcome," said Samuel. On tiny bird legs the woman walked down to the stage, where Samuel bent over to accept the bag. Its yarn handle hung from his claw while she kissed his hand. Around me men and women shouted, "Thank you, Jesus."

Samuel took three more questions. A Marxist graduate student who distrusted white institutions was dismissed. A schoolteacher who wanted more commitment to our youth was applauded. A social worker who wanted to promote direct political action was encouraged. Finally, Samuel said, "Thank you for your love and support. I can feel the hope that lives in this hall. Take that hope, and if you are a registered voter in the city of New York, use that hope to nominate Reverend Elijah Vaughn as your Democratic candidate for mayor. It is time to take the institutions that our graduate student friend questioned tonight, those institutions that have been run by the white man, be he Irish or Italian, Jew or Protestant, and make them our own. The time is ours."

The crowd cheered. As the man in the suit stepped to the microphone to thank everyone for coming, people got up from their seats, ignoring him as they would the final credits to a movie. A crowd gathered at the base of the stage. More women proferred gift bags, and students held out copies of Sam's book for him to sign. The book that had won the Prize. Our book.

As I stood in the back of the auditorium I looked toward Samuel so that he would know I was present. I wanted to think that he gave me a nod as the mob pressed in around him. He lifted the claw in my direction as if to send a kiss with it. Then he turned his gaze to the people at his feet, who longed to touch him, to have just a few private words with him.

Mel and I shuffled out of the theater into the hot cloud of the city street. She touched my elbow, and softly asked, "Can we go to a girl bar downtown tonight?"

"Sure, honey, it's your turn to pick a place," I replied. "Let's beat the crowd, since we don't need to wait around for more autographed copies of the great work."

"You can say that again, girlfriend," she laughed, stepping out on Broadway to raise her arm and flag down a taxi.

It was a relief to be sitting on stools in one of the old, cozy lesbian bars on Hudson Street, even though the place was empty.

"So, what's the deal, Mel? Is every dyke in New York using up her last midweek share on Fire Island?" I took a small sip of a light beer and stared at a heavyset couple in jeans and work shirts who were trying to do what passed for a two-step to a k.d. lang song. The only other customer in the place wore a blond bowl hairdo and a navy blue suit that screamed "Wall Street." She sat at the other end of the long oak bar, crying into a martini glass. The bartender patted her arm.

"It's just a quiet night, almost Labor Day," Mel said. She picked up a matchbook from the stack on the bar, struck a match, and lifted the flame to the tip of her long, thin cigarette. A puff of mentholated smoke drifted toward me. "I guess we're all intrigued by the forbidden other, huh? Including Sam. And you. Remember that old saying?" she asked.

"What old saying?"

"Once you go black, you'll never go back."

"Stupid me. I thought I was just having an affair with a person who happened to be black."

"Sorry to throw a cliché at you."

The door swung open and a young transvestite hobbled in. She wore a pale blue sleeveless satin sheath, with matching bag and pumps. But her wig of layered brown hair was a little crooked, and one rhinestone earring was missing.

"The kind of dress our mothers wore, no? All she needs is a circle pin," I said, watching her sit nervously on a stool at the far end of the bar. Her frosted peach lipstick was smudged, exposing the face of the scared boy that lay beneath.

"I love cross-dressers," said Mel, "but she isn't very good at this yet, is she?"

"Do transvestites usually come to women's bars?"

"Every now and then." We watched her tilt her head back and lift a drink with a frothy top to her lips. Mel sighed. "God, I love queer people. There's probably a cherry in that drink—what is it, a whiskey sour?" She laughed at my impatient sigh. "Sorry, I forgot. Time to talk about the boyfriend."

"It's just that I've never seen Sam get hassled like he did by those teenagers tonight," I said. "He says it's been happening a lot on the road."

"Well, they're obviously not with the Nation of Islam, or the NAACP. Maybe they're agitators?"

A bra strap slipped down the transvestite's arm. She winced as she pushed it back up her shoulder.

"What do you mean?" I asked.

"You know. Divide and conquer. The opposition splits people's loyalties. Like those crazy independent candidates who always went after the black vote, the Hispanic vote, now even the gay vote. Or people who join organizations as troublemakers or informers. Take that bitch Monica who turned out to be a plant in my LABIA group."

"What?"

"Lesbians Are Bitches In Action. It's a direct action group—kiss-ins, wheatpasting flyers, stuff like that. Every time we had a meeting, Monica would push people into strange arguments. Until we figured out that's why she was there."

The two-stepping couple were now leaning against the jukebox necking.

"I think those kids tonight were legit. I just can't figure out why they hate him so much."

"Julia, please, it's not as if the guy has such a great message to deliver to inner-city kids. I think he's lucky they don't charge the stage and carry him off." I opened my mouth to protest and she squeezed my wrist. "Don't argue with me. I can see he's brilliant. I get it. He appeals to the over-thirty crowd's shared experience and makes them feel they can have more, just like he does. It's a great performance. But it's all about sharing the status quo, not changing it. And besides—he's still a creep." I popped a goldfish in my mouth, and sucked the powdered cheese taste out of it without saying a word.

"Look," said Mel, "Why don't we go sit with our friend down there. Show her how to use a lip liner before she reapplies her lipstick? Okay?"

"Okay."

We moved down to the end of the bar. With a flourish of gallantry, Mel struck a match to light the cigarette the transvestite pulled from her beaded purse. The gesture seemed to restore her confidence and she sat more erect, the cigarette held high between her polished fingers. It was only a matter of seconds before we learned that her name was Juliana. It was so close to mine that the next whiskey sour convinced her that we were soulmates. When Mel slipped off her stool to find the bathroom, Juliana turned toward me. I noticed that moving her arm made her wince again.

"Did somebody hurt you, Juliana?" I asked

"No, dear, not really. I just should have left a certain situation before I did tonight."

"I know what you mean. I never leave when I should. It's as if my feet are frozen in place."

"Oh, darling, isn't it the most awful thing? My brain was saying, just go, Juliana, and you'll be all right, but I couldn't follow my own advice. Believe me: stay away from married men."

I spit a mouthful of beer into a napkin.

"You start out thinking it's going to be so romantic—but it's not. You're too angry and disappointed, and it all turns ugly."

I picked up the matchbook that Mel had left on the bar and lit the fresh cigarette Julianna was tapping on her palm. She exhaled a beautiful smoke ring and excused herself to make a phone call. A wave of old hurts flickered across my belly as I ground the match into the ashtray. I thought of hotels I should have checked out of. Restaurants I should have walked out of. Conversations I should have ended. Flights out of town for forbidden rendezvous with Sam that I shouldn't have booked.

Funerals I shouldn't have left. A brother I should have kept a closer eye on.

Mel returned to her bar stool.

"Did you notice anything strange about my brother this summer? Like when we all went out to that house in Quoque for the weekend?" I asked, pushing my full bottle of beer toward her.

"Strange such as—?"

"More depressed than usual? Strung out?"

"The only times I saw him, Fitz was there by his side. He was so good for Corky—could calm him down, keep him straight. Corky seemed to really depend on him. Though I have to admit I never understood what Fitz got out of it himself." She took a slurp from my bottle. "You, I get. The loving older sister. No explanation needed, even when the brother turns psychotic."

"It's not as simple as you think," I said, gesturing to the bartender for a glass of water. I gulped several cold mouthfuls, letting the ice fall against my teeth. "I remember sitting in my parents' backyard one warm twilight last spring. Just as the breezes were becoming warm—when you want to open your mouth and swallow the air like cotton candy. Fitz and I pulled two wrought iron chairs out from under the tarp on the patio, and sat in the dusk watching my brother try to light the grill he'd dragged out from the garage. That's when Fitz had explained to me his way of looking at the world." I took another mouthful of water. Mel waited.

"Fitz had worked out this philosophy," I continued. "That night he told me that we each go through life carrying a bag of bricks on our back. There are sixteen bricks in every bag. Each time you get to take one out, someone will come along whose bag is too heavy. And when that happens, you have to take one of his bricks, and put it in your bag."

"You're kidding me, right?" she asked.

"No. Fitz said that my brother's bag was just way too heavy, even if most of us couldn't see all the bricks there." I shook my glass to dislodge the ice that remained there. "I wonder what he saw. What he knew."

"You think Corky's in some kind of trouble?" asked Mel.

"Yeah, I do. I just need to figure out if it's the obvious stuff, or something more." I swallowed hard, to keep down the acid that started to burn in my stomach like a leaking battery. "Time to go, huh? It's a school night, after all."

Outside the bar, Mel grazed my cheek with a soft kiss and headed for the subway to Brooklyn. I decided to let Beckham & Coates pay for the expensive cab back to the Upper East Side.

At home, I gulped diet ginger ale straight from the bottle, and listened to Sam's voice on the answering machine, instructing me to come to room 1509 at the Peninsula Hotel if I could be there before midnight. I was glad that the clock said 12:20 A.M. I took two of the ulcer pills I'd stolen from my father's medicine cabinet, and tried to go to sleep. The phone rang as I lay in bed, but the caller hung up. I knew it was Sam, angry with me for not showing up in time.

So much for introducing Mel to the great black hope.

7

But Sam was about to work his way into yet another part of my life.

He surprised me on Sunday night, as I sat at the narrow table that doubled as a desk and a dining room, sorting through my papers. Fitz's briefcase sat open before me, and the graded practice tests were fanned out like a hand of cards. I had found a printout tracking results of what seemed to be one class of students at P.S. 95 in Harlem over the past eighteen months. In the July test the kids had improved by 25 to 60 percent. It was incredible. Students who had been failing were now at or above grade level. Fitz was probably just proud of the damn results, I thought. No wonder he didn't want to lose the briefcase. A record like this could help him land a good teaching job. Or at least win him another award.

The phone rang. I muted *60 Minutes* on the television when I heard the voice on the machine.

"Hello, beautiful."

"Sam. I didn't expect to hear from you," I said, grabbing the portable phone from its cradle.

"I think about you more than you know, baby. More than you know."

"Is that right?"

"Right now I'm looking at my schedule and I see the ANB is the day after Labor Day. I'm presenting the awards."

"Yes, I have the invitation right here." I pulled my Filofax out from under a stack of reading tests. "Alliance of Negro Businessmen 125th annual dinner dance. Reverend Vaughn says grace, Samuel Reid Ph.D. gives out the awards. Beckham & Coates has a table. Do you want to sit with us? I could move Jonetta Smiles—"

'No, baby, don't be silly. I have to sit on the dais. But isn't this party taking place in the hotel where your little brother works?"

"Yes. It is. The one and only Pan American Hotel." He remembered I had a brother?

"The same place where that other boy was killed. The teacher."

"I didn't know you noticed. Yes, he was my brother's best friend."

"I pay attention when attention must be paid. When you're hurt, I feel it."

His words brought unexpected tears to my eyes. "I guess I haven't felt that way in a long time, Sam."

"Julia. You're breaking my heart." I didn't answer. "Tell me. Police figure out what happened to that boy?" he asked.

"Not yet. Why? Are you afraid someone will lock you in the freezer?"

"That's not funny, Julia. Especially when you know I have been experiencing difficulties at my speaking engagements. Point is, I wonder if the little brother would give my associate and me a guided tour of the facilities? So that we can plan our own security backup for this ANB event?"

"I can try. There isn't much time before the long weekend. The ANB is the day after Labor Day."

"Any day this week would be fine, beautiful. Any day. Leave the message with my secretary. That's my good girl." A car honked. His cell phone clicked off.

In all the time I had known him he had never once told me he was available any day of the week.

Corky agreed to meet us on Thursday afternoon. It was one of those dark blowy days in late summer when the air keeps going still in anticipation of a thunderstorm that never seems to happen. I escaped a midtown restaurant after lunch with Sylvie Barr, a reading expert from Teachers College, and started walking to the hotel. The sky exploded on my three-dollar umbrella and the city melted around me into a wet stream of red and green and yellow lights. Please let Corky be sober, I thought as my foot sank into a curbside puddle that was as deep as my ankle. My shoes squished as I walked through the lobby to find Samuel. I discovered him sitting erect, his expensive suit never touching the back of the shiny brocade sofa. His skin was smoky from the Easthampton sun he'd been enjoying with his family. He showed no hint of humidity or damp.

"If I didn't know any better, I'd say that you were a film producer," I said.

He rose without a smile and kissed me European-style on both cheeks. "Someone needs to get you a towel," he said, then introduced me to an elegant brown man in a navy blue suit named Calvin Smith. Smith eyed me over the top of the small blue sunglasses that sat on the bridge of his narrow nose.

Trying to smooth my wet linen jacket, which was shriveling upward, I led them to the service elevator. As the doors closed I squeezed Samuel's arm out of sight of Calvin. "Are you okay, Sam?" I asked.

"Yes, Julia. The burdens of life just become heavier when the barometric pressure falls." Since I never could remember when it fell or rose, I just nodded. As I patted my damp hair in place, the doors opened onto the second floor bar.

It was calmer than I'd ever seen it in the service kitchen area. Just a few men in white coats stood by the sink, wiping out metal trays. We moved past the bare steam tables to Corky's cage. The fly strip above his desk was now choked full. Corky hung up the phone when he saw us, and came out of his wire mesh office. At least he looks like he has it together, I thought, noting the blue button-down shirt and the ironed chinos that were straining around his waist. Fat but sober.

I tore some paper towel off a roll sitting on my brother's desk and dabbed at my damp head.

"How do you do, Professor Reid?" Corky stared at the fiberglass hand that hung at Samuel's left side, and then abruptly looked away.

"Fine. Thank you for meeting with us, Christopher."

Calvin shook hands with Corky. "We're interested in knowing about the entrances to the ballroom—from the public areas of the hotel and from the kitchen."

"Sure. Public areas are easy." He pushed open the swinging door in the wall and we stepped into the Grand Ballroom. Two folding walls that could be slid on tracks to divide the room now hung like old shower curtains against the red flocked wallpaper. Crystal hung in beaded loops from the light fixtures. They reminded me of the cheap glass necklaces you buy from street vendors in Venice.

"See those four doors on the long wall? Those are the only entrances from the public areas. They are all along the same hallway. For a big benefit like the ANB, we'll start with a cocktail hour in the Galaxy Room across that hallway, and then move 'em to this ballroom." We all peered at the wall as if we would find writing on it. Corky pushed the door and gestured that we should go back through it.

"Now, we'll go downstairs. Right now, you're in what we call the second floor bar and service kitchen. The food is made downstairs and brought up in those insulated wagons." He gestured toward the stainless steel shelves on wheels. "They're called Queen Marys. Follow me."

We all returned to the dingy elevator I'd arrived in with Samuel and Calvin. Corky pressed "Kitchen 1" and we descended to the basement.

The door opened onto a vast kitchen space that held what seemed like a mile of burners and sinks. There was a long steel counter down the middle, and floor-to-ceiling ovens along one wall. A gray-bearded man in a shiny black suit, beneath which peeked the strings of tzitzit, was praying aloud in Hebrew. At the same time a younger man in a striped T-shirt and yarmulke passed a blowtorch over the burners. He moved to the bank of ovens, and repeated the process in each one. By the sinks were stacks of clean dishes.

We all looked at Corky for an explanation. "I've got a kosher fund-raiser tonight. My caterer Manny Cohen pays his rabbi to fix the kitchen. They've got to dip every dish in hot water, too. What a pain in the ass."

A pink-faced man in a blue and white seersucker suit walked toward us with a long loping gait. His hair was that yellowish tone of gray made darker by ancient hair tonic. He was taller than my brother, and put a familiar hand on his shoulder with a smile.

"Here he is," said Corky. "Mr. Manfred Cohen. A legendary political force in the New York Democratic party as well as the owner of the best kosher catering firm I know. Manny, meet my sister Julia and her friends, Samuel Reid and Calvin Smith. Jule, this is Lee's father."

"Miss Moran," he said, taking my hand and twinkling his pale blue eyes at me, "a true delight. My son, Lee, has told me all about your good work. And of course I know Professor Reid and his famous op-ed pieces. Mr. Smith, hello. Well, excuse me, folks, I must be going." He waved to the man with the blowtorch and floated down the hall.

"That guy practically invented 'kosher-style' catering back in the sixties, when Jews realized they had to serve bar mitzvah food their old-fashioned grandparents would eat. He made a fortune." Corky grinned. "He still handles the real thing, too, of course. I love kosher events. Especially kosher weddings. Jews hardly drink at all. I can sell the same bottle of apricot brandy ten to fifteen times. I give Manny a cut. Of course the rabbis drink scotch."

"Corky, cut it out," I protested.

"Hey, that's how it is. Now look—this kitchen is where all the food is prepared. It's connected through this wide passageway to the supply room, the freezer, and the laundry room. Also, of course, to the regular elevators, for things like room service. Everything in a hotel is on wheels."

We walked down the hallway. We stopped before the yellow police tape, now torn and broken, which still hung in pieces from the door to the freezer room. Two yellow roses tied with ribbon lay on the floor beneath the tape.

"Is that where you found your friend?" asked Samuel.

"Yeah. The waiters keep leaving roses there. It's a real Latino thing, you know? Honor the dead. I told them it has to stop or someone will trip on a fucking flower." He pushed the flowers against the wall with the tip of his shoe. "They won't let me throw away the police tape either."

"When did it happen?" asked Calvin.

"Two weeks, three days ago. He was in the chest that holds the cubes from the ice machine for the bar stations. Someone killed him and stuffed him in there." His voice cracked. "I've ordered a new ice chest. I'll never be able to forget how he looked there."

"Most unfortunate," said Calvin.

"A terrible thing, Christopher," said Sam. "Are the police any closer to knowing who did it?"

"Not yet. But they sure do have their eye on this hotel now, which should help where you're concerned. Unless, of course, the cops make it worse for you guys." He laughed nervously and moved down the hall. "This is the laundry room."

Sam stepped into the room and looked at the shelves of cloths, towels, jackets. Corky stood by his side in front of a shelf marked "L/XL." "I suppose someone could slip in, but he'd have to know his way around. Otherwise our own security would pick him up. And he'd still need to go through my second-floor bar to get directly in or out of the ballroom, unless he was entering the normal way with the other guests. Remember, on a heavy security night like the ANB benefit, no one could make his way out of the hotel from here unless he knew about the secret service elevator."

"I was wondering when you'd get to it," said Calvin in a smooth voice.

"What's that?" asked Samuel.

"Follow me," said Corky, and we filed into the supply room. The cans of tomatoes, chicken stock, tuna fish, and olives were so large that I felt as if we had joined Jack the Beanstalk in the giant's kingdom. At the far end of the room was an elevator door wider than any I'd ever seen.

"This service elevator connects the garage, the loading dock, this pantry, and the second floor bar. It was built around 1960 to carry Kennedy in his limousine from the garage to the ballroom without his having to go through the hotel. He made a big speech that night, and disappeared through the second floor bar. Probably had a babe waiting in the car."

"How did you know about it?" I said to Calvin.

"A brother used it to carry Michael Jackson away after he appeared at a Black Image Award dinner. I hear that Madonna used it once, too."

Corky nodded. "We had started to use it for regular bulk transport—

you know, food for big buffets, huge weddings, and banquets—because it's right on the other side of the kitchen. But we found guys were using the connection between the loading dock and the garage to move large appliances like TVs out of the hotel. So we've limited its use to managers who have a key. Everyone else has to use the regular service elevator on the other side. Look." He turned a key in the panel by the side of the elevator, and the call button went on. When the elevator arrived, we entered its cavernous space.

We could feel the pull of a descent, and the door opened onto the parking garage. Corky pushed another button and we ascended again. When the door opened there was a rush of hot damp air from the loading dock. With a shudder the elevator took us up again and deposited us in a small gray closet I didn't recognize. Then we followed Corky through a door and we were standing outside his cage. Back at the second floor bar.

Corky kept talking while leading us through the service kitchen, through the swinging door, and into the ballroom. He loves this job, I realized with amazement. All this work to feed people rubber chicken. For the kick of giving people a good time, making them happy even if just for a night.

"We may want one of our people in the kitchen. That secret elevator is a problem, especially since it's not exactly a secret. We don't know how many people got their hands on the keys," said Calvin.

"That's fine with me, man, but I don't think your problem is going to be coming through the kitchen, even with that elevator. There are only two doors to the ballroom from there, and I can see them both from my office or from the bar station."

"That didn't help Fitz," I said.

"That was different. Fitz wasn't hurt in the ballroom. He worked in the banquet sales office, remember?" Corky stood in the middle of the ballroom, and winced, as if to say, if only Fitz's desk had been in full safe view on this worn red carpet beneath the crystal lights and the blank video screens. "Look. The problem is going to be that you can't realistically check what people are bringing in. The ANB is huge. It uses the whole ballroom, so people will come through all four doors."

Samuel nodded, his brow furrowed. Corky continued, "Two months ago we had bad trouble here. One of the liquor companies sponsored a rum promotion through one of the black radio stations. The thing was oversold. We had over a thousand Jamaicans in here, drinking all the rum their entry ticket allowed. They were also smoking crack and PCP."

Calvin started to say something, but Corky stopped him. "Look, I work with lots of your people, but these Jamaicans were wacked. Before you know it, some guy who's been waiting too long on line for the bar pulls out his gun and shoots it off into the ceiling. My staff crawled out of this room on their bellies, and barricaded the two doors to the second floor bar with those Queen Marys you saw. I called the cops. They were afraid to go in until it calmed down."

"I didn't hear about that in the news," I said, looking for a bullet hole in the ceiling tiles.

"Of course not. The cops didn't want to admit that they just sat outside waiting for everyone to crash."

Calvin walked to the end of the room and back again as if he were counting paces. Then Corky pushed the door in the wall and we were back in the service kitchen. The close smell of thawing salmon was starting to seep up from the downstairs kitchen. To my dismay, Lee was sitting in the cage with his feet on Corky's desk, speaking Spanish on the telephone. He hung up the phone when he saw us.

"Look, Corky, a rodent in the kitchen," I said.

He ignored me. "Lee Cohen is Manny's son, as well as my friend and an aspiring lawyer who happens to work for the mayor. Lee, this is Professor Samuel Reid. Julia's friend. And his friend, Calvin Smith."

Lee dropped his feet, stood up, and extended his long arm. "A pleasure, Professor. Of course, I know who you are. I've heard you speak. Very exciting."

Calvin did not offer his hand, which made me want to kiss him.

Corky laughed. "Lee has worked for the Bronx Democratic party, Community Board Number 7, the mayor's reelection committee, and assorted federally funded jobs projects. Such a true public servant, you'd never know he grew up in Scarsdale. I'll meet you outside, Lee."

"Okay, I'm looking for my dad, anyway." He planted a big wet kiss on my cheek before pushing through the door to the ballroom. I wiped my face with my hand.

"Would you all like something to eat or drink? I have sandwiches from the buffet for the biotech conference on the eleventh floor." asked Corky.

"No, thank you," replied Calvin. "We must be going."

"Many thanks to you, Christopher," said Samuel with a slight dip of a bow. "My associate will be in touch with you if we have any other concerns."

"Don't hesitate to call," said Corky, perspiring and breathing a little too heavily. "Anytime. You'd be surprised at the things that go on in a hotel like this."

8

I stood in the corner of the Pan American Hotel's Galaxy Room with my friend Gordon, whose drink had just been upset by the ample brown arm of a woman reaching to grab a waiter. From a room across the hall, a band was playing a strangely peppy version of "Take the A Train."

"Look at the gorgeous beads on that dress. Do you realize how much handwork it takes to cover someone who's as big as Nell Carter?" said Gordon. His face glowed with the admiration of an artisan whose own furniture designs were just beginning to make their way into the magazines that mattered.

"Careful, Gordon. She may be Nell Carter."

Beaming, he turned to look at the woman again. I tried to move my toes in the T-strap high heels that I'd charged at Saks that afternoon to go with my short black evening dress. I couldn't tell if the toes were moving, because they were already numb.

"I can't wear these shoes, Gordon," I said, gripping his elbow.

"Just remember to flex your feet every few minutes. Don't give up—they look great! And that V neck is terrific. You should wear it all the time." Gordon tossed his sun-kissed ponytail over the shoulder of his snug Italian suit and gave my hand a squeeze. Though his true passions were hiking and skiing, he was gamely trying to fulfill his duties as my escort. I knew in his heart he believed I'd be happier in flat shoes. But I had been determined to look great tonight, when I would be in the same room as Sam, but not with him. I tried to grab a baby quiche from an hors d'oeuvres tray that went by too fast, but missed.

"I'm not sure those appetizers are worth the struggle," Gordon said, accepting a replacement glass of orange juice from a waiter. I sadly watched several middle-aged black women in sequined jackets bite into their hot little pastries.

My brother weaved his way through the crowd, stopping to pat us both on the back. His eyes were too bright but he didn't seem messed up. Yet. "Hey, you two, we'll be moving into the Grand ballroom soon. Do you like the appetizers?" he asked.

"They go by too fast to tell," I answered. Corky raised his hand and a waiter with a tray miraculously appeared. I picked up a miniature tart and put it in my mouth. It was sweet. "That doesn't taste like quiche," I said.

"Naw, it's sweet potato pie. Great idea, huh? Soul food!"

Gordon chewed politely.

"I'll see you guys later. Have fun watching my sister's married man perform, okay? You get your table numbers from Ella Fitzgerald over there," said Corky, before disappearing into the crowd.

"What's wrong with him?" asked Gordon, his gray eyes wide with shock.

"That is one of the questions that consume my life," I said, taking his arm. "Let's just go find our table."

Once the blue-wigged woman who presided over the guest list directed us to number 47, we shuffled into the ballroom, now a vast sea of skirted round tables. The numbers that rose on steel sticks from bowls of carnations reached as high as the eighties. At the front of the room—the end that I knew was closest to Corky's office—a long table covered with microphones and dinnerware sat on a raised platform. At the other end stood five older black men in white dinner jackets, resting between sets, instruments in hand. I wondered if they would jazz up the interpretations when they saw that this wasn't another kosher wedding.

In front of the dais stood the mayor, the familiar curly black hair sitting like a wig atop the high forehead and pug nose that always reminded me that the iron ruler had once been someone's adorable child. The mayor kept smiling at people and giving the occasional wave while he spoke to an elegant silver-haired man who stood by his side. Clustered around them was the usual assortment of aides, commissioners, and advisers, squirming in their tuxedos. Nearby were a couple of reporters and a bored cameraman from a local news station who clearly didn't think it was worth turning his video camera on yet, despite the mayor's eager smile.

I still hadn't seen Samuel or the Reverend Elijah. I sucked in my stomach and took small steps toward our table, which was in the center of the room. A large-chested woman behind me said, "He has a nerve showing his white ass here. I hope they serve him a watermelon."

"I guess no one's forgiven the mayor for accusing that Brooklyn school board president of having a watermelon mentality, huh?" said Gordon with a devilish arch of his eyebrow.

"Nope, he's still in hot water. That's one of the reasons he has to be here tonight, even though it's the reverend's crowd."

The room was heavy with the sweet smell of an expensive men's cologne that Samuel used. It was a fragrance that had become popular among black men, and I used to savor the ache of recognizing it in a fleeting moment on a subway or in a store. Now it filled the room, choking me. As we reached our table, I turned to Gordon. He was standing behind his chipped gilded chair, grinning with the look of someone who had reached a long-sought destination and found it exactly to his liking.

"Beautiful," he murmured, his eyes following the full figures of black women and their devoted mates. "Just beautiful. All this color and warmth." A frown creased his brow. "So why the armed guard?" he asked, letting a long hand float toward the police who stood near the doorways. I didn't tell him that the reverend and Sam had their own guards in place, as well. Though I couldn't figure who or where they were.

"It's just security because the reverend's officially challenging the mayor in the primary next week. And of course, Hizzoner is here."

"I see. And who are our companions?" He gave a small bow to the short man and woman in woven yellow and red robes and matching round pillbox-style hats who were preparing to sit at the other side of our table.

"This is Professor Adimbe, who founded the Africana studies program at NYU."

I leaned over to shake the hand of the professor and his wife. The two coauthors of my "Leading the Choir" series sat down with their husbands and I trotted to the other side of the table to give them each a kiss. Then my newest superstar signing—Quint B. Sure, a DJ in dreadlocks who did a syndicated call-in show for teens from Philadelphia—arrived and I introduced him to everyone. With the lithe grace of a greyhound, Gordon made his way around the table to ask guests what they wanted to drink, stopping a waiter to place the group's requests. Four ministers from the Nation of Islam walked by, accompanied by wives dressed in elegant brocade with deep-colored chiffon chadors. Gordon looked at the man in the lead, then to me, and said "Is he—?"

I nodded, and took my seat. Two tables away I recognized a woman whose first book I had published. As I raised my hand to greet her, I felt someone squeeze my shoulder, and looked up to see the smiling face of Lee. I sighed.

"Hi, Lee. I believe you've met my old friend Gordon."

Lee held his glass high in the air as he leaned down to kiss me and shake Gordon's hand in one fluid move. I tried not to notice how well Lee filled the tuxedo.

"I didn't think you'd be here, Julia. Aren't you above sordid politics?"

"I'm never above worthy causes, especially when there are authors involved. But what are you doing here? Shouldn't you be studying for the bar exam?"

"I'm here with my dad and his Bronx cronies to show our commitment to the black vote. And I'm working afterwards—I run a group that collects unused food from events like this and delivers it to homeless shelters and welfare moms. It's called U-CAN. We've been in business for over three years now. City contract, big donations and everything."

I was surprised. "That's great, Lee."

"Yeah I'm a great guy, I keep telling you. See you later. I hope you enjoy the speeches." He touched my cheek with a fingertip and winked. Then he waved to someone he knew across the room. With a few deft steps between tables, he was gone.

"I just can't figure that guy out," I said to Gordon. "He does all these good public-interest-type things, but he's a total creep."

"I can see why he gets away with it, though. The creepiness part, I mean." He took a quick lick of white wine without seeming to touch his lips to the rim of the cheap hotel glass. "He's very handsome, in an old-fashioned, ruin-your-life kind of way." As if on cue, the combo started to play Stevie Wonder's "You Are the Sunshine of My Life." I heard scattered applause and looked toward the door. The Reverend Vaughn had finally entered the ballroom.

Each time I saw Elijah Vaughn I was surprised by his smallness, as if I were seeing him for the first time. Somehow it was the part of him that you always forgot, because by the time he took leave of you, the sheer force of his personality had expanded like hot air to fill the room. He was larger than life, yet only five foot three. From thirty feet away he was barely visible through the circle of bodyguards and well-wishers. Four large men in big-shouldered suits stood around him, shifting on their toes like prizefighters in a ring. Above the reverend's shoulder I could make out Sam's square face. He followed with his claw behind the reverend, as if he were using it to steer their course.

"Ah, the mayor is adjusting his bow tie. He must be getting ready for the cameras," said Quint, in a deep voice. I saw Gordon steal an admiring look at the DJ's collarless white shirt and black raw silk jacket. They smiled at each other.

Head tilted back, eyebrows raised in two upside-down Vs, the mayor squeezed through the crowd, as his own pack attempted to follow him. It was like watching two little herds of sheep bump into each other. The mayor shot his arm through the throng of admirers and managed to grab the reverend's hand. He was shaking it wildly as camera bulbs flashed. When he noticed Sam, the mayor shook his hand too.

"I wonder if he's confused about which one is his rival," I said, taking a gulp of white wine that seared all the way down.

"Aren't we all?" quipped Professor Adimbe, raising his glass. "Who do you really want in office? The professor or the reverend?"

I couldn't take my eyes off Samuel. The formality of black tie complemented his solemn features. I longed for him to be sitting near me, at our table. Maybe I'd meet him at his hotel afterward. Make it up to him for all our recent bickering. You catch more flies with honey, my mother had always told me.

"Your man looks good tonight," said Gordon.

"Shhh," I hissed. "Nobody here knows about us."

He rolled his eyes. "Oh, puh-lease, Julia. I'll bet half the women in the room want to claw your eyes out. And you love it."

"Yeah. Me and my secrets. What a thrill to know a public man in private, and never be acknowledged."

"Sounds pretty good to me," he said, clinking my glass with his.

The band began to play "Respect" in a sort of fox-trot tempo. Their increased volume signaled to the men at the front of the room that it was time to sit down. The mayor's pack pulled him back toward their tables, and most of the reverend's crew took the steps to the dais. The bodyguards stayed below.

A heavyset man with a wide face the bluish black color of fountain pen ink wrapped a hand around the standing mike on the dais and began to make introductory remarks. Waiters moved among the tables wielding ladles and tureens of soup. I got up to talk to an editor from another publishing house two tables over, hoping that Sam would see me, but he didn't take his eyes off the speaker at the microphone. Mel waved to me from the 60s-numbered tables near the band, where she was sitting with the author of her successful "A Girlfriend's Guide to" series. The man on the stage announced that the Reverend Elijah Vaughn would be saying grace, and I returned to my seat. The reverend rose and walked in front of the table on the dais. Somehow the tuxedo made him look younger, like a boy acolyte. Until he spoke.

Raising his arms, the reverend began, "Thank you, Lord. For all my brothers and sisters here." He paused for a second.

"For the food we fight to put on our tables." From the rear, someone shouted, "Say it."

"For the food our children need. Not just for their stomachs." A few more voices whispered, "Amen."

"For the food our children require. For their minds. For their hearts." Several men on the platform closed their eyes, lifting their heads heavenward. The reverend continued.

"Our children are hungry. Hungry for love." At the mayor's table I saw two men put down their tumblers of scotch. Two tables away, Lee picked at his salad with his fingers and popped some lettuce in his mouth. His father sat with his hands in his lap, his head cocked to the side. Gordon gazed at the reverend and I was so grateful for his open heart that I squeezed his lean thigh under the table.

"Our children are starving to death. Is there a child born who deserves to be abandoned? NO!" Elijah screamed. "It is our responsibility to give each child what he or she needs. Food. Learning. Care. And love.

"People say I'm crazy for talking about love," he said in a stage whisper. He stepped across the stage, and bent all the way over to his knees in a crouch, as if he had stomach pain. "But if they knew what I mean," he said, and then shot up, with his arms stretching toward the ceiling. "If they knew what I mean by love, they would never call me crazy." A chill prickled up my spine, and my eyes filled. I swayed along with most of the people at the other eighty tables.

"Our children, brothers and sisters, are starving to death. Starving for love." He stopped suddenly, as if to bring himself back down to earth, with all of us. "Remember, my friends. There is no place that God is not." Silence. "Tonight, we break bread with our brothers and sisters in the business community, and we pray that they will help those who have been abandoned by the marketplace. Those who need our LOVE!"

The applause was wild. The waiters who had stopped serving to listen to the reverend resumed ladling seafood bisque out of the large tureens.

The reverend raised his arms for silence. "We're going to eat our meals now. Then, our beloved Brother Samuel Reid will speak to us before the awards are given out. I will say a few words again before we part. Enjoy this blessed evening!" The band broke into a sultry rendition of "Georgia." It was the first song they had played that sounded like something approaching the blues, rather a standard by the Peter Duchin orchestra. Overhead, the necklaces of light dimmed slightly.

The mood of the dinner was upbeat after the reverend's opening. Every now and then I would see Corky gesturing to one of the waiters, or bringing a tray of drinks from the bar station to one of the important tables near the dais. The room buzzed. Laughter and the clink of silverware on plates filled the air. At our table, everyone except Gordon finished the stuffed roast Cornish game hen, and even he ate both his mashed potatoes and mine. I helped myself to his soft dinner roll and let it dissolve in my mouth. While everyone was still eating, I went to say hello to Mel.

"What'd you think of the reverend?"

"He was incredible. I want to work for him. Patti tells me he paid for those two tables just so that his younger staff could participate." She smiled at the young men in Sunday best ordering another round of drinks from a tired-looking waiter.

"My brother seems in control, huh?" I said.

She nodded.

When I made my way through the tables back to my own, I saw Lee engrossed in conversation with a short olive-skinned man who looked young enough to be a college student. Then Lee tapped one of the waiters on the shoulder and followed him to the door to my brother's office and the second floor bar. Going after those leftover hens in the kitchen, I thought, wondering if I really knew Lee Cohen at all, with his command of Spanish and his volunteer work and his relentless energy.

I stood at my chair, looking up at the dais, willing Sam to acknowledge me. His head was lowered and cocked toward the reverend. Elijah smiled at me and gave me a salute. Sam glanced up and our gazes met. His eyes narrowed and his lips pursed in the slightest echo of a kiss, or what I thought was a kiss. Then he returned his attention to the reverend.

"I'd be happy to show you my work anytime. You should come by the studio," Gordon was saying to Quint. He slipped a card from the inside pocket of his evening jacket into Quint's hand. The DJ flashed a radiant smile at him and excused himself to go to the men's room as I sat down.

"Gordon, you're wasting your time. He's married to a beautiful woman," I whispered.

He crossed his slender wrists in his lap as if he were about to lead me in meditation. "White or black?" he asked.

"What difference does it make?"

"Just answer me please, Julia," he said."White or black?"

"She's white," I admitted.

"Uh-huh." He raised his left eyebrow again. "I knew it."

"What do you mean, 'you knew it'? Quint and Karen met in college."

"Julia, you know what I'm talking about. For some people, black or white, there's always someone thinner, blonder, whiter."

"For what kind of person?" I asked.

"Not you. God knows, not me," he laughed, flipping the ponytail. "But, remember my friend Lars? The architect who always had to go home to take care of the dog? Who said he loved me, but then it turned out that I didn't have the money to support him like Mr. Beverly Hills?"

"I didn't mean—"

"Dear Julia, it's okay. I've just learned the hard way to be wary. I'm not buying what our friend Quint is selling. No matter what he says about all those poor little black children. And you should be careful too about your friend Samuel . . . well, never mind." Quint was back in his seat, digging into a piece of pecan pie.

Another hand squeezed my shoulder. A small female hand.

"Julia. It's Sylvie Barr."

"Sylvie." I stood up and gave her cheek a peck. My Teachers College expert.

"I can't stop thinking about your idea for a book on reading for parents. I think the timing couldn't be better." Waiters rushed around her with coffeepots and trays of pie. Like a tiny stubborn bird she stood her ground. A tray skittered over her head and she carefully brushed her blond bob with her hand.

She kept talking about the book in that way new authors can without ever sensing how much they're boring you. At last I cut her off, saying "I can't wait to see the final proposal," my eyes still on the dais. Sam wiped his lips with a white napkin, folded the napkin with his usual precision, and placed the napkin on the table. Then he got up from his chair and leaned over to say something to Elijah.

"With the crisis in the schools, and these damn tests of the mayor's, reading has become an issue," Sylvie Barr ploughed on.

I turned to her. "Tests?"

"Yes, yes, everyone is obsessed with the new scores. But it's absolutely the wrong tack. I can't tell you how frustrating it is for the teachers."

"Maybe we could get together and talk more about it all. I'd love to understand what's been going on."

"Sure, Julia. Classes start this week, so things are crazy. But once we're up and running I'm always available for you. Oops. Looks like I should sit down for the speeches."

The man who had first introduced the reverend came to the microphone. "Once you all have your coffee, our guest speaker, Samuel Reid, the Allen Roberts University Professor at City University, will hand out the prizes for this year's winners of the ANB achievement awards." Sam's seat was empty.

Men don't have to wait in lines to use the bathroom, do they, I wondered. I poured the contents of the creamer into my cup of coffee. Two of the bodyguards standing below the dais left the room. Despite the cream, the coffee set off a series of twitches in my stomach.

Reverend Elijah stepped to the microphone. "While we're waiting for Brother Samuel, why don't we begin with the awards. The first award for Youth Employment Sponsor of the Year goes to Brother Henry Jackson of Color-Me-Proud Paint Stores, Incorporated, of Brooklyn, New York. As you all know, I believe there is no greater gift than supporting our youth. Let's give a shout out to Brother Henry!"

Applause filled the room. Brother Henry brought his wife with him to collect his plaque. She wept on his shoulder while he wept on the reverend's neck.

By the door to the kitchen Corky was talking to a tall man with thick auburn hair. I guessed Army or Navy reserve from the way the man stood erect with his navy suit jacket open, arms clasped tight behind his back, legs slightly apart. While Corky spoke the tall man's eye traveled in a slow line from the dais to the tables at the back of the room and to the dais again. He waved over one of the uniformed cops. When the red-haired man leaned over to speak to the officer, I realized that I had seen him before. He was the man who had stood outside Fitz's funeral, watching my brother. Now he gave some kind of direction to the cop, who listened, nodded, and left the room.

Samuel had not returned to his seat.

Reverend Elijah gave an award to the woman who ran the Harlem Museum of Dance. She accepted in a flowing purple gown.

"Gordon, where do you think Sam is?" I said.

"Don't worry, my vigilent friend. Nothing can happen to him or anyone. This place is more heavily guarded than the Bastille," he replied, patting my arm. I twisted in my seat and looked around the room while the reverend handed a plaque to a beautiful woman in braids who led a girls choir in the Bronx. A table of girls in matching taffeta dresses stood up and did an a capella rendition of the first two bars of "Jesus Is My Savior." The room cheered.

Samuel was nowhere in sight.

I didn't hear the last three awards. I was staring into my glass of melting ice, trying to fight back the nervous bile that was starting to rise in my throat.

Two uniformed cops approached the man who'd been talking to Corky. He shook his head and walked to the end of the dais. The reverend leaned down to hear what the red-haired man had to say. When he stood up, Reverend Vaughn lifted his shoulders, and mouthed, "Now?" The man nodded and the reverend stepped to the microphone.

"My brothers and sisters, our friend and teacher Brother Samuel Reid has been called away on an emergency basis. Given that it is late and we have given out all the awards, we will conclude this annual ANB dinner with a prayer for his well-being. Oh, Lord, watch over our Brother Samuel." There were a few halfhearted Amens. "Now, if you would leave in an orderly fashion through the doors here to my right, we will all be sure to have a peaceful evening." At once questions danced in the air, "Why?" "What's going on, man?" "Where's the brother?" The rising volume of uneasy voices filled our ears like an engine revving.

Voices exploded from the back of the room, where Mel was sitting. When I turned around, a young man who looked like he was with the Nation of Islam—a teenager, really, in wire-framed glasses and a bow tie—was standing and pointing at one of the tables sponsored by the reverend.

"You cannot take care of your own. You feed on each other like vultures," he said in a slow and serious voice.

A barrel-chested boy in a deep purple jacket with a gold chain around his neck stood up and said, "Why you on our ass? You so busy fighting amongst yourselves you can't even see what's goin' on."

"Fighting amongst ourselves? Boy, where is your professor friend right now?"

Purple jacket pushed back his chair, said, "Well, I think the answer to that question begins with the man," and stormed through the tables toward the front of the room. His friends followed.

The nervous chatter around us subsided as the young men planted themselves in front of the mayor's table. The combo stopped its rendition of "Sweet Georgia Brown" at one of the points where the Harlem Globetrotters used to sink a basket.

"Yo, mayor. Where's the professor?" Two cops moved closer to the table.

The mayor stood, shooing away his aides. "I'm afraid I don't know, young man. But if something untoward has happened we will do everything in our power to help him." Purple jacket stomped his feet, while his friends began to yell. The men at the mayor's table were half in and out of their seats.

The reverend marched across the dais. "Stop this. Stop this vile behavior right now. Have some dignity, my brothers. Dignity!"

They stopped as one at the reverend's words. Admonished, they lowered their heads. They marched toward the door where uniformed policemen now stood.

"People. Brother and sisters in struggle. Do not end our evening on an unhappy note. Brother Samuel has simply been called away. Please leave peacefully, now. Honor my request!" shouted the reverend, his arms held high in the air.

As if the Lord himself had requested it, the din lessened. People stood up and began the slow process of herding toward the exit.

I watched the cops position themselves by the exits. Gordon and I shuffled with the crowd.

"Gordon, I'm so sorry."

"It's you I'm worried about, Julia. It's not the first time I've been frisked on my way out of a party."

We made it to the doorway. I stopped. "Damn it, girl," snapped the woman in front of me when I stepped on her heel. "Gordon," I said, reaching for his arm, "first I want to see if my brother knows what's going on."

He twisted around in the hallway and cupped his hand around his mouth. "Shall I wait?"

"No, I'll be okay," I called.

I squeezed through the bodies and walked past the dais toward the door on the other side of the room. Above my head, Reverend Vaughn was sitting at the table, leaning back in his chair, engrossed in conversation with a slender black man I recognized. It was Isaac Lord, who had sat next to me at Sam's Symphony Space lecture. I stopped in front of them. But if they saw me they did not acknowledge it.

When I reached the door to the service kitchen, I lied to the red-faced cop standing there and said that I'd been told to wait in the kitchen. He looked at me for a second, then patted my shoulder and said, "Okay, miss."

I pushed through the soiled brocade wall, and walked toward the cage where my brother sat at his desk, back to me, his head in his hands.

9

Corky sat silently in his office waiting for the police to return. On top of the metal desk was an empty glass coffeepot and a plate of what we used to call "bakery" cookies. Every few seconds Corky popped another seven-layer square or butter swirl into his mouth with a hard flick of his wrist. I sipped a ginger ale and looked at the waiters who were scraping plates and trays before sending them downstairs for cleaning. The only indication that they thought anything was wrong was the fact that no one came over to laugh with my brother or see if he wanted to share a few lines of coke. Instead they spoke in quiet Spanish among themselves.

My eyes drifted to the fly strip above the desk. Someone had changed it. The tall redhead and another man came through the swinging door from the ballroom and entered the cage. Corky sprang up to offer his seat to them. The shorter man took the empty chair, his suit a shade of blue frighteningly close to the vinyl padding he sat on. Corky pushed things out of the way so that the tall man could lean against the desk without sitting in the cookies. There was an exchange about what the men would like to drink—anything you want, Corky kept saying, anything—before my brother raced out to the steam tables, snapping for fresh coffee with milk, no sugar.

"You are?" asked the man who was still standing. I realized that the thick auburn hair was actually faded, like dried flowers left in the sun.

"Julia Moran. Corky's sister."

"Ah. The sister. Nice to meet you, Miss Moran. I'm Detective Thomas Lynch from Midtown North." Corky pushed open the steel door with his hip, a tray in his hands. "You can call me Tom. Your brother and I are already on a first-name basis by now. This is my partner Frank Logan." Logan grunted in his chair, eyes on the cookies.

"You're the detective he's talked about?" I asked.

"Depends on how many he knows." Lynch took a big gulp of black coffee. "Because I'm such a favorite of the captain's, I've also been serving as precinct liaison with the Special Investigations Task Force. Which looks after the interests of well-known public figures at events like this evening's dinner."

"Oh." I felt as if a large spider were gripping the right side of my face.

Lynch continued, "We really don't know if anything has happened here tonight. The professor might have taken a walk. But it's best to talk now in case we need to follow through on anything. Corky, you want your sister here?"

"Absolutely," he said, trying to look casual as he rested against the frame of the cage.

"Okay, then. Frank and I have spoken with several people who were in the ballroom tonight. Mr. Calvin Smith tells us that you knew that Professor Reid was worried about security, and gave the two of them a tour of the premises last Thursday?"

Corky stood up straighter. I was glad he had taken off his tie and undone the top stud of his tuxedo. At least his larynx wouldn't burst if he tried to speak. "Yeah, that's right. He's—uh—a friend of my sister's, and she told me he was concerned about security. So I walked them around."

Logan looked up from the pad he was scribbling on. "You didn't feel the need to include the hotel's director of security?"

I started to reply but Corky put his hand on my arm. "No," he said, "it was just a favor to them. I did mention that we had our own security here at the hotel. But they didn't seem to want it to be too official, if you know what I mean."

"I know Smith. He used to be on the job. He's good people. But he never did like to restrict himself to the regular channels," said Lynch. Logan's hand reached toward the cookie tray and two miniature black-and-whites disappeared. Lynch frowned. "And you, Miss Moran?"

"What about me?"

"You're the connection here to Samuel Reid?"

"Yes. We worked together on several books. I was his editor. We also became friends." I didn't flinch as I stared into the skeptical brown eyes that were flecked with green. Beneath them, delicate violet shadows swung from the ample bridge of his nose to his temples.

"And he asked his editor for help with security?"

"There had been troublemakers at his recent speeches. Even death threats at home. He knew my brother worked here, where the ANB was being held. He just wanted everything to go well for the reverend, especially with the mayor present." I paused and said helpfully, "The primary's next week."

Lynch was rubbing his chin and looking at the ground while I spoke. He cocked his head to the side. "So, let me get this straight. He was afraid of trouble. You provide him with a tour of the facilities. And now, poof, he disappears right before his speech?"

"I don't know what you mean by poof," I said.

"I mean, poof. Without warning." He turned his attention back to my brother. "While your memory's fresh, Corky, did anything strike you as odd tonight? Any special deliveries? disappearances? suspicious people lurking around?"

Corky almost stamped his foot with impatience. "No. Everything was smooth. I even made sure all the floaters were people I already knew. I did alert hotel security to be extra cautious—we've had trouble ourselves with these black groups before."

Lynch ignored Corky's attempt at white bonding. "Security said that the only uses of that special service elevator were regular and authorized: the bread delivery, the van for the food for the homeless, the laundry truck. You can confirm that everything and everyone else went on the regular service elevator?"

Corky nodded. "I told you. I worked extra hard to be sure it would all be fine."

Lynch arched his back in a stretch, running a large hand through the thick hair. An oversized college ring with a crimson stone flashed in the light. "Like I said, we don't even know if anything's wrong here. Professor Reid could have pulled a no-show, met a waitress he liked." He glanced at me, "Or, one of the rival brothers could have taken him for a long drive just to show that the professor and the reverend don't speak for everyone."

"He could have been mugged near the telephones," mumbled Logan, his mouth full.

"That's right, Frank. He could have had a heart attack on his way to the can. We have a lot of checking to do tonight. But whatever happened, I hope that I don't find out that either one of you has conveniently forgotten to tell me something."

"We've told you everything. We both wanted to help Sam," I said, stepping instinctively toward my brother. By my thigh I could feel that once again he was shaking. I took one of his hands and held it tight.

"Like I said, Miss Moran, we don't know yet if the man needs any help at all." Lynch reached into his jacket. "Here's my card. Please be in touch if you think of anything new or if the professor gets in touch with you. We've got at least twenty-four hours before everyone becomes officially concerned and we have a real mess on our hands. Okay?"

I nodded.

"Corky, if it's necessary I'll expect your help in speaking to staff. Who knows if any of this is related to your other incident here," he said in a quiet voice to my brother.

"Sure, anything you need. Anytime."

Lynch opened the door to the cage and the two men walked out through the door to the ballroom.

I turned to my brother.

"You know anything about all this, Corky? If you do, so help me god, I'll—"

"No, Julia, I swear I don't know what the hell's going on." He rubbed his eyes and reached out to me. I felt myself stiffen but let him hold me for a long minute before I pulled away.

"Well, I guess I'll go home and try to sleep. Don't stay up all night here, promise?" I patted his front.

"I promise. Let me walk you to the front of the line to hail a cab. Otherwise you'll have to wait for hours."

For once I didn't argue with him. I didn't want to be near him any longer than I had to.

10

I lay in bed staring at my digital clock, its glowing red numbers slipping past midnight. My head lay near the street end of my narrow room. Usually, air and light from the window gave me enough pleasure to offset the sound of the traffic. But tonight, every slam of a car door, every whine of a car alarm, every downshift of a truck's gears, made me tremble.

Drifting into a light doze, I saw my brother's face, swollen and red. He was pushing Sam down a hallway in a laundry basket. Stuffing Sam into one of the Queen Marys on wheels. Dipping Sam in hot water and saying Hebrew prayers. Then the Hebrew shifted into an insistent vaudeville rhythm. Shave and a haircut. Buzz buzz. Was I dreaming in Yiddish? I opened my eyes and the buzzing continued. Someone was ringing my bell downstairs. The clock said 2:07 A.M.

I looked out the window but in the violet light I saw no one on the stoop or street below. The intercom for the front door was broken, and I had no intention of letting anyone in without knowing who it was. I pulled on my silk robe and walked through the short hallway to the living room, turning on lights as I went. The buzzing had stopped, or at least it wasn't coming from the small panel by the door anymore. For all I knew the bell had gone the way of the intercom.

The jangle of keys skittered near my lock. Then they fell to the floor and I heard a man say, "Fuck." Who had a set of my keys? Only Corky. I looked through the keyhole and saw the top of his shoulders as he strained to pick up what he'd dropped. With a sigh I opened the door. Though he was standing up now he gave the impression that he was moving in place like a tree in the wind. His face was a mottled purply red color, and a sour smell came off him.

"Hey, sis, have a good time tonight?" he said, and pushed by me into the apartment.

"What the hell do you want this time of night, Corky? You're so drunk you can't even stand."

Though his face was pointing toward me, his eyes were not. They stared somewhere behind me, glazed over like the eyes of a fish you decide not to buy. It looked as if the tuxedo from the benefit had been long gone, as there were stains across the front of his jean jacket and down the leg of his khakis. He waved his arms around and kicked the corner of the antique trunk I use as a coffetable.

"You live in a dump. And everyone knows it. You don't even know the things people say about you. I feel sorry for you, you stupid cunt."

"Just get the hell out of here. I don't want to look at you. Go home."

"I don't have to do anything."

"Yeah, you do. Because I'm tired of watching you drink and do coke and god knows what the hell else and then blame other people for how you fuck up."

"I didn't fuck up."

"Oh, really? Then why is Fitz dead, you pathetic little shit?" I regretted the words as I watched his face crumble. But at the same time I wanted to hear what he would tell me.

"What are you talking about? I loved him. Even though I couldn't live up to his standards. The little saint. The absolutely perfect, precious little twat," he said, pursing his lips together. Two white streaks appeared on his red cheeks, as if giant thumbs had wiped them clean. He looked away and then seemed to remember where he was. "I didn't do anything wrong," he shouted at me. "I'm tired of all of you. Blaming me for everything."

"Who's 'all of you,' Corky?"

"You gang up on me. Even you and Lee. You tried to take him away from me. Then you were mad at me when he blew you off. Now he watches me."

"Corky, that's not what happened," I said, made guilty by the pain that twisted his face, "It was a long time ago. We all know it never could have worked."

"What do you know? You and your stupid nigger boyfriend." He took a step back, and put his hands out as if to catch his balance.

"I know that boyfriend's in trouble. And maybe you have something to do with it."

"NO! No, I don't!" he screamed. As if in slow motion, his fist swung through the air and smashed into the small Italian woodcut I'd treasured since going to Rome in my early twenties. The glass shattered, and the wooden frame and its contents slid down the wall to the floor.

"What are you doing? What are you doing, you goddam maniac?" I cried. "I told you last time—no violence. You promised. And now you break one of the only things I own that has any value to me." I crouched over the print and retrieved it from the mess. The glass fell in slivers as I lifted the frame and its backing.

"I'm sorry about the picture. But you're still a bitch."

"Take five minutes to calm down, Corky. Then get out," I said, bent over my paltry treasure in tears.

He fell backward into the armchair, his head rolling like the faces of those ugly novelty dolls that have a coiled spring for a neck. I rested the print on top of the turntable that sat dusty and unused on one of the higher shelves on my bookcase.

"I don't know what happened to him. Everyone in the kitchen was talking but no one would tell me what was going on," he said.

"Who was talking?"

"They don't like me even though they pretend to. Lee had only four guys on. Four guys out. They wore the white coats just like everyone else."

"Who? The guys with the van for the shelter?"

With his finger in the air, he mumbled something to himself that I couldn't make out. Then he bent over toward his shoes. He could barely reach his toes, but it looked as if he were trying to undo his laces.

"Do you want me to help you with your shoes? You can't spend the night on the couch unless you promise to calm down and go to sleep."

He looked up at me as if he were seeing me for the first time.

"What?" he asked.

"I said, are you planning to stay here, and if so, do you need help with your shoes?"

"I don't need anything from you, bitch." He got up and leaned toward me.

"I'm not a bitch. But you're a goddam drunk."

"NO!" With both hands he gave my shoulders a hard push.

"Don't touch me, Corky."

"I'll do whatever the fuck I want."

He made a gurgling noise and shoved me so hard that I lost my balance and fell backward, knocking all the magazines off the trunk as I went.

"Alcoholic fucking bastard," I said, sitting on the floor. My heart was pounding up through my neck and ears.

"I don't have to take this shit," he said, his head down like a dog sniffing for food. He lurched into the kitchen and I heard the refrigerator door open and shut. He emerged with a can of light beer peering out from his jacket pocket. Without looking at me he found the front door, struggled to pull it open, and slammed it behind him so hard that everything in the apartment shook. I was still sitting on the floor with my arms over my head as his footsteps disappeared down the hallway.

My hands were shaking as I secured all the locks, including the dead bolt and the old chain that Corky could probably break if he really tried. I found the dustpan and swept up the glass as best as I could. I was trying not to think, because when I did all I could think was that it might be better for everyone if my brother just went ahead and drank himself to death. My mouth and throat were dry and gritty, like sand. I stood at the kitchen sink, gulping glasses of cold water. Then I went back to bed.

I lay there with my eyes open until eight-thirty, when I decided I might as well get up and go to work.

BLONDER

I am not Booker T.—nor was I meant to be. But if we look at the experiences of our European and Asian and Latino neighbors—if we look at the success of our Jewish friends—we see a great tradition of people helping their own. In America, families help their own.

Do we help our own? Or are we too busy tending to other people—sweeping their floors, feeding their children, entertaining them with our songs? At some point or another, no matter what degree you have or what boardroom you sit in, someone will stop you because you are black. And at that moment, you will go home and say to your black family: from now on, we help our own.

—Samuel Reid, from *A Native Son Bears Witness*

11

I rocked back and forth in my desk chair, staring at the stone curlicue outside the window. A couple of pigeons had decided that they liked the crevice between the gray curl and the sill. Their gurgling rose and fell in a contented rhythm. I fought the urge to open the window and throw a book at them. From the look of the thick paint crusted around the jamb, it was probably impossible to open the window anyway.

"Julia, that was Mallory Snow's office on the line. First bids are due at eleven." I twirled the chair around. Kit stood in my doorway, gripping a file to his chest. He looked at his watch. "It's ten forty-one now," he added.

"First bids?"

"The auction for *Booting the Strap*. By Pierce Lamal?" The toe of his Italian loafer tapped with impatience. "You met him last week? You expressed fervent interest?"

"Oh God. African-American parenting guru. No more corporal punishment. Right?"

"Right. Pat cleared us up to one-fifty."

"Okay. Here's what we'll do," I said. "Take our boilerplate black offer—the one with the paragraph about our reach to the African-American market—and go in at fifty thousand. Standard terms. North America. Sub rights, spell out we want audio. Then fax it."

"Will do. Lunch with Steve Crocus today. You want the Yellowtail Grill at one?"

"Cancel it."

"You canceled last time."

"Kit. I don't care. I can't make chitchat today. Tell him I have food poisoning. Okay?" A pull of disapproval tugged at his brow, but he nodded. "And please take messages for me. I don't want to talk to anyone. Except you-know-who, if he calls."

I turned 160 pages of a manuscript on gospel music without taking in a single word. At noon, Kit delivered his usual neat printout of my messages. I scanned the list, but there wasn't anyone I wanted to hear from. Not even my brother.

"There are only three of you left at the end of the second round. Mallory says the high bid is seventy-five thousand. She's not doing traditional bottom-to-top rounds—says it takes too long. She wants everyone to make their next bid at the same time. Do you want to call her?"

"Seventy-five? Maybe this won't get too crazy. Call her and offer eighty-five."

"Me? If that's what you want."

"You can do it, kiddo. It's good practice for your brilliant future." He smoothed his silk tie and smiled.

I could not bring myself to use the phone. The risk was too great. I knew I'd be sitting there with the receiver crooked between my ear and my shoulder, arguing about reprint splits or first serial rights, at exactly the moment that the red message light flashed on. I was in familiar female territory, a place of anxiety I'd visited first in my teens and returned to many times in adulthood. This dark place had one rule: Keep the line open. He might call.

When the late-afternoon papers came out I traded Diane the receptionist a candy bar for a set of the publicity department's copies. Without even stopping at Mel's office I shut my door and spread them out before me. The *Daily News* asked "WHERE'S SAMMY?" above a picture of Sam in his academic robes receiving some kind of honorary degree. It was an old picture and he was clutching the diploma in front of his chest like the Scarecrow in the Wizard of Oz. Below, the caption read, "Did someone nab the Brains behind the Baptist?" The *Post* screamed "SAM SCRAMS! One-armed prof vanishes at Black Fundraiser." Several organizations, from white supremacists to Afrocentric purists, had claimed credit for the disappearance, but no one seemed to be taking them seriously. The *Post* reserved a special tongue-in-cheek sidebar for the fringe group "Cleopatra's Children," whose spokesman had phoned the paper to explain that Samuel Reid was a white man using skin dye so that he could trick the black community into suicide. The police said they were pursuing all reasonable leads and the FBI was standing by. Sam's wife, Ellsbeth, reported that no demands for ransom had been received. No one had heard from him.

"Julia."

I sighed and looked up again at the diligent Kit.

"There's a police detective here to see you," he said.

"What?"

"Says he called before. I didn't realize he was a cop. Thomas Lynch?"

I looked at the message list, fixed in place on the Lucite clipboard. There he was, between the agent who wanted us to run more ads for his client's book and the novelist who was threatening to sue me for not issuing a paperback of the great work that had failed in hardcover. "T. Lynch. Can you meet today? Please call."

"Jesus Christ, Kit."

Empty paper cups, their damp sides crumpled and stained with lipstick, covered my desk. I swept them into the trash, and shoved the newspapers behind my computer.

"You'd better get him before anyone sees him sitting out there. I hope he's not wearing a uniform," I muttered.

"Before I go," he said, "last round for Lamal, the highest bid was one hundred five. Everyone else has dropped out. Do we want to top?"

"Go to one-ten. Tell Mallory we want to shut this down. I have to get rid of this guy."

Kit returned with the man I'd met the night before at the Pan American hotel. I looked up from the proposal I was pretending to read and smiled with my lips pressed tight together.

"Miss Moran. I'm sorry to surprise you. But the second time I called, the receptionist said you were in and I might as well stop by."

"Not at all, Detective. Come right in."

I stood to shake the large hand. The three of us did not fit very well in my office.

"You mind?" Lynch asked, pulling off his jacket. He handed his navy blazer to Kit, who could not suppress a frown at the sight of the short blue-checked sleeves.

"Please, sit down," I waved at the two fake mission chairs, knowing they were less comfortable than they looked. With a hand cupped over his red knit tie Lynch lowered himself into one and stretched his long legs toward the wall of bookcases. When he glanced at the shelves a strand of thick hair fell forward, softening the line of his high forehead and formidable nose. For a second I saw a flash of the earnest and handsome teenager he must have been. But I willed the image away.

"Lot of books you got there," he said.

"It's what we do. Lot of criminals where you work, I'm sure."

"Not as many as you'd think," he said, lifting a worn leather briefcase to his lap. "Not on display, anyway." He pressed the sides of the brass clasp and pulled a long yellow tablet from the case. He rested the pad on his knees. "Miss Moran. I've been thinking that you and I should have a private conversation about recent events."

"We can try."

"You were intimate, were you not, with both William Fitzgerald and Samuel Reid?"

"Yes, but—"

"My father always used to say, there is no such thing as a coincidence."

"Was your father a detective?"

"No. He was not." His thumb clicked the end of a ballpoint pen. "You and I have never spoken about Fitzgerald. Did you know him well?"

"Well enough to know that he was special. One of the only truly good people I ever met."

"People keep telling me that. And yet, someone wanted him dead. And someone wanted to send a message with him dead."

"Message?"

"I've never had a refrigerated homicide before, Miss Moran. It's not your usual way to dispose of a body." He looked over my shoulder as if the image of Fitz's body was projected in my window. "Putting a person on ice like that. Horrible."

"I agree. It's awful," I said, folding my hands.

He turned the almost-green eyes to me. "So, Miss Moran. No idea why someone would want to send a message?"

"None."

"Wait staff says that Fitzgerald used needles. You know anything about that?"

"I'm sure my brother has already explained, Detective. He was a diabetic. Not a drug user." Two red lights lit up on my phone at the same time. I pressed the button that would block all calls.

"Some people are both."

"Not Fitz."

He wrote something on his pad. "Then it's just your brother and his friend Lee Cohen who are into the recreational pharmaceuticals?"

"I don't know what you're talking about, Detective."

"I've spent a lot of time at the Pan American, Miss Moran. There's no need to mince words."

"Well, they certainly don't use anything you shoot with needles. I think my brother would faint if he had to use a syringe." I hoped. "Why does it matter?"

"Makes people vulnerable. Makes people stupid. Confuses their thinking, their judgment."

"Excuse me." Kit rapped on the door frame. "I hate to interrupt, Julia. But Mallory is on line 403. She says we've won the auction but she's not selling you the book unless you can be bothered to speak with her."

I glared at Kit. He lifted his shoulders and mouthed, "What can I do?"

"Excuse me, Detective, I have to take this call." I breathed deep and picked up the phone. "Mallory, I'm thrilled."

"Where have you been all day? It's not like you to let boy wonder carry the bids in an auction."

"Believe it or not I'm sitting here with a police detective."

"Oh. My. God. You're not being arrested are you?"

"No, Mallory. Just routine follow-up to last night."

"That's right. Mr. Pulitzer went bye bye. Maybe it'll boost his sales."

"Mallory, I have to call you back."

"Why don't you just let me keep audio, then?"

"No. We do a great job with audio. Especially for the African-American market. You know that."

"Best-seller bonuses?"

"We're not doing that so much anymore—"

"Come on, Julia. You did it two weeks ago for the Kove brothers."

The detective had left the mission chair and stood before my bookcases with his hands folded behind his back. He glanced at me.

"Okay, okay. Based on slots on the *Times* Sunday list, totaling twenty-five thousand. We'll work out the details later. Tell Pierce I'm thrilled."

I hung up the phone. Lynch had picked a copy of Sam's book off my shelf and was flipping through it.

"Sorry, Detective."

"Perhaps we should close the door?" he asked. Before I could answer a long arm swung forward and pushed the door shut. "Reid's book was a best-seller, huh?"

"Yes, it was."

"You make it a success?"

"I worked harder than I ever have editing the manuscript, getting people excited in-house." I remembered the notes I'd written to every individual member of the sales force. All forty of them. "It was already selling through word of mouth, and then, of course, it won the Pulitzer. It's a great book, a moving book." I cleared my throat. "You can have that copy if you like."

"Thanks. I shouldn't," he said, bending into the chair again.

"Don't worry. I have plenty. Anyway, I hate to be rude, but I wonder if we could tie things up here?"

"I understand. Let's talk about Samuel Reid for a few minutes. He didn't share with you any special concerns about last night?" he asked.

"Other than security, no."

"But you're close?"

"We are close friends. Why?"

He sighed with the kind of throated moan that usually signals parental impatience. "Miss Moran. The Task Force knows a lot about Samuel Reid because that's what they do. They feed the precincts information as it's relevant to special situations. That's why I know that you and Samuel Reid are—tight. That you would be privy to his plans." Like a pale paw, his freckled hand rested on the copy of Sam's book that he'd placed on the desk.

"Yes, I would have known if he had any intention of skipping the speech. But he didn't. That's why I'm so worried about him now."

"Miss Moran. I'm not trying to embarrass you. But I know you are not platonic friends." His voice tightened on the "not platonic" part. Beneath his upper lip the bulge of his tongue rolled across his teeth. The sweet mix of spearmint chewing gum and Old Spice cologne reached my side of the desk.

"I resent this intrusion into my personal life, Detective. It's not relevant," I snapped.

"It is relevant. You're the one he trusted to show him the secret tunnels, the service elevator."

"His own security people wanted to know where trouble might come from. Did you talk to Calvin Smith?" I folded my arms tight and stared at the phone. All of the lights were blinking, silently.

"Yes I did. He was very insightful."

"And?"

"The thing is, Miss Moran, it just doesn't sit right with Smith, either."

"Of course it doesn't. So what did he say about the people who might want to hurt Sam?"

"That's where you and your brother come in, I'm afraid."

"Corky and I?"

"How are things between you and Reid?"

"What are you talking about?"

"Word is he fell in love with you, almost left his wife for you. But he didn't. Or hasn't." A slight twitch quivered in the soft part of his cheek—the part that was going to slacken with beer and age.

"That's none of your business," I hissed, gripping my sides so hard that my ribs hurt beneath my clenched fists.

"The fact is, Miss Moran, leaving out Reid's wife, who's clearly used to the guy by now, and the crazies who think he's covered himself in shoe polish to keep the blacks from going back to Africa, the person who has most reason to be angry with him is you. And the person who cares the most about you is your brother."

"And we are angry at Sam because—?"

"Once Reid and Smith asked for that security tour, you might have started getting ideas. And if any of the crazies did approach your brother and wanted to cause trouble—well, your brother always needs cash. Take that, and the fact that he's protective of his sister, and you've got a lot of motivation to yank Reid's chain. I have a sister. I can imagine how I'd feel." A manila envelop appeared in his hand.

"Feel about what, Detective? Your sister sleeping with a black man?" I said, pushing back my chair so that I could show him the door.

"No. I can imagine how I'd feel about this."

He peeled back the lip of the envelope and pulled out a handful of glossy photographs. He slid one across the desk. Sam and I were laughing at a dinner benefit for Project Hope from the previous spring. I looked up, puzzled.

"What? I look chunky in that dress?" I said.

He said nothing and threw down a photograph of Sam dancing with a redhead in a strapless dress. It looked innocent enough until you noticed how his pelvis was pressed into hers.

"When was this? A few years ago?" I asked. Calm as a nun.

"No, Miss Moran. Ten months ago."

He tossed down another photograph of Sam standing too close to a short brunette woman in a blue Chanel suit with black trim. His prosthetic hand rested beneath her elbow, and she was gazing up at him. They stood in front of the Mayflower Hotel on Central Park West, which was one of Sam's regular haunts. A separate sour pulse started to throb in my stomach.

Lynch narrated. "Renata Butler. They're on the City University Overseers Committee together. Five months ago they slipped away after a board meeting."

Another photograph. This cop must play a mean hand of poker. Sam and a very thin woman with long blond hair sat at a linen-covered table, their cheeks pressed together for the camera, heads thrown back in laughter. It was hard to say but it looked like they assumed the tablecloth would hide the hand that he had gripped around her inner thigh. Instead, the linen had flapped up in the breeze and exposed the caramel-colored fingers that were digging very clearly into her ivory stocking.

"The Fresh Air Fund Summer Dance," he said.

"Three months ago," I whispered. I could even figure out which night if I tried. Instead I was working very hard at pushing something terrible back deep inside so that I would not fall apart. Especially not in front of this detective who pursed his lips like my cousin Danny. Who looked like my uncle Kevin. Who could probably read my face—just as I'd read his short-sleeved shirt and fading sideburns and hard-won college ring—to know exactly where I came from and how far from there I'd traveled.

Who might even have seen other pictures of me, naked, or worse. "Who took these?" I asked, feeling the heat rush up my neck. "And why?"

"There are more," he said, ignoring my questions as he scooped up the pictures and shuffled them like a deck of cards before placing them back in the folder. "But no need to go through them all now. I just want to be sure that we're straight with one another here. I know all about Reid. And I can see your brother getting a little tuned up and deciding to teach the guy a lesson. Tip off some of those bow tie Nation of Islam boys. Play knight in shining armor. May not have even involved any money changing hands. Just emotional payback."

"No, Detective, I'm afraid you have it all wrong." My mouth tasted like blood, as if a tooth long loose had finally torn free from my gums.

"You mean you and the professor have one of those open relationships?" he said with a sneer of distaste.

"No. Actually, I had no idea Sam was—any of this was going on. So I did not have what you call a motive to hurt Reid. And neither did my brother." I blinked hard and tried to trap the swell of tears by resting my index fingers beneath my bottom lashes. Several drops escaped and fell on my desk in slow, fat plops like early rain. The notes on my conversation with Mallory bled away in a stream of blue. Lynch was silent.

"Don't you want to check that off on your pad?" I said, my voice loud and hard. "Moran did not know Reid was fooling around? Motivation, until today: zero."

"Miss Moran. I am sorry." Flushed with embarrassment or frustration, I couldn't tell which, he dropped the yellow pad and tried to fold himself into the tight space between the desk and the chairs to retrieve it. "Everyone said that no matter what Reid was up to, you knew him better than anyone," he said, struggling to resume his erect position. He fumbled with the pad and the case. I refused to look at him. Instead, I held my eyes on the mound of dried roses that sat in a basket on the top shelf of the bookcase. They had all come from Sam, at different times and for different reasons. The cop kept talking, too fast. "You have to understand. It explained the connections. The hotel, Fitzgerald, Reid, your brother, you. If I can clear up this Reid business fast, then I can focus on Fitzgerald. That's the case I want to close."

"I do understand, Detective. You're just doing your job. But in the future, you should remember that sometimes there is such a thing as a coincidence."

"Right. Why don't we just leave it at that for today?" He coughed into his briefcase. "I'd like to stay in touch. If you remember something Reid told you, or you hear from him, I'd appreciate it if you would give me a call." He stood up and slapped another one of his white cards with the police department logo on the desk, where the photographs had just been.

"Thinner, blonder, whiter," I muttered.

"What was that?"

"Nothing. Something a friend tried to tell me." I steadied my gaze somewhere in the middle of his forehead. "Let me find Kit to show you the way out."

Kit was not at his desk. The paperwork to draw up Lamal's contract already sat in a neat stack, awaiting my signature. Three of the lines on the phone were ringing. I grabbed Lynch's jacket out of the guest closet and led him down the hall to the reception area with the soft blue leather sofa and the low glass table covered with magazines.

"So you'll give me a call if you hear from him, Miss Moran?"

"Absolutely, Detective. And you should do the same." I pressed a call button at the elevator bank, ignoring the hand he extended. As the elevator door opened he was still talking about wanting to head off the Feds, close it himself, have my help. I could care less, I thought, as the door glided shut.

"You okay?" said Diane, with her headset slung around her neck.

"Don't ever tell anyone to stop by to see me without an appointment again, you hear?" I shouted. She jumped as if I'd slapped her. The headset fell behind the chair and she dropped to her knees to pick it up. I stormed down the hall toward my office.

I slammed my door. The pigeons began another round of orgasmic burbling at the window. I threw the copy of Sam's book that Tom Lynch had left on the desk across the room, knocking the standing file off the windowsill. Then I took the signed copies of *A Native Son Bears Witness* that I hid in the bottom of the file cabinet as gifts for prospective authors and flung them like Frisbees at the stacks of paper on my desk. There was a knock and the door opened a crack.

"Julia, Mallory called again. She wants you to confirm those best-seller bonuses by seven," said Kit, trying not to look at the mess on the floor or the streaks of tears on my face.

12

It was the hour when the office was turned over to the thick Polish ladies in faded blue housecoats who rolled their plastic trash bins down the hallway, scrub brushes and rags hanging from the side like bats in a tree. Every now and then the women would call out to each other with a snickering laugh that made me feel we must be very dirty by the standards of the old country. A bow-tied figure appeared in my doorway.

"Julia, I'm so happy to see you. I don't mean to bother you but I've been trying to steal a few minutes of your time for days." The Southern drawl nearly made me jump. Its silver-haired owner stepped into my office and perched on the arm of the chair that I hadn't kicked over. He glanced nervously at the books that were still strewn on the floor.

"What is it, Henry?" I was making a superficial attempt to straighten my desk so that I could meet Mel for a late dinner. I was in no mood to be helpful to one of the textbook editors, even the beloved Henry Rawls. Who cared if his division actually paid all the bills for Beckham & Coates.

"Well, dear, it's about one of your authors. Samuel Reid. He said he'd come on as coauthor for the new reading series. With his name we knew we had a shot at getting Illinois state approval for adoption in the public schools. But I just found out his endorsement would give us a chance at California, too. We've never had the state of California adopt our series before, Julia. People kill for less, you know?"

"Henry, you're not going to be able to get him to do any work right now, you understand that?"

"No work necessary, Julia. He only has to read the material and sign on to let us use his name as a coauthor. Willis and McGee spent years on this project, but they've had to bite the bullet." He twisted a pencil between his hands. "I explained to them that a name like

Reid's gives the book the credibility it needs in the multicultural classroom. We sent him the material six weeks ago. Do you think you could call him?"

"Call him, Henry? Do you read the papers? No one knows where the hell he is!" I found the *Daily News* on the floor behind my chair and tossed it at him. He slipped his reading glasses out of his pocket and scanned the headline.

"Oh my. Do you think something untoward has happened?"

"Henry, I don't know. But I will certainly tell you if I find out."

"This may ruin everything. We need to have him onboard now, before the college reps get out there to sell. We go to press next month because we have to ship the examination copies at the first of the year to lock in the orders for next fall." He looked as if he was going to cry.

"Call Penny, his secretary." I scribbled a number on a blue Post-it. "Maybe he's already given her the letter to type. He endorses lots of things without anguishing over it, you know?"

"Thank you, sweetheart. Go home now. You look exhausted." He blew me a kiss from the door and disappeared.

It was true that exhaustion pounded behind my eyes. But I kept my date to meet Mel at the little French bistro that we loved in Murray Hill. It was our quiet old-fashioned place in a quiet old-fashioned neighborhood. I passed up the best steak frites in town, and settled for spoonfuls of the mashed potatoes that came with the roast chicken. Mel was spreading steak tartare on toast points with an expression approaching rapture.

"You know, Jule, they really prepare this dish to perfection here. It's just the right amount. They have tiny capers, not the big ones. And of course the meat is exquisite. Hmm." She had gone to the health club before dinner and her cheeks glowed with the flush of exercise and delight.

I didn't answer. Mel took a delicate sip of Chateauneuf du Pape from her glass, let it linger in her mouth for just a second, and then swallowed. The small diamond in her right ear sparkled in the candlelight.

"You were quite the talk of the office today," she said. "First the detective. Then you screamed at Diane. And of course you threw all those books around in such a rage that even Kit was afraid to clean up after you. Good thing Pat wasn't in." I rolled my eyes and sucked on another spoonful of mashed potatoes. "I don't mean to sound unsympathetic, Julia. But are you really surprised about the other women?"

"Of course I'm surprised. And stunned. And hurt." I put down my spoon and took a large gulp of red wine.

"It's just that he's so completely awful. He stands you up. He forgets your birthday. What am I saying." She slapped her forehead. "I forgot! He's married to someone else."

I swallowed another mouthful of wine. "He did not forget my birthday. The roses just came a day late."

"Right, Julia. He's a great guy. That's why the cop has photos of him with a dozen other women in the past year alone."

"Maybe this dinner was a mistake."

"Don't get all pouty on me."

"Then don't sit there saying 'I told you so.' "

"I won't. Even though I did. Because"—she licked a smear of raw meat off her finger—"the point is not whether I saw it coming. The point is, can you see it now? If you ask me, those photos are a blessing in disguise. Get mad, and say good riddance."

"Well I can't exactly say good-bye when the guy is MIA. He might be dead."

"No chance. If someone wanted him dead it would have happened by now. Trust me. I've thought of it myself." She grinned.

"Well, it would be easier to stop worrying if the whole mess hadn't happened in Corky's hotel. That's why the damn cop came to see me at work."

"It has nothing to do with Corky's hotel. Last night he was on top of everything, cheerful and sober," said Mel.

"Well, he didn't stay sober," I said. "He was so drunk when he got to my apartment he won't remember being there."

"He'll dry out. And then apologize with his tail between his legs. Just like he always does."

"Maybe. But he's been crazy, ever since Fitz died. Last night was like witnessing a psychotic breakdown." I emptied the bottle of wine into my glass. I liked the way it was dulling the pain below my breastbone.

"Julia. You have to let your brother grieve. He found his best friend dead."

"I know, I know. But there's more to it than that."

"Maybe. But that's a lot, in itself. Five extra bricks in his bag, at least. Right now, tonight, why don't we focus on you? Here's saying good-bye to Samuel Reid." She saluted me with her glass.

At the table next to us, a man in a tight pinstripe suit exploded with the arrival of his date's entrée. "You call this a portion? At these prices?" he shouted at the waiter, pointing at the little pile of raw meat she had ordered. His face was as red as the ground beef.

"Monsieur, most people cannot eat more than that. It is very fine, very rich, I assure you," replied the Algerian waiter.

"Tell him, honey, you want more than that, don't you?" urged the man in pinstripes. Honey shrugged her pink-clad shoulders.

Boyfriend picked up the plate, handed it to the waiter, and said, "Bring us more of that tartar stuff. Presto. I'm going to the head." He stood up and stomped away.

The woman smiled at us from beneath her frosted blond bangs. "Aren't men silly? He does this every time we go out."

"You're joking," said Mel. "Perhaps you should try dinner with me sometime. I'd never force you to eat anything you don't want." The woman blushed and concentrated on buttering her roll. I wrapped two surreptitious fingers around the stem of Mel's wineglass and slid it toward me. While Mel leaned over to say something else to Honey, I took three large gulps.

Mel picked up her glass and raised it to her mouth, not realizing it was empty. She stopped and looked at me, twirling the glass by the stem so that the remaining drops slid around its sides. "Someone's been drinking in my glass," she laughed, "and I'm cutting her off." She signaled to the waiter for our check. "Besides, I don't think it's a Grand Marnier kind of night, do you?"

"Nah." The waiter placed the bill on the table with an elegant bow. I threw my corporate credit card on the bill. "My top author is causing me extreme stress. Let B&C pay."

The man returned, adjusting his belt, to find his date staring at a mountain of raw meat. "You got any ketchup or Worcestershire to put on this stuff?" he demanded, pulling the plate toward his side of the table. Mel pulled on her jacket and winked at the woman. Honey stared after her as we picked our way through the tables.

Outside, Mel placed her arm around my shoulder. The wine had warmed me and loosened my knees. I was overcome with the realization that I fit perfectly in the curve of her waist.

"Shall I hail a cab for you, babe?" she asked, unaware of my new insight.

"I guess so," I leaned into her. "Would you like to share one?"

"I live in Brooklyn, Julia."

"I know." I smiled.

She pressed her hand to my cheek. "How many times have I tried to weasel this very invitation from you? And now you ask me home? I think I'll wait until the damsel is not in so much distress."

"I'm not in distress."

"Yes, you are. But I'll take a rain check." She placed a gentle kiss on my lips. "With pleasure." She raised an arm to hail a cab for me. "Go home, Jule, and take a hot bath. There's nothing else you can do tonight."

The taxi sped up an empty First Avenue, magically in sync with the green lights for nearly thirty blocks. I opened the window as far as it would go—which was only six inches. Why did they keep the windows from going all the way down? Had someone on the news reported an epidemic of people who jumped out of moving cabs? I leaned my head against the glass like a family dog in a station wagon, hoping to be revived by the small stream of air. The feeble breeze failed to erase the bitter smell of the pine fragrance tree that hung from the rearview mirror.

I left the cab at the corner of my block so I could buy ginger ale at the all-night grocery. Outside, the grandfather of the Korean proprietors nodded to me as he sprayed the tired flowers with a hose. There was a movement in the air that hinted of autumn, and the straggly sidewalk trees, encircled by little iron fences, rustled their thin arms in the breeze. As I approached my building I spotted a figure squatting on the stoop with his arms wrapped around his head. When I reached the bottom step he lifted his head. Beneath the wool cap, glassy eyes stared through me. His brown skin was mottled like an overripe pear. A crackhead.

My door key was clenched between my fingers. I tried to shake the red wine out of my head and concentrate on the situation before me. What was I going to do with the key in my hand? Poke him?

I looked down the street to see if there was a neighbor in sight, instantly reverting to the suburban version of fight-or-flight: the search for a white person in a sports shirt to offer safe passage. A tall light-skinned black man emerged from a car parked twenty feet away and walked toward me. He wore a small woven skullcap and a leather pea coat, and his boots clicked on the sidewalk as he neared me. I almost ran back to the corner, but my feet were frozen.

"What's the problem, Miss Julie?"

I stepped backward away from him, my head high and my eyes on the street. The tall man looked down at the figure on the steps.

"I see. Afraid of a brother down on his luck? Tsk, tsk, Miss Julie. You being such a friend of our people and all." He walked up the steps, touched the man's thigh, and said, "Move on now, bro, move on." He slipped a bill in the man's scabby hand. The sad figure shuffled down the steps and across the street.

"I don't know you," I said, trying to retrieve my toughest St. Vito's Grammar School voice. "How do you know my name?"

"You may not know me, Miss Julie, but you have met me. We sat next to each other at Symphony Space. My name is Isaac Lord. Remember?"

Shame swept through me. "God. I'm sorry." I fought to focus my eyes in what would seem like a sober gaze. "But what are you doing here?"

"Reverend Vaughn wants to keep a protective eye on Samuel's jewel. In case of a surprise appearance. You know. 'Julie, Julie, Julie, do you love me?' " His feet slid back and forth in an awkward set of moves that I guessed was an imitation of a white person dancing.

"It's Jul-i-a. And I have no idea where Samuel is."

"That is probably correct, Miss Julie. But he knows where you are. So do his enemies. Though you may find this difficult to believe, the reverend also wants you to be safe. Go safely, now."

He followed me up the stoop with calm, languid steps. His jacket crinkled like wax paper as his arm reached behind me to catch the heavy frame of the outer door, and I breathed the rich smell of the leather while I groped for the mail key on the ring in my hand. All I wanted to do was crash through the inside door and run up the stairs away from him. But something in me knew I owed it to both of us to retrieve my mail without fussing. If he was lying, it wouldn't matter anyway. My fingers tightened around the roll of circulars and envelopes I pulled from the mailbox. Lord waited as I riffled through the stack.

"All bills," I said lamely.

"Nothing from our friend Professor Reid?" he asked.

I flipped through the envelopes again. "No."

He bowed his head, slightly, and turned away. I pushed inside and made a fast climb to the safety of my apartment.

Breathing hard, I went to my bedroom window and looked at the street below. Isaac Lord stood beneath a streetlight, smoking a cigarette. I lowered the blinds and walked back through the hall and the living room to the narrow slice of cupboards and appliances that served as my kitchen. Off a high shelf I took a bottle of Maker's Mark that I kept for Sam, poured it over a glass filled with ice, and sipped at the sweet, numbing brown liquid. At first the bourbon burned when it met the red wine. But after a few shudders, it went down.

13

If this is how Corky feels all the time, no wonder he's so moody, I thought, sipping milky iced coffee, pretending to myself that I hadn't ever shared a hangover with him. A sludge of undissolved sugar slipped through the straw and crunched between my teeth. It took two sweating, waxy cups to get me through the mail and messages. I stared at the colored notes from Kit that danced all over my desk, reminding me to approve flap copy, run P and Ls, draft tip sheets. It was going to be a long day.

I'd spent most of the night sipping bourbon and smoking Camel Lights from an old pack that I kept in the freezer, staring out my bedroom window at the tall man who kept watch over me from the sidewalk. Now I was fighting to breathe in a tinny cloud, the telephone receiver unsteady in my hand. Corky still hadn't called to apologize for Tuesday night. I waited until eleven o'clock to dial his number at the hotel. Only voice mail, again. We tried to have lunch together every Thursday. Where was he?

Contact lenses sat like iron weights on my eyes. I squeezed some drops and blinked at the crack of gray sky outside my window. Maybe the long walk to Corky's office would help. I hated to make it easy for him. But it was better to do something than to sit, waiting. I pushed my chair back and stood up. The sudden motion sent a flash of pain between my eyes. I headed for the aspirin I knew was in Mel's desk drawer, but her office lights were off. In the dark, a bald man with silver rings in his nose and his lips and his ears was clicking through a presentation that glowed from the laptop he'd placed on the edge of her desk. He seemed to be talking about the history of tattooes, or tanks. I couldn't tell which. She sat with her chin on her hand, looking bored. I waved and she curled her fingers back in response. At least she wasn't angry about my drinking all the wine last night, or our awkward parting.

I left the Beckham & Coates office on 24th Street and headed north on Broadway. It was a cool, damp day and the clouds hung low, as if we'd all pulled an old pilled blanket over our heads. I marched past the rows of pocketbook and electronics wholesalers in Little Korea, through the Coney Island lights of the retailers in Herald Square, by the store windows filled with exotic buttons and trims on Sixth Avenue. At Bryant Park, I stopped to consider whether I should buy a knish and sit in one of the delicate chairs that dotted the green next to the library. An old lady in a warm-up suit slick with grease hobbled up to me to ask if I could spare a few dollars for her hairdresser. I walked away. Then I stopped, remembering how badly I'd treated the man sitting on my stoop the night before. I usually kept a few singles in my pocket for such encounters—something Fitz had persuaded all of us to do in a flush of New Year's resolutions two years earlier. It was a tiny act of charity I'd sworn to continue, in his memory, forever. And I'd already forgotten. I found the woman, handed her the five-dollar bill in my wallet, and kept walking.

Finally I reached the Pan American Hotel. When I walked into the lobby I was shocked by a blast of cold air. No one yet realized it was time to turn down the air-conditioning. Guests stood in line at the reception desk rubbing their arms and wrapping their sweatshirts around their necks. I found my way to the service elevator and pressed the button for the second floor bar.

Corky's cage was empty. Two men in white jackets stood by the steam tables speaking Spanish, their backs to me. I recognized Tino, the headwaiter. The older man by his side looked at me with tired eyes, and elbowed Tino.

"How you doing, Miss Moran?" asked Tino.

"I'm supposed to have lunch with my brother. Is he downstairs?"

"Mr. Christopher no come in since Tuesday," said the older man.

"Has he called?

"No. But I tell boss he sick. Is okay." He gave a little "okay" circle with his callused thumb and middle finger, and said something to Tino that I couldn't understand. Then he walked away.

No call for the second day. Oh god. So it wasn't just embarrassment that had kept him from calling me. He hadn't made it out of the house yet. Not even to work. The one thing he never missed, no matter what, was work. I shook off a chill.

"They should turn down this air-conditioning, huh?" I said. I looked inside the cage as if I would find some sign of my brother there. "Anyway, I need to leave him a message. Can you open the door?" I asked Tino.

"No one is supposed to go in. Because of whiskey. Bad scene two weeks ago. You know."

"Yeah, I know, but I'm sure Corky won't mind if you let me use his desk for a minute."

He shrugged, and pulled a ring of keys from his pocket. The door whined open. On top of the metal desk sat an open cardboard box that announced it once held twelve 64-ounce cans of plum tomatoes. A trophy peeked out from the top. I looked at Tino.

"Senor Fitzgerald's things. They clean out his office." He made an abbreviated sign of the cross and left me alone.

I dumped my bag on the floor and approached the box. The trophy for the 1991 Quarter Mile Dash at Miles College rested precariously above a loose jumble of things. Fitz had been so tidy, so organized. He would be horrified to see this mess. One by one, I removed the contents of the box so that I could repack it the way he would have wanted.

A scratched brass plaque mounted on synthetic wood that said "Number One Greek Softball League 1992 Psi Upsilon." A beat-up electric calculator with a roll of paper tape. Two wide, pale green pads with many columns, the kind accountants use. A heavy silver St. Christopher medal on a cheap dog tag chain. A pamphlet from the Big Brother Program of New York City, with phone numbers written on it. The book *Words to Live By* by Arthur Thomas, S.J., which flopped open on a paperback spine weak with use. A framed photograph of Fitz's mother with her nine children from the late seventies, judging from the clothing. A stained navy blue tie embroidered with red ducks in flight. A lead crystal triangle engraved "Volunteer of the Year, 1999." Pencils and pens with mismatched caps. A blue vinyl-covered ring binder stamped with a "W" corporate logo, its edges frayed, with pockets inside.

All that remains of the days spent at a desk. I looked at the short stocky mom in the photo, surrounded by her freckled brood of boys in wide ties and girls in plaid knit dresses. Tiny Fitz, the youngest, grinned a toothless smile by her side. I wiped the dust off the glass with my finger. Carefully, I returned each item to the box, beginning with the square and the heavy. Before slipping the blue binder next to the crystal award, I hesitated. I opened it flat on the desk. Inside the front sleeve a glossy flyer announced: "U-CAN: Helping Others to Help Themselves." Behind it was a dog-eared photocopy of "Guidelines for U-CAN Volunteer Tutors," with sections highlighted in yellow marker. Toward the middle I found an official-looking document of thin paper stapled up the side, "Report on Manhattan County Reading Scores Grades 1–6." The rest of the binder was stuffed with tests like the ones in the portfolio I had at home.

So Fitz had been one of Lee's army of tutors. That must have been where he'd won his award. I flipped the pocketed pages over the rings again, not knowing what to look for. Perhaps Fitz had misplaced this binder, was looking for it when he left the other papers with Corky. Maybe that's what the problem had been. Have you seen my binder? Or else something in the binder belonged with something in the briefcase. I looked around to see if anyone was watching me. Tino and the old man were talking to another waiter at the far end of the steam tables. They were being polite, in case I did want to take a bottle of Johnny Walker.

"This is exactly what my brother wanted me to look at," I said to no one in particular, and shoved the binder into my own briefcase. I picked up the photograph and the plaque, and continued packing. After I'd rolled the tie around the St. Christopher medal and carefully wedged them next to the calculator, I grabbed a piece of paper and a red Magic Marker.

"Corky, please call your sister. She loves you," I wrote. The desk drawer did not respond to my tug. The intruder's crowbar had jammed it with the kind of violent dents you see on cars that need major bodywork. I pulled my arm away from the cold touch of the chair's metal arm. With a pushpin from a jar on the desk I tacked my note to the crowded bulletin board.

I stared at the large plastic calendar, willing it to tell me something I did not already know. But the ANB dinner was marked in the same purple felt pen as all the other nonkosher evening events. My initials were marked in small orange letters for lunch today. My brother was nothing if not organized. So where was he?

I snapped my briefcase shut and adjusted the strap on my shoulder. The added weight of the binder pressed the leather deep into my skin. Pulling the cage door shut, I walked toward the elevator. "Thanks for everything," I called out. The men in white smiled at me and waved. An older man with a loose pink face also raised his hand. I recognized Manny Cohen. He took a step toward me, but I popped in the elevator as the doors opened. I escaped the lobby through the exit closest to the Seventh Avenue subway at 50th Street.

Back at my office, I collapsed into my desk chair. I opened Fitz's binder again, but black spots swam over the pages of the U-CAN guide like the tadpoles Corky used to catch in a jar of swamp water. I closed my eyes, pressed my head into my chest, and tried to fill my lungs with air.

I'd tried to forget what drinking did the day after. I had almost forgotten it all—the sweet hum of the whiskey, the fleeting mania, the crash of exhaustion. No one wants to admit that there are plenty of happy memories mixed in with the sorrows and the agonies of too much booze and drugs. Nights filled with the kind of laughter that hurts your belly. Jokes that you can't remember in the morning that made you knock over the bowl of peanuts at the bar. Dreams confessed in the morning's early light that no one ever mocks you for. I understood all too well the untested pleasures of the bar stool pipe dream. What I had learned was that I couldn't handle the self-recriminations the day after. Of course Corky had learned to push the morning after into one long tomorrow.

But there had been a stretch of time in my twenties when I could drink six or seven scotch and sodas by my brother's side without blinking. When a taste of his drugs or a snifter of his brandy provided an easy release from all my years of good girl behavior. Just as I'd tutored him through biology and algebra, he'd found me to be a willing pupil in the ways of self-medication. We had strengthened the bonds of childhood with the false glue of manic three A.M. confessions. But that glue just wasn't holding us together anymore.

Kit knocked on the door that I had left ajar by only a few inches. I bolted upright and tried to look as if I were reading the proposal on my desk. "Come in."

"Julia, I hate to bother you, but that woman from Teachers College says you keep missing each other. Sylvie Barr. I can tell her you're in a meeting if you don't want to talk to her."

"No, it's okay. Thanks, Kit."

"Okay then. She's on my line, 402."

I picked up the phone. "Sylvie. Thanks for calling back. I've been trying to reach you."

"I warned you this was a crazy week here, Julia. First week of classes."

"Yes, I know. I'm sorry." I tried to recall what I wanted from her. "I'm interested in learning more about those city tests you mentioned."

"Yes, our mayor's great panacea. 'Hey, kids, pass this test so that I can prove I'm doing something for education in this town.' Even though most children still can't read at grade level. Makes me mad as blazes. But what exactly can I tell you?"

I looked at Fitz's open binder. "I'm interested in how different schools cope with the pressure. Extra measures, like this tutoring group U-CAN. Have you heard of them?"

"You bet. They took everyone by surprise last spring—they won the city contract for a special federally funded program devoted to after-school reading instruction. Beat out older tutoring programs like Literacy Pals and Children's Helpers. I have to hand it to them."

"Hand it to them? They're actually good at what they do?"

"They've had incredible results. Of course who knows if they can keep it going. City contracts can be the kiss of death for creative organizations. But everyone wants to get on that treadmill. Once the city has you in their system, it's actually harder to stop the money coming than it was to start it in the first place."

"Amazing. I know the person in charge of U-CAN."

"Really? I didn't know you were so connected to the reading world, Julia! Perhaps you'd be interested to read the presentation that accompanied their bid. It may give you some ideas for that book we talked about. I'll send it over to you. I was one of the city's ten outside consultants."

"I'd love to see it, Sylvie."

"Read it this weekend. But I can't get together until next week. The new students command all my attention right now."

"Next week, then."

I hung up the phone. Every day I learned more about Lee's apparent success as a servant of the people. Never would I have expected the Don Juan of Scarsdale to do so much good for so many. I slipped the U-CAN papers back in the sleeve of the binder and closed it with a sigh.

I looked around my office. The wake of my tantrum over Sam was still in evidence, with confused piles in place of my usual neat stacks, and no sign of the legendary Moran to-do list with its seven categories of activity. If Lee Cohen could run a successful nonprofit agency, the least I could do was keep my own house in order. I put the phone on do-not-disturb, asked Kit to get a dumpster from facilities, and kicked my shoes off and under my desk.

14

By 7 p.m., the newest round of proposals sat neatly piled in my aluminum baskets. The waist-high black plastic dumpster was filled with used manila folders and out-of-date catalogs and draft manuscripts of books published long ago. Wrappers from cheese peanut butter crackers and empty cans of Diet Pepsi peeked from the top of the smaller trash can beneath my desk. A bottle of Mylanta sat open next to the computer. I took a long swig and returned to the task of smoothing out the crumpled pages of the signed copies of *A Native Son Bears Witness* that I'd used as Frisbees. A familiar voice barked from my door.

"Moran, who the hell is responsible for this?"

The figure of Pat Muldoon, Publisher, filled my doorway, her short curly hair almost brushing the top of the door frame. If only Pat had been born in the age of professional women's basketball. She could have made millions endorsing cereal and sneakers. But instead here she towered in her green rayon pantsuit, fighting to make a book publishing company profitable in the age of cable TV and the Internet.

"Hi, Pat. I'm just doing some end-of-summer cleanup."

"No. This book, Moran." The ugly cover of Fred Stone's *There Used to Be a Neighborhood Here* shook between her thick fingers.

"I am. I mean, I inherited it from Eve Barrington when she left. Don't worry. We won't be publishing crap like that anymore."

"Crap!" she shouted with a force that made the books on my shelves tremble. "Do you look at the large quantity orders on the daily sales report? It's in a fourth printing already, for crissakes."

"Those are special sales. The conservative think tanks buy hundreds at a time."

"Great! Nonreturnable sales! Just what this place needs. Have you signed up his next one?"

"Not really," I stammered. "I didn't think we wanted to do any more of these rants about how the world's been going to hell in a handbasket since the sixties—"

"Look," she leaned over my desk so that I was forced to drop my head back to look up at her, as if I were stuck in the front row at the movies. Beneath her perfume I caught the scent of the cigarettes that she still smoked at a terrifying rate behind the closed door of her office, though the building had long been a designated no-smoking zone. "All this soft stuff is fine, Julia. Your black books are doing okay. But you need some franchises. These conservative nutheads buy books. Not like they used to back when Melvin ran the place," she said, referring to the former publisher, "but they're still a tight-knit crowd. And they have plenty of cash to spend. So get this guy's next book, okay?"

"You bet," I replied.

She straightened and flashed her bleached white teeth in the famous grin that made each one of us believe, mistakenly, that she was our friend. In the doorway she stopped and twisted around to launch one final instruction. "I believe there's a Hamilton Institute Event tonight in honor of Mr. Stone? His editor should be there." The swish of panty hose rubbing on mighty thighs sounded as she walked down the hall to find her next victim.

Tonight, of all nights—an evening organized by the city's richest and most powerful conservative foundation, after I'd been perspiring over my trash all afternoon. I slipped on my shoes and ran to the women's room to survey the damage. I was wearing a simple navy blue rayon dress with a jacket that had sleeves cropped at the elbow. The dress was crumpled, but not everywhere. I would look like a used tablecloth only from the back. As for my face—powder and red lipstick could probably hide the worst, especially at night.

With a damp tissue I wiped away the ghost of antacid from the side of my mouth. Slowly I massaged the ivory cream of a concealer stick into the bluish shadows beneath my eyes. I dulled the shine of my nose and forehead with powder, and added another sweep of blush and mascara to give definition to my now-Kabuki pale face. With a red pencil I drew the outline of perfect conservative lips, and blotted my lipstick three times, just as Mel said the models do. Back in my office, I sprayed too much perfume on my neck, bent over from the waist to shake my hair, and slipped on the higher-heeled evening shoes I kept in my desk drawer. I dug out the Hamilton Institute invitation from the box where Kit dropped all invites and announcements, and shoved it in my purse. On my way out I stopped in Mel's doorway. What looked like hundreds of photographs of corsets were spread out on the desk in front of her.

"Want to come with me to a Hamilton Institute reception for Fred Stone's book?"

"And miss the joy of sorting out Susie Snow's art plan for *The Hidden History of Underwear*? No way." She looked up over the top of the sleek tortoise reading glasses that I suspected she didn't really need. "Why in hell would you go to a Hamilton Institute anything?"

"Pat says I have to."

"You need franchises, huh?" She stabbed her finger at the air in front of her with a demonic grin.

"Yep. My turn to save the company. See ya."

As I waited by the elevator, Henry Rawls walked by with an armful of page proofs. "Good news, Julia, " he said. "Professor Reid's secretary did have a letter for us ready to go in the mail. She faxed it this morning. You're a lifesaver." He kissed my cheek with a soft, moist peck that stank of tobacco. "Going out on the town? You haven't looked this glamorous in weeks. It suits you." He disappeared around the corner as I tried to smile what would look like a mysterious Republican smile.

When I emerged from our office building I stopped to admire the deserted sweep of Broadway crossing Fifth Avenue in front of the Flatiron Building. A few dogs yapped in the twilight from the run in Madison Square Park. Their lucky owners stood by the fence, hands in pockets, chatting about who knows what. Brands of chow? How happy I'd be to stand by their sides, instead of on my way to a room full of strangers. I inhaled deep to summon my nerve, and flagged a yellow cab to take me uptown.

I entered the sensible redbrick front of the Harvard Club and stood for a minute in the crimson-carpeted entryway. I knew that the Hamilton Institute events were held in a large meeting room upstairs, but it was still early and I wanted to avoid the stress of coctail-hour mingling as long as possible. I decided to pay a visit to the stuffed heads that gave the club its warm and cuddly Teddy Roosevelt feeling. I made my way through the grill room, where old men slathered cheddar cheese spread on pretzels and drank Manhattans over ancient card games, and planted myself in the middle of the great room that was lined with portraits of old college presidents and mounted treasures of safaris gone by. As I stared into the eyes of a distressed-looking tiger head, the strong smell of lavender made me sneeze. I grabbed a paper napkin printed with a crimson "H" from a waiter. Across the room a man in a light gray suit sat in a leather armchair, reading a newspaper beneath an elephant with very long tusks. His pale suit, silk socks, and pinky ring stood out with a dandyish brightness amid the dark attire of the other guests, but he looked perfectly at home. A woman in a sleeveless sheath skipped toward him.

"If it isn't Manfred Cohen," she said as he stood up to shake her hand. "Where is that handsome son of yours tonight?"

I froze. Lowering my face into an elaborate procedure with the paper napkin, I started to turn away from them.

"Busy as a bee, Bitsy, busy as a bee. Can't keep track of that boy during election season. Say, is that my friend Miss Moran?" he called.

I abandoned the napkin and smiled into the pale sparkle of Manny's blue eyes. "Why, hello Mr. Cohen. What are you doing here?"

"I always come out for the Hamilton events. And yourself?"

"Supporting a house author. Fred Stone."

"Have you met Bitsy Stephens?" he said. Bitsy squinted at my dress. Another sleeveless wonder buzzed to her side. "And Cornelia Valence. Meet Julia Moran." The two women smiled without parting their lips.

Manny lowered his face toward mine. "I'm a lucky man to see you twice in one day," he murmured. "Weren't you looking for your charming brother this afternoon?"

"I was picking something up for him. He has the flu."

"Really? Couldn't be what they call the Irish flu, now, could it?"

"Manfred," interrupted Cornelia with a firm bejeweled hand on his sleeve, "do you know that black man from Yale who disappeared? He and I sit on the Lewis Foundation committee together. What a delightful person. So very . . . charismatic. Very."

"Yes, Corn, I've met him," said Manny. "Miss Moran has worked with him as well, haven't you?"

I nodded. Corn must have found me very rude, because I was staring at her face, trying to figure out if she was the blonde sitting at the table with Sam in the photograph Detective Lynch had shown me. "He was just as smart as a whip," she said, avoiding my gaze. "Not all obsessed with other black people like so many of them are. We both agreed the poor come in many shapes and sizes, not just hues. In fact, we gave a nice grant to that boy of yours for his program to feed the homeless, tutor little children, and all that. What's it called? WE R?"

"U-CAN," I offered.

"Yes, we did. Enough to help them get things rolling and secure that city contract," she said.

"Corn, you are a true patroness of the needy." Manny took her hand and found a place to kiss it between the diamond rings.

"Well, I have to be heading upstairs," I said. "Ta ta."

I left them and made my way to a small elevator with walls that were newly painted in a hue more cherry red than crimson. On the second floor I followed the worn red carpeting to the Eliot Room. Luckily for me, the panel discussion was already well under way. At linen-covered tables sat men in navy suits and women in gold-buttoned jackets of beige or blue, attentively listening to the woman who was speaking from a microphone on the dais.

"Fred's book exposes the horrible legacy of the sixties social welfare system. We've created a population that believes it has rights but no responsibilities," she read from the paper gripped tightly in her hands.

Here we go, I thought.

"We're left holding the bag, paying for lavish social uplift programs. Imagine a high school that provides lush day care facilities for unwed teenage mothers, rather than making pregnancy onerous. Why aren't we punishing the serial impregnators?"

The audience applauded. Even the serial impregnators.

"We need to teach this population, marginalized and chaotic, to embrace the middle-class values that keep our society stable." Her plastic headband slid off her head as she gave the crowd an excited nod.

The audience stood and clapped again with such fervor that a moderator had to ask everyone for quiet before introducing the final speaker, a Mr. John Walker. Walker was tanned and silvery and handsome in a familiar, too-much-time-spent-on-the-golf-course way. But the way his yellow tie popped out against his white shirt made my eyes hurt. I headed for the coffee urns on the other side of the room. I flipped down the handle on the one marked "decaf," but nothing happened.

"Allow me," said a deep voice. Isaac Lord tipped the pot forward so that a trickle of brown liquid flowed into my cup.

The cup clanged on the crimson-rimmed saucer as I placed it on the table. "Funny to see you here," I said, trying not to sound as nervous as I felt. "Or is it just that you'll follow me anywhere?"

"These people are very powerful. It's important to know what they're saying."

"What they're saying is awful. They talk as if poor people are some kind of nasty foreign bird nesting on their window air-conditioning units."

"But you publish them?"

"You know I've worked hard to take the list in a new direction. But I inherited Stone. My boss made me come." I raised my eyes from the mauve diamond pattern that crossed the center of his silk tie. "I'm sorry I was so spooked last night." My cheeks burned. "Guess that's a poor choice of words."

He laughed. "Not at all. Sorry I came up on you without warning. Be prepared, though—we will continue to keep an eye on you."

"And Sam?"

"Sam, when he shows, indeed. Come. I'd like to introduce you to someone." He took my hand and led me to a table in the last row near the door. A fiftyish black woman with very manicured hair sat erect in a coral knit suit. Her fingers toyed with the strand of pearls around her neck.

"Julia Moran, this is Dean Harriet Perth of Columbia."

"Pleased to meet you," I gushed, thrilled to be so close to this year's Parker Genius Award winner. She nodded and put a finger to her lips to silence me. From the podium Mr. Walker was becoming animated.

"Four years ago we set out on a new course in the city of New York," he boomed. "Now it's time to take the next plunge. To create a culture of accountability, a culture of choice, a culture of control. In education we want results, not rules!"

He won even more applause than Ms. Headband had.

"What's all this about?" I whispered to Isaac.

"This man owns Walker Communications," he said. "The company that puts paid advertising in every classroom on the 'free' TVs it gives to schools. Now he's running for-profit schools throughout the Southeast. The mayor is backing him to take over six city schools—uptown and in the Bronx."

"Wasn't he with the mayor at the ANB?" I remembered aloud when I looked hard at the silver hair. Isaac nodded.

"The mayor of the twenty-first century must be an entrepreneur!" Walker pounded the podium. "Let's hear it for our favorite entrepreneur."

The mayor rose from his seat at a table near the front of the room. The crowd came as close to cheering as it had since the Yale game of 1981. He waved his arm in jerking movements and when the applause wouldn't stop he bounded up to the podium.

"It's not my night, folks, or my dear friend John Walker's. Tonight belongs to Fred Stone, a great scholar and writer. No speeches—just remember that everyone has to buy a copy of Fred's book in order to get that free Hamilton Institute drink! So pull out your checkbooks."

There was a roar of thirsty laughter. As the applause died out, people began to stream toward the table where Fred Stone stood behind a stack of books. It was actually located just next to the bar that had been silently rolled in during the final speech.

"Nice touch," said Isaac. "Does the liquor boost sales?"

"I'm afraid I have to let Fred know I'm here," I said. "Dean Perth, I hope we can speak later."

"We're not staying to socialize," she said in a regal voice. I looked in despair at Isaac, who gave me the slightest hint of a wink. I pushed my way across the room to Fred's side. A sheen of perspiration clung to his bald head.

"Congratulations, Fred. It's quite a turnout."

"Julia! I'm so surprised. I didn't think you—well, this is wonderful."

"We're so proud of you, Fred," I said, turning my back to the woman who was clutching four copies of his book to her chest. "I know it's not the right time to talk, but I want you to know I'm already thinking about the follow-up. Perhaps"—I looked at the tall figure of Mr. Walker crossing the room—"*There Used to Be a High School Here*?"

"Yes, yes," he gurgled, reaching into the wrinkled pockets of his khaki suit to find a pen, "That's just what I was telling Eddie here."

"Here, Fred, my man, sit down so you can sign these babies," urged the short man by his side. He pulled out a seat and tucked Fred in behind the table. As people thrust their books forward, he opened them to the title page so that Fred could quickly sign them.

Once Fred had a rhythm going, the man called Eddie turned toward me, bouncing on his toes with an insistent energy. His honey-colored skin was as smooth as a boy's, though it sat atop a body that looked as if it belonged to someone middle aged who was already going a little soft around the edges. He flashed a smile at me and shot out a hand.

"Eduardo Saldivar," he said, "But everyone calls me Eddie."

"Nice to meet you, Eddie. Have I seen you before?" I asked, keeping my eye on Fred.

"I started as a speechwriter for the mayor when I got out of college. Now I'm a special assistant on education policy." The slightest beat of a Puerto Rican accent danced beneath his words.

"You must know my friend Lee Cohen, then."

"Sure, sure, Lee's my buddy, my man," he insisted. "We're like this." He raised two crossed fingers and smiled.

"Didn't I just read about your office in the *New York Times*? Advocating the use of corporal punishment in the public schools?" I asked.

His brown eyes crackled with mischievous electricity. "People love that shit, don't they? Gets them to pay attention." He moved closer and cocked his head toward Fred, who was trying to sign fast enough to keep his customers happy. "So what goes on, hey? We thought that Beckham & Coates was pulling away from the Hamilton Institute."

"Oh no," I cooed, "we're always commited to the free marketplace of ideas."

A slick of black hair fell forward and a frown creased his brow, as if he wasn't sure whether or not I was making fun of him. The crowd behind him seemed to surge in a wave that bumped him toward me. The well-known head of black curls appeared behind him.

"Eddie, my boy," said the mayor, slapping one hand on each of Saldivar's shoulders, "How's it going, *nino*?"

Saldivar stood up straight and buttoned the top button of his suit. "Great, sir. I was just talking to—"

"This is the lady publisher, isn't it? Miss Moran?" said the mayor with a tight smile.

Startled, I raced back over every publishing party of the past year, trying to remember if I'd ever been introduced to the mayor. I knew that my mind wasn't working at its best with a hangover. But the only time I knew we'd been in the same room was the night Sam disappeared.

"Eddie, why don't you leave the two of us alone for a few minutes?" said the mayor. Eddie nodded and resumed his post by Fred's side, opening books.

"Lovely to meet you," I said, reaching for a mayoral hand that did not appear.

"Eddie is brilliant. And so very ambitious," he answered, ignoring my confusion and steering me toward the abandoned tables near the microphone. "I'd be lost without him. God knows he feeds me the right Spanish phrases when I need them." He stopped.

"I have to admit I'm surprised that you know who I am," I pressed.

"Ah," he said with an impatient flap of his hand. "It's a small world. In fact, I hope you won't mind if I bring up a business matter in the midst of the festivities?"

"Business? I'm flattered, Your Honor," I said, slightly relieved, in my deepest "I only have eyes for you" voice. I almost forgave myself for thinking, sign up the mayor and Pat's really going to have to sweeten your bonus next year.

"You were Samuel Reid's editor, were you not?" he asked.

"Yes. For *A Native Son Bears Witness.*"

"You and Reid were close, no?

"Editors and authors can work closely, the way Sam and I did. But when the author is as busy as you are, we bring in a writer."

He cocked his palm in a wave to someone across the room. When he continued he spoke in a voice so low I had to concentrate to hear what he was saying. "Lee Cohen told me all about your work with Reid. Cohen knew you'd be worried, wanted me to assure you we're on the case."

"On Sam's case?" I faltered on the words.

"I'm deeply concerned about Reid's disappearance. The police will do everything in their power to find him," he said, punctuating the sentence with a practiced tightening of the mayoral jaw.

"Why are you telling me this?"

"Why? Because I want to put your mind at ease, Miss Moran."

"But according to the police I've met, there might not be anything to worry about," I said. The hard crackle of my voice did not fit with the happy martinied hum of the room. "Besides, Sam's disappearence doesn't exactly hurt your campaign, does it?"

"Ah, Miss Moran. You must understand. I love the game, the race. I hate anything that gets in the way of the race." His hand went to his tie, which did not need straightening. "Of course, it's rare that someone with Reid's brains gets involved with the game of politics." He stepped too close to me, so that I was forced to see the hairs in his nose. "I don't suppose you've heard from your friend since he dropped out, have you?"

"What?"

"Or, anyone else? Say, some disgruntled associate of his?"

Isaac flashed through my mind. "I don't know what you're talking about."

"The world is filled with unscrupulous people. I wouldn't want anyone to pressure you. Try to involve you in some wild-goose chase."

"I'm not interested in any chase that involves Sam, wild or not."

"Glad to hear it, then, glad to hear it." He squeezed the soft part of my arm—the part I hated—a little too hard and a little too long. "It's always best to let the system do its job. We're doing everything we can for Reid. So try not to worry too much, Miss Moran. Great to meet the literary lioness." He gave my arm one last squeeze as if it were a damaged orange, and walked away to embrace the woman who hated impregnators and two of her friends.

I looked around the room, trying to steady the flutter in my neck. Fred was still signing books, while Eddie Saldivar's hand was wrapped tight around the waist of a woman old enough to be his grandmother. Isaac Lord was nowhere in sight. So many people had sought me out, and yet I had never felt so alone.

It was hard to keep looking over people's shoulders as if I were searching for a long-lost best friend. I was afraid that the next person whose eyes locked with mine would want to talk about Sam, too. Of course, I was used to being with him at this sort of function. We'd catch each other's eyes from opposite sides of the room, pass by each other with a brush of the arm or thigh, slip in and out of each other's conversations with deliberate casualness. Sam loved nothing more than playing games in the company of rich, successful people. But I had no idea what kind of game had now pushed him onto everyone's mind.

Searching for the refuge of a powder room, I stopped to pick a plain cracker from an elaborate cheese board. Behind me, two women were talking about someone and his date. Pausing to wipe my fingers on another H-stamped napkin, I listened.

"Can you believe he brings her out in public? With her hanging all over him? When his wife gets wind of it, it's going to be very expensive for him. Very."

I saw myself with Sam at the New York Public Library Benefit, laughing in his arms on the dance floor. We had timed our departures fifteen minutes apart, and met in the black limousine waiting outside. With the press of a button the window in the middle of the car had glided shut to protect us from the view of the driver. Sinking into the backseat I'd felt Sam's fingers sliding under my skirt, inside my stockings, ripping a hole in them, tearing them, before we had reached my apartment. But at 3 A.M. he'd risen from the bed, after hours of heated lovemaking, to leave. A hotel was preferable to sleeping in my bed. Never get too close. Never take off the T-shirt, the prosthesis. Never stay. And here I was, surrounded by strangers, missing him, despite the hurt.

It was time to go home. Manny and the mayor were talking to each other over a fruit platter as I walked toward the stairway. Manny was holding a bunch of red grapes, popping one grape in his mouth at a time, while the mayor twirled his empty glass at a waiter, signaling for a refill. When he caught my eye, Manny lowered the grapes and prodded the mayor with his elbow. They both waved to me like boys being left at summer camp. Bitsy stepped toward Manny to introduce him to another small woman in a silk sheath. As they stood there, each woman placing a perfect little hand in one of Manny's, I slipped down the crimson-carpeted stairs.

The doorman of the club tipped his hat to me. When the taxi deposited me at my stoop, one of Isaac's crew did the same thing from the curb, where he kept watch.

15

I didn't check my mail until the next morning, when I was on my way to work. That's when I discovered the postcard.

It slid out of the box into my hands. A shot of Louis Armstrong, trumpet to his lips, from 1926, with the Hot Fives posed behind him. The message, in a familiar scrawl, said, "Miss Me Baby? Hang in there. Everything is copacetic. S." I slipped the card between a phone bill and an overdue notice from a credit card company and looked out at the sidewalk. A skinny teenager leaned against Isaac's red car, peeling tinfoil back from a soft roll that was swollen thick with egg. He licked ketchup and cheese off his hand before leaning into a large bite. I ran back up the stairs to my apartment.

Sam loved sending little notes that were supposed to win him forgiveness for his latest transgression. But the postmark on this one had Wednesday's date—the day after he had disappeared. Now I didn't know what to make of the question I'd heard from so many people over the past three days. Have you heard from Sam? It looked as if I had. Maybe I could redeem myself with Isaac by sharing the news with him. Unless, of course, the card was some kind of trick. I stared at the handwriting, the cramped letters I'd once prided myself on being able to decipher. It looked real enough.

So Sam had made contact. But not my brother. I picked up the phone. It was Friday, Corky's most important day at the Pan American—the day he liked to start early to prepare for the weekend assault of tourists and weddings. I dialed the second floor bar and let the phone ring until Tino finally answered. He'd still had no word from Corky, but all the weekend deliveries had arrived on time, as if my brother had placed the orders himself. I chewed on a crust of toast I'd left sitting on a flowered plate, and figured out what I should do next.

There was no way around it. Isaac could wait. This morning I had to go to Queens to wake my brother from his bender. It was time for him to face whatever he was hiding from—including me. I bypasssed Kit's questions by calling direct into his voice mail to say I would be at home working on the Davison manuscript. He should email Pat to tell her what I was up to and to say that Fred's event had been a big success. I ran out of my apartment before he or anyone could call me back. Downstairs, I avoided the eyes of the egg-eater and hurried down the street toward the subway.

Soon I was sitting on the E train, head rolled forward like a broken doll, headed for Kew Gardens. I was battling my own private hell: the movement of the train was aggravating the unstable pulse in my stomach that made me Mylanta's best customer. Sam's postcard threatened to jump from the outside pocket of my bag, where I'd put it for safekeeping. Every few minutes I flicked its edge with the nail of my index finger, to make sure it was still there. I tried to ignore the churning in my gut as we hurtled forward.

Three soft furry Indian women sat in saris across from me. One smiled at me and then returned to the animated conversation that trilled above the chug of the train. With a sigh I popped another chalky peppermint tablet. Once we hit the outdoors on the elevated track it would be better. No more fluorescent lights, no more braking in darkness for unseen obstacles. As we swung out of the tunnel into the daylight, the chug of the train began to sing to me. Somebody needs me. I wonder who. Doo-doo-dee-doo. Sky, the tops of buildings flashed by the window. Time to breathe again. Clear the mind. Solve the problem.

Kew Gardens, at last. I stepped onto the platform and followed the thick white shoes of four nurses to the stairs. They sang good-bye to each other in West Indian accents and parted at the sidewalk. I looked around to get my bearings. No Royal Gardens of Kew here but a faded urban strip. A low row of storefronts that looked as if they belonged in a Hopper painting were now covered with gaudy signs announcing the usual jeans and rotisserie chickens and sneakers. Behind them towered apartment buildings of crumbly brown brick with pretty casement windows and Tudor ornamentation near the rooftops. Gentility.

Which way was Corky's? I hesitated, trying to re-create the route we'd taken when I had last accompanied him home. I turned right and walked down a very un-Manhattan street shaded by thick trees that had refused to relinquish a leaf to the encroaching autumn. A block of the Tudor apartment buildings gave way to stuccoed two-family houses. I thought I remembered turning left at the third stop sign. There it was—Corky's blue Toyota, retrieved from the lot where my brother had drunkenly abandoned it, sat snugly by the curb. Lee's beat-up Pinto was parked a few cars away, though his precious Saab was nowhere in sight. I trotted down the street and ran up the steps to the door on the left side of number 42, where I pressed the buzzer marked "Cohen/Moran."

Nobody answered. I waited and rang again. I dug in my pocketbook for the eight-ball key chain Corky had left with me for emergencies. The round ball felt good in my hand, the way a smooth stone does, and as I held it I wondered if I was ready for what I might find inside. The old trees that lined the sidewalk swayed as one in the breeze. I closed my eyes and listened to the heavy rustle of the leaves. It was an old sound that reminded me of summers, and of home. I knew what I had to do. I turned the key in the lock and opened the outside door.

Stained beige carpet led up the stairs to Lee's apartment and to the door on the right that was Corky's. Though it wasn't quite legal, given the zoning of the block, their side of the house was subdivided into two separate dwellings. Stacks of mail addressed mostly to Lee sat on a small iron table that had once been intended for a patio. I went back outside and checked the mailbox, pulling out more bills and circulars addressed to both Lee and Corky. It didn't look like either one of them had been around in days. Even Lee's latest issue of *Penthouse* was still in its brown mailing wrapper.

Nothing happened when I pounded on the door to Corky's apartment. From the street I heard the angry honking of a car. Heels clicked on the sidewalk, followed by the jangle of a dog's lead. I turned the key and opened the door, slowly. The room was dark and smelled like pickles. I called my brother's name, but no one answered. I flipped on the light switch by the door. The old plaid sofa from my parents' den—where Corky had seduced so many girls in his youth—presided calmly over the coffee table where copies of *Sports Illustrated* and *Time* sat in neat stacks. On the opposite wall was a prefab unit that held a TV and stereo and a handful of books that looked like almanacs or yearbooks. I examined the shelves. Since I'd last been there, Corky had framed photographs of my parents and the four of us with my grandmother and carefully placed them on the top shelf. I was surprised to see that they were flanked by several of his track trophies. On the middle shelf, in a sterling frame, sat a photograph of Fitz, Lee, and Corky, standing arm in arm on the porch steps of an old white frame house. Smiling boys in sunglasses and khaki shorts. Little Fitz was between the two taller boys; it looked as if they were lifting him off the ground in their arms. Over their heads someone had pasted a balloon that said 'All for one and one for all."

I walked to the kitchen and dining area that stretched like an L from the end of the living room. In the middle of the dining room table sat a round lazy Susan that held several different pepper mills. A Formica-topped island separated the dining area from the kitchen, where there was a wall of full-sized appliances in that once popular pea soup color. To my cramped Manhattan eye this looked like surburban comfort and I was surprised all over again to think that Corky liked it so much. There was a coffee cup in the sink and the cold remains of a pot of coffee on the counter. The refrigerator held eggs, juice, and a couple of bottles of flavored vodka; the freezer had only ice trays and a clear Ziploc bag swollen full of marijuana. I remembered the tense order of Corky's teenaged bedroom. Even stoned out of his mind he kept his albums lined up tightly on the shelf in strict alphabetical order.

I moved on to the bathroom and bedroom. Hanging over the shower rod were a couple of used towels, all of them dry. Green bottles of Polo cologne and shaving cream and lotion sat in a basket atop the toilet. The bed was made with a paisley comforter and matching pillows—also discarded by our mother from her eighties collection. I flipped through a pile of magazines by the side of Corky's bed. One was a copy of the *New York Times Sunday Magazine* opened to a profile of Sam. Beneath it was an old *New York Magazine* with a cover story on Reverend Vaughn. Had Corky been boning up on the subject of Sam for the wrong reason? Or just trying to impress me, his big sister? I opened his drawers and found nothing but pens and tape and old credit card receipts on top, socks and underwear and shirts on the bottom.

The light on the answering machine was blinking. I pressed play and listened to the unheard messages: seven from me, two from work, one from our mother, one from Lee on Tuesday afternoon, saying, "Hey Buddy, see you at that black fund-raiser at the hotel tonight. The mayor's kept me busy. Haven't been home in days. Let's party later. Bye." That meant no one had listened to them since the day Sam disappeared. Where was my baby brother?

I returned to the kitchen and poured myself a glass of water. Then I sat down at the table to confront my feelings of panic and failure. I pictured myself standing on street corners, handing out fliers with Corky's photograph copied on them. Of course, there was no need for fliers if he was deliberately hiding from me. And the world. I gave the lazy Susan a hard spin. Behind the salt and pepper mills sat my brother's leather address book. I flipped through it, not knowing what to look for. Some connection eluded me. I slipped the address book in my bag anyway, a souvenir of my fruitless mission.

The water in the plastic tumbler tasted of chlorine. I poured it down the drain and placed the empty cup in the sink next to the coffee mug. I walked through the apartment, trying to find a trace, a sign that would tell me what was going on in my brother's life. I stopped before the photograph of the three musketeers on the bookshelf. I picked up the silver frame, already dented in the top left corner. Fitz's head was tilted back in glee, as if the camera had caught his friends in the act of tickling him. Corky was grinning with wide Groucho Marx eyes, the way he used to when beer still made him funny instead of angry. Almost against my will, my eyes rested on the tall figure on the left. Lee was wearing a shirt I recognized all too well—the same worn pink button-down he'd had on one hot July night the summer after they'd graduated from college.

I remembered how Lee had looked as he climbed out of the small lima bean–shaped pool that sat steps below the stone patio behind my parents' house. The wavy hair had clung wet to his forehead, so that for a second he'd looked like a giant-sized ten-year-old boy. But the plaid swimming trunks that clung to his groin confirmed he'd left childhood far behind. The smooth shoulders were broad as a beam, like the athlete that he was, but he'd already started to go a little soft in the waist. He had grabbed for the shirt to cover up his budding handles, the way a self-conscious teenage girl might wrap a towel around her bare thighs.

"What's with the frayed cuffs, Lee?" I'd said, laughing. "Trying to look like a WASP?"

"Come on, Jule," he'd whined. "Whaddya talking about?"

"I thought nice Jewish boys always wore crisp new shirts, not family heirlooms."

The sweet smell of pot had drifted over from the umbrella-topped table where Corky was rolling joints with two other friends. Fitz had been busy as usual, fanning the coals on the grill with a newspaper. A car honked from the driveway and the cackle of girls' voices rang through the night. Clearly my brother had taken advantage of my parents' vacation to arrange a little party for his friends.

"Guess I'll be seeing you guys later," I'd barked in older-sister fashion, retreating to my room upstairs with a book and a perspiring bottle of pinot grigio.

Hours later, when the squeals and jumping and giggles and blues music had subsided to the occasional splash, and I was lying on my stomach in the dark of my bedroom, the door had opened. I'd smelled chlorine and beer and deodorant soap as his fingers slipped beneath the sleeveless T-shirt I was wearing. Full lips had found the back of my neck.

"I'm here, Jule," he'd whispered. "Right where you wanted me to be." His mouth was slippery and soft inside, like I'd always imagined my own would be. It was the first time in my life that my body had actually hurt with desire.

"Hello," shouted a voice from the door of the apartment. "You home, Corky?"

I slammed the picture on the shelf so hard that it didn't stand up. With a clumsy jerk I sat it on its fin and turned around.

"Lee," I breathed. "What are you doing here?"

"I live upstairs, remember? I had to change my suit." He waved the tan jacket he held by the collar at me. "I saw Corky's door open and I thought, oh good, he's finally home."

I stared at him, confused. His face and shoulders were a shadowed silhouette against the brightness of the entryway. I squeezed my eyes tight for a second.

"The question is, why are you here?" he asked, stepping out of the glare of the door into the darkness of the apartment. "Is something wrong?"

"I'm looking for my brother," I said. "When did you last see him?"

"Tuesday night. After the benefit. But we both drank a few too many and had what I guess you'd call a fight. Though now I'm not sure why." He looked around the apartment. "He's such a neat freak you'd never know if he was here or not, huh?"

"Corky stopped by my apartment late that night, completely tanked. It must have been after you saw him. What did you fight about?"

"I told you, Jule. I don't know." He threw the jacket on the plaid sofa and walked over to the sink in the kitchen. He turned the right tap and cupped his hands beneath the running water. As if he were dying of thirst he lowered his face to the cold water and kept throwing handfuls on his face, slurping from what was in his hands, until I wanted to scream at him to stop. Finally, he turned off the water and blotted his face on the stiff towel that hung on the refrigerator door. Small curls of damp hair licked his forehead.

"What did you fight about, Lee?" I repeated, resisting the impulse to touch his hair.

"I told him that I was worried about him. That he should clean up his act, pay attention." He looked up from the towel. "This thing with Fitzgerald has freaked me out, Jule. Somebody had to be really angry to do that to him. Almost as angry as my father is with me right now."

"But why, Lee? Angry about what?"

He breathed deep, the way a child does before bursting into tears. When he looked at me the hard golden eyes went soft, like they'd been years ago. "You have no idea how seriously some people take things, Jule. The pressure is unreal. I just wish everyone would chill out, you know?" His voice cracked.

"But why is your father upset with you? He seems to dote on you."

"Aw." He folded the towel into a small tight bundle and placed it on the counter. "My dad's always wound up around primary time. This one should have been a piece of cake but that reverend made it complicated."

"Is that why the mayor is paying so much attention to Sam? I can't believe that you told him I, of all people, was worried. He even approached me about it."

"What are you talking about?"

"I met the mayor last night at a reception. Your little friend Eddie, too."

The light in his eyes went out. "Yeah. My dear friends and associates." He swept up his jacket from the chair. "I'm sure Corky's just crashed somewhere. Maybe he picked up a girl. Speaking of which, want to come upstairs to see my etchings?" he asked with an exaggerated wiggle of his eyebrows.

"No. Thanks. I have to get back home."

"Okay." A few beads of the water that still clung to his temples stole down the side of his face. "It's just that, for a split second, when I walked in, your face—"

"My face what, Lee?"

"Your face said . . . You looked so happy to see me." He blew a sad kiss with the tips of his fingers and closed the flimsy door behind him. I heard the thump of his feet going up the stairs, the slamming of his door.

I stood, alone, in my brother's apartment. I looked at the tidy magazines, the photographs so proudly positioned on the shelf. From above, the scream of a rock radio station began to pound through the ceiling. I considered running upstairs after Lee.

Instead, I locked the door and hurried down the street. Near the subway station I saw a gypsy cab, and threw myself in front of it, relieved to avoid the train. Sailing across the 59th Street Bridge, I clutched the door handle and looked upriver at the curve of gray buildings. Lookin' for love and feelin' Groovy, I hummed to myself.

But the subway rhythm returned, and I couldn't shake its tortured tune from my mind.

Somebody needs me. I wonder who. Who can it be worries me.

16

Redial. Redial. Redial.

So I passed my hours at home that Friday afternoon. Machines. Voice mail. The long, languorous rings of unanswered phones. The pages of Corky's open address book fluttered in the breeze of the fan that was supposed to move the air around my apartment. But none of the numbers led to him. I slammed the book shut on its swollen hinges and slipped Sam's forbidden home number from its hiding place in my wallet. If he'd sent me that postcard, then maybe he, at least, was safely home. An automated but nasal female announced that the number had been changed and was unlisted at the party's request. At least a live operator hadn't conveyed the embarrassing news. I threw the slip of paper, worn thin at the folds, into the trash.

The telephone did ring at last, shattering the stale silence. But the voice on the line belonged to the one person I didn't want to talk to. Until I found my brother, I wanted to avoid Detective Lynch and his insinuations. Yet here he was, no-nonsense, practical. He had a surprising development, something important in hand. Could I come to the station, take a look, tell him what I think, nothing more, forty-five minutes, see you then?

Of course, I said yes. I showered and pulled my wet hair back in a ponytail, just like I used to do almost every day in high school. But sitting in a taxi, chilled by the damp lump tied at the nape of my neck, I felt the unease of a teenager in trouble. Seeing Lee like that, letting myself worry about him, had been like tearing into an old scar with dirty nails. And I wasn't about to let Detective Lynch see what I was feeling, no matter what he had to tell me. The cabdriver braked at an intersection and my teeth bit hard into the dry mush of my tongue.

The Midtown North police station was an unadorned building of pale yellow stone on 54th Street between Eighth and Ninth Avenues.

It sat next to a low brick garage on a block that was strangely empty of people and traffic. A row of police cars was parked diagonally into the curb, like a fallen stack of bright blue dominoes. After squeezing through the tight entrance, its walls covered with framed lists of precinct personnel and what looked like Boy Scout badges, I walked smack into a folding table that blocked off the counters where people went about their business. Someone had written "Stop Here" in Magic Marker on a piece of poster board and taped it to the table. Behind the red-faced man posted at the table, the place did not look like the lively hubbub of eccentric public servants I was used to seeing on television. Its mood was more like the Department of Motor Vehicles on a medium-slow day.

What it did feel was male. Very navy blue and very male and much younger than I had expected. A group of cops passed by, leaning into each other like large blue birds. "So, Harry, the wife forgive you yet?" asked one, laughing, before they disappeared behind the door to my left. The man sitting at the card table looked up from his copy of the *Post* and asked if he could help me. He directed me to another man at the counter behind him, who called upstairs. Finally, a heavyset man with a steel gray comb-over (the desk sergeant? I tried to remember from the movies) took pity on me and led me up a flight of industrial green stairs to a frosted-glass door marked "Detectives."

Tom Lynch sat in the far corner of a dingy room at a desk that jutted out from the wall beneath a tall dirty window. Four of the other five desks in the room were empty. At one of them a thin man chewed on a pencil with the phone cradled under his chin, a bound computer printout spread open in front of him. He looked up, glanced at me with a blank expression, and returned to his printout. Lynch kept reading, his head resting in his left hand, a navy blazer swinging on the back of the chair in time to the slight rocking motion of his leg.

Comb-over coughed. "Lynch, you have a visitor."

He looked up and glanced at his watch. "Jeez Louise," he said. Then he wiped his hands on a paper napkin and unfolded his tall body from the chair. He extended his hand. "Miss Moran. I'm sorry I didn't see you. I didn't realize it was already after five. Thanks, Fernandez."

Comb-over grunted and left. "Sit down, please, over here. Can I get you some of our wonderful coffee?" Lynch asked, leading me toward the space around his desk as if we were entering a private office. His moves hinted of former glories in CYO basketball, torso and long arms slightly bent, body too close to mine. I held myself stiff, willing him to realize that I didn't have the ball and back away.

"Lots of milk, no sugar, please," I replied. I lowered myself into a molded plastic chair. Next to me was an identical chair, almost invisible beneath a stack of files and papers. A navy blue sweat suit was folded on top of the pile. Other tidy towers of files covered the floor, the desk, and a small filing cabinet. His neatness stood out from the disarray of the rest of the room and reminded me of my brother's own compulsive stacks.

Lynch placed a thin paper napkin on the desk and planted the full cardboard cup in its center with a delicate flourish. I took a sip and forced myself to swallow the gray liquid, which was not even warm. Next to my cup, the ribboned fragment of a shell-shaped Italian pastry sat on a small paper plate. It was my favorite in the assortment my grandfather used to bring on holidays.

"Sfogliatelle, not doughnuts?" I asked.

"My mother's Italian." He shrugged. "What can I say?"

"Mine too."

"No kidding. Ever try DiMonti's on Arthur Avenue in the Bronx?"

"Only ones my grandfather would eat." I caught myself smiling and turned away to avoid the happy spark of recognition in his eyes.

"Right. If you don't mind, Miss Moran, I'd like to show you something we received this morning. This way, please," he said, standing. He ushered me to the hall with his hand on my elbow. "It's a videotape. Left at the front desk wrapped in brown paper, with my name on it. All the guys thought it was a porn tape. Can you imagine? For me? To the right, please." We entered a small room with a VCR and beat-up looking television. He pulled a metal chair from a stack in the corner, and unfolded it for me. I sat down and waited for him to put the tape in the machine. He perched on the edge of another folding chair.

Static hissed on the television screen and then Sam's face and shoulders appeared. It looked like he was wearing the shirt from his tux without the jacket or tie. He began to speak.

"This is Samuel Reid. I am in safe hands and I have not been hurt. I will be returned to my wife and family as soon as the mayoral candidacy of Reverend Elijah Vaughn is withdrawn. Please do not attempt to find me or I will be killed. Thank you."

The video camera moved back a foot or so to show Samuel's arms and waist. The good arm reached across his abdomen and held the elbow of the prosthesis, which hung by his left side. It was a familiar Samuel pose. Behind him you could make out a brick wall with some graffitti on it, a gray metal door, and the top of a green dumpster.

Relief wrestled with anger. Sam was alive. He was being held against his will, which was a strange sort of vindication. But even his kidnapping lines mentioned another woman. Okay. His wife. We sat in silence on the folding chairs for several minutes until Lynch made one of his nervous little coughs.

"Well, how does Reid look to you?" he asked.

"To me he looks alive. For 'how,' you should ask his wife."

"We already have. She can ID him as her husband, but she's not what you'd call expansive. You have a different perspective on how the prof behaves. Does he look like he's on drugs? drunk? under duress?"

"He seems strained but calm. I wouldn't guess drugs but it's hard to say. He's not looking straight into the camera, which would be more his style. But isn't that what you'd expect? He must be terrified."

"Terrified? You think so?"

"What's that supposed to mean?" I asked.

"I mean, he doesn't look too terrified to me. To me, he looks bored. But go on. Tell me. Did anything look familiar?"

"Why would it? It's not as if I know where he is."

"Miss Moran, I'm not asking if you know where he is. What I am asking is, do you recognize something about Reid's surroundings or what he's said. Something that would help us to place where he is, or how he got there. Even the slightest association or connection would help."

He rewound the tape and played it again, freezing the frame at the end of the short speech so that the image of Sam grabbing his elbow quivered on the set in front of us. I stared at a blotch on the wall behind his shoulder, thinking, was there a building in New York that didn't look like this from the back? Brick wall. Dumpster. I shook my head no.

Lynch repositioned himself on the small folding chair, almost losing his balance as he pushed his legs even further apart. "Did Reid ever say anything that would lead you to believe he would make a tape like this on his own? Any fight with the reverend?" he asked.

"No. I've told you before. He is Elijah's biggest supporter. Ask the reverend himself."

"We have, Miss Moran. We have. The reverend received a copy at his home this morning and together we have analyzed it as thoroughly as if it were a verse of the Bible." He rubbed his eyes. "One more obvious question. Did you receive a copy of this tape?"

"No. I would have told you right away if I did." It occurred to me that I should have mentioned the postcard by now. But I felt like I owed it to Isaac to tell him first. Besides, I still didn't know if I liked this cop, the way he plowed through complicated questions as if they had simple answers. Not to mention the fact that he might have spent some time looking at photographs of me doing things I knew he'd been raised to abhor.

Lynch opened his mouth to say something, but didn't. He sighed and pushed himself up from the chair. I followed him back down the green corridor.

"This video creates a mess," he said as he walked past two cops in uniform. "If it was really made under threat of harm, then I have to bring in the Feds. Who are eager to jump in."

"What do you mean 'really'?"

He ignored my question. "As far as I can tell there are only two copies in circulation. So I have to ask you not to discuss it with anyone. We'd like to keep the press from sniffing it out, if we can help it. The reverend has offered to withdraw if we feel that Reid's life is really in danger. Only a few days left before the primary."

We were back in the squad room, standing by his tidy desk.

"Maybe you should see if the mayor has one of these tapes," I said. "Maybe he made the original."

"Not likely, Miss Moran. The mayor has been riding our asses on this one—if you'll excuse my French. Says it makes the whole process look bad, blah, blah, blah. Now with the tape he's completely furious. Wants to know what we know, hour by the hour. He says no politician can tolerate this kind of 'coercive bullshit.' Electoral terrorism, I think he calls it."

"Yeah, I know. He loves the race. But he's the one who stands to gain if the reverend withdraws."

"Miss Moran, you've got to understand that this tape is too weird. No legit politician would indulge in this kind of Mickey Mouse shit. There are a million ways for a politician to be crooked. Nobody goes around making movies about it."

"Then I guess you need to find out who's interested in Mickey Mouse shit."

"No kidding. That's why I would like to talk to your brother again, about this and another matter. But I've had trouble getting through to him."

"Yeah, well, he has a crazy schedule," I said.

So the police were looking for Corky, too. The elastic band in my stomach started snapping uncontrollably. I sank into the swivel chair and grabbed the edge of the desk to stop myself from rolling across the room.

"Are you all right, Miss Moran?" he asked.

"I'm just exhausted. Like I told you." I lowered my head to my knees. "And call me Julia, okay? I'm so tired of people calling me 'Miss.' " In a minute the spinning would stop.

He squatted by my side and touched my wrist.

"Julia. Okay. You want a glass of water? Something to eat?"

"I don't want to eat anything."

"No problem. Then just sit here a little while."

I folded my arms tight against my stomach, and murmured, "Okay, Detective."

"It's Thomas Peter. But everyone calls me Tom."

"Fine. Tom."

He disappeared. I closed my eyes and begged the room to stand still. From somewhere behind me came a forgotten sound. As if I were sitting outside the grammar school principal's office. The clacking of a typewriter. A man swore. The clacking resumed.

When I sat up, Tom was pouring mineral water from a plastic bottle into a small paper cup. I took it from him and swallowed.

"Look, I didn't have time for lunch today. I know a place. Come sit with me. It's around the corner," said Tom. He looked embarrassed. But the crow's-feet around his eyes were furrowed in something resembling kindness.

"Okay. I mean, no." I breathed deep. "Maybe. Just for a little while."

I left the station with Tom Lynch's firm hand steering me by the elbow.

17

Outside, the workday was ending. Tom guided us through the press of six o'clock people to a restaurant on Ninth Avenue called McMullen's. I was delivered to a booth of wine-colored leather bound tight by brass studs. The table was covered with stiff white linen, cool and crisp to the touch. Near the front, the bar was three-deep with men. Whenever the door opened, the evening sun flashed in an arc across their backs, lighting the cigarette smoke into a golden cloud.

"Suits. After-work crowd. They'll be gone in two hours," said Tom. He shrugged off his jacket and glared at the bar.

"Where there's an Irish bar, there's a pack of men avoiding the women in their lives," I answered, unfolding my napkin. Over Tom's head, the dark wood paneling was covered with framed photographs. In a wave of sunlight, I could make out Kennedys, a former governor of New York, a couple of senators, and a small red-haired man standing in front of a castle, presumably in Ireland. When the door closed and the light disappeared, so did the faces in the photographs.

"You're probably used to nicer places than this, huh?" Tom asked, watching me.

"Are you kidding? This is just like all the restaurants I ever went to growing up. I feel like I should be having a Shirley Temple and beef consommé." I sighed. "Or a scotch, neat, water on the side."

The short man from the castle photograph appeared by our side. "Good evening to you, New York's finest. Who's the lovely lady?" he asked Tom.

"Miss Julia Moran. Meet William McMullen, proprietor."

"Pleased to meet you, Lady Julia. It's about time, too, Mr. T.!" he laughed, turning up the dial on the faded brogue and jabbing Tom's arm with his pen. Tom ordered a Harp on draft. I asked for a club soda with lime.

"I used to romanticize the Irish," I said, as a red-jacketed waiter who looked about twelve set down our drinks. "But the older I get the more awful I think they are."

"How could you, Lady Julia? Aren't you forgetting the poetry? The lost kings?" said Tom, with his mug lifted high in a toast.

"The alcoholism, the tempers, the repression. . . . " I said. Mean laughter erupted from the bar. "An entire philosophy of life that can be boiled down to the phrase 'Suck it up.' "

"Is that your favorite? Mine's 'SPS.' " He took a long gulp of beer from the frosted glass. " 'Self-praise stinks,' as my father liked to remind us, whenever we got an 'A' on a test or won a game." He handed me an enormous menu of gold-embossed green vinyl. I stared at the frightening array of offerings. It was a long list: shrimp teriyaki, veal parmigiano, and turkey enchiladas.

"The only things worth eating here are chicken pot pie, fish and chips, or Dublin broil," Tom suggested, not opening his menu.

" 'Dublin' broil? When do they pass around the hat for the IRA collection?"

"Very funny, Julia Catharine Moran."

The underaged waiter returned to take our order. I repeated my chicken pot pie request three times before he could understand me well enough to write it down on his pad.

"So many of the patrons here look like my father," I said, looking at the crowded tables. Plump pink faces straining above white collars. Freckled hands resting on tumblers of whiskey. Not a glass of fresh-squeezed fruit juice or a cup of decaf cappucino in sight. Tom pushed a soft roll into his mouth and stretched his back against the upholstered leather seat. He looked comfortable, which annoyed me.

"So, Detective, why did you want me to see that video?" I asked.

He swallowed the bread with a gulp. "It's Tom. And I told you. I wanted to know if anyone had mentioned something like it to you, or if you had received a copy."

"You could have just asked me that on the phone."

"I don't like to ask people important questions when I can't see their faces. Don't forget, I also wanted to know if you saw anything you recognized."

"Why? Do you think my brother and I made the tape in a rage to defend my maidenhood?"

"No. You could say that I have abandoned that line of inquiry." He took a long swallow of beer and pulled his lips back from his gums with a sigh. "The truth is, I don't believe the Reid situation is serious. Trust me, there's some kind of foolishness at the heart of it. But it's high profile. Even the mayor's on our case. And it pisses me off because I have to give it my attention while other cases go uncleared. Like the murder of your friend."

I pulled the pocketbook to my lap and flicked Sam's postcard beneath the cover of the white linen cloth. "Sam's disappearance is a high priority, Tom," I said deliberately, "because he's a public figure. An important African-American public figure who receives death threats from crazies, black as well as white. This could be some kind of sick hate crime."

"See what I mean? You're like everyone else. You think the guy's some kind of tragic genius or something. Even now."

"I still think he's one of the most voracious, but one of the most undaunted men I've ever known." I brushed crumbs from the bread across the cool linen onto the floor. "It's a kind of genius."

"Is that why you did it?"

"Did what? Get involved with a man who's black?"

"No. You keep saying that. I mean get involved with a man who's married."

I looked away at the middle-aged men who filled the restaurant. Kind faces. Hard little priest-trained hearts. Wouldn't everyone be so disappointed in me? "I didn't exactly fill out an order form and check off 'married,' Tom. I fell for the man, his energy, his talent. I didn't want doctor, lawyer, Indian chief. I didn't want this." I flapped my hand toward the other diners.

"I read the guy's book, the one you had in your office," he said, tearing another roll into little pieces. "It was pretty good. He's no Ralph Ellison or anything. But a nice combination of personal stories and big, encouraging ideas. I wondered how much of that was you, how much was Reid."

"You read *A Native Son Bears Witness*?"

"Yeah, Didn't they tell you? Now we have to be able to read to get into the police academy."

Proprietor Billy interrupted us to supervise the red-jacketed boy as he put the plates of food in front of us. Tom couldn't suppress a smile of anticipation at the sight of his meal: dark brown gravy glistening over brussel sprouts and mashed potatoes and meat. Hand trembling, I broke the crust on my casserole and let the hot steam bathe my face. The peas and carrots and chicken inside swam in a golden sauce. I wanted to join them.

"As far as I'm concerned," he said, "Reid is just a jerk. Black or white, genius or fraud, if he's in trouble, it's what he deserves. But William Fitzgerald didn't deserve what happened to him, did he?" He examined a large forkful of meat and potato and put it in his mouth.

"No. He didn't. Maybe he'd still be alive if he hadn't come to work at the Pan American. Corky just wanted to help him out, pay him a nice salary for six months, since he was so determined to teach in the public schools." As soon as the words were out of my mouth I regretted them, in case they cast a shadow on my brother. I hurried to explain, "Fitz had no support, financial or otherwise, from his family. The widowed sainted mother had no money. And she was angry that her precious baby was going to waste his genius on the 'coloreds,' as she called them."

"That kid's death is eating away at me. That's why I'm looking for your brother," said Tom.

Gazing into the chicken pot pie, I carefully lifted a spoon of the warm goo, my fingers gripped tight around the stem. "You can't possibly think that Corky had anything to do with Fitz's death," I said, still staring at my spoon.

"Not for a minute. I saw how distraught he was the day he found Fitzgerald. Weeping over the little guy. Trying to put a jacket on his frozen body. But they knew a lot of the same people. I need your brother to talk to me again about Fitzgerald's friends. Not to mention, he should be careful himself. Keep his head up. If I could get him to return my phone calls."

"You think my brother's in danger?" I said, fighting not to picture what Corky had looked like as he tried to thaw Fitz's dead body.

"Might be."

"Why?"

Tom looked to either side of us, then cut his chin toward me with a conspiratorial jerk. "At first, because of the head injury, I figured Fitzgerald died in an altercation that got out of hand. Maybe a crime of passion, someone lost his temper. So we were looking at the ex-husband of his current girlfriend. Jealous Mexican guy."

I blinked at him. I hadn't even known that Fitz had a girlfriend.

"But turns out the ex-husband's gone home to visit his mother for a month. In the meantime we get a surprising report from Forensics. Fitzgerald didn't die just from the blow to the head. Autopsy showed massive overdose of insulin. The hit on the head came after he was too weak to resist. So someone really wanted the poor guy dead. Planned it out."

"So it had to be someone who knew him? Knew about the diabetes?"

"Looks that way."

"Oh god." Something tightened in my chest. "And you still don't know why that someone wanted to kill him?"

"I have ideas. Maybe he was too goody-two-shoes for the Dominicans your brother does business with, or the night staff who depend on your brother for blow. But had to be someone close enough to know about the needles."

I put my fork down. My eyes burned and I had to blot them quickly with the napkin, which was too thick for the job. I wiped my fingers on my thigh and trained my eyes on a picture of Teddy Kennedy kissing a cardinal in full dress. "Now you've got me panicked about Corky. I think he's on a bender right now."

"Problem is, someone as messed up as your brother might not know when he's in trouble. And you can't trust him to be alert to what's going on around him."

"You can too trust Corky."

"Julia. You cannot trust a drunk. Believe me, I know. My father drank. His whole life. I'd hear him come in at 3, 4, 5 A.M. and my mother would scream at him. Until she got too tired to scream. Then she became hard. Took pills. Anything to help her sleep through it all."

He took a sip of beer. I dipped a piece of roll in the golden sauce and sucked on it.

"Every time it got bad, that guy promised to stop. And he would for a while. Then, one day when I'm at the academy, I stop home in the middle of the afternoon and find him with one of the floosies from the corner bar. She's passed out on the couch. In my mother's home." The idea of it made his face red with anger, still.

"What'd you do?"

"I picked him up and threw him down the front steps. I told him if he comes back, I'll kill him. He never lived with us again."

"And your mother?"

"She kept on self-medicating, until she died."

"I'm sorry, Tom."

"Can't do anything about it now." He looked across the room and shrugged. He had pushed the pain back down, deep. Submerged it so far he didn't have to acknowledge the weight of what he had told me. "Drinkers can't be loyal, Julia. And the most important thing I learned in the service is that loyalty matters. My CO used to say, 'Give me incompetence over disloyalty any day. Incompetence I can fix with instruction.' "

He turned his attention to the knife he held in his right hand, and smeared potato and gravy on the last chunk of steak left on his plate. He gave the meat a slow, deliberate chew.

"Okay. So Corky can't be trusted when he's drinking. But I'm still worried about him," I said.

"Bingo, Julia. We should be worried about him. I've got an uncleared murder, and this wacky disappearance. And only two things connect them: Both men knew you. And they both came to no good at the Pan American Hotel."

My brother's fiefdom. Where he presided as the king of food and beverage. The unspoken fact hung in the air between us. I shook my head, trying to sort out all the new information, fighting to clear my ears. They rang with a strange new buzz. Maybe it was the laughter from the bar. Or maybe it was the idea of someone messing with Fitz's insulin.

"Have you talked to Lee Cohen? He was also close to Fitz, might know who Fitz knew."

"I talked to him, sure. He didn't have too much to say. Of course, it might have been because he got at least ten calls on his damn cell phone from his father while we were speaking." He tapped his nose. "Just remember, though, the word on the insulin is not for public consumption. No one knows outside the house. Okay?"

I nodded, though I could feel my face crumbling.

Tom reached across the table and brushed my finger with the hand that wore the college ring. "If your brother has taken off for a few days before, then let's not jump the gun. I'll talk to his staff at the hotel again, keep an eye out for him, okay?" With his spoon he scooped up crust and chicken from the dish I'd abandoned in front of me.

Tom had another beer while I sipped mint tea. He was happy to have the audience, for the chance to tell his story and explain his small disillusionments to someone new. Too happy, really, for my mood. It wasn't his fault. He didn't know how many times I'd been here before, listening. Now my own worries threatened to drown out his tales of Fordham and ROTC and the army and the police academy. I hardly noticed the way he poured my tea, and ordered bread pudding to soothe my stomach, and asked a few careful questions about my family and my job.

When the check came, Tom reached for it with a swiftness that told me he needed to be in charge. I let him have what he needed. As we waited for the credit card receipt, the piped-in music switched from orchestral arrangements of movie themes to Frank Sinatra singing "Fly Me to the Moon."

"When I was a kid I thought this would be on the soundtrack to my adult life," I said softly. "Along with the sound of women laughing and cocktail glasses clinking and the smell of men's aftershave. Like one of my parents' Saturday night parties."

"Yeah? I always thought mine would smell like steak on the grill. There'd be a ball game on the radio. Women in white bermuda shorts and those little colored sandals. Sunday afternoons."

He emptied his glass of beer. I looked at his face. The hazel eyes were soft in a way that belied the strength of the high forehead and the long nose. The tender blue shadows beneath his eyes, the fading hair, the cheeks beginning to soften into jowls, placed him well on the other side of forty. Closer to fifty, even. And there was still a sadness there. A solitary soul longing for a life he couldn't quite grab tight in his hand. Maybe we were more alike than I suspected.

He offered to escort me home, but I refused. "Let me hail you a cab, then," he said, raising his arm. A yellow taxi pulled up to the curb. Damp lips brushed my cheek, and for a second I found myself caught in the Old Spice bitterness of his day-old shirt. After an awkward hug we stepped away from each other.

"Thanks for dinner, Tom."

He opened the door and stood leaning on it as I tumbled into the cab. "Take care of yourself, now. If you hear from your brother, tell him to give me a call, okay?" He slipped the driver a bill, and said something to him I couldn't hear.

A Haitian radio station was playing, and the lilt of the Caribbean French sang as we glided through an empty Central Park. Around us the lush trees whispered in the breeze with the glitter of the buildings behind them. I could almost hear the clink of those highball glasses on the bright terraces. But nothing could soothe the poison that was seeping through my thoughts. I did not want to lose my brother. But for the first time, I was afraid that the tide of trouble was too strong for him. Or for me to help him. And as for Sam?

Black man. Irish man. Homicide chief.

Soon we were at my door. A short, round-faced man who wasn't Isaac stood under the streetlamp, smoking a cigarette and rocking his head to whatever he heard on the earphones that hung around his chin. I asked the cabbie to wait until I was inside, with the door closed safely behind me.

18

People moving out. People moving in. Because of the color of their skin.

The Temptations sang to me from the radio. Yo, Julia. Give us those syncopated white girl moves you do when you're alone on Saturday mornings listening to the "Motown Marathon." But I was in no mood to join them. I was trying to rouse myself for a morning of schmoozing and scouting at the Hip Hop Council. I'd been looking forward to the council for weeks—it was, after all, my kind of scene, much too vibrant and multihued a venue for the severe devotees of the Hamilton Institute. But as I paced back and forth, trying to be sure I could walk in my mules, my mind kept playing over the events of the past week. Always I returned to the image of my brother, weaving like a clown in my doorway. Sam's postcard. That strange and scary home movie. At some point today, I was going to have to talk to Isaac Lord.

I clicked off the radio and stood for a final check in front of the mirror. I shook the earrings that were as large as I could manage, gave a tug to my black cropped pants, and blotted my lipstick. A hard rap sounded at my door. When I opened it, a man with stiff brown hair was standing with his toes so flush to the doorjamb that I could smell his hair gel.

"Zoran, what can I do for you?" The super gleamed in a tight blue T-shirt and shorts. I had never noticed before how sculpted his arm and leg muscles were. Only the black nylon socks gave away that he was from Croatia.

"I sign for you!" he announced, holding out an oversized manila envelop. Kit's initials were scribbled above the Beckham & Coates address on the label.

"You keep beating old Mrs. Bellini to the special deliveries, she'll lose her will to live," I said, taking another step back. "She likes to keep watch for packages from the second floor window."

"I sign for you! Yesterday. Messenger boy," he said, waving the package at me.

"Okay. Hold on." He grabbed the door while I scrambled for cash. In the pocket of the raincoat that was hanging on the coat rack I found a balled-up five-dollar bill. I smoothed it out and handed it to him.

"Thank you. Any time!" he said. I smiled and counted to ten so that he would disappear down the stairs. Then I made my way after him.

I stood on the stoop, adjusting to the damp heat. The same egg-eating teenager was back, wearing far too many clothes for the weather. He looked up from the cigarette he was lighting, his eyes taking in my shoes as I shuffled over to him.

"Hi, my name's Julia Moran."

He gave me a long wordless dip of a nod, as if his thin neck were as flexible as a flamingo's.

"I need to find Isaac Lord. Any idea where I can reach him?"

"He's at the Hip Hop Council today."

"You're kidding. I'm on my way over there right now."

"You goin'? To the Hilton Hotel?" He pulled a rolled-up *Daily News* out of his oversized back pocket and showed me the day's headline: "When God Meets Gangsta: Churchmen and Rappers Face Off on the Future of Hip Hop."

I opened the paper and scanned the copy. Lamont Tyler, head of Bad Boy Records, was sponsoring the three-day extravaganza to promote the peacemaking power of rap. Too bad that the first day had resulted in a fistfight between one of the leading ministers of the Nation of Islam and a white rapper from Buffalo. "Isaac's there now?" I asked.

"reverend's on a panel," he explained. Since I'd taken a meteoric rise in his estimation, he gave me Isaac's cell phone number. Before I left, he even leant me his own phone so that I didn't have to go back upstairs to leave Isaac a message saying I'd find him at the Hilton.

I flagged a taxi on Second Avenue and tore into Kit's package. The miraculous assistant had sent me the highlights of the day I'd missed. Phone messages from authors and agents and colleagues in other departments were neatly typed. But still no word from my brother. Or from Sam. I crumpled the sheet of paper in a ball and stuffed it in the envelope.

There was more: Two new book proposals from top agents. "V. Interesting," Kit had written with a swirl on the one he preferred, a letter from Migs Petite pitching the story of an autistic woman's climb to the top of Mount Everest. Kit thrilled when Migs deigned to share her proposals with us. It had motivated him to photocopy all the latest reviews of *Amazing Grace*, our exposé of sexual misconduct in a black Baptist church that was hovering at the bottom of the best-seller list, and to mark with a yellow highlighter pen the phrases that would work best excerpted in an ad. At the bottom of the pile, a note from Sylvie Barr was clipped to the front of a fat blue plastic sleeve. "J—Here's the U-CAN proposal that won the city contract last year. Your friend Roberta should be proud. Let's talk on Monday. SB." The paper fell out of my hand as the taxi swerved to avoid a battered station wagon filled with paint cans and poles and bundled canvas.

My friend Roberta? I didn't know anyone named Roberta. I retrieved the packet from the floor of the cab and scanned the grant application form. The type had started to blur and wave from being copied so many times. But it had been submitted by one Roberta Jones, Director. On the second page I found the organization's board of directors. There was the person I knew as the head of U-CAN: Leopold M. Cohen, Treasurer. Had Lee's father pushed his son out of the top spot in his own organization? No wonder Lee was so upset.

I scanned the proposal, or what there was of it. The text was short on exposition, long on testimonials and faded color copies of smiling children. I looked at one: a little boy in a white shirt and a plaid clip-on tie, holding a copy of a Ninja Turtles paperback, above the caption, "Scott Malcolmson says, I can!" A foldout table charted the rise in reading scores in ten U-CAN centers over a three-year period. Scores went up in every case, in schools so bad four of them had been targeted for takeover by the state. Sylvie was right. U-CAN had almost nothing to say about its method (One-on-one attention! Stories kids can relate to!) and a lot to say about its impressive results.

"You want I pull in, missy?" asked the turbaned driver, looking in dismay at the stretch limousines and taxis clogging the circular driveway in front of the Hilton. I stuffed the papers in my bag, paid him, and jumped out of the cab at the corner.

The Hilton was one of the Pan American's main midtown competitors. It sat two blocks north of Radio City Music Hall, looking like it had been airlifted from St. Louis or Atlanta to sit amid the corporate towers of the Avenue of the Americas. Over the years I'd been there for events that ranged from gatherings of literature professors to press conferences for science journalists. Now the participants of the Hip Hop Council had invaded its tight carpeted spaces in a blaze of golden-chained glory that left the tourists in the lobby looking as dazed as if they'd woken in an episode of *The Twilight Zone*.

I maneuvered through a maze of journalists with press passes on beaded chains around their necks. A writer I knew stopped me and asked when we could have a drink to talk about his new idea for a profile of one of my authors. I told him to call me on Monday to set a date. Behind the concierge desk stood a nervous man, a scrap of toilet paper fluttering from the shaving cut on his chin. When I asked for a program he directed me to the registration table upstairs. The short escalator landed me in a mirrored space designed for milling outside the ballrooms that doubled as meeting rooms. The area was crowded with a buzzing mix of musicians, recording executives, ministers, and bodyguards. People were passing around CDs like business cards.

Behind a skirted table sat a doe-eyed woman who was showing a lot of dusky skin above and below her tiny elasticized tube top. She held her fingers over her mouth like a fan so that you could see the miniature tiger painted on each nail.

"Any programs left?" I asked.

She raised an etched eyebrow at me. "Who's asking?"

"Samuel Reid's publisher." I threw a business card on the table.

She flipped through a thick stapled list of registrants. "I see your company here, but not you."

"I know I registered. What name do you have?"

"Pat Muldoon?" she said, giving several beats to the "doon."

"Really?" I said, trying to hide my surprise. "She's my boss. I'm sure they paid for both of us." She shrugged and reached under the table. "We ran out of the printed versions. Here's the copy—it's more up-to-date anyway."

I grabbed the smudgy copy of the program and found myself a small clear space of wall to lean on. As I was flipping through the pages, looking for the reverend's session, a voice boomed above the din of the crowd.

"It's Julia Moran!" shouted Pat, as if she were announcing my appearance on a game show. "You know Malefa Mfume, don't you?" she said, patting the shoulder of the elegant black woman by her side.

I nodded at the editor-in-chief of the Sugar Hill imprint, the African-American line at one of our main competitors that Pat was always urging me to watch out for.

"You're Samuel Reid's editor, right?" smiled Malefa, with a delicate flick of her beaded extensions.

"Yes. Is Melinda speaking today?" I asked, referring to the bestselling black spirituality guru that Malefa had discovered long before daytime TV made her a household name.

"We're on our way there now. She does a beautiful presentation called 'The Heart—and Soul—of Rap.' Would you like to join us?" she purred.

"Sorry, I'm booked."

"Next time, then. Lovely to meet you."

"Same here," I said. Pat flashed the white teeth at me for a second and then turned her eyes to Malefa as if she were transfixed by a holy light that she saw there. They made their way down the hall, Pat awkwardly tilting over her right shoulder to speak to Malefa while they walked. Except for the occasional pro-basketball-height bodyguard, Pat's head remained the tallest in the crowd.

So it looked as if we'd soon be welcoming another top editor of black books to Beckham & Coates. One who had said in a much-debated interview in *Essence* that you have to be black to read black.

Franchises.

I returned to my stapled copy until I found the morning's sessions. Below a seminar on nonviolent conflict resolution run by a former gang leader I found a panel devoted to the question "Is Hip Hop Good for Black Youth?" Reverend Vaughn was one of the speakers on the panel. Sam was also listed, as one of the respondents. I found the President's Ballroom and pushed my way into the packed room.

"You can't deny our youth the right to be heard, the right to make art of their experience . . . the right to get paid!" shouted a man I recognized as the head of a rap recording label. "Hip hop is now a global industry. It's the most popular music form today!"

The room cheered. Reverend Vaughn patted the hand of the congresswoman sitting next to him on the dais and stood up. Standing, he was still not much taller than the table.

"You're right, Brother Michael. Our children deserve to be heard. But think about the price we pay for selling the world these violent, negative images. White people are always happy to see black boys degrade themselves: gold teeth, blunts and forties, ugly talk about women . . . I don't think the harm caused one hundred thousand black children is obviated by the opportunity for one hundred black men to become billionaires." The room was silent. "Remember, it is the black boy wearing gangsta clothes who is stopped by the police, not little white Johnny in the suburbs. Why should self-denigration be our only form of self-expression?"

A woman stood up in the back of the room and shouted, "Say it, brother!" First one, then two, then many hands joined in applause.

Rap star Tuf N Reddy leaned forward from his seat at the other end of the platform and almost swallowed the microphone. In the nasal snarl that had made him famous, he intoned, "The reverend has love but he's got the story all wrong/ You can't stop the boys when their hearts are bursting with song/Our moms is on dope we got no where to turn/Is it really our fault that the man wants to see us burn?"

A whoop sounded from a group of teenagers sitting on the left side of the room. Several of them began to sing the opening "Mother, mother," from Marvin Gaye's "What's Going On," which Tuf N Reddy had sampled in his first platinum hit.

I caught a whiff of the sweet musk of Sam's cologne to my right. My pulse jumped, despite everything.

"Same old story. The younger generation must make its own way," said a familiar voice that was not Sam.

I turned to face Isaac Lord. "I'm glad you found me," I said, "but I have to admit that I'm thrilled I got the chance to see Tuf N Reddy first."

The recording mogul started to argue with the congresswoman.

"Perhaps we should step outside?" said Isaac. We pushed through the crowd at the back of the room and made our way to the middle of the milling area. "I got your message, Miss Julie. Why are you so eager to see me all of a sudden?"

"I want to talk to you about something that arrived in the mail." I flashed the postcard at him. "I got this before Detective Lynch showed me the videotape."

"Let's go downstairs," he said, brushing the air with a slow hand as if he were removing a large cobweb from the top of the escalator.

In the crowded lobby bar two low club chairs presented themselves to us, empty. Isaac pulled one out for me, ignoring the throngs of people angling for a seat. We sank into them and ordered drinks.

"May I see that card?" I handed him the postcard. He pushed his glasses down his nose to examine the postmark.

"Wednesday," I said. "Two days ago."

"Did Brother Samuel ever tell you to expect this?" he asked.

"No. Why would he?"

He wrapped a hand around the salted nuts that sat in a bowl on the table between us. "Samuel never spoke to you about the ANB? I find it hard to believe that he would keep his plans from you, of all people."

"Well, you'd be surprised by all the things he didn't share with me." I picked a single cashew from the bowl. "But he did tell me he was worried about security. He even asked my brother to give him a tour of the premises. Which he did." The waitress placed a ginger ale on a napkin in front of Isaac. I took the tea bag out of the empty cup she left me and dropped it in the small aluminum pot of tepid water.

"I see." He placed the postcard on the table, slipping it just beneath the rim of the bowl of nuts. "Time for full disclosure, then."

I began to choke on the stale pulverized nut that was coating the back of my throat.

"It was a typical Reid show. Foolish, I always said to Elijah," he continued. "And melodramatic. But Reid had to have his way. Keep everyone guessing for twenty-four hours. A major black public figure disappears and no one sees him, even though he is in their midst. He walks right out of a public event at a major hotel in a waiter's uniform. Over the course of a day he could be a cab driver, a homeless man, a rider on the subway."

"Sam planned this whole thing?" I croaked, thinking of how he'd eyed the linen closet in the basement of the Pan American.

"Remember, I said this was to be a twenty-four-hour tale. The police, though warned of the security problems, do not protect our hero. For a day he is invisible. An award-winning black journalist stands ready to chronicle the story for the paper of record. This all happens a week before the mayoral primary. The ramifications are resounding."

"You're saying that Sam used me, and my brother, to stage a little PR show for the reverend? That his bodyguard sent that detective after me, to humiliate me, while Sam was off telling a sad little story about race relations to the *New York Times*? You can all go to hell," I said, pushing up from my seat.

"Wait," said Isaac, putting his hand on mine. "Samuel never arrived at the appointed place to meet the journalist. And the videotape, Miss Julie, was not part of the plan. We are perplexed by the tape."

I sat down again. "Meaning what—?"

"Meaning something has gone terribly wrong."

I took a gulp of cold tea and looked around the lobby. We were surrounded by young men of many shades and sizes, wearing porkpie hats and do-rags and studded chains, laughing and clasping fingers in complicated handshakes and blowing loud kisses at the women who seemed to follow them like lithe birds. In dress and style they were as mannered as characters in a French farce. Yet how happy and normal they seemed, compared to the strange story unfolding before me.

"That's why the date on the postcard is so important," said Isaac.

"But Sam could have put it in any mail slot in the hotel that Tuesday night."

"I suppose."

"And you staged the little stakeout outside my apartment because you were hoping that Sam would just show up there?"

"We were. But now Elijah and I are also concerned about you. Believe it or not."

"I don't know what to believe." Pat's scrubby gray head passed by above the potted palms to our left. "The betrayals just keep piling up." My voice cracked.

He took a delicate sip of ginger ale and waited for me to collect myself.

"If Sam has got my brother in some kind of trouble, intentionally or not . . . I'll kill him," I said. "Better yet, I'll call his wife."

"Understood."

"Does the detective—Tom Lynch—know about this, plan, of Sam's?"

"Had to tell him, once that tape showed up. I was with Elijah when he reviewed the tape with Lynch." He lifted his shoulders, as if to say, go figure.

No wonder Tom had been so contemptuous of Sam, so lacking in concern. Or respect. "So now what do we do?"

"Lynch pursues whatever leads he has. We watch and wait. And the reverend contemplates whether or not to withdraw."

My hands twitched and I squeezed them between my legs. "I can't stand waiting. So why do I spend so much of my life doing it?"

We were interrupted by three young men in cheap black suits who stopped by our table to shake hands with Isaac. The shortest one, with a shaved head and a nose ring, grinned at me and ran his tongue over his lips.

A cloud of disapproval crossed Isaac's brow. He waved them off. They moved away, bouncing into each other with affectionate shoves, like cubs. Though Isaac's eyes followed them, his mind seemed far away. "When I was young, barely twenty, I spent a year in Paris," he said. "Exciting days for all of us. There were so many black people in Paris, so many young people. If you were an African American, the thing to do was to make an African friend, because the Africans could speak French. So I came to know my good friend from Mali, Claude. He and I would go to the famous bookstore, Shakespeare and Company, on the Left Bank. It was always filled with tourists, all these girls, ooh la la! Claude would use his French to pick up the Canadians. I'd stick to the Americans." His tired eyes lifted at the memory. "Those days were my first taste of something new. Now I wonder, how do you teach people to live with freedom? That is the question."

"Do you have to teach them?"

"Freedom is a heavy yoke, as a wise man said."

"Isaac—do you think you have to be black to read black?" I blurted out.

"Come, come, Miss Julie. You know better than that. Do you have to be British to read Shakespeare?" He smiled. He placed several bills under the check. "Shall we?" We stood up to go.

At the entrance to the hotel we stopped. "Miss Julie, let us stay close. Let each other know what we discover. And I am sorry for your pain. Truly," said Isaac.

"Then I want you to do two favors for me."

"Name them."

"One, stop calling me 'Miss.' I'm Julia. Jul-ee-a. From now on."

"Noted, Julia," he said.

"Two, do you know anything about a woman named Roberta Jones? She's supposed to be the director of a group called U-CAN."

"Roberta?" A flicker of surprise danced in his eyes. "An excellent woman. I've known her for so many years, she'd be angry if I put a number on it. But we were at City College together during the Ocean Hill/Brownsville battles. Those were turbulent times."

"How did she get to be head of this tutoring group? Did she push out Lee Cohen? He's an old friend of my brother's, you know."

A low roar sounded from the other end of the narrow lobby. Isaac peered in the direction of the shouts and the laughter and frowned. "The reverend's coming," he said, "I have to get down there."

"But—"

"Look," he said, pulling a pen and an elegant leatherbound pad from the inner pocket of his jacket. He wrote something on a slip of paper as thin as airmail stationery and handed it to me. "Roberta's real passion is helping people find employment in the Bronx. This is her work number and address. Why don't you talk to her yourself? I think you'll find that she can answer all your questions."

"I don't know what questions—"

"Talk to her," he urged. "I don't want to be the bearer of all bad tidings. And then let's you and I connect later this weekend." He extended his hand. I took it and held it tight. Then I wrapped my arm around his neck for a quick, fierce hug. And a stolen breath of the cologne that now made me feel sadder than ever.

19

I stopped on the corner of 51st Street and Avenue of the Americas. The afternoon stretched ahead of me, hot and empty as the office plazas in the Saturday sun. An old man wading through the still water of a turned-off fountain, collecting the coins that sat at the bottom of the dirty turquoise pool, yelled at me to get away from his money. I looked at the address Isaac had written down for me. It was the same Job Corps office Lee had worked at earlier in the summer on Kingsbridge Road in the Bronx. He'd been so happy with himself and the job. Now I remembered the despair in his eyes when he'd found me in Corky's apartment. Something must have gone terribly wrong for him to lose control of his project. And Isaac had dared me to find out what it was. I headed for the D stop at Rockefeller Center to catch the subway to the Bronx.

If only I hadn't pushed Corky to give Sam that tour of the hotel, I fumed. We might have thwarted Sam and his ridiculous scheme. A train finally pulled into the station. I pushed ahead of the tourists whose caps said they were heading for Yankee Stadium and took one of the few remaining seats for myself. I tried to take my mind off Sam by reading the rest of the U-CAN proposal. Several pages were devoted to the usual list of educators, congressmen, and philanthropists who had agreed to lend their name to the project. A special note thanked John Walker, the man I'd heard at the Hamilton Institute, for printing and paper. But on the twenty-plus-person advisory board popped out that damn name. Samuel Reid, Ph.D.

Sam gave his name not just to book and TV consulting projects that paid him lots of money, but to a dizzying array of boards and causes. He answered every letter from every cook and janitor and teacher who wrote to him; he replied to every invitation to sit on an honorary committee. So I wasn't surprised that he'd never mentioned

U-CAN to me among all his other worthy causes. But Lee had been strangely silent about the fact. Of course, as dear Corn had pointed out the other night, Sam also donated money to U-CAN when he sat on the Lewis Foundation board. It was classic Samuel Reid style. Put your name on one advisory board and then sit on another board and give the first one a grant. I didn't write these rules, he would laugh. White men did. The words rang in my memory, in that persuasive, mocking voice. I stuffed the U-CAN proposal back in my bag and tried to shut out the voice by concentrating on the chug of the train. Doo-doo-dee-doo.

When I reached Poe Cottage on Kingsbridge Road, a flock of slender Japanese people in Bermuda shorts and logoed sports shirts were standing in front of it, shouting "Nevermore, nevermore." Across the street was the storefront that Lee had so proudly pointed out to me a few weeks ago. I walked as purposefully as I could through the explosion of sound that filled the sidewalk: the horns of Latin music layered over the voice of a rap singer I didn't recognize. When I pushed the Job Corps door open a bell jangled, as if I were walking into an old-fashioned pharmacy or candy store.

It was a quiet and ordered refuge from the street outside. A teenage boy sat in front of one of four computers on a long Formica table that extended most of the length of the room. Shelves filled with books hung above the table; next to it was a tall stand holding a state-of-the-art flat screen television. Beneath the storefront window to my left were two faded orange sofas, with fifties-style foam cushions resting on chipped white metal frames. A blond wooden desk sat like a barricade between the front door and the computers.

"I'm looking for Roberta Jones," I called out to the boy at the computer.

"Miss Jones in the back. She'll be right out."

I stood, watching him type an email. The screensaver on the other monitors and the TV flashed a blue "W."

"You better start liking yourself, girl, because if you don't, no one else will. I feel nothing but hatred coming off of you." Two women emerged from a door behind the computer stations. The first was young, with thick braided extensions and an oversized shirt that hung over wide jeans. Her head was down, as if she couldn't take her eyes off her own sneakers. The speaker followed behind her. I caught a flash of white clothing.

"Now, Loraine, you go think about what I'm saying to you, you hear? I cannot help you if you will not help yourself." Loraine stomped out and the bell rang behind me. "What can I do for you?" asked the woman in white.

"I'm looking for Roberta Jones."

"You're looking at her." Indeed, I was. Roberta Jones was, simply, gorgeous. She stared at me with wide-set eyes and pursed full lips that were stained with coral. Long straightened hair curled in a flip at her shoulders, held back with a pink and orange headband. The white pique suit and fuschia silk top hugged a slender body above long, perfect legs. I could not imagine balancing, let alone walking, in the white sling-back sandals with black patent leather toes that said Chanel.

"I'm Julia Moran, a friend of Isaac Lord's. He suggested I talk to you about U-CAN."

"Ah yes. I've heard of you. You're the one he says is a 'special' friend of Samuel Reid's aren't you?" She sat down behind her desk and crossed her legs. I sat in the thick oak school chair opposite her.

"I'm Sam's editor, yes."

"I've known old Sam since he was in graduate school. Guess he hasn't changed much since then. Can't turn the leopard's spots, right?" She laughed and flared her nostrils as if she was hearing one of her favorite jokes for the tenth time. I felt as if I had soiled myself in front of her.

I flailed ahead despite the stinging in my cheeks. "Well, I'm not here to talk about Sam. I'm here to talk about another person we both know. Lee Cohen."

"My, my, my. You know all the charmers, don't you?" Still chuckling, she dabbed an eye with a tissue.

"You're now the official director of U-CAN. Is Lee upset about that?"

"Not at all. It's still his baby, for better or worse. Besides, I spend most of my time here in the Bronx helping people get themselves ready to go to work."

"But then why are you named as the director on the federal grant application?"

"Look. The Cohens wanted to secure a woman of color to be the head of their tutoring group. That way they would be eligible for WBM status."

"WB what?"

"Women, Black and 'other' Minorities. It's a kind of affirmative action for federal grants. Please don't look so shocked. It's quid pro quo—I get Manny's support for my work here. He gets the contract for his son's organization. And Elijah gets a friend on the inside to see what's going on."

"Why does Elijah need someone on the inside of U-CAN?"

Her face softened a bit. "You don't see it, do you? That why Isaac sent you to me?"

"Doesn't U-CAN get good results? I thought everyone loved them."

"They're the flavor of the month, no doubt about it. But all I know is, when I want my kids to learn, I make damn sure they're in a school where they're going to get a serious education from trained teachers. Not some volunteers with picture books. You get my drift?"

"I've known some of the tutors. They were completely devoted. And there are major foundations who've given U-CAN big grants."

"That's my point. Tell me, lady publisher, why this group gets more money, more support than the actual teachers in the classrooms. Free equipment from bigwigs like the head of Walker Communications. How come nobody cares that the kids only seem to read well at test time?"

The bell jangled again. Two teenage girls came in, one holding a baby. "I'm here for my appointment, Miss Jones," said the shorter one, shifting the baby from one hip to the other.

"Excuse me, I really must get back to work," said Roberta, rising from her chair.

"I hope we can speak more another time," I said, but she had already turned her back to me.

"How you holding up, Corinne?" she said, in the honey and vinegar voice. I slipped one of the cards from the Lucite holder on her desk and walked out the door.

On the sidewalk outside, someone was waiting for me, leaning against a black sedan.

"Well, well," said Manny Cohen, unfolding his arms. "Look who's visiting the Bronx. Come for a ride, Miss Moran, and see the operation."

My body was rigid in the back of the Lincoln Town Car as it sailed around the walled perimeter of the Botanical Gardens. I realized we were going around in a circle the second time we passed the stone lions flanking the entrance to the Bronx Zoo. Manny Cohen leaned against the soft upholstered seat, his legs stretched comfortably in front of him, while he concluded negotiations for dinner with his wife, Pearl, on the car phone. Even his car smelled of lavender.

"Forgive me, Miss Moran. Married life. Each party must compromise. My wife hates politics; I hate dinner parties. So we each do a little of both. Between you and me I think she does more politics than I do dinners." He shook his freckled head in disbelief at his own good fortune. "A beautiful girl like you should be married, Miss Moran. You must be awfully picky."

"I just haven't met the right person."

"Miss Moran, there is no right person. Trust me. Everyone must compromise. I hardly knew my wife when I met her, and we're together forty years this November. Get married, Miss Moran. The human animal is not meant to live alone."

I am trying, I thought. And I am not a girl. I looked out the window. Now we were floating down the leafy expanse of Pelham Parkway. Orthodox couples strolled on the green meridian that divided the parkway, long-skirted girls and solemn boys walking by their sides.

"Now that I've kidnapped you, why don't you tell me what prompts this visit to Ms. Jones?"

What would he believe? "I'm really looking for Lee. He said he'd be working at the Job Corps office through September." I swallowed the beginning of a sneeze, and pressed the window button on the armrest nearest to me. Nothing happened.

"This could be your lucky day. He usually stops by the offices on a Saturday." Without seeming to move his finger he pressed a button on the armrest on his side of the car. My window glided down a few inches. "You don't want too much wind." He smiled.

My hair flew in my eyes. "When do you think he'll be coming by?"

"Impossible to pin him down during primary season, I'm afraid. What is it, exactly," he asked, folding his hands on the knee of his crossed leg, "that makes you so eager to track him down?"

"Well," I said, as we made a turn and slipped beneath an elevated train track, "I wanted to clarify a few points about U-CAN." I recognized the tall silhouette of a hospital, and realized with relief that I knew exactly where we were. I turned to Manny and shined my biggest editor's smile. "My boss is thinking that we should publish a book for parents about the U-CAN approach. Maybe do it on a crash schedule for the spring list, before summer school starts." The lie impressed me even as it rolled out of my mouth.

"Fantastic!" he clapped his hands together. "The whole thing's a stroke of genius, wouldn't you say? Come in, come in. See the Morris Park Democratic Club."

The car had stopped in front of a storefront on a busy street near the El. Plastic banners of red, white, and blue hung on nylon cords, their tips ruffling in the slight breeze. Inside, a circle of old desks faced each other, topped by phones and typewriters. Several computer screens glowed from a corner. A bearded man in khakis stood at a phone, arguing with the person on the other end. Three middle-aged women sat together folding fliers, their fat arms resting in front of them on the top of a large table. They all waved to Manny, then kept on folding and talking to each other. White message slips were fixed in a clip on a tall thin metal rod that sat on one of the desks. Manny removed the slips from the clip without breaking his stride. I followed him across the room and up a narrow stairwell.

His office was large enough to hold a long sofa of dark leather and an old walnut desk. Next to a leather pencil holder sat a cut glass bowl of candies wrapped in cellophane, like you'd find in a pediatrician's office. He gave the rod on the blinds a quick twist to tighten the slats against the afternoon sun. Dust danced in the narrow slants of light that sliced across the opposite wall, which was covered with photographs. Manny was in almost all of the pictures, hugging men I assumed were politicians. In some of the pictures he wore a yarmulke.

"Sit, please, Miss Moran," he said, gesturing toward the sofa. "Would you like a Coke? It's still hot as Hades here. My wife tells me not to wear seersucker after Labor Day, but how could I put on a wool suit in this heat, I ask you?"

"A Coke would be great."

He bent over to extract a can from a small refrigerator by the desk. Two styrofoam cups appeared. He handed me a cup and sat down in the wooden swivel chair behind the desk. I perched myself on the edge of the leather sofa.

"Everyone's out campaigning today. They'll gather back here later on," he said. "So we'll have a little time to talk." He read the slips and waved one at me. "I'm afraid it looks as if Leopold won't be joining us."

"Don't let me take up your time, then," I replied, tensing my thighs on the leather. "Especially on a Saturday."

"Sit, sit." He gazed at a yellowing, five-foot-tall map of New York City pinned to the wall. "I've always had to work on Saturday. People of my generation were not as observant as our parents. Today the young people flirt with religion. When their lives are comfortable, they find meaning in the letter of the law. But they still don't have the tight bonds that we had. Family. Neighborhood. Are there even any neighborhoods left that you'd call Jewish, except for where these meshuga Hasidim live?"

"But Lee loves community. Family. Friends," I said.

Manny broke away from the map and his memories. "Leopold is blessed with remarkable people skills. Not so much brainpower—how he finished that goyish law school I still can't imagine. But he has people smarts. So I help him where I can. Why else did I pull this borough away from those damn Irish—if you'll excuse my saying so—if not to pass on the fruits of my labors to my only son? It wasn't for those damn Hispanics and Koreans, I can tell you." He slowly untwisted the wrapper from a yellow candy he'd plucked out of the bowl on his desk. "A book on U-CAN. Now that would really put Leopold's name on the map."

"Yes. We'd have to find him a writer—of course. He's much too busy to write it himself."

"I told Pearl that her son would have a great future in this side of the family business. Not food and beverage—ach!—such a terrible way to make a living. Your clients are never happy. I only took over my father's firm because my brother didn't return from the War. . . . The food business is better left to ingratiating souls like your lovely brother. Is Christopher over the flu, by the way?"

"Flu?" I repeated.

"You said he was ill. The other night at the Harvard Club." He smoothed the candy wrapper flat on the desk and neatly folded it.

"Oh." I flapped my hand at him as if I were one of the fat ladies downstairs. "That seems like ages ago. He's fine. Feeling much better. Great, actually."

"Glad to hear it. We've been concerned about Christopher, Leopold and I."

"Yes, they've really been leaning on each other so much since Fitz was killed."

"Of course."

I concentrated on his eyes, cloudy and pale. They narrowed ever so slightly, as if he were trying to remember an old telephone number or the name of his first grade teacher. Without warning, he stood up and closed the door.

"American boys do treasure their friendships. Too much so, for my taste," he continued. He finally popped the lemon drop that had been sitting naked on a coaster in his mouth and sat down again. "Tell me, Miss Moran. What did the police want to talk to you about yesterday?"

"How did you know I talked to the police yesterday?" I said, staring at the door.

He shrugged, rolling the candy into his left cheek, where it bulged like a Ping-Pong ball caught in a loose net. "I've been working in this city a long time, Miss Moran. I understand that Detective Lynch was very eager to see you. What was on his mind?"

"He wanted to talk to people who knew Samuel Reid."

"I see. Nothing new on that front? The disappearing professor?" His right eyebrow shot up, lifting the loose skin above his eye like a drawstring tightening a pouch.

I swallowed my warm Coke and glared back. "Nothing at all."

"Strange. A strange case." He shook his head. He snapped, almost too eagerly and clumsily. "Say—isn't Lynch also investigating what happened to the Fitzgerald boy? Any news there?"

"None. That I know about, anyway. It's awful." I leaned toward the candy bowl and rummaged through the assortment so that I would not have to look into his eyes again.

"William Fitzgerald was a mensch. He did wonderful work for Lee's organization. We could give him a dedication page in the book."

"In memoriam." I nodded. I abandoned the candy dish and leaned back into the leather sofa, which was far too close to the ground for comfort. "No reds. My favorite." I crossed my legs and twisted my body so that I was facing the door to the stairwell. I was trying to figure out if he had locked it, but I couldn't see whether there was a bolt beneath the old brass knob.

"Leopold couldn't put any other tutors in that East Harlem school. Those parents carried on so about Fitzgerald." He rolled his eyes. "I'm a successful man, Miss Moran, but I've never had that effect on people. People adore the do-gooders. The idealists."

"But, Mr. Cohen, Lee is also a do-gooder. After all, wasn't U-CAN his idea?"

"Yes, his brainchild, the dear boy. Education is the buzzword right now. Look at all the trouble it's caused the mayor. Until now—with the new standardized tests, the extra tutoring programs, the new charter school referendum coming up. Let's face it: If Leopold's tutors can do better than the teachers in the damn union, then who's to say what a state-of-the-art private company could do, eh?"

"The possibilities are mind-boggling," I agreed.

He folded his hands on the desk in front of him. "So. What did you want to ask Leopold about U-CAN?"

"Well." I pulled a palm-sized spiral notebook out of my purse. I flipped open its orange vinyl cover to a grocery list I'd made two weeks ago, and wrote a checkmark next to the word "milk" with studied concentration. "There are so many. First of all, the advisory board. Will they give their support to the book?"

"Absolutely. I'm sure of it. Especially if you're the editor, no?" He winked.

"Wonderful," I said. "And can we use some of the actual students for publicity?" I asked.

"Of course, of course. I can see it now. Put the kids on *Oprah*. One of each kind. It's brilliant!" With his arms resting on the chair he spun himself around in a happy little half twirl. "I know some backers who might be willing to help with extra money for advertising, promotion, things like that."

"That leaves my central question: Should Lee be the public face of U-CAN? Now that his brainchild has been taken over by someone else?"

"What?" he swallowed the end of his lemon drop.

"Roberta Jones is the director of U-CAN. At least that's what it says on the application for the special federal contract."

"Miss Jones? You just met her. She's lovely, isn't she?"

"She is, indeed."

"Leopold still runs U-CAN. Don't you worry about the paperwork ."

"But you used Roberta's name to get WBM status for the federal contract, didn't you?"

"That isn't your concern," he said, his voice crackling with impatience.

"And she's such a mediagenic figure. We might actually sell more books with her picture on the cover."

"What are you talking about?" He stood up.

"I'm just saying that with a beautiful black woman—"

"Are you threatening to steal my son's good work?" His hands pumped angrily by his sides. "To take credit away from him?"

"There is no need to shout at me, Mr. Cohen."

"I will not let my son be interfered with, do you hear?" His voice screeched. As he jerked his arms, strands of hair came loose around his ears. In the slits of light they glowed around his head in a faded halo. "Everything has led to this moment, for Leopold to take his due. U-CAN is his!" he screamed. He kicked the desk and the styrofoam cup bounced off and rolled away.

"Then are you saying the grant application was fraudulent?"

His fists stopped midair. "No, Miss Moran," he said with a tight smile. "I am saying how happy we all are to be working with Miss Roberta Jones. Miss Jones has asked Leopold to be her spokesman." He held out the candy dish to me. "There is a red one right there on the left, near the rim."

"No, thank you. I've had enough."

"Miss Moran, remember what I said: I am a pragmatist, not a do-gooder." He smoothed back his hair with the palm of his hand. Then he walked to a small sink in the corner and washed his hands while he spoke. "I owe my success to three principles my beloved father taught me. First, never expect anything from a weak man, a man who is slave to his vices. Second, never push a man too far beyond his abilities. Third, never mix business with the bedroom." He threw a paper towel in a bin beneath the sink.

"Fourth, keep your enemies closer than your friends."

"Miss Moran, you make it sound as if we're in a gangster movie."

"I do have an Italian grandfather."

"How could I forget? Irish and Italian? Now that used to be considered an interracial marriage!" he chuckled.

"I don't want to take any more of your valuable time, Mr. Cohen," I said, snapping my little notebook shut and slipping it inside the zippered pocket of my bag. "I'm so glad we cleared the air about Roberta. If you like the book idea I'll go ahead and try to find a writer to work with Lee."

"Fantastic." He clapped again. Smoothly he slid the seersucker jacket off the back of his chair and pulled it on over the short-sleeved white shirt. He was long-limbed like his son, with a more advanced touch of dinner roll squish around the middle. He probably had a subscription to the symphony and a good seat at one of the best Reform temples. A prosperous Jewish man of a certain New York vintage. I liked everything he stood for. Except for the calculated rage that was uniquely his own—as if he always had his eyes trained on something coming that I couldn't even see.

He stopped so abruptly in front of the door that I stepped on one of his shoes. "I know you publish books by the great thinkers of our day, Miss Moran. I hope I didn't seem insensitive about Reid's disappearance. You know the man well, no?"

"We worked on his big book together," I said, inching back to create space between us. "It's terrible not to know what's happened to him."

"As I said, it's all very strange. But it's always difficult to comprehend what's going on with the blacks. I've met the fellow. He seemed sharp. Not as sharp as he thought he was, of course. The schvartzes never are." He raised his spotted hand to my face and deliberately pushed a strand of hair behind my ear. "You know, Miss Moran. You can do much better than that."

I recoiled from his close lemoned breath. The narrowing leer in his eyes made me wonder what his son had told him about me. He turned on his heel, and opened the door.

"After the election we should all get together," he called over his shoulder as he led the way down the stairs. Lee and your brother and your lovely self. You could come up to the house."

"Yes. The boys are so much fun together."

"The boys, as you call them, are men now. Each of them could use a little more smarts, a little more chutzpah, if you ask me. May the heavens hear us!" As he walked by the desk with the message wand he waved his hand at the ceiling. "Though I confess, I have great hopes for my son. There are a few weak spots in the marble. But it's such beautiful marble, no?"

"Yes, he's certainly in demand."

"His time will free up after the primary. It's been a pleasure, Miss Moran." He held the door to the sidewalk. "Please let my driver return you to Manhattan."

"No, I can take the subway. It's okay."

"Miss Moran, I insist." He stood by the open door of the Town Car. "Don't forget, now, you need a husband. I have a good reputation as a matchmaker. Just give me a call when you're ready."

"I don't think I need—"

"Just remember, Miss Moran. Keep an open mind. But remember what I said. You can do much better. Go carefully now. And remember rule number three."

The driver folded his jacket and placed it on the seat beside him. Manny Cohen stood slightly stooped on the sidewalk, his hands in the pockets of his seersucker pants.

I couldn't figure out how Manny knew about my visit to Tom Lynch's office, or how he'd found me at the Job Corps office. I had no idea if the news of the videotape about Sam had already reached him. But I did know that he was breaking rule number two by expecting so much from his son.

20

Where to, ma'am?" asked the driver, turning around in his seat. He clicked off the radio before starting the engine.

"That's okay," I called out. "Leave the game on. And the window down."

"Thanks, lady. Yankees versus Red Sox. Top of the sixth. No score."

I told him my address and sank into the upholstery. I was so relieved to be out of Manny's clutches that I was grateful even for a getaway car provided by him. Seeing Manny unravel like that had made me understand some of what I'd seen in Lee's eyes. How many times had the father unleashed that temper at his son—the son who was doomed to crumble beneath the force of all that ambition, that drive.

The bitter tastes of disappointment and hurt and fear lingered in my mouth beneath the cloying sweetness of hard candy. I closed my eyes and listened to the click and swoosh of baseball on the radio. I'd heard that real fans preferred to listen to a game than to watch it on TV. But to me it was just a background track, a summer sound I associated with transistor radios at the beach or in the backyard. A boys' sound. Of course, summer was a boys' season. I remembered Corky and Fitz as kids, when we had just moved to Westchester from the Bronx. Running shirtless in the heat, pounding their taut little torsos like Tarzan as they circled our new yard in a frenzy. Boys were not afraid of summers' ills—they had none of the terror of bees and burns that had always left me sitting in the shade of a tree with my dolls.

On the radio, the announcer's voice became excited as someone made it to second base. The last time I'd been to a baseball game, I'd been with Corky and Fitz. Still in college, they had reveled in the challenge of teaching me to keep score. I could still picture Fitz drawing small straight lines in every box of the scorecard, while my brother shelled peanuts and threw them in his mouth at a fast, regular pace that seemed to defy the principles of digestion. It had been a long time since I'd shared that kind of simple companionship with my brother. And I would never again have it with Fitz.

The crowd cheered. I sat up and realized that we were in Manhattan. "Home run, Yankees." The driver smiled.

"That's great," I said, shaking my head to clear it. The scent of lavender was in my mouth and my nose and my eyes. I rubbed my arms. The smell seemed to get stronger. "You know what, I'll get out at Second Avenue, okay?"

"You sure, lady?" I nodded. He glided to the curb and I jumped out. It was already the beginning of dusk, and I had to face the long evening that lay ahead. Three years of involvement with a married man distorts your sense of what constitutes a social life. Saturday is often the quietest night of the week. For most of the affair I had liked it that way. But now I was in no mood to relish my independence.

I ran into the Empire of Food for a few provisions, making my way through the weekend crowds of single men with carrying cases of light beer and single women pushing wagons of fat-free chocolate cakes. Telltale plastic bags holding video rentals peeked from almost every cart. I endured the maddening slowness of the express checkout and walked down my block, looking for one of Isaac's crew. A muscled man in a snug T-shirt and do-rag who was definitely tougher-looking than the morning's teenager leaned against a silver SUV with his arms folded. Relieved, for a change, to see him, I waved and headed upstairs.

I put away the few groceries, leaving out Triscuits and a block of generic supermarket cheddar cheese. Salty fatty bland food. I opened a bottle of Cote du Rhone and poured some into a glass. I took a small sip, battling the flutter in my stomach that said, you are in deep trouble. "What's happened to me?" I whispered to no one.

Your baby brother is missing. Your lover lied to you, about so many things. And now he is gone. Your friend was killed by someone who knew him well. And you are alone. I sensed movement in the living room. Something dark passed by the window to the left of the sofa. Or did it. I jumped into the kitchen and hid myself behind the doorway, watching the window. Nothing happpened. I took a small step into the room. Still nothing. I knelt on the sofa, faced the window, and pushed it open. The cable wire, hanging from the roof down the side of the old building, was slapping against it in the breeze.

Calm down, Julia. I held my head in my hands and closed my eyes. It actually made me dizzy to be alone in the dark muck of my own thoughts. I felt as if I were swimming in strong currents that kept washing me up on different patches of dirty beach. How I would have loved to talk with someone about how the patches fit into a shoreline. But there was no someone. I opened my eyes. Tom Lynch was probably sitting somewhere alone too, watching a ball game or reading a book of military history. But then, he wasn't scared like I was. No one was watching him the way that Isaac, and now Manny Cohen, watched me.

Someone must have watched Fitz, too, known just the right moment to get him alone and give him the fatal injection that would slow him into shock, to drag him into the ice locker so that he would be there when my brother opened it the next day. Fitz was a loner, just like Tom. Just like me. Yes, his movements must have been carefully watched. I cut a piece of cheese and reached into the box for the oily, corrugated crackers. I couldn't hold them still unless I had a whole hand wrapped around them.

A loud bang exploded from my bedroom. I picked up a five-pound hand weight that lay unused beneath the end table, and edged through the hallway. Without turning on the light, I went to the locked window that faced the street and peered out. I couldn't see anything. The bang exploded again. I looked down to the sidewalk. A homeless man was hitting the side of a car with something that looked like a metal pipe. The man in the T-shirt who worked for Isaac was walking toward him.

I returned to the living room. The old building creaked and sighed. A woosh of air blew through the open window. The wet smell of the wind said a storm was coming. I flicked on the televison to watch the local news. The mayor was being interviewed in front of a fried dough stand at a feast in Little Italy. "Our democratic process guarantees all candidates the right to run for office. It's unfortunate that tensions in the black community have led to the alleged abduction of Samuel Reid, who has been a staunch supporter of the Reverend Elijah Vaughn. Of course I continue to believe that I am the person who can unite all races and creeds in this wonderful city of ours." Boys in "Kiss me, I'm Italian" T-shirts waved at the camera from behind the mayor's head. I muted the sound with the remote control. The word was out. So much for Tom wanting to keep the news of Sam's "kidnapping" from the press.

I picked up the stack of magazines that was sitting on top of the answering machine, and saw for the first time that the light was flashing. How could I have forgotten to check? One hang-up. My mother wondering if I'd heard from my brother. Gordon calling to say, "Hello, darling, how are those feet? Want to see the new Godard at the Angelika?" Mel confirming brunch the next day. I smiled and took a small sip of the wine.

Then a voice I didn't recognize. At first. "I'm sorry, Julia. I didn't mean to cause so much trouble. But I'm too afraid to move. I love you, Jule." A choking sort of sob. Click.

My brother had finally called. And he was afraid.

The separate pulse in my stomach quickened. My chest groaned and heaved with a will of its own. I surrendered to the pressure building from within, the pain exploding from my stomach. I only made it as far as the kitchen sink when I started to vomit up something redder than the wine.

I doused a dish towel in running water and held it to my face. Then I rewound the tape, pulled it from the machine, and curled myself up in a ball. That night I rocked myself into a shallow sleep on the narrow sofa. Sometime around two in the morning I was wakened by a clap of thunder, and I pulled the old blue blanket around me. I stayed there all night, afraid to go near the bedroom window where I could see the men watching from the street. Or worse, let them see me.

21

At least you know that Corky's alive," said Mel. She was standing in the entry to my kitchen, pouring a thin stream of honey into a bowl of yogurt. She disappeared and returned with a red wooden tray that held tea, toast, plum jam, and the yogurt. With the deft moves of someone who once spent a summer waitressing at the Kosciusko Catskills Inn, she swiped all the papers and magazines off the trunk with her foot and placed the tray on it. I tried to remember where she could have found the tray.

"Why don't you tell that detective that your brother called?" she asked, handing me a mug. "Maybe he can trace the call."

"I'm not saying anything to Tom Lynch until I know for sure that Corky hasn't done anything wrong." I took a sip of the tea. It tasted of apricots.

"You don't know that? In your heart?"

"No. I don't." I shifted in the lumpy wing chair I'd had since childhood. Through the canvas slipcover I could feel a spring pinching me. "I don't have a clue where he'll come out in all this."

"But you can always trust Corky," she pressed.

I thought about what Tom had said. Drinkers can't be loyal. "I'm just facing the possibilities, Mel. My instincts about people haven't proven too accurate lately." She handed the bowl of honey and yogurt to me. "No thanks. I can't keep any food down. I think I have an ulcer."

"Try this. It's sweet and thick. Maple vanilla yogurt from the Farmer's Market."

I took a spoonful and swallowed. It tasted like paste. Mel smeared some jam on a piece of toast. "You know, Jule, they say that ulcers are caused by bacteria that can be zapped by that pink stuff—what's it called?"

"Pepto-Bismol."

"Yeah. Funny. Everyone has a bottle in the medicine cabinet, but I've never seen anyone really use it."

"You've just never known anyone who needed it before," I said, picturing my brother chugging from the extra-large bottle he kept in his desk drawer at work. Fear for his safety cramped my insides again. "You know what? I want to go to church. To light a candle."

"You what?" she asked through a mouthful of yogurt. "Not pray, not meditate, but light a candle?"

"I can't explain why, I just need to do it," I answered. "Let's walk over to Loyola, please."

"You're so lucky that I'm a Polack," she said. "I spent my whole childhood surrounded by crazy women lighting candles. Let's go. Maybe the fresh air will clear your head."

It was the first Sunday after Labor Day and the streets of the Upper East Side were filled once again with blond people in khakis. The old women with shopping carts who had owned the sidewalks in July had disappeared. "How do you stand it up here?" asked Mel, after five frosted-haired women on their way to brunch refused to break ranks to let her pass.

"Cheapest rent I could find," I answered.

"Figures," she laughed. We kept walking until we reached the severe facade of St. Ignatius Loyola Church on Park Avenue.

"Ah, Jesuits," I said. "The intellectual aristocracy of Catholics. My father spoke of them so reverentially that I was almost voting age before I realized that the Inquisition was their idea."

Men in dark suits stood at the bottom of the stairs. Pallbearers? I wondered. No one has funerals on a Sunday morning. The church doors opened and a throng spilled down the steps: men with thinning hair in navy blue blazers and sports shirts, tanned women in brightly colored sweaters and flat shoes. There were people laughing, and children held on shoulders, and a sense of goodwill that you could almost reach out and touch. It felt like a childhood Sunday and suddenly I wanted one again, desperately. Comics. Jelly doughnuts. *The Wonderful World of Disney*.

To my surprise, a familiar head of receding black curls with the telltale white sideburns appeared in the church's central doorway. It was the mayor. Silver-haired Mr. Walker was by his side, with his arm around the shoulder of a woman whose small face was overwhelmed by a massive halo of ash blond hair. Behind us some cameras clicked and I stopped Mel by the elbow.

"Look who's here. This isn't his usual pre-election working-class beat," I said.

"Well, he needs this crowd to come out and vote for him in November, even if they don't bother with the primary this week. Besides, imagine what he still has time to do today: Mass in Queens, a barbecue in Brooklyn, cocktails in Staten Island. . . . "

"And the Bronx is covered, " I said, nodding at Lee Cohen, who stood on the steps surrounded by several young women wearing sweater sets that all seemed to be variations on the theme of ice blue.

He picked his way through the crowd in his usual languid fashion, as if no one was jostling him or touching him or offering him a baby. A natural politician. I remembered his father's pride. People smarts. He caught my eye and waved. But when he lifted his sunglassess I was shocked to see the circles beneath his eyes. His face was gray in the midday sun.

"Julia, great to see you again. How are you holding up, sweetheart?" he asked, hugging me while keeping an eye on the people around us.

"I'm okay, Lee. You've met my friend, Mel?"

He surveyed her over the top of his sunglasses. She wrapped her hand around his and gave it a strong pump.

"No word about that professor, huh? Terrible for him, but I have to say it hasn't done the mayor any harm." He leaned over in a conspiratorial way and spoke out of the side of his mouth, as if each word was for our ears only. "As my father would say, 'those schvartzes just can't keep peace amongst themselves, can they?' Anyway, I'm exhausted. I haven't been home in days and now I've got to go to a brunch in frigging Staten Island." He patted his nose with a tissue as if he had hay fever.

"Lee, I've been wanting to talk you," I forced myself to say.

"I know, babe. My dad told me about the book idea. Sounds great. But this isn't the time. Jeez. Here comes the Frito Bandito. This guy is driving me crazy."

Eddie Saldivar strutted by. "Hola, Julia, long time no see." He raced ahead of the mayor to open the door of the limousine.

"Any word from your brother yet?" Lee asked, watching Saldivar.

"Actually—"

"Don't worry, Jule. You know he'll turn up. Gotta run." He spun around and glided through the remaining clusters of people to the mayor's side. Lee said something in his ear, and the mayor waved his hand in my direction.

We watched the cars pull away. "Let's get out of here. I'll light an imaginary candle in the park," I said. Mel and I crossed 84th Street toward Madison Avenue.

"What book was he talking about?" asked Mel.

"Oh, just a lie I told his father. That I wanted to do a book on his tutoring group. You know, everybody's a sucker for the idea of a book contract—even people as smart and duplicitous as Manny Cohen."

Groups of thin people speaking European languages strolled on the avenue, stopping in front of each shop window with the kind of rapt attention usually reserved for great paintings in art museums.

Mel and I passed them and entered the park at 79th Street. We walked without any destination in mind, cutting across the patches of fading grass and the concrete paths, so that more than one rollerblader swore as he swerved to avoid us. When we reached the bronze statue of Alice in Wonderland, Mel grinned at the children in blue and red and yellow sweatshirts who scrambled all over the toad-stool. "I love this spot. Let's stop here," she said. I plopped next to her on a bench, facing the small pond dotted with toy sailboats. The images of childhood made me feel vulnerable, and small.

"Even Pat is turning on me, you know," I admitted. "She was at the Hip Hop Council yesterday with Malefa Mfume. The head of Sugar Hill. You'd think they were in love the way Pat couldn't take her eyes off her." A chocolate Labrador gallumphed to my side. The dog sniffed my hands. When I patted her neck she jumped up with her paws on my knees and licked my face. I breathed in the big smelly dog licks.

"Julia, do not let that dog kiss you." Mel gave a shove to the dog's thick torso. "Talk to me instead." The Labrador lay down by Mel's feet. A woman holding a little boy on the toadstool clucked at the dog and shrugged apologetically. Mel absently scratched the dog between her ears. "You're too important to B & C, Jule. Don't worry about Pat now, when there's so much else going on."

"No one ever stays too important to Pat. Except the glamorous fiction editors like Leigh Fleming. La dee fucking da."

"I can't stand Leigh. How can you trust anyone who greets you by shouting your whole name?"

"Tell me about it. She always sounds surprised to see me, as if I've just returned from Siberia. Does she do that to you? Mel Du-BROW-ski!"

"Julia Mo-RAN!" She laughed, but I knew she was angry because she got up to buy a hot dog with onions and mustard from one of the vendors clustered by the path. She offered me a bite, but I shook my head, no. She broke off the end and tossed it in the air for the Labrador to catch. A circle of brown leaves rustled at our feet.

"Let's go back to your place," she said. "We'll get you settled and then I'll take off from there later this afternoon. I have to go to a reading tonight."

In front of my building, Mel waved at the chubby teenager standing across the street by the red car. He lowered his earphones and waved back. After we climbed the stairs, I unlocked my apartment door and kicked it open the way cops do on TV. Mel rolled her eyes and walked in ahead of me. "Julia. You are losing it," she said. "There's no one here except the cockroach in your kitchen sink."

I opened the closet door in the hallway and looked inside. She groaned. "That's it, Julia. Here's what we're going to do. You are going to take a nap. I am going to sit in the living room and do the crossword puzzle. Okay?" I nodded.

I poured a seltzer and walked to the front of the apartment. I knew that she was right. At least part of my paranoia could be explained by the fact that I hadn't really slept enough the night before. But I didn't want to lie down. I assumed my sentry perch on the end of my bed by the windowsill. I was trying to figure out why Lee looked so nervous, as if he were being chased.

Through an open window across the street I could see the clock light on a VCR flashing. Someone had turned the machine off and on again without setting the clock. It was just a silent green beep but I didn't like it. I sipped the cool bubbles and wondered for the first time in days how Samuel was actually doing. He would hate the fact that his screwed-up plans, this kidnapping, was helping the mayor.

The VCR blinked. Would I ever do something mundane like rent a movie again? The only video I'd seen in weeks was the one of Sam in front of the garbage can.

I closed my eyes to shut out the annoying wink. A slight breeze caressed my face. I heard the distant muffle of horns honking. A car drove by and someone spoke heated Spanish under the insistent blare of Latin music. I tried to fix the image of Sam in my head, as if I were already losing the reality of him. I had seen him more ways than I could count, but now all I could think of was the video I'd seen at Tom Lynch's precinct house. The boomchaca of the music pulled away. In my mind, Sam started to fade but the wall behind him became clearer. Familiar, even. Then I knew.

I opened my eyes and walked to the living room. Mel was lying on the sofa with the *New York Times Magazine* propped on a pillow on her stomach.

"I thought you were taking a nap," she said without looking up from her crossword.

"I can't. I just figured out where the videotape of Samuel Reid was made."

22

I clicked off after leaving two messages for Isaac on his cell phone.

"Come on, Julia. Call that Roberta woman."

"It's late on a Sunday afternoon, Mel. There's no way she'll be there."

"Then let's just go up and see for ourselves. If you're right, we'll call that cop and let him take it from there."

"What about your reading?"

"I've never missed one of Bobbie's before. She'll just have to live with it. This is too exciting. What do we take, the D train?"

"Slow down, Mel. It just doesn't make sense. I mean, I think I'm right, but I can't figure out why."

Mel was already leaving a message about a stomach flu with someone at the Union Square Barnes and Noble. She hung up the phone with a triumphant smile.

I said, "I'm not taking the subway to the Bronx on a Sunday night. With the weekend construction and the slow schedules we'll be waiting around forever."

"Use the car service," she suggested. "I'll bet you have a couple of vouchers tucked away somewhere don't you?"

I nodded. There was actually one hidden in every bag I owned. For emergencies, of course.

Thirty minutes later we found ourselves sitting in a dented black Cadillac with bad suspension, headed back to the Job Corps offices I'd visited the day before.

"Are you ladies sure you wanna get out here?" asked the driver. In the rearview mirror the skin around his eyes looked like a bruised banana. His stained green jacket pulled tight beneath the arms.

"We're sure. Will you wait for us?" I asked.

"I don't wait for no funny business, lady. Company policy."

"It's no funny business. We're just checking something. I'll give you the voucher when we get back," I countered. He sighed and turned on the radio.

"Isn't this going to attract attention, Julia? The ladies from Manhattan descending from their chariot?" said Mel.

"Everyone who lives up here uses a livery service, Mel. There are no medallion cabs in the Bronx."

Dusk was settling on Kingsbridge Avenue with the spent exhaustion of a Sunday night. Poe Cottage looked small and tired in the half-light and graffitti-covered metal grates were pulled down over the storefronts across from it. Only a take-out chicken place, a bar with a neon shamrock in the window, and a corner bodega were still open. Though the sidewalks were empty, it was noisy. Babies cried from windows, girls laughed in doorways, rap music thundered from invisible cars.

"Let's go around the back," I said. I fished in my bag for the flashlight I'd brought, and tugged at Mel to follow me around the corner.

The whine of burning rubber yelled behind us. We turned to see the Cadillac pull away.

"Great, Mel. Just great. What are we going to do now?"

"It's early, Jule. We can take the subway home."

I looked at two boys who were leaning against a streetlight outside the bodega, smoking cigarettes. "Fine. This way."

I passed the light over the alleyway Lee had parked in that hot Saturday morning when Corky sat in the front seat of the Pinto, stewing in his hangover. Only a couple of weeks before, and so long ago. Now, round dark shapes skittered across the ground.

"Jesus Christ, Julia. Rats. I wish I wasn't wearing sandals," Mel muttered.

I squeezed her hand and moved the flashlight over the garbage bins. "I don't know. These dumpsters look like every other dumpster to me."

"Didn't you say the symbol was painted above—how about over there?"

I turned the feeble beam on the wall above our shoulders. The bricks were so crumbled and worn that they seemed to be peeling off the building. And there it was. Painted over the flaking wall was the same sign I'd seen behind Sam's head in the videotape. Large purple lines in a checkerboard, contained in a circle. If he stood right here, in front of the dumpster, the symbol would be just to the right of his head. As it was.

I pounded on the back door that Lee had used, but there was no answer. "I don't think anyone's inside. But they must have made the video right here. I just can't believe it's Lee Cohen."

"Or Roberta," said Mel.

The thought actually made me laugh for the first time in days. "That would be divine justice, Sam being pushed around by a tough black woman. Let's go. I want to call Tom Lynch."

We turned around and found ourselves facing a dark man wielding a long curved knife. A wool cap was pulled low over his forehead. "My, my, my. What brings these two fine snowflakes to the 'hood?"

The knife he held looked large enough to be a farm implement for harvesting wheat. "We're just checking on this address. A friend of mine works here," I said. Mel glared at me as if the polite explanation was final proof of my insanity.

"That right? I bet it's not the nasty sista up front. She don't seem too friendly to me."

"Do you want our wallets?" asked Mel, "We'll hand them over to you if you'll let us go."

"Lookkee here, little bulldyke, I don't take no orders from you." He sliced the knife in the air in front of her neck, and she retracted her head into her shoulders like a scared cat. He rolled back his cap an inch and I could see eyes were veined with red, like marbles. He swayed ever so slightly in place. I wondered if the two of us could knock him over.

"What is it you want from us?" I asked, staring at the unsteady glint of the knife.

"I think the brother wants to apologize for bothering the ladies," said a deep voice from the shadows. The end of a gun emerged in the dim light, held by one of the men I recognized from the ground patrol outside my apartment. Isaac Lord stood next to him.

The man in the wool cap looked confused. The hand holding the knife fell to his side. "I didn't know this was yours, man. No dissrespect intended."

"I don't want you messing with these people. Now get on out of here before we fuck you up real bad. Oh, and I'll take the blade."

The man dropped the knife and ran away into the darkness. From the street the thump of a radio bass line pierced the night and faded away again.

"This isn't the first time you've come to my rescue," I said to Isaac Lord. "Thanks a lot."

"Foolish of you to come up here alone. You should have waited for me."

"I did call," I said. "But I didn't want to waste time"

"Julia, this neighborhood shuts down at sunset. Then it is feeding ground for people who survive like those rats over there—on garbage and filth and blood. So tell me what your message meant. What is it in this alley that links the Cohens with our unfortunate friend Professor Reid?"

"Look, Isaac." My hands still shaking, I waved the flashlight over the door. In the quivering light the quadrant smiled down on us. "Do you remember seeing this in the video?"

"Safety to those who pass here," said Isaac quietly.

"But what does it mean now?" asked the man to Isaac's left.

"It means, Louis, we have another interesting connection between Brother Samuel and a certain aspiring young politician." He looked at me.

"Christ, I just saw Lee this afternoon," I muttered.

"Julia, why don't I give you and your friend here a ride back to Manhattan? Looks like we need to continue our conversation about Brother Samuel. Not to mention Mr. Lee Cohen and his father."

Mel climbed into the backseat of the red Porsche, and I slid into the passenger seat in the front. Louis waved to us from the sidewalk.

"Put your seat belts on, please," Isaac said firmly. He turned over the key in the ignition, inserted a Miles Davis CD—*Sketches of Spain*—in the stereo, and drove us out of the Bronx via the Third Avenue Bridge. No toll.

23

The three of us sat in a booth at the Mount Olympus coffee shop on Second Avenue and 92nd Street. Mel piled extra slices of red onion on her cheeseburger deluxe and opened her mouth wide around the stack. Ketchup splurted onto her fingers. Isaac added four spoons of sugar to his coffee, carefully stirring each one into his drink before adding the next. I slid my mug of tea in a slick of water on the pink Formica tabletop. A new kind of dread was taking root in my bowels.

"So I assume your friend Roberta hasn't seen Sam hanging around the garbage cans out back of her office?" I said.

"No, she has not," Isaac answered, rubbing his eyes with his fingers. "We now have a much greater sea of troubles than we expected. A vast sea of troubles, indeed."

Mel pushed her french fries across the table. Isaac returned his glasses to the bridge of his nose, peered at the fries, selected one, and delicately dipped it in the pleated paper cup of ketchup. The waitress slid a thick plate of lemon meringue pie in front of him. I asked for more hot water for my mint tea and she grunted.

"So, let's talk about that alley. Why would anyone connected with that Job Corps office want to harm Sam?" I asked.

He rolled up his sleeves, took a huge mouthful of pie, and began his story. "Let's go back to the beginning. Why is Lee Cohen, the devoted public servant, here, there, and everywhere? Because his daddy has fought long and hard for control. The Italians have Queens and Staten Island, the Irish and the Jews fight over Brooklyn and Manhattan. But the Jews have had the Bronx since before the Koch administration."

"Yes, and the Irish had it before them," I said. "So what?"

"Remember," said Isaac, "that Manfred Cohen is the man who helped to deliver the Bronx for the mayor in the last election. He and his crew invalidated every ballot petition that Frankie Saldivar put forward when he was running for borough president."

"Saldivar? Eddie's father?"

"One and the same. Eddie's position as one of the mayor's youthful inner circle is part of the payback to his *padre*."

"No kidding. My brother and Lee actually worked on invalidating those ballots once for a summer job."

"What about the reverend? All these powerful old machine politicians must hate him," said Mel.

"*Bien sûr*, my lovely Melanie. That is why we try to fight back in kind. With information about how crooked the whole crew is. Which is"—he shot his index finger toward me—"where the Cohens really come into our story. They are as crooked as an old tree."

"How do you mean?" I asked.

"Take a hard look at U-CAN. Started out as a kind of Meals on Wheels for the homeless. Get food from restaurants, hotels, some donations. Give to those who need it. Sounds great, does it not? But Lee Cohen has no experience. He uses the operation to move drugs. Launder money."

"What?"

"More goes in than comes out. The donated food and time and grants exceed the costs. After all, most of the labor is free. But the real business for sonny boy is in the extras. Access to the downtrodden and all their weaknesses. Get my jist?"

"How do you know this?" pressed Mel, taking a forkful of Isaac's pie.

"We know, Miss Melanie. We know. But that's not the half of it. That, I'm sorry to say, would just be business as usual. Now, the son finishes law school. The group he founded while still in college wins support from the community. Not to mention foundations with cash. He wants to add to the original plan. And what is the most popular topic in city politics today?"

"Education," I whispered, licking a bit of lemon filling off my finger.

"A-plus to Sister Julia. Education. So two years ago Lee adds a teaching operation. Tutoring for selected locations. Children on public assistance. His vision is an all-in-one operation—someday a social worker and tutor from U-CAN in every inner-city neighborhood."

"There's a whole trend toward these all-in-one, on-site social service centers. They did a special on TV—"

"Yes, yes, yes. He's very shrewd, our Lee. A man of the moment. So he begins with tutoring in several carefully chosen districts where the scores are abominable. If the reading scores go up where Cohen's group has been—if they go up higher than in the city overall—then maybe the mayor is right. Maybe the city should privatize school contracts. Maybe not."

"So, the old machine Democrats get cozy with the conservative right-wingers?" I said.

"Exactly," said Isaac. "At the very least, higher scores make the mayor's boy look good. Which makes the mayor look good. And the poor little black and brown babies have a better chance of making it in the world. Everybody wins."

"Higher scores also mean that U-CAN gets the contract for the after-school reading program. The special federally funded city program," I said.

"That's right." Isaac nodded.

"Once they have a black woman listed as director. Roberta Jones."

"Yes. You know all about that now." He toasted me with his mug.

"Let me get this straight," said Mel. "We hate the Cohens. We really hate Lee Cohen. But if he gets the job done, and the scores do go up, what's the problem?"

"There's no doubt that the higher scores are delivered, Miss Melanie. The U-CAN groups beat the city average by quite a bit. But the cost is high."

"How high a cost? The tutors are overpaid?" she asked.

"No. The tutors—when they exist—are volunteers. Trained by other volunteers. The cost is paid by the children."

Syvlie Barr had recently said something like that to me. So, in fact, had Roberta Jones. "Is that what Roberta meant when she said the kids could only read well at test time?" I asked.

His eyes narrowed and he fixed their golden glint on me. "In the schools where U-CAN operated, 40 percent of the students who used to fail were reading above grade level within a year," he said. "The rest all reached grade level. Every one of them. The children, the teachers, the families were elated. But if you hand some of those children a *See Spot Run* book, they hold it upside down."

"That can't be true, Isaac. Even if they know the answers in advance they have to be able to read the questions. Let's be fair," said Mel.

"Fair? Fair? None of this is fair. Never has been, woman." He slapped the pink tabletop. "These children took their damn tests. I know the teachers, the mothers. These children did not cheat, they did not know the answers in advance. So we conclude that someone has gone to great lengths to make it look as if they did better than was possible. Someone contrived to give these children higher scores than they could possibly get on their own."

"How? How could that happen? These tests are graded far away, probably in Albany," I said.

"I just want to be sure I understand what you're saying," interrupted Mel. "U-CAN didn't even bother to teach the students to memorize the answers in advance? After the fact someone just made sure the scores looked good?" Mel asked.

"That's right," said Isaac.

The disgrace, the cynicism, the evil of it, settled heavily upon each of us. No one spoke while the waitress poured more water into the mug in front of me.

"You're absolutely sure of this?" I asked when she'd moved on to the next booth.

"We know many of the teachers, the social workers, the mothers. A minister who is close to Reverend Elijah came to him with a heavy heart. For as you can imagine, the implications of such a scandal are ugly. Were the news made public, who will really suffer? The politicians? No, the children, and their families, and our people as a whole. Tarred once again with the brush of ignorance and stupidity."

"What's the reverend's take on all of this?"

"Elijah believes that this is one of the most cynical acts ever perpetrated against our children. If he can establish for a fact the chain of events, he is prepared to risk the bad publicity for the students involved. Of course, he doesn't mind the bad publicity for the mayor, either," he allowed with a wince of a smile. "But many pieces of the puzzle still elude us. The only fact we can determine is that many of the children tutored by U-CAN cannot read any better than they did before. Whereas throughout the city, children who were not taught by these fools actually made modest gains."

"And what about Sam?" asked Mel.

"Brother Samuel is indignant. However, he insists it would not be fair to the students involved to reveal to the public that the grades are false. It would make the children, and their regular teachers, look like failures. Tests, he says, are just another tool of oppression."

" 'One man's C is another man's A,' " I quoted.

"Julia, you know your man better than you realize," said Isaac. "You understand that he is perhaps more of a politician than the politician."

" 'White men made the rules. I just learn how to play by them,' " I answered.

"It's a tough call," said Mel. "You want to punish the people who cheated the children, without punishing the children."

"Exactly."

"And you don't know how to trace what happened? You have no evidence, other than the children themselves?" I asked.

"We have suspicions, surmisings, deductions, and a fact or two, which Miss Jones is trying to substantiate. Perhaps there is a hacker who gets into the grading computer. But we cannot prove anything without knowing specific details about the U-CAN group and how it works."

"You need to talk to someone who's worked inside the U-CAN organization since the beginning. Like someone who tutored for them," said Mel. I stopped pressing my tired tea bag with a teaspoon and placed it in the saucer. Something cold and sharp started to ache behind my eyes, as if I'd eaten an ice cream cone too fast.

"In fact, one of the tutors did approach Reverend Elijah," said

Isaac. "Someone who was doing canvassing for us this summer. He knew something was terribly wrong. Had his students' exercises to compare to the tests they took the next day. Couldn't believe the discrepancy in performance. I hear he said things were even worse than we thought."

"So where is this tutor?" I asked quietly.

"He said we wouldn't hear from him again until just before Labor Day. But the holiday came and went."

"Isaac," I said. My tongue was not moving very well. It felt as if it were stuck to the roof of my mouth. "Did you know that my friend William Fitzgerald, who was murdered, found dead in the freezer at my brother's hotel, worked for U-CAN? That he was a close friend of Lee Cohen's?"

"No, Julia, I did not. But our source's name was Arthur Thomas. I never did meet him in person."

Arthur Thomas. The Jesuit who wrote *Words to Live By.* Fitz's favorite book.

"That's the name of one of Fitz's favorite authors, Isaac. It's a Jesuit who's been dead for fifty years." Tears spilled down my cheeks. Mel pulled three thin paper napkins from the cannister and gave two of them to me. The third she kept for herself.

"You're certain?" he asked.

I nodded.

"Then you must tell the police right away."

I crumbled my wet napkins in a tight ball and threw them on the empty pie dish. "Tom Lynch already knows that Fitz was killed by an insulin overdose. Given to him by someone who knew about his diabetes. What he doesn't know is that I have something Fitz left with my brother just before he died. Those papers you mentioned, practice tests and stuff. I had no idea they were this important." My throat was closing so that it was hard to speak. "I can't believe I've been feeling so sorry for Lee, when all along he'd killed his own friend."

"Oh god. This might explain what happened to Fitz," said Mel, grabbing my hand tight beneath the table. "But I still don't see what it has to do with Samuel Reid."

"What we are now afraid of, Miss Mel, is that either Lee Cohen got wind of Reid's plans the night of the ANB, or Reid tried to take on the boy himself. And put himself in danger doing so. That would explain that fool videotape," said Isaac.

"Why would Samuel go off on his own like that? Without involving you?" asked Mel.

"As Julia can attest, Brother Samuel believes he is the Head Negro in Charge—especially when it comes to dealing with the white establishment. He persuaded Reverend Elijah not to go to the news media to break the story of the U-CAN scandal before the primary. Said we needed to have our facts in impeccable order first. Only then could we be assured that we were giving the children what they deserved."

"Don't forget Sam's name is on the advisory board of U-CAN. So he's probably doubly infuriated, because he feels tricked. He also sat on one of the foundations that gave them money. Makes the personal stakes higher," I said.

"Indeed." He selected a toothpick from the wrapped assortment in a dish on the table.

"It would be Sam's style to confront someone like Lee Cohen, try to make him see reason, cut a deal for special resources for the kids," I said, sniffling. "It doesn't surprise me he wanted the reverend to avoid the press."

"Sounds like Sam is in way over his head," said Mel. Isaac bowed his head to her.

"What I don't understand is this: the Cohens are everywhere. We've seen them all over town. They're not acting like they're standing guard over someone they've kidnapped," I said.

"Don't mean a thing, Sister Julia. Manpower is always for sale."

"I hope to god my brother isn't helping Lee in some harebrained plot." Mel patted my thigh. "I want to be certain of that before I talk to Lynch."

The waitress slapped a check down on the table. Isaac waved away my ten dollars. "Sort out the baby brother first, if you can. But remember, he might be in danger."

I nodded, trying to rub out the pain that shot down the sides of my face. "Now I know why Manny Cohen was so eager to get me alone, grill me. And why Lee looks so guilty whenever he sees me." I looked at my hands and tried to steady the tremor I saw there. They seemed far away, as if they belonged to someone else. "Let me try one more time to find my brother. Then you and I should connect tomorrow and talk to the police, okay?"

"At least you and I finally have all of our cards on the table. Word is bond, right?"

I squeezed my eyes shut so that he wouldn't see any more tears, and nodded. "Word," I said. He grabbed my hands and held them tight between his.

Mel waited. "Isaac, can I ask you a personal question," she said, after I'd returned my hands to my lap.

"Sure, baby."

"Do you like Samuel Reid?"

"No, Miss Melanie, I do not. Never have." He slid a toothpick with a fringed yellow cellophane tail out of the back of his mouth. "But that doesn't mean I think the brother deserves to end up in a freezer, either."

24

"A man was hunched over his knees on my stoop, leaning into the railing as if it would hide him from passersby. The same sad crackhead as last week? I inched closer. When he raised his face, the eyes were glazed and red, but the skin, though dirty, was white. It was the swollen lump that my brother Corky had become.

I turned back to the street and waved to Isaac, who sat in his car waiting for my sign. He gave a gentle tap of a honk and drove off to take Mel home to Brooklyn. A teenager talking on a cell phone also waved at Isaac's car from the other side of the street. I faced the stinking figure who sat on my stairs.

"Where the hell have you been? No one's been able to find you for almost a week. You made me sick with worry, you selfish bastard. For all I know you're a murderer, or a kidnapper. I've never hated you so much in my whole life."

I swung my leg back and kicked him in the thigh. I liked the way the hard thud felt. So I did it again. And again.

"Stop it. You're hurting me." He threw his arms up over his head. I remembered how he'd cower as a boy when my father went after him, and stopped my foot in midair.

"And what's the deal with the desperate phone call. What was I supposed to do with that?"

"I'm sorry, Jule. I really am. But it's not as if I've been having what you'd call a wonderful time. Can I come up? Please?" His voice was hoarse. "I'm sober now. I promise."

I gave him one more small kick in the leg. Then I extended my hands and pulled the heft of him from the stone step. He followed me up the stairs, stopping for breath at each landing. When we reached my apartment door he was covered with a film of perspiration that gave off a strange sour smell. I pushed him into the living room.

Silently I filled a large glass with ice and Diet Pepsi and handed it to him. He sat on the edge of the sofa and held on to its arm as if he were afraid he'd fall off.

"So?" I said.

"I'm sorry about the call. I was scared and I got drunk again. So Gramma kicked me out."

"Grandma?"

"Yeah. Last time we were there she told me I was in trouble. Just like Uncle Stephen had been. She said if I ever wanted to dry out in a safe place, I could do it at her apartment. What day is it, anyway?"

"Sunday night. Actually early Monday morning by now."

He winced. "When I left here on Tuesday night I was fucked up. But I actually straightened up a little. Or it felt that way. I had coffee and a sandwich somewhere around the corner. Then I hooked up with Lee in one of his favorite dives downtown. You know, one of those places where we can score blow without any hassle."

I stared at him, my arms closed tight against my body like the shell of a rotten clam.

"Once I got there, Lee lit into me," he continued. "He said I must feel awful for ruining the banquet, that the Dominicans I owe money to grabbed your boyfriend to scare me. I told him he was full of shit and he kept asking when I was going to tell him the truth." He cracked an ice cube with his back teeth.

"So, then?"

"So, then he wanted to know if Fitz had given me anything before he died. He got very angry when I said, no, nothing. He said I should stop hiding things from him, because he could make things look very bad for me. As if I had murdered Fitz myself." He wiped his eyes with the heel of his hand. "He said that Fitz died of insulin shock. Someone injected him with ten times the insulin he needed."

"That's what Detective Lynch told me, Corky."

"I didn't do that, sis."

"I know that." I might as well say it. "You realize that there's only one way Lee would know that?"

"He said that his father had a friend in the police department.

That's how he found out. But I didn't believe him. Especially when he said the cops just might find insulin and needles in my desk at work."

"What did you do?"

"He went to the bathroom. And I ran out of there. I went to the kind of dive not even Lee could ever find. A piss-stinking room, where you buy your booze a bottle at a time. Old drunks sitting in their own shit. It made any after-hours place you've ever been in look like the Oak Room at the Plaza." He emptied the glass with one long swallow.

He was sniffling now. I was tempted to go to his side and put my arm around his big damp smelly body. But I couldn't touch him. Not this time. No one had put a gun to his head to make him drink. "So, I'm supposed to feel sorry for you because you couldn't stop yourself from blacking out for a whole week?"

"I didn't stay there for a week. I told you. I tried to drink but I couldn't get Lee's face out of my head. I had never seen him that way. Twisted and red and screaming. And I knew there was something wrong about him knowing how Fitz had died. I couldn't shake it."

He continued, "So I put my finger down my throat and made myself throw up as much of the booze as possible. Then I bought a black coffee and a bottle of water. And I walked. For hours. I walked all the way from the Lower East Side to the Rockefeller Center subway stop. It was morning by the time I got there so I called Fredo, the old waiter I trust, from a pay phone and told him I was sick. And not to let anyone in my office."

"Tino let me in."

"Yeah, Fredo told me when I called in on Thursday. That was okay. Then I called Gramma and asked if I could come stay with her. She said yes and I got on the subway for Bedford Park. I stayed in Stephen's room and helped her do stuff around the apartment. Threw out crap like Stephen's shoes. You wouldn't believe it. There were bugs living in them—she couldn't see well enough to realize what a mess it was."

"And you couldn't call me to let me know you were okay?"

"To be honest, Jule, I didn't want you to know where I was. In case anyone put pressure on you to find out. It could be more dangerous for you. And for Gramma. Besides, I had to do some thinking on my own."

Corky had never told me he needed to think. Ever. "So what happened last night?"

"Like I said, I panicked. I realized I couldn't stay there hiding forever. I have to go back to work. Get on with my life. So I drank some of Gramma's scotch. Stupid." He shook his head. "I called her already to apologize. Told her I'd be staying here tonight."

I got up and took his glass to the kitchen to refill it with ice and soda. My mind was swimming. I handed Corky his glass and held another filled with ice to my forehead to fight the midnight heat that had closed in on us after last night's storm.

"The thing is, I still don't understand why. What could Fitz have done that would make Lee so angry?" he moaned.

I sat down next to him and told him the long story of U-CAN, including the videotape of Samuel.

"Jesus Christ."

"So you had no idea?" I asked. "You weren't in on it?"

"Are you kidding me? This is way beyond me. It sounds like it's beyond Lee, too." He broke another ice cube between his teeth. "Still no word from Reid himself?"

"None. I did get a postcard from him, but I think he must have mailed it from the hotel that night."

"Would Manny be stupid enough to kill him too?"

"Manny? Why do you say Manny?"

"Julia. Lee didn't care enough about any of it—U-CAN, the mayor, the election—to kill someone."

"I think you're wrong, Corky. He's cutthroat and ambitious. And desperate to please Daddy. Maybe you can't see that side of him. You're too close."

"But Fitz, Julia. Fitz." He spoke in a still, quiet voice I didn't recognize. "You know, sometimes Fitz would get so depressed about the diabetes. He'd say, why should I bother, just so I can go blind when I'm fifty like my cousin Larry did? We'd tell him, no, things are different now, but when he was depressed, he wouldn't listen. One night at our fraternity house there was this big party. A girl Fitz liked, Janie Coughlin, got drunk and went off with Moose—you remember

Moose? He's a dentist now. Anyway, Fitz threw his kit of needles and insulin in the trash, poured himself a beer from the keg, and sat on the porch, moaning, 'I don't care, I don't care.' " Corky took a careful sip of his soda and put the glass down. "It was Lee who stopped him. Lee just took that plastic cup out of Fitz's hand, put his arm around him, and said, 'You can't, buddy. We need you.' And Lee led him upstairs to the bathroom, and gave him the shot himself. It was the first time any of us gave Fitz his shot. After that, Lee or I would do it for him sometimes. Last spring Lee offered to pay for him to get that new system, with the digital monitor, that doesn't rely on old-fashioned needles."

"I never knew that side of Lee. Or Fitz. I never knew Fitz to be despondent."

"Despondent?" he snorted. "Yeah. That's a good word for it. Despondent. He used to call it the valley of despair. That's why he read all those inspirational books and stuff."

"*Words to Live By*."

"More like words to die by." He shook his head as if he were trying to clear water out of his ears. "The thing is, Jule, I know Lee would know how to do it. You've told me why he'd do it. But I still can't believe he would do it."

"But some part of your brain knows it could be true, Corky. That's why you left the after-hours bar."

"That, and a lot of other things. I'd never been so angry at Lee. Except for when he slept with you. I was so pissed at him then—I'd told him to stay away. I knew he'd only hurt you like he did all the rest of them. But he had this thing for you."

"Well, it was mutual. I had a thing for him, too. So don't waste time hating him for that. I should have known better."

"For a while there I wondered if you had changed him. But he couldn't stick with it. And the truth is I was glad because I'd felt so left out. I wanted both of you back." My brother's swollen eyes rested on the print he had knocked off the wall a week before. Its frame and the longer pieces of shattered glass were still leaning against the wall behind the bookcase. "I'm sorry about scaring you that night, Julia. And I'm sorry for being so unreliable in general. All that's going to change."

"Gee. Already up to the 'making amends' step, Corky?" I said. But my sarcasm had no effect on him. There was something different about him. I looked at his bloated face, his once-curly hair, his thickened middle. Then I realized what it was. He was calm. Not nervous like an abused dog who'd been rescued from the street. I gently put my arm around his neck, and planted a kiss on his cheek. He held me for minute, and let out a sigh so deep it nearly rattled my windows.

"Can I stay here, Julia?"

"Okay. But same house rules Grandma has."

"That's fair."

"Then go take a quick shower and I'll set up the pullout couch."

"You have any of those old shirts of Dad's?"

"Sure. Let me get one."

I maneuvered the awkward frame of the bed out across the small living room and snapped clean sheets onto the thin mattress. I shook one of my bed pillows into a clean case and held it to my face. The fresh smell promised cleaner, happier times. Just like my brother was looking forward to. But in case he didn't succeed, I wanted to be sure that I had Fitz's evidence. Quickly I slid the portfolio from its resting place above the albums and brought it to my bedroom, where I hid it beneath my bed. As I returned to the living room, Corky emerged from the bathroom in a long cotton shirt of pale blue.

"You seem different, Corky. Sadder but more in control."

"That's how I feel. Remember Uncle Tutti?"

"Of course I do." My mother's uncle Tutti had been the philosopher of our dinner table. He would remove a gnawed olive pit from his mouth and place it on his salad plate with the deliberate air of a man who knows just how much pain he can tolerate. "'I've been sad, and I've been anxious, but believe me—'"

"'Sad is better than anxious,'" finished my brother. "He was right, too."

The pullout bed groaned as his large body fell onto the mattress supported by its slender legs. I kissed his forehead.

"Sleep well, sis. I love you."

"Love you too, Corky. In the morning, we'll talk about what we should do next."

Alone at last in my room, I sank onto the bed. When I closed my eyes, small white lights flashed. My limbs were heavy but my mind danced away without me, like a discarded candy wrapper lifted in the breeze.

Corky was safe. And if he was telling me the truth, he had nothing to do with Lee and Sam and the whole sad story. But Sam. Sam. Had he taken on too much this time? He hadn't realized that the Cohens were beyond his solitary reach. But his boldness, his stubborn bravery melted away some of my anger.

Starbursts of exhaustion flashed again in my brain. I feared that I was falling, falling, falling out of the window to the street below. My heart raced with a shallow, tired flutter. I knew only one thing could calm me enough to sleep. My hand was already between my legs. My middle finger moved to the spot it knew better than any other, and began to circle slowly.

I'd banished longing for Sam since Tom Lynch had shown me those photographs. But now Sam's insistent passion seized my imagination. What he'd do with his tongue. How he'd enter me from behind. How I would be his slave. Then I relived the one time he had been maddeningly slow instead of frantic. He'd used his silk Hermes tie to fix my hands over my head in the Ritz Carlton in Boston. And then he'd entered me carefully, deliberately, coolly, building to a slow frenzy. As I remembered, my legs parted and my body arched toward the ceiling. I was the center of the world. My finger moved more quickly to release the ache.

As I finished, a car alarm gave a shriek and continued to scream for several minutes. Two thoughts penetrated my consciousness before I fell asleep.

I wondered if I'd ever hold Samuel Reid—in my mouth, in my hand, inside me—again.

And I wondered how long Manny Cohen's eye had been fixed on Sam, waiting for the chance to pounce.

WHITER

People come to me and ask: Why do you focus so much on ideas like "economic indicators"? Why don't you speak to our pain? How can we make our way in the world of work when white people keep us from making our way to the corner?

I know this pain. Every black man does. When I see flashing police headlights, I am still afraid. And that kind of fear can shut a man down, keep his head low, his hopes diminished.

Yet I still maintain that the most effective way to ease that hurt is to make ourselves present in the society's institutions. That is why the single greatest change in the past thirty years has been the growth of the black middle class. We must keep taking our place at the table, eating a piece of that pie.

I still believe that there is enough pie for us all. That is why I am proud to be a centrist. That is what I am, that is what comes to me most naturally. You could call me the last good integrationist.

—Samuel Reid, from the conclusion to *A Native Son Bears Witness*

25

Schoolteachers always rise early.

So Sylvie Barr assured me when I called her home before the seven o'clock buzz of my alarm went off on Monday morning. I must have scared her, because she agreed to meet at my office at nine on the dot. Just as long as she was on time for the ten-thirty symposium she was moderating at the Bank Street School, up near Columbia. I returned the phone to its cradle and lifted my face toward the small fan that whirred from the top of the painted green dresser. Though my window was open, the air hung so hot and wet that it hurt to breathe. I lifted my arms and tried to inhale in a sad imitation of a deep yoga warm-up. To enlist Sylvie's help, I would need a cool head.

The screech of pipes from the other end of the apartment told me that my brother was already awake and in the shower. I slid my bare heel along the zippered edge of the briefcase tucked beneath my bed, and pushed it further back into the dust with a little kick. Please, I prayed, let Corky forget to ask about Fitz's papers, so I can bring them to Sylvie. It would be easier if I just hid beneath the sheets and pretended to be asleep. But I wanted to be sure my brother was ready for the day ahead. That he could still find that place in his mind where he touched metal to stay calm, just as he had in the basement when we were kids. After another long minute I stood up and walked to the living room.

Water beaded everywhere. It dripped in the corners of the windows and from the tops of the walls where they met the ceiling. Streaks of it slipped down the blank face of the television set. Corky emerged from the bathroom tucking another of my father's old shirts into his khakis.

"Next time you decide to take a sauna instead of a shower you should open the windows," I said, patting down his collar.

"Do I really look that bad?"

I twisted his second button into a threadbare hole. "Nah. You look great."

"I need to look like I've got my act together when I go into the Pan American, make sure I still have my job. Then I've got to find Lee."

"Lee? Corky, the guy murdered your best friend. The person you need to talk to is Tom Lynch. The cop."

"I told you last night, Jule. Lee would never hurt Fitz. And you don't know for certain that he did. I want to give him a chance to explain it all to me. Then I'll call Lynch. I made some coffee. You want a cup?"

"No, thanks. Corky, I don't think—"

"Julia. Promise me this. I talk to Lee first."

"Okay," I relented. "But for god's sake, be careful."

He gulped black coffee from a chipped red mug. "Time we did a little refurbishing for you, huh? A guy could break a tooth on your china."

"I'll remember to get my mind back on housewares. When things settle down."

"Yeah. When things settle down." He chugged the rest of the coffee as if it were a cold beer and slammed the empty mug on the counter. Then he wrapped his arms around me in a hard squeeze. His neck, already damp with perspiration, gave off the feminine scent of my lemon verbena soap.

"Gotta go. Remember—no talking to Lynch until I call you later today," he said, patting his back pocket for his wallet. I shut the door behind him, and poured a splash of cranberry juice into a glass of seltzer.

How long would Corky be able to keep up his new sober, sensible routine? How long before he wavered and started drinking again? The odds were against him if he actually found Lee, who would greet him with a line of coke, a double scotch, and a thousand excuses. At least the briefcase was still mine. But I couldn't carry Corky under my arm to keep him safe.

I turned on the shower taps and stood beneath a dribble of almost cool water, hoping it would clear the steam out of the apartment. It didn't work. I had to wipe a corner of the bathroom mirror clear with my towel in order to see my reflection. A tired face stared back at me, with crevices around the eyes I didn't recognize. Like footprints left on a beach at high noon, the shallow crow's-feet that would become the deep tracks of my middle age were etched hard and dark beneath the glare of the fluorescent bulb. It was not the face that Sam had first met all those years ago. I turned away from the mirror. In the bedroom I stepped into a calf-length black cotton skirt, slipped on sandals, and draped my linen jacket over Fitz's portfolio. Wet hair sat heavy on my neck as I marched down the stairs with my own briefcase flapping on my shoulder.

One of Isaac's crew stood outside. When he saw me, he spit the ice cubes from his mouth back into a limp wax-coated cup. "G' mornin', lady."

"Good morning. Stay cool today," I answered and headed west for the subway.

I did not remember the last time I had been at my office at eight-fifteen in the morning. Newspapers and magazines wrapped in clear plastic sat unopened on the receptionist's desk. The hallway was a dark blur. I knew that most of the offices along the corridor would not be fully illuminated until well after 10 A.M., when the publishing day began. A sole desk lamp shed a halo of light from one of the assistant's pods in the center of the floor.

Kit sat reading the *New York Times*, nibbling on a power muffin that looked as if it were made of twigs and small rocks.

"Hey, Julia, you're early. How was your weekend?"

"Good, Kit. Sylvie Barr's coming in at nine."

He lowered his newspaper and peered at the calendar pinned on the cork wall of his pod. "I don't have her down."

"No. You don't. I made the appointment myself. Would you keep an eye out for her? You can show her right in as soon as she arrives."

In my drawer I found the binder I'd taken from the box at the Pan American, and placed it on my desk, next to Fitz's briefcase. At ten minutes to the hour, Kit appeared in my door with Sylvie. Once we had settled her in a chair with a cup of black coffee, I turned to him. "Absolutely no phone calls, Kit. None."

I closed the door and pressed the button in the middle of the doorknob that was supposed to lock it. It sprang back. Again I pushed it in, again it popped back out. Sylvie's eyes widened as I dragged the empty guest chair to the door and jammed it beneath the doorknob.

"Julia, what on earth is going on?"

"I don't want anyone to interrupt us. This is a real crisis."

"So I gather. Your phone call this morning sounded a little hysterical, if I may say so."

"I need your help, Sylvie," I said, giving the chair a final heave with my hip. "I've unearthed an awful mess with the city reading tests. And you're the only person I know who understands the education world from the inside out."

"You know how I hate those tests. I'd be happy to hear they're a mess."

I walked around the desk and returned to my chair. "Okay. Remember the tutoring group that won the federal grant from your committee? U-CAN?"

"Of course I do. In fact, the mayor couldn't stop talking about them at the convocation for new graduate students last week. Back to basics. Back to basics. My god, he's a broken record."

"Last week you told me it was U-CAN's results that impressed everyone. Not anything special about their approach to teaching." My fingers curled tight around Fitz's briefcase.

"That's right. The method, as far as I can tell, is basically old-fashioned drill. They claim to focus on sound groups, with a higher success rate than phonics or whole language. But most of us figured that it was the one-on-one attention that produced the results. We gave them the grant simply because the U-CAN students performed so well."

"Then what would you say if if I told you that their results are phoney?"

"Phoney?" She leaned forward and placed her cardboard cup of coffee on my desk. Once the cup was out of her hands she shook her fingers as if they'd been scorched.

"Yes. Their scores on those city tests far exceed what the kids could attain on their own."

"If you're saying there are some discrepancies, I would be disappointed but not surprised. We've all heard stories of the teacher who stands behind a student and points a finger to the right answer. Comes with the territory these days. So much is riding on these damn tests. That's why I despise them."

"I don't mean teachers who help out with a few answers, Sylvie. I mean scores that bear no relation to the kids' abilities. Like kids who can't read at all, scoring above grade level."

"Why would any teacher risk it? The children would be exposed as soon as they reached the next grade level."

"U-CAN has nothing to do with the regular teachers, Sylvie. It's a nonprofit agency in search of contracts and donations. They even committed fraud by claiming a black woman was the director."

"She's not?"

"No," I said. "The director is one Lee Cohen. A white man I've known since high school."

Two red spots started to burn high on her cheeks. "So much for the WBM status. And to think they're taking over reading instruction in three pilot schools this fall. The teachers were desperate for help, anything to fight the mayor's plans to turn them over to a private contractor. I could spit."

"Walk me through the grading, Sylvie. How is it done?"

"All standardized tests are scored by private companies. You know, the way ETS in Princeton runs the College Boards."

Someone knocked at my door.

"I'm busy," I called out. Whoever was at the door turned the knob and pushed it. The chair wobbled but held firm. "Go away!" I shouted. "This is a private meeting. Continue," I said to Sylvie. "Please."

Sylvie coughed into her hand, and patted her chest. "I don't recall offhand the name of the firm responsible for scoring the new city reading tests—they've only been in place for a year and a half. I do know that once the exams are collected, they're supposed to be sealed and sent by every individual school to the same PO box in Albany."

"Do any kids take the tests on computer?"

"Not yet. Just too expensive to implement. Until someone like John Walker plows private money into his damn charter schools."

"So, if you wanted to make the students' performance look better, what would you do: send substitute tests? Or alter the grades where they're scored?"

"What an awful question." She squinted and looked over my shoulder to the window with the stone curlicue, just as Tom Lynch had done. "The fact is, it would be tidier to send false tests. It would be harder to trace than if someone went into the computer system and changed the grades after the fact. You'd have more control. The teachers themselves wouldn't need to know. Or at least not all of them." Her eyes met mine. "You may not understand this, but I know with every inch of my being that you could not convince large numbers of teachers to do this."

"I do understand, Sylvie. But remember, we're not talking about large numbers of teachers. We're dealing with people who probably want to make regular teachers look bad, you know?" I dragged open the zipper of Fitz's case and handed her the top stack of papers. She flipped through them, shaking her head at all the corrections marked in red. "What would you make of these?" I asked.

"Kids in trouble. Terrible problems with basic comprehension. But these are just practice tests, aren't they?" she said, her eyes carefully moving down each page.

"Yes. Though a week later these students did very well on the city exams, compared to other schools."

She looked at the covers of the answer booklets and the list of names Fitz had marked up. "These are from PS 95? Their students topped the city's placement tests in August. Where did you get them?"

"They belonged to a friend of my brother's. A young teacher who was tutoring for U-CAN. He suspected something was wrong. This also belonged to him." I handed her the binder I'd found in the box in Corky's office. "Those are from another U-CAN school that did well—PS 127 in the Bronx. What I want to know, Sylvie, is this: can you help figure out how it was done?"

"The very idea of this makes me shake with rage, Julia. I can't see straight."

"I understand. But we need to concentrate on proof. That's the only thing that will put a stop to it all."

She bowed her head and carressed the narrow bridge of her nose between her thumb and forefinger. I knew from our days working together on her first book that this meant I needed to be quiet for several minutes. When she lifted her head, she was ready.

Sylvie had a plan. She would check the names of the students on Fitz's list against the computer printouts of June and August test results that were now sitting as doorstops on the floor of her office. Then she would call the teachers whose students' scores were unusually high on the pretense of inviting them to a reading conference. She would also do some general snooping among her colleagues about the schools that had done well. Most important, she would find out exactly how the tests were mailed to Albany.

"What about this Roberta Jones?" she asked. "Should one of us speak to her?"

"A friend of mine is going to see her today," I said. "She actually does great work with teens in the Bronx."

"Then, in the meantime, Julia, you should meet more of the actual U-CAN tutors. They're the ones who have seen how it all works up close. What about this friend of your brother's? What else can he tell you?"

"Nothing, Sylvie. He's dead now."

She looked at the papers in her lap. "The man these belonged to is dead?"

"Yes. He was murdered. Murdered because of what he found out. Maybe even because of what you have in your hands. There's a lot at stake here. Power. Control. Money."

The red spots on her cheeks burned brighter and met a flush that swept up from her neck.

"I have to warn you, Sylvie. There are dangerous people looking for what's in that briefcase."

"Sure," she snorted, "how handy at contract negotiation time if members of the teachers' union are underperforming the volunteers. It's worth killing for, isn't it?" I was silent. "Tell me, Julia. What was his name? The tutor?"

"William Fitzgerald. His nickname was Fitz."

"And he was a good person?"

"The best. A teacher, in fact. A born teacher."

"A teacher who died because he wanted to protect the children?" She swept the papers into the briefcase and tugged the zipper shut. "Then we must punish those who killed him. And make sure he did not suffer in vain, Julia. That is our task." She stood up and shoved Fitz's binder into her own formidable satchel, which looked like the kind of bag doctors used to bring on house calls. "Good thing no one ever thinks there's anything worth stealing at Teachers College."

"I can't tell you how much it means to me to have your help."

"It means something to all of us." She gave my arm one of those little pinches that teachers give to show support or affection. Then she stretched up on her toes and pecked a quick, precise kiss on my cheek. I wanted to hug her, but couldn't overcome an ancient childhood taboo against touching the teacher. Instead, I took her weightless beige raincoat off the hook on the back of my door and held it open so that she could easily slip her small arms into its sleeves. She gathered up her newspaper and the zippered portfolio along with her bag and stopped for a minute to gaze at my shelves.

"Books are such wonderful friends," she said. *A Native Son Bears Witness* stared at us from the top shelf, where I'd placed it on a display stand out of throwing range. The gold sticker announcing the Pulitzer curled above Sam's left ear. "You know, Julia, I do remember reading an article about U-CAN in *Instructor* magazine. If I'm not mistaken, Samuel Reid was mentioned as a big proponent of their techniques. Said it was guaranteed to help inner-city children. Some nonsense about rap culture and oral learning. As if black children can't learn the same way everyone else does."

"Sam?" I said, dislodging the chair from its barricade position at the door. "I didn't think he knew anything about reading pedagogy."

"I'm sure he doesn't. But you know what it's like. The endorsements from the big names mean everything. Especially today."

"Yes, the publishers play the same game." Hadn't Henry Rawls dreamed of locking in California adoptions just by tacking Sam's name to his project? I opened my office door. Kit stood at his desk sorting the internal mail. He held an envelope high in front of his face so I wouldn't see that he was staring at us as I led Sylvie down the hallway.

"Don't forget, Julia. Go to U-CAN headquarters as soon as you can and try to talk to some of those other tutors. Who knows what they'll be able to tell you?" She gave me a small salute, Fitz's portfolio held tight to her chest, as the elevator doors closed on her.

Diane sat at her desk tearing plastic off the out-of-town newspapers and the weekly magazines. The strong smell of a bacon, egg, and cheese on a roll filled the reception area. I spied the telltale ball of foil and waxed paper next to her computer.

"You're the early bird today," said Diane. "Whaddya having, some kind of power breakfast?"

Leigh Fleming stormed by without lifting her sunglasses or saying hello.

"Leigh Fleming!" I shouted. She aimed the sunglasses at me and mumbled something before continuing down the hall. Diane stuck out her tongue at Leigh's back. I inhaled the rich bacon smell and considered asking Diane for a bite. Instead, I grabbed a *Times* to take to my office. On the front page was a picture of the mayor sitting in a classroom, listening to fifth graders read aloud.

Corky's address book was still in my bag. Under Lee's name was a phone number, but no address for U-CAN. I walked to the hallway and tugged the thick Manhattan phone book off the shelf of reference books near the filing cabinets. Like any nonprofit agency happy to take contributions, U-CAN was listed in the white pages: 167 E 28th Street. Kit, ever curious, opened a drawer near me and carefully fingered the plastic tabs that separated the different hanging files, as if he were searching for something that was very difficult to find. I wrote the U-CAN address on a slip of paper and returned to my office without saying a word to him.

I began to assemble what I needed for my U-CAN excursion: a notepad, business cards, my antacid tablets, my Filofax. As I reached for the phone to dial Corky's number, it began to ring. Kit knew I didn't want to be disturbed, but my eleven o'clock appointment had arrived. The author from New Zealand. Had I forgotten scheduling the meeting by fax with the London agent? I groaned and quickly smeared my mouth with some pink lipstick. I pulled the proposal from pile number two on my desk. I hadn't read more than the first three lines.

"If you're not up to it, I'd be happy to take the meeting for you. I read a copy of the proposal over the weekend and thought it was fantastic." Kit now stood on the other side of my desk. His eyes gleamed with helpfulness.

"That won't be necessary. But you can rework the Rasheed flap copy as I've marked it. If we don't move it on we'll miss the bound book date."

"Sure thing." He took the copy from my outbox.

For an hour Former Brigadier Commander Sneed of Her Majesty's Service told me about the positive benefits to health and spirit conferred by the secret magic of Sri Lanka. All I needed to do was ask him to recount the history of his own fascination with the subject. His white brows—sprouting like weeds above his purple face—wiggled in delight at my enthusiasm. He clasped my hands and hugged me to his plain white muslin tunic before we parted.

Kit stood by the water cooler, his arms filled with files, watching the Commander bow a good-bye to me from the lobby.

"You seduced another one, Julia. I don't know how you do it."

"First lesson of being an editor, Kit. Keep asking someone about himself, and he'll think you're the most brilliant, interesting person in the world." I slid the strap of my bag across my shoulder. "I might be gone for a couple of hours. Please get a number from my brother when he calls."

26

I stopped at the dog run in Madison Square Park. Stood there by the doggies and breathed deep to clear my head, chewing on some honey-roasted cashews from the man with the cart that said "Nuts about Nuts." I wasn't sure what, if anything, I would find at the U-CAN office. But Sylvie was right. I needed to see it, feel it, for myself. Talk to the staff. Try to understand if anyone else knew what Lee was up to.

A mutt with a chewed-off ear sniffed a terrier as two sleek greyhounds bounded back and forth. The sun had failed to break through the morning's clouds, so the fur of the dogs and the green of the leaves quivered as bright spots of color against the shadowless dust and concrete. At least the air had cooled a bit. Dog smell and the sweet caramel burn of the nuts mixed with a hint of autumn's hopeful chill. I'd yearned for a dog as long as I could remember wanting anything. But with Corky's allergies a dog would have killed him, or so my mother had always insisted. As a teenager I'd fantasized about those grown-up autumns when I'd have a dog the red of the falling leaves by one side, a tall serious man by the other. But here I was, still alone, still gazing at other people's dogs.

Other people's men too. Damn Samuel Reid. Maybe I'd just fallen for my own tricks: asked him lots of questions about himself and mistaken it for a relationship. I remembered the manuscript of *A Native Son Bears Witness*, my notes scribbled on every page, hundreds of blue and green Post-its waving like little flags of love. It had been my job to probe, to query. His job: simply to respond.

The one-eared dog jumped up on the wooden face and barked at me. I threw him a cashew. It was time to find out what was happening at 167 E 28th Street. I dumped the rest of the nuts in a bin by the park's northeast corner and headed for the U-CAN office.

At 28th Street, Lexington Avenue was undergoing an Indian explosion. The air was filled with the pungent smells of simmering restaurant sauces mixed with the dry aroma of the groceries with their bins of spices and lentils and rice. Stores with windows displaying bright saris of pink and turquoise alternated with the occasional cheap framing shop. East of the avenue the transvestite hookers and vagrants were oblivious to the gentrification that was nipping at the margins of their neighborhood. Two men lay passed out on the sidewalk in front of a storefront that advertised, "Checks and Money Orders Cashed/Wire $$$ with Western Union Here." I counted the building numbers and realized that number 167 was a residential hotel. The Miles Standish. Of course. One of the last hotels to house mothers with children on public assistance, along with other Title A residents. U-Can was based here as part of its master plan to provide "help around the clock to those who need it most."

A fat woman with skin the color of black licorice leaned against a stone column outside the entrance to the hotel. Three toddlers sprouting braids tied with little plastic balls played hide-and-seek around her legs, squealing with excitement. I smiled but no one smiled back. There was nothing to do but climb the cracked marble steps and go inside.

I had actually been to the Miles Standish years before. The lobby had the same dank smell I remembered from my days as a Children's Aid Society volunteer. The shouts of unseen children still echoed from the stairwell, the air still choked with the stink of old take-out food. Behind the sagging front desk, a short Indian man stared at me with blank eyes. Where was the office that organized the food donations? The tutoring? "Mr.Cohen?" I repeated. He shook his head. "U-CAN?" He jerked his thumb toward a door next to the stairwell. "U-CAN" was painted on it in block letters of red and blue.

I knocked on the door. No answer. Then I turned the knob. Locked. A bulletin board hung on the wall by the door. Typed announcements about church services, school lunches, and government programs were pinned neatly in place. An August calendar announced, "Food deliveries this week." No update for September in sight. There was a sign-up sheet for appointments; next to it a string that must have once held a pencil dangled from a thumbtack.

"Scuse me. You the new tutor?"

I turned around. A pretty woman who didn't look more than seventeen years old stood with her hands on her hips. She glared at me beneath a soft cloud of unbraided hair that smelled of mango.

"I said, are you the new tutor? 'Cas if you are, then I have a few things I want to say to you."

"I don't work for U-CAN."

"You with social services, then?"

"No. I'm trying to find someone who works here."

"Well, forget it. They don't open that office until after school ends. When they open it at all."

She turned on her heel and walked away. I followed her across the lobby and outside to the steps. "I'd actually love to talk to you about U-CAN if you have a minute," I said.

The woman adjusted her jeweled plastic hairband, took a crumpled pack of menthol cigarettes out of the back pocket of her jeans, and lit the cigarette with a pink disposable lighter. With a long drag, she folded her arms and shook her hair in the breeze.

"My name's Julia. Julia Moran. I could buy you lunch or something," I suggested gently, afraid of offending her.

"Pretty name. Julia. My sister's little girl is called Julianna."

"I'm trying to figure out what goes on with U-CAN. See if they deserve a grant."

"A grant? Like in money? Ha!" She blew a large smoke ring and we both watched it float away. "I don't have much of an appetite. You got twenty bucks?"

"Yeah. I guess."

"Okay. I'll take that. Instead of lunch."

"What's your name?"

"Taneesha. Taneesha Diamond. Let's take a walk." She threw the cigarette on the ground, and cocked her head toward the avenue. I followed her down Lexington and south across 23rd Street to the green finery of Gramercy Park. She leaned against the iron fence, rested the heel of her left foot against the bottom rail, and lit another cigarette. "I like it here. You know why?"

"Because it's beautiful?"

"Sure, it's pretty. But that's not why. I like it because no one can go in that park without a key. Not you neither. None of us can go in." She shook her head, laughed to herself.

I stood by her side looking at the forbidden rosebushes dropping summer's last petals in the swell of the breeze. A squirrel danced around my feet and ran in between the rails. "So, Taneesha, tell me what's going on with that U-CAN office? Why did you want to meet the new tutor?" I asked.

"Because the last one they had for the older group couldn't do shit. My boy, Cornel, he had to show her how to do the homework so that she wouldn't have the other kids doing it wrong. I mean, she was nice and all—every now and then she'd take them to the movies. Movies didn't hurt Cornel. He did real good in school last year. But this year I want someone who knows what she's doing."

"Are all the tutors like that?"

"That's the thing. Some do okay. Paris, my younger boy, his reading grades went way up. So the tutor for his group must have done something right. Even though he still needs Cornel to help him with his homework."

"Ever see the man who runs U-CAN? Tall white guy, about thirty? Eye for the ladies?"

"You mean Mr. Lee?"

"Yes. Lee Cohen."

"Oh sure. A couple of my girlfriends think he's fine. Oh, Lee, oh, Lee, baby, they say. I think he's full of himself."

"So do I." A smile pulled at the corner of her mouth. "So do you see a lot of him? Mr. Lee?" I pressed.

"Comes and goes. Comes and goes. Been around a lot the past week or two."

With the primary tomorrow? "Doing what? Setting up the schedule for the new school year?"

"Not him. Tutors come once or twice a week. They check in the office around three. Once a month Miss Jones comes, gives advice on benefits, food stamps, special school programs. Mr. Lee, he likes the food side. Makes him feel like hot shit to feed hungry people. Easier than math homework, too. You know what I mean?" She shook her head and picked a shred of tobacco from her front tooth. "And I must say. The food always comes."

"You sure? There's no schedule posted this month."

"Sure I'm sure. We know when they're here."

"Were they here last week—the day after Labor Day?" I found a linty cashew in my pocket and tossed it to the squirrel.

"I think so. Wait. Let me think now—yes, it came, but it was late. The kids were starting school and had to get up early for the bus. Paris was disappointed. Mr. Lee give me a baby chicken, said I should go upstairs with him. But I don't fall for his shit. He'd need more than a little chicken to get me upstairs, you know?"

"What's upstairs?"

"His private room. For when he works late, he says."

"Do you know where it is?'

"Of course I do, girl. Every woman here knows. He keeps it on the best floor, where there are some of those old vets. That's where my friend Laraine got to know him. Room 315. Says he has a little bed up there and everything. Lots of pillows, she said. I think they should give those rooms to us with kids, you know? They got new bathrooms."

"What does he do in room 315?"

She rolled her eyes at me. "Can I have my twenty dollars now?"

I pulled out two of the three tens in my wallet and handed them to her. We walked back to the hotel. She stopped at the foot of the steps.

"So if I want to find Lee, do I just go knock on the door of his private room?"

"Honey, you can get the key from old Ravi if you tell him you're doing work for Mr. Lee. Just say it's overtime."

"Just like that? He'll give it to me?"

"Sure, if you're a woman who ain't bad-looking, he'll give it to you." Her raised eyebrow told me to take the compliment.

I smiled. "Okay. Thanks." I took a step and twisted around. "Should I take the elevator or the stairs to the third floor?"

"Elevator stinks, but the stairways are worse. People smoking, doing dope. Rat shit. For you, elevator's the way to go."

"I'm sorry. About the rat shit and everything."

"Yeah, me too." She shrugged, and turned to go.

"Thanks for all your help," I called after her as she walked down the block to join the women who stood smoking outside the check-cashing place. Then I returned to the front desk.

"I need the key for Mr. Lee Cohen's room. I'm doing some work for him and he told me to meet him upstairs. Overtime."

Ravi lifted his eyes from a styrofoam tray of curry and wiped a smear of yellow sauce from the side of his mouth with a square of paper towel. "Okay, miss, no problem. You should have told me you work for Mr. Lee," he said, throwing the key on the counter. "You don't look like most of the girls who do overtime for him, you know?"

In a folding chair by the elevator a security guard nodded over his OTB sheet. I pressed the call button for the elevator.

I was on my own.

27

Taneesha was right. The elevator reeked of urine and stale french fries and marijuana. On its walls the shadows of old graffiti floated behind fresh slashes of violet spray paint. I was glad I was only going to the third floor.

The elevator groaned and spit me into a dark hall, lit only by the two bulbs that flickered overhead. Cheap pine cleaner burned my nose. There was no flocked wallpaper, no helpful Hilton arrow pointing to "Rooms 301–317." A cat howled behind the door across from the elevator. I swallowed hard. Silly white girl, Sam had always called me. Maybe he was right. Hungry, desperate cat nails scratched at the door as I walked past.

I followed the hallway that stretched to my left and tried to make out the room numbers. Painters had worked around them for years, rather than go to the trouble of redoing them with each new job. Now each door looked as if a large thumb had left a dirty smudge in its middle. As I peered at one, a finger protruded from its peephole and wiggled at me. Someone said something in Spanish and laughed. I jerked away and looked up and down the hall, afraid the door was about to open. When nothing happened, I continued down the dark corridor.

The building was laid out like a U, so I turned left again. More of the lights here were still working and I could see that the floor beneath my feet wasn't linoleum but old terrazzo tile. A sign of happier days at the Miles Standish. Room 315 was in the middle of the hallway on my right. There was nothing to indicate that it was any different from the other rooms. A sliver of light shone at the base of the door. The afternoon sunlight? Or one of Lee's local girlfriends? With the key gripped in my hand, I leaned against the door and strained to listen.

A radio was playing. Charlie Parker. The weekly bebop show on WBGO.

"I told you. I can't deal with this right now," shouted Lee Cohen. The radio clicked off. "Geez. I cannot stand that jazz shit," he whined.

No one responded. There was silence for a few seconds as he listened to someone on the other end of the telephone.

"Okay. Okay," he answered. "We'll talk later. Right now I'm late for the mayor's press conference. I'm on my way out the door. Yeah. Later." The cell phone snapped shut. Was he talking to my brother?

I ran down the hall and around the corner, relieved by the silent tread of my rubber-soled sandals. Whatever Lee was doing in there, he wouldn't be happy to find me lurking outside his door. I wasn't in any mood to confront him alone, either. But once he was gone I wanted to see what I could find in that room.

I flattened my back against the grimy plaster wall, listening for Lee to leave the apartment. An old man in a frayed bathrobe and slippers closed the door to the garbage disposal at the end of the corridor and shuffled toward me. I put my finger to my lips to signal that we should be quiet. He stopped in front of a door to my left. I waved, rolling the fingers of my right hand the way I'd do to entertain a baby. His mouth opened in a crooked smile that revealed he had no top teeth. In a long, loose twitch, his tongue flopped over his lower lip. I waved again and mouthed "bye bye." He waved back. Then he turned the doorknob and disappeared.

The key felt heavy and cold in my hand, wet from perspiration.

To my right, a door slammed shut and a bolt turned with a rusty screech. The leather soles of Lee's expensive loafers slapped against the tile as he hurried toward the elevator I had just left. I twisted my head around the corner to be sure that he was really gone. A tall flash of navy blue disappeared in the dark at the end of the hall. The key fell out of my hand and clanged on the hard terrazzo floor.

I listened for the sound of Lee's feet returning. Nothing. The elevator door rumbled open and shut. I leaned around the corner. No one was there.

Damn yourself, Julia, I whispered. I wrapped my fingers around the cold metal, and walked to the door of room 315. My hand was shaking so hard I could not get the key to meet the keyhole. It dawned on me that I might find a strung-out girl in Lee's bed. Still, I had to go in. I tightened my left hand around the right to steady it, and forced the key into the lock. The key fit the hole but at first I could not make it go inside.

Then in it slid. I twisted to the left, but could not move it. When I tried the right, it clicked over. I turned the knob, and slowly pushed the door open.

Two small patches of afternoon glare bounced through the window and blinded me for a second. When my eyes adjusted from the dark of the hallway, I could make out a small room that was someone's idea of bordello elegance. Red velvet curtains, lots of velvet pillows on a brass bed. A brocade loveseat flanked a small desk beneath the window.

A man sat at the desk with his back to me, fiddling with the dials on a compact stereo that sat next to an open laptop. Beneath the red cotton turtleneck I could make out the line of a strap that crossed his left shoulder. The room smelled of garlic, no doubt from whatever had been in the white cardboard take-out containers that filled the brass trash can. A musky kind of men's cologne hung behind the garlic.

"Forget something, man?" said the person at the desk.

He turned around. I stared into a pair of familiar brown eyes.

"Sam," I hissed.

"Julia?" The brow that was usually so smooth curled into a knot. "What the hell are you doing here?"

"That's what I'm dying to ask you." The restless notes of Charlie Parker's horn broke through the static of the radio as I stood in the doorway, waiting for Sam to say something. Surely he was too smart to be ambushed by Lee, of all people. But why wasn't he running for the door? "You can explain how it happened once we're out of here," I said. "Come on, let's go."

I watched him push his face into a smile. "That addle-headed white boy didn't tell me you were coming up. What a sight for sore eyes you are."

"He doesn't know I'm here, Sam. Do I have to prop this door open? It must have some kind of trick dead bolt, right?"

"No, beautiful, don't be silly." He walked toward me with both arms extended, as if I were a late Christmas present he was going to open. With his good hand on my wrist, he pushed the door shut with his claw. "You and I need a little privacy after all this time, don't you think?" He cocked his head and pressed his open mouth against mine. His hand slid up my arm to my breast while his soft lips swallowed me, his tongue searching for the familiar places.

Over his shoulder I stared at the closed door, horrified that he'd so easily squandered my hard-won gift of liberation. I pushed him away. "Not now, Sam. What's wrong with you? Don't you want to get out of here?"

"In due time, Julia, in due time. First I want to get reacquainted with my girl. You know what I mean," he said, tilting his head toward the bed. But the look in his eyes was not seductive. It was hard and determined, as if he were about to undertake an onerous task.

I stepped toward the curved brass bed frame, my eyes taking in the crowded room. A portable phone sat on the desk behind the laptop. "Sam, that addle-headed white boy, as you call him, is a murderer. So why are you so calm when he's locked you in this ridiculous room? Doesn't that phone work?" I made for the desk, not wanting to believe the truth that was settling in on me like a thick fog.

He blocked my way, took my hand, and pulled me to the shiny brocade loveseat that was stuffed against the wall. Our knees touched as we perched against the wall of decorative pillows. From the radio, the saxophone was beginning to sound frantic.

He held tight to my hand and looked at a point beyond my knees. He spoke so slowly that at first I wondered if he'd been drugged. "Julia. The Cohens and I know each other very well. You might say that we've become business associates."

"No, Sam. No." I tugged my hand out of his. "You must not realize: they are completely crooked. U-CAN is a total fraud." I looked in his eyes for sign of reaction. “But you already know that, don’t you?” I continued. “That’s why you told Elijah you had a plan.”

“That fool Isaac Lord talking to you?”

“That’s what you wanted him to do, isn’t it? That’s why you sent me the postcard—as a sign that you were safe.”

“That’s right, baby. Satchmo and the Hot Five. What did I do, to be so black and blue?” For a second, he flashed the old Samuel smile, as if the postcard were a private joke between us.

“Why the hell didn’t you tell me what was going on? A detective came and grilled me about us, accused my brother of hurting you. . . . ” There was too much to say. I stopped.

He dropped his head toward his chest, as if he were gazing at his shoes. He breathed in deep, and exhaled so deeply that the moan seemed to push him to his feet. There was no hint of a smile when he stood up.

“The original idea was brilliant: I’d disappear from the banquet, emerge unscathed at one of the locales serviced by the lovely Cohen boy here, and tell my story to the paper of record. Blow the horn on this U-CAN situation and tell a moving tale of darkness at the same time. Discredit the mayor’s people just before the election. All for the glory of Brother Elijah, of course.” He pulled the chair out from the desk, turned it to face me, and sat down again.

“So what happened?” I asked, fighting to concentrate on his words instead of the fear that was churning inside me. I looked at the closed door, again.

“Before the night of the ANB Manfred Cohen invited me to dinner. One thing led to another. As he pointed out, I had been on the foundation that approved a substantial grant for sonny boy’s charity. And I had endorsed the U-CAN method in public.” He pulled his right foot up over his left knee, and rested his claw on a spotless new sneaker. “Manny said he would make it worth my while to forget about U-CAN. Said if I’d go a step further and withdraw my support from Elijah, he’d connect me to political people with real power. The men who write the checks. You might say the ANB presented itself as a dramatic opportunity to cross over.”

"Manny convinced you to betray the reverend? After everything you and Elijah built together?" I choked to think of what Manny had known as I sat there on his leather sofa, sucking on hard candy.

"I wouldn't put it that way, Julia. I simply strengthened my own contacts outside the circle. Time to leave home, take my place at the larger table, you know?" He spoke with the kind of formal deliberation that made me think he'd been repeating the line to himself over and over as he ate Chinese food.

"That's bullshit, Sam. You didn't just change sides. You made a video saying you might be killed. You tried to force the reverend to withdraw from the election."

"That fool tape. Sonny boy got carried away. Thinks he's Martin Scorcese with the damn video camera. You ask me, too much powder up his nose has burned the brain cells." To my horror, he laughed, shaking his head in bemusement.

I got up from the loveseat and walked as far away from him as I could get in the tiny room. "These people murdered my friend, William Fitzgerald, just because he threatened to expose them. Doesn't that mean anything to you?"

"That's not true, baby—"

"I thought we were partners in crime. But you've lied about everything. From when you first plotted your little PR stunt with Elijah to this ridiculous alliance with the Cohens. Not to mention the string of socialites you've been fucking."

"Look here, Julia." He stood up and pushed the chair behind him with his heel. "I am not married to you."

I stared at him. We had been careening toward this moment for a long time. I could never have imagined that it would happen in such strange circumstances. But now that it had arrived, a kind of perverse thrill was hurling me forward, headlong, on the tidal wave of my own anger.

"That's right, Sam. You are not married to me. I'm just someone you use when it suits your purposes. Just like you used me to get inside my brother's hotel."

"What an exaggerated sense of your own importance you have, Julia." The fingers of his hand twitched by his side. "Especially since you're the one who's been riding my coattails to get ahead. What is it that I could possibly need you for?"

"You tell me, Mister Pulitzer. Could it be that you needed me to write your goddam book for you?" I moved near the wall, so that the bed was between us.

"How dare you. You arrogant little bitch. I was writing books long before I met you."

"Come on, Sam. You didn't even look at the final manuscript before it went to the copyeditor. You never saw the page proofs." My mouth was dry. "You still don't know what chapter six says."

"I've always relied on research assistants, editors, to take care of the details," he said, through gritted teeth. "That's your job. The ideas, the sentiments, are mine."

"The sentiments? Don't make me puke! I even wrote the acknowledgments for you." I had never said it before. But now it was too late to stop. "I deliberately left my name out. It was a test. To see if you'd read them. Because I knew if you did, you'd have to at least stick my name in there, after all the work I'd done." I was panting, as if I'd run a long race. "But you didn't. Because you never read the acknowledgments, did you? You can't even say your own thank-yous."

He lunged across the bed, balancing on his knees and his good hand. "You little bitch. You can't stand the fact that I'm the one who's famous. Successful. And you're not."

"What I can't stand is the fact that you're a fraud." He howled in fury. I ran around the bed away from him.

The door swung open and I almost tripped into the arms of Lee Cohen. His bloodshot eyes widened at the sight of me. Then he shut the door with a manic flourish that told me he was very high. He dangled in the air the key I'd left sitting in the door. "Break it up, lovebirds. Did someone forget something? Could it be our surprise visitor, Julia Moran?" I reached out to grab the key but he pulled it away and slipped it his left pocket. "No tickee, no key, Miss Julee. I knew it had to be you when Ravi asked how I liked the busty white chick who had come to see me."

"She was just asking me about your lovely videotape, Leopold. I guess it's playing at all the local theaters," said Sam, sitting on the edge of the bed, fighting for calm.

"I should have known she could get that over-the-hill cop to tell her anything." Lee swept the back of his hand across his nose. The bottom lid of his left eye twitched uncontrollably, almost in time to the saxophone. "What the hell are you doing here, Julia?"

"I was just doing some research on worthy charities, Lee. I had no idea I'd find all of you so cozy here in the Miles Standish."

"I've got to call my father." Lee pulled a cell phone from his pocket and punched in some numbers. In a little-boy voice he asked someone if his dad was around. Whoever it was made him smile. "Okay, Mrs. B., I'll try him there in five minutes," he said, and hung up. Then he pulled a yellow glass vial out of his jacket pocket. He unfolded the black plastic spoon in its cap and dialed another number. Sam stepped toward me, stretching his arms over his head. We spoke quietly, like parents whose child has caught them in the middle of a screaming argument.

"What exactly did they promise you, Sam?" I asked.

"Next year: a cultural affairs spot in the new city administration. Down the road: you never know. Department of Education, the Senate. But. . . . " He looked away from me toward Lee, who was frantically flipping through a small pocket address book.

"But what?"

His voice lowered. "I did not expect to be sequestered like this. I agreed to confuse the reverend, dismantle the attack on U-CAN. Now I am losing patience."

Lee screamed, "Damn it to hell," and stamped his feet. He threw the address book on the desk and faced the venetian blinds with the phone cradled beneath his left ear. He shoved the small black spoon up one of his nostrils and snorted. It hung there for a second, forgotten, while he dialed another number.

"Then why don't you leave? You could walk out any time," I said, averting my eyes from the spectacle of Lee.

"No, I cannot. Mr. Cohen senior has made it impossible for me to leave."

"Impossible? How?"

"He has information which in the wrong hands would do me great harm. Unsavory stories. Unsubstantiated, but unsavory." Sam shivered. "My lecture fees would plummet. I would have no political prospects."

"Blackmail? Your new 'business associates' are blackmailing you? About what?"

"That's not important," he said. A vein pulsed in his left temple.

"Sam. What's wrong with you? You know all the dirt on their little charity here. Just get up and walk out."

"I cannot."

"Sam—"

"I will not."

"You're being taken for a fool."

"I am NOT a fool. Elijah Vaughn is the fool." Something hard and high that I had never heard before twisted in his throat.

Lee swore at another answering machine and snapped his phone shut. A rash of red hives was spreading up the side of his face to meet the pulsing eye. The insistent frenzy of the bebop sax on the radio was boring into my brain. Suddenly I was exhausted, as if my blood pressure had taken a dive. It was time to leave.

"Great to see the two of you, but I've gotta go. Back to work."

"You're not going anywhere, Jule," said Lee. "Until I find my father you are keeping your nosy little ass right here."

"Lee, I don't have anything to do with you and your father."

"I'm sure Sam would be happy to have you stay here," said Lee. "Maybe you can do a better job satisfying him than the ladies downstairs have been able to. After all, he has a predilection for white girls and they're in short supply at the Miles Standish."

"Sam, would you tell him to get out of my way?" I looked at Sam, who had perched again on the edge of the bed. He did not take his eyes off a velvet pillow he bounced in his lap. He said nothing.

The two men who had figured so intimately in my life, at different times, were now tied inextricably to each other in this tiny velvet box of a room. And I was trapped with them, as if we were all waiting to go onstage for a nightmare segment of *This Is Your Life*. "I don't want to be near either one of you," I said. "You deserve each other."

"Julia, you are staying here," said Sam, rising from the bed.

"No, Sam, I am not. I am doing what you should have done the minute you met the lovely Cohen family. What I should have done when I first met you." I made for the door. Lee grabbed my arm and turned me back into the room.

"Let go of me, you asshole," I shouted.

"Stop it, Jule," said Lee, with another stamp of his foot.

"Help! Someone!"

"Damn it, woman!" Samuel tossed the pillow across the room like a football. Then he raised his good arm behind him and swung his hand against the side of my head. The force of the blow toppled me onto the bed. I lay crumpled in a heap on top of the pillows. When I opened my eyes, little black stars floated in a wave across my left eye. The wave rolled with every move of my head.

"Damn it, Reid, damn it. What are you doing?" whined Lee, his arms flapping.

"What have you done to my eye?" I started to cry. "I can't see."

"Get her out of here," said Sam. "I cannot stand being around women who are hysterical. Especially not in these close quarters."

"Okay, okay. I'll take her upstairs."

A heavy pain spread out across my face and neck. Everything above my neck felt burning hot, as if I were on fire. Lee opened the door of a mini refrigerator beneath the desk and pulled out a bottle of water. Then he opened the desk drawer and something metal glinted. "Come on, princess, you're checking into the Miles Standish." He snapped a handcuff around my left hand and clicked it shut on his right. He tugged hard enough to lift me to my feet.

"Don't try anything stupid or I'll hit you again," said Sam.

Lee picked up the water bottle and dangled it from his fingers by its neck. The metal cuff dug into my wrist when I pulled away from him.

I turned toward Sam. "Are you really going to let him do this to me?" I asked.

His eyes were cold, unblinking. Black dots of ink on a cartoon hero.

"I hate you, Sam."

"No you don't, baby. You like me just fine."

I kicked his thigh with the heel of of my right foot. He looked in disgust at the dust mark I left on his black sweatpants.

"Get her away from me before I mess her up bad," he said.

I spit as hard as I could, but my saliva fell in a sad little puddle on the floor. Sam grunted and dove toward me.

"Just cut it out, prof," shouted Lee. With a hard yank he pulled me out of the room. The door slammed behind us.

No one bothered to lock it.

28

Lee dragged me to the elevator and pressed the up button. As we waited he scraped the floor with his feet like a nervous horse. I twisted my head toward the door with the finger that had wagged at me before. But there was no one in sight.

"You should never have come here, Jule," he said. I pulled again on the handcuff and he gave a hard, sharp tug. "Please, stop it," he continued. "Don't make things more screwed up than they are. That professor is a pain in the ass. And my dad is so pissed off at me about the video thing, he's barely talking to me. I just thought it was a creative touch, you know? Something that Frito Bandito would never have the balls to do."

I tugged my arm away from his, again. He pulled back with a hard jerk as if I were a bad dog. At the same time, he kept on talking in the patter I remembered from when we would sit on bar stools with our second round of drinks in front of us. "Everyone at City Hall is bent out of shape about that Reverend Elijah guy. There shouldn't have been anyone challenging the mayor this year. But the people who love the reverend are the exact same people who hate the mayor. Really hate him." He made a snorting noise and swallowed hard. Wet streaks dribbled from his nose. "So when Fitz hooked up with the reverend, and was going to tell him everything, it looked like my friend was creating more trouble for the mayor. My dad too. I had to try to fix it, you know?" He pleaded with me, his face glistening with sweat.

"Is that why you killed Fitz?" I swallowed hard.

"Kill Fitz? Me? No way, Julia. No fucking way. I wouldn't hurt Fitzgerald if he showed up at my door with three cops. I loved that guy." With his free hand he brushed at his eyes, where a few stray tears had started to roll. "Besides, he never knew enough of the details to prove anything. Just smart hunches. My father was pissed off, though. Said I trusted goys too much. Can you believe that? About my own fraternity brother. So my dad goes and gets involved with this wacko professor friend of yours."

"But you told Corky you knew how Fitz was killed. You knew it was an insulin overdose."

"My dad saw the police report. He told me. I just wanted to fuck with your brother's head. See if Fitz had told him anything before he died. Did he?"

"No, Lee. Not a thing."

"So then where's Corky been? He disappears for a week and suddenly he calls me five times today. Like I have time to deal with him right now."

The elevator door opened and he pulled me into the empty car. The floor shifted in waves beneath me as the car lurched upward.

"Where are we going now?" I asked.

"I'm putting you in a room upstairs, Julia. It's not pretty but it's not going to kill you, either. After the polls are closed tomorrow I'll let you out. I just need for everything to calm down until the primary's over."

"I don't care when you let me out—today, tomorrow, or next week. I'm going straight to the cops."

"The cops. Straight to the cops," he mimicked me in a shrill voice, pursing his lips and tilting his head from side to side. "Go ahead, Jule. You go talk to your cop friends. Then you'll find out that I've already warned them about your obsession with Reid. That includes the detective you're so wet for. After all, who do you think tipped him about your boyfriend's little infidelities?"

Tom. Tom had talked to Lee. My bowels shifted. "Is that what you've got on Sam? His sex life? Who cares?"

"The New York ladies are the tip of the iceberg, Julia. Your man has an unhealthy approach to the noble profession of teaching."

"Right. I bet you say that about all the men your father blackmails."

"Don't make me barf. When Reid heard what my dad could do for him, he practically came all over himself. It was his idea to screw the reverend the night of the ANB dinner. And he was right about one thing—in kitchen whites, no one noticed him. He just slid a tray into a U-CAN van and off we went."

The elevator opened on a darker floor than the one we'd been on. There was no overhead light in the first strip of hall. There was an overpowering smell of something rotten, like boiling bones.

"Welcome to the funhouse, Julia."

The stink filled my mouth. "What are you going to do, Lee? Not kill me like you didn't kill Fitz?" My entire body began to tremble from the inside out. "Help!" I tried to shout, though my voice came out like a wounded crow's.

"Don't bother, Jule." He pulled me around the full U and stopped in front of room 1221. Why was no one ever in these hallways? Lee gripped the water bottle beneath his arm and groped inside his jacket for a ring of keys. Once he'd opened the door he flicked on a switch with his elbow. In the dim light from a dirty bulb overhead I could see a narrow bed frame with a striped mattress and a set of drawers. In the corner were pieces of crumpled foil, tin cans cut in half, and small colored caps that I recognized as drug works only from watching cop shows on television. Lee slipped a smaller key into the handcuffs and released me from them.

He dropped the handcuffs into the side pocket of his jacket. Then, he almost knocked me to the ground as he wrapped his arms around me and pulled me to him. I twisted away with all my strength but only made it halfway before his arms locked tight beneath my breasts. My back was pressed against his front. I had forgotten how tall he was.

"I'm scared, Jule," he whispered.

"Me too."

"Everything was fine before. I said to Fitz, we both help the underprivileged. We just have different methods. Now he's gone. Your brother hates me."

"If you didn't kill Fitz, Corky won't hate you. But you haven't said who did."

"I'm sorry Reid hit you."

"Is that supposed to make me feel better?" I struggled to slide out of his grasp but he squeezed so hard I was afraid he'd break a rib. I started kicking backward at his shins.

"I don't mind rough play but I'd never hit a woman. Not like Reid. That is, unless she wanted me to. What did you say once? It's all about surrender?" He moved his hips slowly, seeking a point of entry. He stopped and urged himself between the full cheeks of my behind. It flashed through my mind that I might have already soiled myself. "Do you remember saying that, Julia?" he whined, in that high, insistent voice I had learned to avoid.

"Yes, Lee. I remember."

"You want to fuck, Julia? For old times' sake?" He warmed the back of my neck with his fast, sour breath.

"Are you crazy, Lee? Now, when you're scaring me to death? Stop it."

He grabbed the fabric of my skirt in one hand and started sliding it up my thigh. "No stockings, huh, Jule? You always did love summertime. Those gauzy shirts." He maneuvered us toward the bed and pushed me down onto it. My face was pressed against a mattress thick with smell. I clawed at the oily stripes to get away from the deadweight of his body. He plucked at my underpants. "Remember how I snuck into your room that night? When your parents were away?"

The coke had killed whatever he might have mustered of an erection. I felt him flapping and tried to roll away. "Lee. You don't want to do this. Get off me."

A phone rang and he sat up. He pulled the cell phone out of his jacket pocket and unfolded it. I rolled over onto my back but he swung his leg over my belly to hold me in place. A fold of blue and red striped boxer shorts stuck out from his open fly. I remembered that he was the first man I had ever known who wore boxers instead of briefs. At the time, I had marveled at the youthful pretension of it. A choke of tears filled my throat.

"Hello. Dad? Yeah, I've got a situation. Yes, it's her. You do? Okay. I will. I will. I'll call you after I leave." He tucked himself into his pants and zipped his fly. "I guess I'll have to take a rain check, Jule."

"You're not really going to leave me here, are you?"

"My dad says I should tie you up. I guess I could handcuff you to the bed."

"Is that really what you want to do to me? What happened to 'for old times' sake'?"

We stared at each other. His eyelid was twitching again and his cheek was mottled red. But his glassy eyes looked as sad as I felt.

"No, Julia. I don't want to leave you so you can't move. If I don't use the handcuffs will you sit here quietly, please?"

"You don't have to do this, Lee. Your father will never know if you let me go. I'll just go back to work." I watched him hesitate and plowed ahead, hoping my cocaine-style chatter would touch him somewhere. "Then I need to go to the eye doctor because everything I see with my left eye is swimming like a lava lamp. That's all I want to do, Lee. You know you can trust me."

"I'm sorry, Jule. I really am. It's all getting out of control. Just sit here please and be quiet. Please." He pumped his fists at his side, just as his father had done in his office, and raised his voice into a pleading screech. "Please. Just. Sit. Still."

"Lee," I pressed. "Don't go. Talk to me. You're just upset that—"

"No. I shouldn't have done that. I'm sorry. I only wanted to see . . . if it could be like the old days. Before you liked black men better."

"Better? Better than what?"

He walked to the door and turned around. "I'm leaving the water as a good faith gesture, Jule. For old times' sake." He actually smiled. "Sorry there's no food, but that won't kill you. . . . Be good. I'll come see you later."

"Lee. Don't go. I need to know who else has a key to this room. Does Ravi? Some drug dealer? Your father?"

The door closed and the key turned from the outside. I ran to it and pounded against it with my fists, calling his name. The easy shuffle of his footsteps faded away down the hall.

29

A dry scratching sound skittered up and across the wall behind my head. When the scratching slowed to a march, the mice moved into formation. Two straight lines. The mice wore old-fashioned military jackets with epaulets on the shoulders. They chewed the roaches in time to the march, and the roaches hung from their mouths as they walked. A whistle shrieked. The mice grew bigger until their jackets burst. One by one the gray feet lost their fur and turned into fiberglass claws. The claws started swinging at my face. Scraping my cheeks. Poking at my eyes.

I shouted and sat up, gasping for air. I ran my fingers over my face. There were no rat bites. Only a bit of blood in the corners of my lips, which were dry and cracked.

From far away two horns screamed at each other. A siren swelled and broke up the fight. I lifted myself from the dirty mattress and went to the window, hopeful that rescue had arrived. There was wire mesh inside the glass, like you see in the windows of old schools and hospitals for the insane. I pressed my face against it, but all I could make out through the mesh and the grime was the dark shape of the fire escape on the other side of the glass. The high whine of the siren moved on past the hotel and faded down a distant unseen street.

My satchel was still strapped across me like a Girl Scout's banner. Kit was right. I should have become as high-tech as the average American twelve-year-old and bought a cell phone. But instead I was locked in this filthy hole with my address book, lipstick, keys, and an ATM card. I twisted out from under the bag and laid it on the bed.

Lee's water bottle beckoned from the top of the dresser. I pulled the chain that hung from a shadeless lamp of dotted milk glass, and examined the bottle close to the light of the weak bulb. The manufacturer's seal was still unbroken. I broke the plastic cap, took a small sip, and waited to see if anything happened to me. I recited my childhood address, phone number, and the names of my grammar school teachers from Sister Annunciata to Mr. Delaquilla. After a few minutes passed, I repeated the same. Once I'd decided that the water was free of poison, I drank half of it in long, gasping swallows. With my mouth around the rim of the plastic bottle, I caught a flash of a swollen, unfamiliar face. I leaned toward the jagged piece of broken mirror that tilted precariously in a wooden frame covered with flower decals that someone had tried, unsuccessfully, to peel off. A purple welt had forced my left eye shut. I raised my hand to my cheek and touched the bruise that Sam had left there. When I turned my head, another shower of black spots fell across my field of vision.

Behind me the light from the window was fading. How long before Manny Cohen sent someone to deal with me more efficiently than his son had done? Or would it be Sam who made his way up to the twelfth floor? Sam might be letting Lee call the shots for the moment; but Sam would never have left me in this room without handcuffing me to the bed. And beating me first.

I walked on unsteady feet to the door, and turned the knob again. Nothing happened. I braced my feet against the bottom of the door, and pulled. I leaned into it with my shoulder, and pushed. There was no give. Though the door looked as fragile and beat-up as the cracked plaster walls, it responded as if it were made of lead or iron. I threw my body against it one more time. From the hallway I heard laughter. "Help!" I shouted, pounding on the door, "Help me!" The laughter in the hallway turned to a howl. A woman moaned, "No, no. I told you. I didn't do it all. Please, no." There was a loud crash and then silence. I stood, listening, praying that whoever was out there didn't have a key to room 1221. Clearly, my neighbors had their own problems. I was going to have to find my own way out. And it wasn't going to be through the door.

I returned to the window. A torn paper shade hung from the top like an old flag. On my toes, I maneuvered the roller out of its sockets. The wooden frame around the top and bottom panes was thick with hardened bubbles of dirty paint, but the dandruff of flakes on the sill told me that the window had been opened at least once since the last paint job. I squatted and pushed up against the lower window with all my strength. It didn't move. I traced my finger across its wooden frame, feeling for a lock. The arm of the lock had disappeared. Instead there was a nail at each end, hammered deep below the surface of the wood to keep the window shut. "Dammit it to hell," I cried, pounding the dirty wall with my hands.

Break the window. Or dig out the nails. I looked at the wire mesh. It floated innocently across the glass, like an ancient net suspended in amber. But I suspected it would stay fixed in place even if I smashed the glass. On the other hand, I wasn't sure I could extract the nails. If I could, it would be easier to climb out an open window than a broken one. I only hoped the fire escape was in one piece. But before I attacked the nails, I needed to pee.

I flicked on the light switch in the bathroom. The toilet contained no water; just the dried, caked remains of what I hoped was human waste. Someone had ripped the mirrored door off the medicine cabinet, leaving the hinges bent and the bare shelves battered. A dark shape skated across the curtainless tub. Its long, rimmed tail disappeared into a hole that gaped from the rotted grouting beneath the tap. Droppings sat in a pile near the drain. Behind the tub's broken tiles giggled a sinister squeal.

I slammed the door shut. The catch wouldn't hold so the door drifted open. I closed it again. It opened again. I decided to slide the dresser in front of the bathroom door. It was made of a heavy wood like oak, and hard to move. But better not to be worrying about the rats. Perspiration dripped into my eyes as I grunted with the effort of pushing. When I was done, I kicked the bottom drawer, which would have felt more satisfying if it hadn't accentuated the pain in my bladder. No rats allowed, I said aloud, so just forget about using the toilet for now. From the bag that lay on the bed, I extracted my house keys and a travel pack of tissues. I blotted my face with one of the tissues. Then I dampened another one with the bottled water and held the soggy clump to my left eye. The world still rolled in a wave of black stars when I blinked. I closed the eye and practiced focusing on my hand. It was easier to see with the left eye shut.

I pulled the bed frame closer to the window, and climbed on top of it. With the keys knotted in my hand, and my left eye squeezed tight, I started to scrape at the paint around the nail in the right corner of the window. Before I'd scraped very much, my hands started shaking. I would never make it out if I let terror overwhelm me. To help me concentrate, I began to sing in the cracked off-key voice I usually reserved for the shower. Doing the Pips' sections as well as Gladys Knight's kept me focused.

L.A. proved too much for the man—

Too much for the man.

I worked down through the layers of old paint and rotten wood around the nail so that I could get a hold of its head. My fingers slipped off. I tried again, but my soft fingers couldn't grip the metal. I needed something to help me grab the nail. I lifted my skirt, pulled off my underpants, and wrapped some of the ribbed cotton around the rusty nail. It resisted at first but then turned in place and I was able to ease it out of the dense wood with hard, slow pulls. When I had the entire nail out, I could see why I'd had to struggle. It was bent in the middle as if it were a pipe cleaner for a kid's science experiment. I repeated the process at the other end of the window, standing on the rusted bed frame, bare-assed, scraping at a nail, singing "Midnight Train to Georgia."

The second nail came out more easily than the first.

I dragged the bed away and gave the window a strong shove. It still resisted my pushes. I looked down at my sandals. I stepped out of one and hit the frame with it, but it just flopped like a piece of stale celery. These shoes would be no substitute for a hammer. Instead, I made a fist and pounded all around the rim of the frame with small hard punches. I gave an enormous heave, exhaled with a groan, and raised the window by six inches or so. With my hands underneath the frame, I bent my knees and pushed up with all the strength I had. The window moved again, so that it was now open as high as my chin. I leaned out and breathed the damp air. In the dusk of the early evening the street seemed very far away. The lights of offices and apartments dotted the twilight. A flat purple rain cloud sat overhead like a pancake waiting for syrup. Dizzy, I pulled my head back inside.

Nerves and Lee's bottled water stabbed my urethra with another sharp jab. I would have to relieve myself before going anywhere. A rusted waste bin sat in the corner near the tin cans. I looked inside it to be sure it didn't house any animal life, and planted it in the middle of the room. I hitched up the long skirt around my waist and squatted over the garbage can, in the time-honored approach recommended by mothers and nuns for use in public lavatories on school trips. With my bare behind in the air, the sound of my own pee plonking against the side of the can did not fill me with confidence. I fought tears again, and won. I took another tissue to wipe myself, and used the last one to pat my eyes. Then I looked at my underpants. Above the right hip was a ring of soot from the nails. Otherwise they were fine. I slipped them back on.

I slung the satchel across my chest again, tightening the strap and twisting the bag to rest on my back. I inhaled slowly and exhaled on a count of ten. In the hallway outside room 1221, running footsteps thudded by, and a boy called out to someone named Frankie to wait up. I touched my cheek where it hurt. I breathed deep one more time, and faced the window.

I crawled out over the sill, my hands groping for the iron railing. On my knees, I felt my way across the grill to the opening that gave access to the first length of ladder. The opening was bigger than I'd expected and I almost slipped down the first few steps. My hands were slick with perspiration but I was afraid to release even one of them to wipe dry on my shirt. One glance below and the ground rose up to meet me. Would I be able to move? I stood with my feet planted on the steps beneath me, my forehead resting on the steps above. At least out here in the deepening twilight I couldn't see the black stars in my eye.

No choice, Julia. You climb down or you don't. You stay here frozen on the fire escape until the primary is over tomorrow, or until someone comes back to kill you, whichever comes first. The deep roar of thunder shook the metal frame. My skirt flapped around my legs in a gust of hot wind that signaled rain was near. This was not the place to be in a storm. I decided I should pull the skirt away from my legs as I descended. I rolled the bottom up and tucked it into the waist-band so my legs were free, and started singing again. This time, in a kind of whispered falsetto, the Spinners. "It's a Shame."

At last I began the slow descent alongside the twelve stories of the Miles Standish Hotel, inching backwards down the zigzagging ladders of the fire escape. Sorry, Lee. I couldn't sit still and be quiet. Not even for old times' sake.

At each story I had to inch my way across the grate to begin the next ladder. Most people probably did this easily; I hugged the building as I crossed back. It gave the residents a strange view of my legs, but I didn't care. Sam's room, at least, was in the front of the building. Two stories down, my knee hit a brown-leaved plant sitting on a sill; a few floors later, a window was propped open with the blue top of a large styrofoam cooler, which almost tripped me. If anyone saw me, no one cared. A woman yelled, a child cried; the laughter of television competed with the rumble of the thunder. As I made my way down, step by step, the honking of horns grew louder. I was drawing closer to traffic. Finally, I was at the end.

One of the things you never notice about fire escapes is that they end so high off the ground. When I reached the last rung I remembered that they're always floating overhead when you walk below them on the street. Never right down there at eye level. Far below me were two dumpsters and, no doubt, more rodents. I tugged on the ladder that was supposed to slide down closer to the sidewalk, but it refused to move. Clutching the rusted rung in front of me, I jumped on the step, and heard only the jangling of the metal straining above me. Fat drops of rain began to plop on my face and arms. My metal perch was going to become slippery soon.

I pulled the bag onto my chest and kept a hand on the railing while I climbed over it to get to the outside of the ladder. I turned myself around on the step to face the ground. I didn't know the best way to jump. When I tried to picture what a leap to safety looks like, I could only remember movie images of men sailing off cliffs in slow motion, their arms in the air. I thought I knew that I didn't want to land on a limb or my head. So, I folded my arms, tucked my head, and bent my knees. "Hail, Mary," I whispered, and pushed myself off the fire escape.

To my surprise, I landed on my feet before falling over onto my side. At first I lay there. But as the rain began to stream over me, I pushed myself up from the wet gravel. I was able to roll my head back and forth. My fingers moved when I wiggled them in the air. With my chest folded over my knees, I slowly rolled up to standing position the way we did at the end of aerobics class. Both legs kicked, both arms swung in a full circle. My right leg was scraped but otherwise everything seemed intact. I pulled down my skirt, brushed the dirt off my leg, tucked in my torn shirt, and smoothed my hair behind my ears. Then I ran as fast as I could. Within a few seconds I was on Park Avenue South, surrounded by cars and people and restaurants and lights, as if nothing had ever happened.

30

When I returned to Tom Lynch's desk wearing the sweatpants and T-shirt he had given me, he was chewing on the cuticle of his right thumb, frowning at someone on the telephone. He gestured for me to sit down in the empty plastic chair.

"Yeah, that's right," he said to the person on the other end. With the phone still crooked beneath his chin, he bent forward, opened the bottom drawer of his desk, and tugged at something stuck behind the tightly packed manila folders. He straightened and handed me a plastic bag that said "Key Food" in large blue and red letters. I put my soaking wet skirt and ripped blouse in the bag. "I appreciate it, sergeant," he said, rubbing his eyes. "Thanks. Okay. Right. Ten, fifteen minutes, max. They should wait for me outside. But no one leaves that hotel." He hung up the phone and shook his head at me. "So. How you doing?"

"Getting stiff. It feels better to be cleaned up. I'm worried about my eye."

"Probably just a little blood floating around. You can still see out of it, right?"

I covered my right eye and circled the left one around his pod. The careful stacks of folders still covered every surface inch, from corner to corner.

"No telescoping, no patches of blackness?" he asked.

"I can see everything. But there are spots in front of it all. Like black flecks floating in oil."

"You could get a doc to check it out. He'll tell you what I'm telling you. Happens all the time on the job." He stood up and adjusted the gun holster that hugged the right side of his belt. I had never noticed the gun before, digging into his waist. "There's a lot I need to talk to you about, Julia. But right now I have to get to that hotel before your pals figure out you're gone and pull a disappearing act." He swept his jacket off the back of the chair, and patted its inside pocket. "I'll have one of the guys downstairs drive you home."

"No. I want to come. I want to see their faces when you walk in."

"I need you to go home and get that briefcase that belonged to Fitzgerald."

"I don't have it."

His voice hardened in frustration. "It's late in the day to be jerking me around, Julia."

"I'm telling you the truth. I gave it to someone I trust for safekeeping. A teacher. We can get it tomorrow. Don't make me go home until you've arrested Lee. Please."

He hesitated.

"I know my way around there. I can save you time," I pleaded.

"Okay. Come on then. We can talk in the car. But once we get there it's my show. You have to promise to do exactly what I say."

"I promise."

He stopped in front of the man I'd seen before, sitting two desks down from his. "Frank, you ride with car forty-three? Meet us there in ten?" Frank grunted his assent without taking his eyes off the *New York Post* open on his desk.

I followed Tom down the stairs and through the lobby. It was much more crowded than it had been the first time I'd been in the station. The patriarch of what seemed to be a large family was arguing in Spanish with the desk sergeant. As I pushed my way through a knot of children, someone made a loud clucking sound followed by a hiss. I looked at two women with bleached orange hair who were sitting on the same wooden bench I'd occupied the week before. The one on the left pointed at me and started laughing. Her friend curled a stringy arm that was covered in tattoos and clenched her fist to say "f— you." I mouthed "f— you too" and hurried out the door, hitching up Tom's long sweatpants as I walked so that I wouldn't trip. He was already opening the doors of a turquoise Cadillac with a white padded roof that was nestled between two police cars. I sank into the springless passenger seat.

"I guess the police logo on this T-shirt won't win me any popularity contests?" I asked.

"Depends on where you go, doesn't it?" he said.

A laminated card with the Irish blessing hung on a faded blue satin ribbon from the rearview mirror. I flicked it with my index finger.

"And don't bust my chops about the Irish thing," he said. "I bought the car from my uncle Mike and he says it's good luck. Put your seat belt on."

We turned into downtown traffic on Ninth Avenue, where the bright windows of the restaurants slipped by. Vegetarian. Greek. Mexican. Chinese. It's a small world after all, pulsed the veins in my temples. My right leg twitched so hard my knee slammed into the glove compartment.

"Jumpy?" Tom asked, leaning out the window to assess the traffic. "Frigging tunnel. " He made a wide left around a stopped taxi that a middle-aged couple were climbing into, and headed down 44th Street. "Isaac Lord came to see me today. Told me about your little trip to the Bronx yesterday. I wish you'd called me before you went off on your own like that."

"I just wanted to make sure I was right before I dragged you up there."

"Yeah, well—if only you and Lord had talked to each other sooner. Or—god forbid—talked to me." He drummed his hands on the steering wheel.

"We did talk. Several times," I said. "He's been practically stalking me at my apartment."

"Well, if you'd mentioned that to me I would have told you to trust him. He's good people. When I met with him and the reverend about that stupid videotape, he told me he was keeping an eye on you."

I studied Tom's profile. The strong nose and shock of hair seemed to have softened with exhaustion. So he'd known all weekend about Isaac's patrol outside my building.

"Of course, I've been dicking around," he continued, "going after the sous-chef who once had an argument with Fitzgerald, thinking he might have killed the guy. Frigging waste of time. But hey—I'm just the detective investigating the case."

I said nothing. A police radio hissed from the dashboard and a female voice issued a string of numbers that didn't make sense to me. Tom ignored the radio.

"And what about this briefcase, Julia?" he asked. "Why the silent treatment about the briefcase? You never said a word about it on Friday." He was fighting to keep the note of injury out of his voice, but I heard it anyway.

"I had no idea it was evidence until last night. You never mentioned there was anything funny with U-CAN. Isaac said the police blew him off when he went to see them."

The SUV in front of us stopped short and he braked. "Come on, Julia, anything a murdered man has given someone for safekeeping the night before he dies is evidence. I don't need to tell you that. But you probably wanted to be sure your brother wasn't involved in something bad and I can understand that, even though it was the wrong thing to do." He sighed, then continued. "As for U-CAN—fraud on that scale would be subject to a long-term investigation. Involve the District Attorney's office and everything." The car inched forward. "But murder is different. Murder is my job."

"Fitz was a U-CAN volunteer," I pointed out.

"I know. I knew that. But I didn't pay attention to it. My mistake. Entirely. Didn't help that he used that phony name. Arthur Thomas. Trying to keep his friends off his trail, I guess. Even when I met with Elijah and Isaac last week—they had no idea the guy who contacted them was the same one who'd been killed. None of us put it together." He braked the car again at a yellow light on Sixth Avenue. The cars behind us honked furiously. He turned his face toward me for the first time since we'd sat down in the car. His red brows were knit tight. "So what exactly is in this briefcase?"

"It's packed with practice tests, lists of names, results Fitz was tracking. The day before he died Fitz said he wanted Corky to hold on to it, that he needed Corky's help with something. But Corky never had a chance to find out what it was about. He gave it to me to keep for him."

"And where is the prodigal brother now?" Something metallic in his voice told me he was not pleased.

"He showed up at my apartment last night. He's been hiding from Lee Cohen all week. At my grandmother's."

"Well, I'll need to talk to him. And, of course, I need the briefcase."

"I guess I'd feel better about handing it over if Lee hadn't told me how chummy the two of you have become. Lee said he's the one who told you about Sam's infidelities, gave you all those horrible photographs of the other women."

Tom shot through the intersection, and braked again. Taxis crawled up against us on all sides like lobsters in an overcrowded tank at a Chinese restaurant.

"First of all, Julia, you do not have a choice about giving me the briefcase. How you feel about it does not matter one iota to this investigation. But, second—because personally I do care how you feel—I'll tell you that today was the first and only time I've heard from Lee Cohen since I interviewed him about the Fitzgerald murder weeks ago. Not that I asked him the right questions back then," he snorted. A flush burned in patches on his pale cheeks. "Today he left a long message on my voice mail at home, of all places, saying that you were harrassing him. That you'd become obsessed with him because you were convinced he knew where Samuel Reid was. That you had your brother's problem with booze."

"That's absurd."

"No kidding. The guy was strung out, not making sense. When you showed up at the station, the penny dropped." He shifted to park and gunned the engine. "I'm just a cop trying to do his job, Julia. I don't have anything to do with the Cohens."

"Then tell me. Did they send you those photographs of Sam with other women?"

"Captain handed the file to me. Some the 'celebrity watch' Task Force took with our own people. Some of the really ugly background stuff was supposed to come from a private investigator who said he's worked for the wife. I didn't question where it came from.

I just read it all to get a handle on why the guy might have disappeared."

"What is the ugly background material?"

"You don't need to know all that right now."

"Yes, I do. Need to know. Everything."

Tom sighed, put the gear in drive, and took the car forward half a block before we stopped again. He gripped the top of the steering wheel with both freckled hands. While he spoke he looked straight ahead through the windshield. "Couple of arrests in high school. No big deal, kid stuff, cases dropped. Except for one charge of attempted rape. Victim was his cousin. Never went to court."

"Arlene? He told me he used to be obsessed with her. She was a good girl. Church choir."

"There's a dropped sexual assault charge in college. Early seventies, everyone's into sex and drugs, who knows what was really going on. Then a pattern develops in graduate school. Sexual harassment problems everywhere. Undergraduate filed a complaint at that big midwestern university he used to work at."

"Michigan," I said quietly. Horns honked all around us.

"Worst was just before he came to CUNY. At Princeton a group of female graduate students tried to sue the university. Very ugly stuff. He was threatening to fail women who didn't comply, that kind of thing. There were fifteen women in the suit." He shot an embarrassed glance at me.

I looked away and out the window at the sidewalk. A homeless man was rummaging through a trash can.

"I'm sorry," he said. His voice was gruff but I knew he meant it.

The homeless man dropped two empty Pespi cans into his shopping cart and rolled on to the next garbage can. Something sickly sweet coated my tongue. It tasted like Sam.

"Thank you, Tom." I lifted my head toward the streetlamp. I blinked my left eye and watched the shower of black spots slide across the light.

"Thanks? For giving you such rotten news?"

"It's not bad news. Not anymore."

"If you say so." A long whistle blew between his teeth. "I hate to do this, but we've really got to get a move on. I'm going to use the siren to get us down there, okay?" he said.

"Yes. Let's go."

He picked up the radio that had been sputtering police codes and said something into it. Then he pulled a light bubble from beneath the seat and slapped it on the hood of the car over his head. The wail of the siren began. Cars slid to the left and to the right to get out of our way on Fifth Avenue. Even the empty tourist buses in front of the Empire State Building hesitated, and waited for us to pass before moving on to wherever it was that they slept at night. Within minutes Tom and I were in front of the Miles Standish Hotel, which I'd left only a few hours before.

31

The steps to the Miles Standish were crowded with women, even though it was almost midnight when we arrived. They sat on the balustrade dangling their feet or leaned against the cracked pillar smoking cigarettes, waving their hands in front of their faces as if it would cool them in the heavy air that hung after the storm. Their eyes rested briefly on Tom with the indifference of people used to seeing strange men in suits walk in and out of their home. Without missing a beat of their conversations they took him in and turned back to each other. I looked for Taneesha in the crowd, but couldn't find her.

"I can't believe I spent the afternoon feeling like the only person here," I said.

A police car pulled up behind one that was already parked at the curb. A cop so young he still had pimples was leaning on the hood of the parked car, trying hard to look casual and tough beneath the gaze of the women who sat above him like birds on a telephone wire. His partner, on the other hand, was smiling and talking to three women who had circled around him, cigarettes erect in their hands.

"Good, Frank's here," said Tom.

The man who'd been reading the newspaper and another detective in wrinkled jacket and tie walked toward us, followed by four men in uniforms.

Tom gathered the group around him. "We'll start with the room Reid's supposed to be in, then take a look at the hole they locked Miss Moran in. Remember, despite the clothes, Miss Moran is not on the job, she's just here to show us where they trapped her, so keep an eye out for her. Frank, Joe, and Ronnie—come with me. O'Reilly and—what is it?—Morales, stay down here in the lobby. Remember: nobody leaves the hotel no matter how pissed off they get about it."

Tom flashed his badge at Ravi's replacement at the front desk. The night clerk was taller than his daytime counterpart. He put down his Big Mac and squinted at the badge.

"Room 315," I announced. "And 1221."

The clerk handed Tom a set of keys. "Twelve twenty-one not nice. Not clean." He resumed eating.

"Seen anything funny the past few days?" asked Tom.

The clerk shrugged and wiped his mouth with the back of his hand.

Frank turned his attention to the security guard by the elevator. "Did you notice the fella who runs the U-CAN office around here today?"

The guard clicked off the small radio that was playing Beethoven's Sixth Symphony from the floor by his feet. "I just came on at eleven. Haven't seen nobody," he said in a rolling French Haitian accent. "But Mr. Cohen, he is almost never here late at night."

"Thanks, buddy," said Frank. "If you see him come down without us, alert my friends over there, okay?"

The guard nodded. Tom pressed the elevator button.

In the humidity the smells of fast food and human waste were thicker than before. But this time I did not cover my mouth. Instead I breathed deep to steady the nervous itch in the back of my throat. Teenage laughter came from the stairwell, distinguished from the afternoon's high childish voices by the seductive pitch of a girl cooing, "Ow. Stop that."

"Just think, the little darlings only went back to school last week," snarled the older and thicker of the two policemen as we entered the elevator. "God forbid their mothers make them go to bed before midnight."

"Take it easy, Joe," said Tom, who kept ramming the third floor button with his thumb.

The elevator door jerked open. The third floor was as I had left it. No one had replaced the burnt-out bulbs in the first leg of the corridor. But it did not seem as sinister as it had in the afternoon. Television laughter erupted at regular beats behind the closed doors as the five of us walked down the small and shabby hallway. Something foul burned on a hot plate.

We stopped in front of room 315, where we could also hear a television. Tom motioned to me to stay a few doors behind. The two cops moved to opposite sides of the door without saying a word. Frank put his hand on his belt. Tom gave a hard, solid knock to the door. No one answered. Tom knocked again. "This is the police. Please open the door."

Still no answer. I fought a smile. Take that, Sam.

From under his jacket Tom pulled out the gun that had been strapped to his waist. The way his hand wrapped around the cold heft of the metal frightened me. I flinched in anticipation, thinking he might shoot his way in, but first he turned the knob. It opened. From the television, a studio audience laughed. Tom gave the door a small kick. Then he entered the room in a stiff awkward pose, gun ahead of him, the two men in blue behind him.

"Oh, jeez," he cried.

I pushed through the two men. At the head of the bed sat Lee Cohen. He looked as if he had fallen asleep against the colored velvet pillows while watching the small television propped on the desk. Except, that is, for the fact that his almond eyes were half open. Three crooked lines of coke were set out on a mirror on the nightstand by his side. The room smelled like a day-old dirty diaper.

Tom walked to the side of the bed and pressed Lee's wrist with his fingertips. "He's dead, Julia."

"No. He can't be," I cried. I moved toward the bed but Tom raised his palm to stop me.

He leaned in front of the pale face and gave the slightest touch to the right shoulder. I saw a purply impression on the front of Lee's neck and what looked like a flush emerging from the top of his open collar. Tom released the shoulder and slipped a pen underneath the sleeve of the gray jacket. He lifted the sleeve as if to flex the arm, but it didn't go very far.

"Frank, call this in," said Tom. "We need the scene roped off and forensics in here ASAP. Alert the ME and get her in here now. I'd say he's been dead four to six hours. He's still warm, starting to get stiff. Julia, you saw him this afternoon, right? Who knows if that phone call I received was really even from him, poor bastard."

The distant rumble of thunder joined the television laughter. I tried not to stare at the mottled face that I could now see was tilted too stiffly above the pillows. After what had happened that afternoon, I wouldn't have expected to be upset by what I saw. But I was sick for the depressed boy who could not bring himself to cuff me to the bed. The one whose best days were already gone by his twentieth birthday, and who wanted you to like him no matter what he did.

"There's an impression across the foot of the bed. That lamp is turned over. Our victim doesn't look like he was in a struggle, but somebody else was. Doesn't look like anyone went through this window," said Tom. He glanced at the air conditioner that was bolted beneath the window frame. "He could have just popped a heart valve from all the blow, but I don't like the welt, the pale face. My gut tells me that someone went for the carotids. Instant cardiac arrest, if you know what you're doing. Ronnie, we need to start interviewing every person on this floor, in this hotel."

"Okay, Boss."

"Julia, I've got to ask you to leave this room now. I'm sorry."

I looked at Lee's long body on the bed. His arms hung by his side with the languid grace that had always been one of his secret weapons. I wanted to shake him, to see him blink and sit up and offer us a line. "Are you sure he's dead, Tom?"

"I'm sure." He pulled my arm and walked me into the hall. Eyes peered at us from doors cracked open as far as the latch chains would allow. When Tom bent down and stared at one of them, all the doors shut without a sound.

"I don't understand. Where's Sam?" I said.

"Good question, Julia. And when did he leave? According to you, Reid could have left here at any time. Did he finally just make a run for it? Or did he take a swing at the kid himself?"

"Sam was frustrated, angry with Lee," I agreed. "But I don't think he'd risk pissing Manny off right now. Of course, we know he has a strong swing." I rubbed my eye.

"I'd also like to know where the reverend's tough guys were tonight. I'll have to talk to Isaac Lord, just to be sure," said Tom, with a deep frown. The pouches beneath his eyes flared a dark purple. "Safe to say that your brother's too tapped out for revenge these days?"

"My god, Tom. Lee was his best friend. The second one killed in the past month."

"Well, for a bunch of fancy college boys from the suburbs, your brother and his buddies are not doing too well. Their mortality rate is topping Bed-Stuy."

His words stung. I understood his frustration with me, his anger at the waste of another life. But a wave of dislike for the old Irish sarcasm surged within me.

"Frank," he called into the room. "Take Joe and check out the room upstairs where Cohen locked Miss Moran. Let's make sure someone didn't lock the professor in there."

"Can I leave now?" I asked Tom.

"Actually, since you've come this far, it would be worth looking at that room upstairs with Frank once he's made sure it's clear. Tell him if anything's changed since you were there. I have to wait here for the ME and the forensics team. Then I'll have one of the guys drive you home. You must be exhausted."

I said nothing. "Hey, I'm sorry," he whispered. He grabbed my hand and gave it a hard squeeze. I let my hand sit in his for a second before pulling it away. Then I walked back to the fetid elevator with Frank and Joe.

I stood again in the room where Lee had trapped me, repeating my story to Frank. The yellow cord of a police lamp in a metal cage snaked around our feet on the floor. In its harsh light, room 1221 was about as threatening as a shoe box. The nails I'd extracted from the window with such effort lay on the floor like discarded thumbtacks. Frank circled the room, patting the dresser that stood askew in front of the bathroom door, raising his eyebrow at the contents of the waste bin. I asked him not to include the waste bin in his notes. He grunted and flipped his spiral pad shut. I stepped over the cord of the lamp and slipped past several policemen in the hallway. Solo rides on the elevator no longer scared me. Tom was too busy to notice and I didn't want to be escorted home by another strange policeman whose jacket was too tight under the arms. I just wanted to rest my head against the anonymous vinyl of the backseat of a taxicab.

The elevator door opened on a much busier lobby than the one we'd entered. The hotel residents had been roused by the drama of policemen knocking on their doors to ask questions about what they'd seen. A few cops stormed through the lobby carrying boxes of what I assumed were evidence-collecting tools. Women stood in circles, talking and laughing and holding their children by the arm. A couple of the old vets in bathrobes and slippers blinked in astonishment.

Taneesha emerged from the stairwell. I called out her name, but she disappeared into the crowd as quickly as she'd appeared, her soft hair flowing behind her. I made my way to Park Avenue South and hailed a cab.

At the first red light I slid back in the seat of the taxi, the plastic bag of clothes clenched under my arm. From the radio, a DJ was counting down the top songs of the 1980s. Madonna wanted to dress me up in her love. Lee had once danced to this song in my first Brooklyn apartment, wearing only a towel. I could hear the sound of his laughter as he snapped the damp towel around my legs, locker–room style, before we both collapsed naked on the bed.

"Is this the block, lady? What number?"

I wiped my eyes with the bottom of my police T-shirt and paid the driver. My legs were stiff as I pulled myself out of the cab. I stopped on the sidewalk to stamp some life into them. The man I recognized as Louis from our misbegotten trip to the Bronx stood across the street, smoking a cigarette. He flashed a gold tooth at me and I waved. Then I slowly climbed the three flights of stairs to my apartment, holding tight to the rail so that my weak legs wouldn't give way.

At last I would be alone. Alone to cry and tend to my wounds. But when I opened the door, the living room was filled with the hulk of my brother's body on the pullout couch, the sheet wound tight around him. The window fan whined as if it were gasping for air. I watched Corky's big back rise and fall to be sure he was breathing, just as I used to do from the edge of his crib. I was afraid that the news of Lee's death would break him. Just thinking about saying the words out loud made my eyes fill. I stepped into the kitchen and saw the note Corky had taped to the refrigerator:

> J—I feel safe here for now, okay? Don't worry, I won't stay forever. There's apple pie from a banquet in the fridge. I still have my job (thank god!). Sylvie Barr will try you at work tomorrow. Guy named Isaac called and said he'd call early a.m. Love you, C.

The clock on the coffeepot said 1:10 A.M. I stretched the spine of a plastic ice tray and released its cubes into a bowl. Then I pulled a striped cotton towel from the wobbly top drawer and wrapped it around a pile of the cubes. I stood in the dark, holding the cold towel to my eye. Maybe I could wait until the morning to tell him.

"What's going on, sis?" Corky said from the kitchen doorway. I turned to face him. His face hung heavy with sleep. He was wearing the same old shirt I'd found for him last night.

"Someone hit me. Samuel Reid, in fact."

"Sam? You found him? Where? Way to go. Is that why you've got the police clothes on?" He rubbed his eyes.

"Sort of."

"But why would Sam hit you?"

"Turns out he didn't want me to find him." I took the glass pitcher of filtered water out of the refrigerator and filled two glasses. I handed them to Corky, touched his shoulder and steered him back to the sofabed. "Sit down, Corky. I have some bad news."

The bed frame squealed as he sank into the thin mattress. He took a big slurp from one of the glasses and then put both of them on the trunk he'd had to slide out of the middle of the room in order to open the bed. I moved the glasses to the crowded end table and sat on the edge of the trunk.

"You're making me nervous, Julia," he said. "What's going on? Is Gramma okay?"

"Grandma's fine, Corky." I stared at the fur on his calves and tried to swallow. "It's Lee. He's dead."

"What do you mean he's dead? He left me a message at work this afternoon while I was going over inventory. Said we'd talk tomorrow."

"Well, now he's dead. I saw him. Lying there." The memory made me wince. "I'm so sorry, Corky."

Tears spilled out of my brother's puffy eyes. "Dead from what? From doing too much blow? I told him he was doing too much."

"They don't know yet. It might have been a heart attack. There were lines laid out on a mirror, untouched. But it looked more like he'd been hit in the neck. You know—one of those karate chops to a pressure point or something."

"The carotids? Someone slammed him in the carotids? Who? A dealer?" He breathed fast. "Reid? Now I will kill him."

"No one knows yet, Corky. I don't think it was Sam. But it could have been."

"First Fitz. Now Lee. My two best friends are dead." He punched the bed with his fists until the frame screeched. "Who am I kidding? The second one dead probably killed the first."

I grabbed one of the fists and held it tight. "You should know this, Corky. When I talked to Lee today, he said he didn't kill Fitz. He said he knew about the insulin because his father told him the results of the police lab report."

"You believed him?"

I lifted a corner of the sheet to wipe the tears that streamed down his face. "I don't know if I believe his father. But yes, I believed Lee. He said he loved Fitz."

He pushed off the bed and stood up, punching one hand into the other as if he was throwing a baseball into a glove. "I am going to find out who did this to Lee. And to Fitz, too."

"At this point I think we should let the cops do their job, Corky."

"Why? Because they've done such a great job so far?"

He was starting to breathe fast and hard. Head down, he headed for the kitchen. A deep rutting sound came from him as he methodically opened and closed each one of my kitchen cabinets.

"What are you going to do now, Corky, drink a bottle of whiskey and start breaking things?" I shouted. "The bourbon is above the refrigerator. There are three more framed prints in my bedroom."

He appeared in the doorway. "You just can't let go of that, can you? Even with what just happened?"

"Not really, no. And it's not going to happen again in my home. I don't care if every person you ever knew has died. So choose."

He closed his eyes and inhaled slowly. "What I'm looking for is decaffeinated coffee. Do you have any?"

"Yes. In the refrigerator. Glass jar on the left."

I heard the clang of glass and metal, the sucking rubber thud of the refrigerator door closing. The tap ran and water slurped into the coffeemaker. I got up from my perch and joined him in the kitchen, where I filled a small enameled pot with milk. I turned the flame on low to warm the milk.

"He was my friend, too, Corky."

"I know." He untied the twist on a plastic bag and popped two dried apricots in his mouth. He chewed them slowly, as the tears rolled down his cheeks. "So tell me where he was when you saw him, and what happened with Reid."

I told Corky the story of my day, as clearly as I could. I left out what Lee had tried to do in the room on the twelfth floor.

"Thank god you're okay." He reached out his arm and pulled me to him. "I don't know what I'd do if you hadn't made it out of that room. That fucking wacko. What the hell was he thinking?"

"I don't think Lee had thought anything through for a long time, Corky. He was just desperate to please his father. You were right—he was in way over his head." I turned off the flame beneath the pot and poured hot milk into the mugs. Corky filled them to the brim with the decaf.

"So the detective wants the briefcase, huh?" he said, returning to the living room. "I just want to check out what's in it one more time before we give it to him. I have a hunch about something."

"Actually, I gave it to the woman who called today. Sylvie Barr.

She's an education expert at Teachers College. Very well connected throughout the city." I tried to sound casual. "She's going to help us verify the U-CAN stats."

"You handed the last thing Fitz gave me to a complete stranger?"

"Whoa, Corky. You handed it over to me, remember? And she's not a stranger."

"You still shouldn't have done that. We need to get it back. Maybe I have some ideas of my own about what it all means, you know?"

The truth was I didn't care about his ideas. I hadn't trusted anything he had thought or said for a long time. But I was too tired to have an argument. "I'll talk to Sylvie tomorrow, Corky. First thing." I led him back to the living room, and stood aside so he could maneuver his way around the mattress.

"I've been thinking," he said, nervously tapping his foot on the small bit of floor next to the bed. "The grade thing with U-CAN was a mess but easy enough to stop at any time. So why go after Fitz because of it? But there was this other guy who had really pissed off Fitz—someone who was handing out a lot of favors to people who needed jobs—"

"Why don't we pursue that tomorrow?" I interrupted him. "I'm too upset to play Nancy Drew right now. My brain has shut down. I can't make it move from A to B."

"Okay," he said in a tight, quiet voice. He stopped his foot midtap and lifted both legs onto the mattress. My heart hurt to look at him, sitting ramrod straight on the sofabed with his legs stretched out in front of him. I went to his side and squeezed onto the bed next to him.

"I've been so angry at Lee," he said when I took his hand. "But we were, you know, like brothers. I never thought I'd have to get married and have kids and get old without him around." He placed his mug on the end table and grabbed one of the bed pillows, holding it to his chest with both arms wrapped tight as if he were embracing a favorite old stuffed animal. With a cry, he curled forward and stayed on my lap for a long time, shaking with long sobs for his dead friend.

I stared at the clock until the numbers slipped well past three, patting his thick neck, not really knowing what it was that kept me from crying along with him.

32

The round smell of strong coffee reassured me. It cut through the cloud of fine mist that had settled on my windowsill, the residue of last night's storm. As I lay in bed, the deep bass voice of the announcer on the classical radio station floated from the other end of the apartment and lingered overhead. I felt a flicker of hope, that the worst was over. Time to get up. I pulled Tom's sweatpants over my sore legs and went in search of caffeine.

The living room was empty. The bed was folded back into the sofa, and the cushions were plumped in place. From the stereo, the DJ warned of cloudy weather and then began to describe the cast of the new recording of *Don Giovanni* that he was going to play later in the morning. My copy of the *New York Times* had been read but was neatly refolded on the coffee table. Corky must have gone downstairs to get it. But he was already gone.

No new note on the refrigerator, but the plate in the sink told me he'd had toast. Maybe he'd promised his boss he'd start getting there early in the morning. It was already close to nine.

I scanned the Metro section of the Tuesday *Times* but could find no mention of yesterday's homicide at the Miles Standish Hotel. The paper did cheerfully remind readers to vote in today's primary. A heavier-than-usual turnout was expected for the Democratic mayoral contest. The mayor and Reverend Vaughn smiled from near-identical podiums in side-by-side photos. The sole Republican candidate, the smiling right-to-life grandmother, and the Green Party challenger waved from smaller boxes beneath them.

I opened the refrigerator to get some milk to heat for the coffee. Damn it. We'd finished it the night before. And it had been a long time since I'd been able to drink black coffee. From the brass coat rack I grabbed an old nylon windbreaker. I pulled it over my head while I limped down the stairs. For the first time in a week there was no red car, no Isaac, waiting outside on the curb. I squinted across the street to see if one of his crew was taking cover from the rain in a doorway. There was so much to tell Isaac about what had happened since he'd delivered me to my door on Sunday night. Serves me right, I thought. Now he has better things to do.

At the corner deli I bought a quart of milk and a copy of the *Daily News*. The mist swelled into fat droplets. I pulled up the nylon hood and hurried down the street with my head bent into my chest. Halfway down the block, a man in a green army surplus jacket stepped out from a doorway and stood in front of me. His body was twisted with palsy, but he managed to extend a hand in front of me.

"Spare some change, miss?"

"Sorry, no, I don't have any." I walked around him, ignoring the pink palm.

Something pulled at the back of my windbreaker.

"What's the matter, baby? Don't you recognize your sweetheart when he's down and out?"

Samuel Reid's face appeared beneath a newspaper folded like a pirate's hat on his head. Despite the kiss of gray stubble on his chin, he exuded vigor. The sight of him shot through me: the insistent light in his eyes, the curve of his persuasive mouth. Only the ripped jacket and unlaced rubber galoshes told me what part he was playing today.

"You don't look very happy to see me," he said.

"That's one way of putting it." I moved to go but he danced in front of me.

"Come on, baby. Stop and talk to me. I want to know if you're okay."

"Okay? As in, did I escape from that shithole room Lee locked me in? As in, can I see out of my left eye where you hit me?" I hissed. "Please, Sam, don't make me want to choke you. Because I honestly never want to touch you again."

"I knew you could get yourself out of a jam, Julia. I had faith in you."

"I used to have faith in you, Sam. But it's gone. So, why don't you go call one of your other girlfriends? Or maybe a couple of abused graduate students?"

Cars whistled in the wet street behind us as the rain deepened. "You're talking nonsense, Julia."

"No, I'm not. Remember? I am not married to you." I wiped my streaming face on the back of my hand and turned to go. With his good hand he pulled me beneath the blue canopy that hung in front of the high-rise a few yards away. In the entryway the doorman adjusted his jacket and eyed us from his podium.

"You don't know what I've been through," insisted Sam.

I pulled my arms away from him and stepped away. "Let me guess. Killing Lee Cohen? Hiding from the cops?"

"What are you talking about? I'm trying to get as far as possible from that crazy Cohen family. That's why I'm here. I need your help." He rubbed the wet fiberglass claw against a dry patch of his jacket, beneath his arm.

"You made your bed, Sam. Go lie in it. You know. With the men who write the checks."

"The Cohens pressured me, Julia. They gave me no choice. But I don't like the way they do business. Not at all." He threw to the ground the now-sodden newspaper that clung to his head. A small piece of wet paper stuck in his hair above the left temple.

"Sam. There is no more 'they.' Lee Cohen is dead. Didn't you hear me? He was found dead in that hotel room you shared with him."

"Dead? Oh Lord. Oh dear Lord." He massaged his eyes with his hand. "It gets worse and worse. That poor boy."

I shivered and folded my arms tight against my chest. "What's wrong? Didn't you kill him?"

"Me? Woman, have you been listening? I'm afraid of these people." His hand trembled as he reached into an inside pocket for a cigarette and a red plastic lighter. He lit the cigarette and inhaled so deeply I could hear the suck of the smoke filling his lungs. "I was sitting in that fleabag hotel, listening to the little cokehead yammer on the phone, when another young man appeared at the door. Very uptight, lost his temper in Spanish. Needless to say, he was extremely agitated by my presence." He took another drag of the cigarette. I had never seen Sam, the health freak, smoke before. " 'This is not helping the situation,' said this other man, and then he lunged for the Cohen boy. He was short but strong. I didn't like the look of things so I threw the lamp at them and made a run for it."

"You need to tell all of this to the police, Samuel. You should go see a detective named Tom Lynch in the Midtown North precinct."

"Have you already told this detective that you saw me in that hotel room?"

"You bet I did."

"Damn. What about Elijah? Or Isaac Lord? You talked to either of them?"

"Not yet."

"Look here, Julia. I'm not interested in the cops. I want you to help me out with Elijah. You're the only one who saw me in that hotel room. You can talk to him, make him see it a little differently. Emphasize that they used force to keep me there." He threw the cigarette to the ground and stamped it into the wet pavement. "If the Cohen boy's dead it helps my case, don't you think? Makes it clear how dangerous it was."

"And why would I want to lie to Elijah for you?"

"Julia. These Cohens worked for the mayor of New York. And look what happened to them. If someone would go to the trouble of killing that stupid boy, there's no telling what they would do to me. Even if they don't hurt me, they could try to pin that Leopold's death on me."

"You betrayed Elijah, Sam. He's not going to help you now."

"Yes he will. He will if I tell him how sorry I am, how misled I was. I know how to ask a church man for forgiveness, Julia. He won't let me go down."

"Elijah may be a church man, Samuel, but he's not a stupid man. Any more than I am a stupid woman."

"I am begging you, Julia. Elijah will trust you. You have such a way with words. With people. Remember how you handled Omar Babi that night at '21'? Only you could soothe the savage beast, calm that man before he threw another glass of champagne at me." He closed his hand around mine. Slowly, his middle finger circled the center of my palm. "Remember how we danced in the fountain later that night, singing our heads off? My Lady Julia. Remarkable. Truly remarkable." He hummed a few notes of an Isley Brothers song with his eyes half closed. " 'Ain't no place I'd rather be, than with you.' I am going to make it right between us, Julia. Trust me."

A low pain swelled inside me, filling my throat and my eyes and my nose. With my free hand I picked the scrap of newspaper from his hair and flicked it into the wet breeze. It danced in the air for a second and then disappeared in a puddle at my feet.

"Julia. I'm scared to death." He dropped on one knee, managing to avoid the puddle. "Take me upstairs and let us call Elijah. You cannot leave me hanging out here. I am a desperate man. I don't want to be someone else's black boy." He blinked several times. The muscles around his mouth pulled in a little tug, containing the hint of a yawn.

The pain swelled again in another wave. It began with a stab so deep and sharp, I actually thought my heart had cramped. I closed my eyes. When I opened them, a curtain of black spots fell in front of Sam's face.

"Sam," I said, slowly pulling my hand out of his. "I will not help you."

I pulled the hood of my jacket over my head, and ran to the stoop of my building. A small waterfall was flowing down the steps and collecting in an undrained pool at my feet. I grabbed the rail and pulled myself over the gulf of water.

When I turned around to look at him, he was gone.

33

I climbed into the old tub and turned the reluctant enamel taps to the right. Zoran had adjusted the water pressure so that the spray of the shower now stung like needles. I bent over and placed my hands on my knees to stretch my back. I stayed there, the hot water slicing into my shoulders and curling into streams that filled my mouth and nose, until I was certain that enough time had passed for Sam to leave the block.

Beneath my skull, my head felt as light and spongy as cotton candy. I realized it had been more than a day since I'd had any food. With my hair swept up in a towel and another one wrapped around my body I popped an English muffin in the toaster. On the counter was the soggy copy of the *Daily News*. The mayor smiled at me from the front page, wearing a Yankees cap. Inside there was still no mention of Lee Cohen's death. I buttered the English muffin and took a large bite. The sound of the buzzer from the front door sent the scrap I hadn't eaten flying out of my hand.

Dear God. Don't let it be him. I pressed the intercom button by the door, hoping that Zoran had fixed it as he'd promised.

"Who is it?"

"Isaac Lord. Can I come up?"

"Thank God it's you. Third floor in the front."

I hit the release for the lock, and pulled on jeans and a cotton sweater. A hard fast knock rapped on my door before I had finished dragging a comb through my wet hair. I opened the door as far as the chain allowed and peered at Isaac, then slid the chain out of its groove and waved him in. The room looked very small around him.

"Where the hell have you been, Isaac? You follow me everywhere and then you're gone when I need you?"

"Sister Julia. There's been a young man watching your door the past twenty-four hours. Besides, I thought you'd had enough of my knight-in-shining-armor routine?"

"Well, I'm very happy to see you now," I said. I took one of his large, dry hands in both of mine and squeezed tight. "I sure could have used some help yesterday. Or even this morning. You won't believe what's happened." I released his hand and wrung mine together like an old dish towel. "I don't really know where to begin."

"Don't agitate yourself repeating the sad story. No need. The noble detective Thomas phoned me early this morning. Told me about your travails, that fool Reid. The unfortunate Cohen boy." He removed his damp leather jacket and carefully hung it by the small chain at its neck on the empty hook of the coat rack. Then he sat on the sofa and crossed his long legs.

"I'm glad not to say it all again. But that reminds me," I said, raising the coffeepot in the air. He nodded, yes.

"What's with the male bonding?" I continued. "You went to see Tom yesterday even though we agreed you'd wait until after I talked to my brother." On the trunk in front of him I placed a mug of coffee, a paper napkin, the sugar bowl, and a teaspoon.

"I called your office yesterday afternoon, Julia. When your assistant said he didn't know where you were, I didn't like the sound of it. Made no sense to wait to set the record straight," he answered, counting three teaspoons of sugar into his cup. "Besides, I did see the prodigal brother sitting on your stoop Sunday night."

"Then I just hope Tom leaves my brother alone."

He stirred the coffee with slow circles of the teaspoon. "Brother Tom takes his job—and you—very seriously. Time for all of us to work together, I think. He even asked me to keep an eye on you today. Good thing I already know the ins and outs of the assignment, no?"

"To be honest, Isaac, I don't know what more could happen."

"I'm not so sure about that, Julia. Did you know you have a visitor downstairs?"

"Oh god. I don't want to see him again." I sank into the armchair.

"Again? I just followed him here myself."

"Sam?"

"No. Manfred Cohen. His driver's been circling the block looking for a parking space. When he finally opted for the long yellow line by the fire hydrant, I took the liberty of asking him what he wanted. Says he wants to talk to the last person to see his son alive."

"I'm not the last person to see Lee. Sam was. And whoever killed him." A small ribbon of perspiration glided down my back. I reached over and depressed the button on the fan that sat on the floor by my chair. The folded newspaper began to ruffle with the rhythm of the fan. "Sam was here, you know. I ran into him on the street on my way back from the deli. He's disguised as a street person."

"You don't say." He wrapped his hand around the mug as if it were a small paper cup and finished the sweet coffee in two gulps. "I think the cat's lost his mind."

"He wanted me to talk to you and the reverend on his behalf. Say the Cohens really did kidnap him." I shook my head. "How persuasive do you think I'd be on that score?"

"Not very. Pictures speak louder than words." He reached toward me and touched his finger to my left cheekbone, making a clucking sound with his tongue. "Shame on him. Shame."

I looked away, embarrassed. "I told him I couldn't help him. That is, I won't help him. What you do is your own business, of course. He said Elijah wouldn't let him 'go down.' "

"Elijah Vaughn, if you must know, would like to see Samuel Reid rot on hot coals in Hades. Not very Christian and forgiving of him, but after all, he's only human." He stood up. "So, Julia, do you have any interest in speaking to the grieving father? If so, I will accompany you. If not, I'll send him on his way."

"I can't say I want to. But I feel like I should. For Lee, strange as it sounds."

"Then, let's go. You tell the man what you can."

The same driver who'd listened to the ball game with me now stood outside the Town Car in a long black coat, holding a small umbrella. When he saw us walking down the steps of my building, he bent over and opened the car's back door, holding it wide as if we would climb in.

"I don't think so," I said, "I'm more comfortable out here."

The driver extended a gloved hand into the car. A voice cracked, "I can do it myself, you idiot."

Two black wing tip shoes, newly reheeled, appeared, followed by two bony knees covered in gray pinstripes. Then two wrinkled hands clutched the frame of the door and Manny pulled himself out of the car. He was folded into himself, like a crumpled piece of paper. The pink face had gone completely gray.

"They killed my boy, Miss Moran."

"I'm so sorry, Mr. Cohen."

"It isn't natural for a man to bury his own child." He gripped the door of the car and reached into the backseat with his other hand. "They gave me his things." He shook a plastic Ziploc bag that held a wallet, a watch, and a college ring. "Is this all that a life amounts to?" he cried.

"It's awful. I know." I looked at Isaac, but his eyes were trained across the street.

Manny threw the bag onto the backseat of the car. "You saw my son just before he was killed, Miss Moran."

"With all due respect, Mr. Cohen, he was locking me in a room against my will at the time. As you may recall. You were on the other end of his cell phone."

"This is no time for melodrama, Miss Moran. We both know that my son was much too fond of you to cause you any harm. Right now I need you to think hard: Did you see anyone else in that hotel? Did my son say anything about people who might hurt him, who had frightened him?"

"Nothing you don't know, Mr. Cohen. He said you were angry about the video with Samuel Reid. That's all." Manny pressed his lips tight and shook his head, so that the skin of his jowls flapped loose. "Sam was really the last one to see him alive, you know," I reminded him.

"Hah! That obsequious schvarzte. He wouldn't have the balls to put a hand on my son."

Isaac coughed, an eyebrow raised high.

"I don't think Sam hurt Lee, Mr. Cohen," I said, "but he did see someone else attack him. He told me so this morning."

"Who, who was it?" he demanded, clutching my hand.

"I have no idea what the man's name is. Young, short, I think he said. Spoke Spanish—swore at Lee in Spanish before jumping him."

"Aaaagh," screamed Manny Cohen. He let go of my hand and pounded the roof of his car with his fists. "I knew it! I knew it! Those bastards." He collapsed onto the car, his head in his hands.

"What? Who was it?" I asked, putting my hand on his shoulder.

"Time to talk to the detectives, Mr. Cohen, if you ask me," said Isaac.

"No," said Manny, straightening. "No police. They won't be able to do what is called for." A dark smear of water and soot drippped from his forehead. From his breast pocket he pulled a white handkerchief, which he calmly unfolded. He wiped his face and the sleeves that were damp from the roof of the car, and then folded the handkerchief again. "A father must take responsibility for his son."

"Mr. Cohen, what can you possibly do by yourself? This whole situation has gone too far for that," I protested.

"Miss Moran. Come to the primary party tonight and you'll see what I mean," he said, in a high, excited voice that suddenly sounded like his son's.

"What party?"

"Tonight. At the Pan American. We always have the postelection parties there. Your brother will be running the affair."

"But—"

"Miss Moran, you've been more than helpful. Thank you." He patted my shoulder, and extended his hand to Isaac, who kept his arms folded. "I understand," said Manny with a nod. "But Miss Moran, I hope I shall see you tonight. In memory of Leopold. *Ohav v'shalom.*"

He disappeared into the dark recess of his car. The driver gave us a small bow and took his place at the wheel. Isaac and I stood together in the drizzle and watched them glide away down the street.

"I'm afraid he's gone mad with grief," I said.

"Grief don't make him a better man, Miss Julie," said Isaac.

"I know." I sighed. "We should warn Tom that Manny's planning to create a scene tonight. Also tell him Sam's on the loose."

"I'm happy to oblige. Do you want to go to the precinct together?"

"To be honest, I don't want to go anywhere near that Midtown North station right now. I'll try to reach him on the phone."

"All right then. I'll pay our friend a visit, just in case," he said. "But don't take offense if one of my boys keeps an eye on you." He whistled and a short man in an oversized yellow slicker waved from across the street.

"Fine with me. Tell him to keep Sam away from my door."

"Will do," he said, walking toward my stoop.

"No wonder my brother left for work so early, if he's running the mayor's primary party tonight."

"You going?"

"I wasn't planning to. But now I think I will. I want to see what Manny's going to do, or try to do. What about you?"

"I'll be uptown with Elijah. His party's at Sylvia's. You're always welcome there, you know, Sister Julia."

I knew I shouldn't risk Pat's wrath by staying home from work again, but I couldn't face the prospect of pretending to care about the details of the office day. I called into Kit's voice mail and told the machine I'd been taken ill without providing any details of my symptoms. Once I'd left messages for Tom and Corky and Sylvie and Mel, I was lifted by a sensation of freedom. At last, a few hours would be mine. I needed to walk, be among people, let normalcy tingle in my bones. I slid another English muffin in the toaster. While it heated I rummaged in my closet for the rubber-soled clogs I'd need to navigate the lakes that collect at street corners after a New York storm.

The rain had stopped, but it hadn't gone. It sat in a swollen cloud overhead, and the air below was thick and chilled. The street smelled of old eggs and cigarettes. I decided to stretch out my sore leg by heading for the Park, and then circle back to the Al Smith Middle

School to vote. I didn't know if the man Isaac had posted across the street would follow me, and I didn't care. I craved the majesty of Fifth Avenue, the curving facades and the imposing stone walls.

I made my way among the gilded ladies on their way to prelunch hair appointments and the tight-lipped decorators talking to clients on cell phones and the floppy tourists in their neon rain slickers. A breeze lifted the branches of the trees on the park side of Fifth Avenue and as the leaves shook they showered me with leftover droplets of the morning's rain.

At the fountains of the Metropolitan Museum of Art, I stopped. Two European teenagers had rolled up their jeans and were splashing their feet in the water, squealing nonsense at each other in a language that was all their own. Years ago I had done the same with Sam, kicking and singing while the limousine idled at the curb, the driver waiting for us to be done. It was the same night he had spoken of this morning. I remembered how cold my feet had been, how he'd rubbed them warm in the car with his one hand. The gesture had touched me more than the dance in the fountain. Those had been our very earliest days together. Now, at last, we were finished.

I looked all around. Any one of the men on the street could be Samuel. Was that him, sitting on a bench, rummaging through a wastebasket, talking to a streetlight, opening a newspaper? A man in an army surplus jacket walked by, talking to himself. We caught each other's gaze, breaking the cardinal New York rule prohibiting eye contact. He glanced at my thick shoes, muttered, "Those are some ugly motherfucking boats," and moved on. I laughed out loud in relief.

But I needed to get away. There were too many Sams here. The traffic light began to blink red. I ran across Fifth Avenue to make the light. Despite the throbbing in my leg, I kept running, crossing Madison and then Park without stopping. At Lexington Avenue the screams of children in a playground told me I was getting close to the school and the polls.

Gasping for breath, I entered the old granite building and followed the trail of small signs to the gymnasium. The room smelled of ancient wax and dust. It wasn't very crowded at midday, and election volunteers drank coffee and milled in small groups, the gentle drone of their conversations punctuated by the occasional groan of a lever being pulled behind one of the green curtains. A tiny woman with bright red hair and matching lipstick waved to me from the table for surnames beginning with L through R. She compared my signature to the one in the oversized book, holding tight to the eyeglasses that sat on her nose, even though they were attached to a chain around her neck.

Behind the curtain. Such a simple, primitive, way to register a preference. Flip the little knobs, then swing the lever, the curtain will open, you're done. I read the incumbent mayor's line, and carefully flipped all the switches in Elijah Vaughn's row. Then I pulled the large lever, nervous as always that it might not work.

When I left the booth, a young olive-skinned man bounced on his heels, waiting for his turn. He reminded me of someone. But I couldn't figure out who.

34

Mel stood in the lobby of the Pan American, a slim pillar of black against the ugly patterned carpet. She stamped out her cigarette in the sand of the single ashtray that passed for a smoking zone by the bar.

"Thank god you're here," she said. "A group of Italian nuns were sitting over there for twenty minutes. I was weak with desire. Ready to follow them to the *Sound of Music* revival, even."

"And you stayed?" I asked as we walked toward the elevator. "I'm honored. I doubt five hundred middle-aged Democrats can compete."

"After what you've been through? It's the least I can do," she said, giving my hand a squeeze. "But for all the bumps and bruises, you look pretty good. Your face is, I don't know, more relaxed."

"I'm following Fitz's philosophy. I just dumped half a dozen bricks out of my bag—but they hurt on the way out."

The elevator door opened. We stepped in between two bellhops who were delivering luggage carts packed with suitcases and garment bags. I wiggled my toes in the T-strap high heels that I was still trying to break in, and grimaced.

"Sensible shoes, Julia. Someday I will convert you. To sensible shoes," said Mel.

When we reached the third floor the party was already at a high pitch. The Grand Ballroom had disappeared beneath a sea of people. Round-faced men in shiny suits talked to each other, ignoring their women in colored cocktail dresses that had filmy bits attached at the shoulders. Overhead hung a swarm of red, white, and blue balloons, their ribbons dancing like tails in the cross breezes.

"Nasty perfume," said Mel, wrinkling her nose. The voices roared.

"No tables," I said. "For this crowd I guess it's just an open bar and a couple of hors d'oeuvres to soak it all up."

We pushed our way further into the room. I took a deep breath, and realized that the disinfectant smell was not cheap perfume. It was the unmistakable scent I recognized from a lifetime of baptisms and anniversaries and Thanksgivings and First Holy Communion parties. Whiskey overlayed with breath mints. Not Manny Cohen's kind of crowd.

Cheers erupted behind us. The mayor had appeared in the same door we'd entered, surrounded by cameras and sycophants and bodyguards. There were too many people crowded around him for the group to move very far into the room. But the mayor looked through them and locked his eyes on mine. With one hard push he broke away from his circle and headed for me. I turned to escape, but the net of people behind me bounced me back toward him. A damp hand closed around my arm, and twisted me around to face him. Up close the bitter smell of scotch and sweat filled my nose.

"Miss Moran. Great to see you again." He smiled, pressing a wet whiskeyed mouth to my ear. "Soon we can talk about that book." The crowd closed in on him and swept him away like ants carrying a crumb of conquest.

"I don't think so," I snarled, to no one.

Mel raised her palms to ask what had happened, but she couldn't hear my answer. The band had swelled into an earsplitting rendition of "Happy Days Are Here Again." In the far corner of the room, a group of men began to chant, "Four More Years, Four More Years" in a bedraggled kind of drunken unison. A blond man with a spotty red face climbed on the platform where the musicians sat. He tapped the microphone that stood on a stand in front of them. By his side stood Eddie Saldivar, bouncing on his small feet. So that was who the man at the polls had reminded me of. Eddie grinned and waved to someone across the room.

"Ladies and gentlemen. Ladies and gentlemen." The blond man's small voice did not make much impact. He must have Lee's job now, I thought, as he tried to win the crowd's attention. He rapped on the microphone and the whine of feedback induced an irritated silence, marked by the clinking of glasses, a rash of coughs, and a laugh from the corner. Eddie frowned in disapproval and clasped his hands behind his back so that the muscles in his upper arms strained beneath his suit. His upper body was broader and stronger-looking than I would have expected. He stood in a quiet, disciplined stance. It was a posture I associated with karate and other martial arts.

The muscles in my legs snapped like an old rubber band that had been stretched too far. I grabbed Mel's arm so that I wouldn't fall down. She patted my hand without looking at me.

"The polls are now closed," said the man at the microphone. "All day long we've heard reports of record turnout for a local primary. Now the exit polls and the earliest counts indicate that our favorite mayor has the Democratic nomination once again! The networks will announce his victory momentarily. Hip hip hooray!"

Sam had described the man who attacked Lee as short and strong, speaking Spanish. And there he was, standing on the stage. The mayor's special deputy assistant for education. No wonder Manny had recognized the brief description I'd repeated to him. He'd known instantly who had murdered his son.

The crowd roared, "Hip hip hooray." Mel leaned into my ear and said, "There's your brother." On the other side of the room, Corky stood outside the door to the service bar and kitchen. He gave us a curt wave without relaxing the solemn expression on his face.

"Mel, I think that's the man who killed Lee Cohen," I said, fighting to steady my knees. "On the stage."

"What?" she asked, her hand to her ear, as the crowd boomed again.

"We have to find Tom Lynch." I twisted around to see if he was anywhere in sight.

"And now, the next mayor of the City of New York!" said the voice at the microphone. The band played a drum scat. Tss, da da Tss, da da Tss. Loud applause and cheers exploded as the mayor made his way across the room. The video cameras following him fed larger-than-life footage to the two screens that flanked the dais. He stepped on the platform and suddenly there were three of him grinning at us like an overaged altar boy. What was left of the dark curls sprang out from behind his ears. He held his arms tight by his sides, his fists clenched with excitement.

"Ladies and gentleman. Tonight, I am honored to accept our party's nomination for mayor of the greatest city in the world."

The room cheered. Saldivar stood erect. His hands had moved. Now he held them tight in front of his crotch.

"I do not take lightly your trust, your vote of confidence. And I am grateful to those of you who work so hard on my behalf."

"How grateful?" shouted a man from the back. Everyone laughed.

"This has been a particularly difficult campaign. We have had remarkable triumphs, but also heartbreaking tragedy." He adjusted his face so that the smile of victory disappeared.

With my hand on Mel's shoulder, I pushed myself up on my toes to see if I could find Tom Lynch's red head in the crowd.

"A young man of promise was killed while he was hard at work helping our city's neediest. He was one of my beloved aides, and the son of our party's loyal associate chairman in the Bronx. Many of you knew him well. A moment of silence please for Lee Cohen, may he rest in peace." Saldivar lowered his head and made a sign of the cross. Next to me a red-faced woman in pink sparkles did the same, sniffling. People shifted uncomfortably.

I looked at Saldivar. He lifted his head from its devotional bow and fixed his calm gaze on the back of the room, as if he were looking for someone. This time the loose spasm in my legs shot up through my back.

The mayor continued, "The threat of coercion reared its ugly head—a respected scholar, writer, and speaker was taken from our midst in an ill-fated attempt to force the hand of democracy. Luckily, Samuel Reid has been returned unharmed to the safety of his home and friends. A warm hand please for Professor Reid and his wife, Elsbeth. Sam and Becky, come on up."

The confused crowd offered a smattering of weak applause. A black man in an impeccable charcoal suit and tie bounded up the steps, followed by a slower-moving heavyset woman in an unflattering cardigan studded with silver beads. Saldivar stepped back to make room for them on the platform. Sam took his place by the mayor's side, holding the hand of the woman by his side. Husband and wife beamed together. So Sam had decided to be someone's black boy after all. And that someone was the mayor.

"Oh my god. She's white," Mel said.

"Who is?" I asked.

"And fat."

"What?"

"His wife. His wife. I always assumed she was black. Thin and beautiful and black. With a long neck like a tribal princess."

"That was the first wife," I said, watching Sam step into the spotlight, again.

"Professor Reid's colleague and friend, the Reverend Elijah Vaughn, fought a tough campaign," continued the mayor from the microphone. "Although we have won, his efforts compel me to make both a confession and a proposal."

The waves in my left eye began to roll in time to the now-rapid beat of my heart. Sam's face flashed on the screens flanking the podium. His head was tilted slightly to the side in the pose he had always described with contemptuous laughter as, "the meek black man listens to the wise white one."

"I've learned so much from my challenger, Reverend Vaughn. I want to extend my thanks to him for enhancing my awareness of issues affecting the black community. In my next term I will be creating a special deputyship for African-American affairs. And to fill that role I have selected the man known as the reverend's secret weapon, the brains behind the Baptist, Professor Samuel Reid. Will you please welcome Samuel Reid as the newest member of my administration? Professor Reid, our city needs your help, our party needs your help, I need your help!" The mayor threw his arms around Samuel, who embraced him like a long-lost brother. Then Sam raised his wife's hand, and together they bowed their heads. The audience took its cue and cheered. Saldivar clapped, still smiling.

My lipstick started to itch.

The mayor's voice boomed. "Professor Reid will use his expertise to help us make sure every child gets the education he or she deserves, starting with our charter school referendum. But first, everybody, let's have fun and drink up. Because tomorrow, we have work to do!"

The electric piano and the bass began familiar Motown chords. The Isley Brothers.

"I have to find Tom. The police detective," I shouted into Mel's ear. "That man standing behind the mayor is the one who killed Lee. Sam knows it and I'm sure the mayor does too. That's what I've been trying to tell you."

The room began to throb. Arms waved in the air and hips swung from side to side in the happy awkward bounce of white people dancing. The mayor skipped down from the dais, imitating the band. " 'I'm taking care of business, woman, can't you see,' " he sang with his head back, mouth open wide and angry like a teenager imitating a rock star. Then he slipped into the crowd, elbows swinging by his sides. Sam and his wife followed, and one by one people joined them, grabbing each other's hips to form a conga line. The line snaked through the crowd. I caught a glimpse of Sam's prosthesis swinging above the teased hair and bald heads. Suddenly he was just a few feet away from me. He winked and blew me a kiss with his good hand. Then he slid that hand around his wife's waist and they disappeared again.

I stood, staring. A round woman in green sequins battered me with her hip, almost knocking me over. Around us formed a circle of boys in their twenties, faces red from exertion and booze. Mel's hand shot through them to rescue me. With a heave she pulled us away from one who was trying to grab her to join the conga line.

"I can't move," I mouthed at Mel.

"Aim for Corky's office. You know—the second floor bar." She pointed across the room.

She held my hand high in the air as she danced through the crowd. I weaved behind her, looking for familiar faces. Once I caught a glimpse of Tom Lynch, but the conga line swept me away from him. Finally Mel and I gave a united shove, and the crowd spit us out to a clearing on the other side of the room. We stopped to catch our breath by the decimated buffet table that stood like an abandoned battle site against the wall. In front of it stood the mayor, surrounded by a circle of well-wishers. He was holding a small pleated paper plate and a canoli, which was half in his mouth. At the sight of us he threw the plate on the table and wiped his hands on a napkin.

"Manny!" he mumbled, while swallowing the pastry. I looked behind me. Manny Cohen stood in a tan raincoat that had seen better days. It hung loose and open, revealing a flash of faded plaid lining.

"Manny!" repeated the mayor, "I've been looking all over for you. I'm so sorry about your boy. We had a moment of silence tonight in his honor."

"Sorry? Sorry? You should be sorry!" Manny walked past me and planted himself face-to-face with the mayor. A couple of the navy blue–blazered aides moved closer. Eddie Saldivar stood back by the table, sipping something from a styrofoam cup. "You killed my boy," said Manny, poking the mayor in the chest.

"Manny, what are you talking about?"

"Tell them. Tell them why we were an embarrassment to you. Mr. I can-help-the-blacks-as-well-as-anyone. Mr. I'll-have-a-deputy-colored-mayor. Where would you be now without us? These Jews from the Bronx that you don't need anymore?"

"Manny, please get a grip on yourself."

"You killed him as well as if you held his soft throat in your own hands. I know your people. You think I don't know who can hurt that way? Senor Tough Guy over there?"

"I know you're grieving, Manny, but this is crazy. One of the scum in that welfare hotel probably killed him. Let's face it"—he leaned closer—"we all know he had a drug problem."

"No, listen to me, you ignorant mick. You tell everyone here what's been going on, or I'll tell them for you." He reached into his coat as if he were about to serve the mayor with a subpoena.

The metal of the gun glinted in the light reflected off the chandelier. Screams shrieked from the buffet table. Above our shoulders the singer's eyes went buggy at the sight of the gun and he waved his arms to stop the band mid-chord. Once the bass guitar and electric piano whined off, the entire room froze like a stop-time scene in a movie musical. A woman started to cry.

"Don't come near me!" Manny swung the pistol around him, scattering us like balls on a pool table that had been expertly hit. "I am only interested in Hizzoner here. None of you will be hurt."

"Manny, my friend, we've got to talk," said the mayor, taking a step toward him.

"Talk yourself, you bastard," said the old man. "Tell everyone what my son was doing for you, and why you feared him. Your cops don't want to believe me. Maybe they need to hear it straight from the horse's mouth." The only sound was the deadly click of the gun cocking.

"Manny, you've got it all wrong."

"God forgive me," said Manny, raising the gun to meet the mayor's eyes.

Something swift and dark kicked Manny's legs from behind. He fell to the ground as if a hole had opened beneath him. The old man landed with his limbs askew, like a rag doll. The gun slipped out of his hands and a uniformed policeman kicked it away while another called for an ambulance on his walkie-talkie.

Eddie Saldivar stepped over Manny as if he were a bag of trash and stretched his neck by rotating his head round in a slow circle, like a gymnast. The mayor threw his arms around his assistant.

"O my god. You saved my life, Eddie. You saved my life."

Several men who'd been standing behind the mayor embraced Saldivar, and then the woman who'd been the first to cry waddled up and started patting him. Within seconds a small crowd had formed around him, muttering, "Way to go, Eddie."

Manny lay in a crumpled heap of raincoat on the ballroom carpeting. Tears slid down his defeated face, which was turned toward the buffet table, twisted in pain. Tom Lynch squatted by his side and felt his wrist.

"He broke my leg," moaned Manny. "The one who killed my son."

"I don't think so, Mr. Cohen," said Tom. Corky handed Tom a tablecloth, which he folded and placed beneath Manny's head. Behind them, Sam stared at the man on the floor with a twitch of his nostril that conveyed more distaste than concern. He took his wife's hand and led her toward the exit.

"Mr. Cohen," I heard myself saying, bending to my knees. "Are you okay?"

Corky came to my side. Together, he and Mel lifted me by the elbows and walked me away from the old man lying on the floor.

35

Deranged by grief over his son's death, eh?" said a thin cop with the shadow of a beard on his blue-white cheeks.

I sat on the edge of the dais, my feet dangling like a child's. Behind me, the band members were snapping shut their cases. They scurried off the platform and tried not to look as if they were running for the exit. I could not take my eyes off the mayor, who was about to be whisked away by his entourage.

"That's the only explanation that makes sense," he said to the cop. "For god's sake—we'd been the best of friends for thirty years." He shook his head and walked away without saying good-bye to anyone. Three of his assistants, including the pimply blonde who'd been at the microphone, waited for him to leave the ballroom. Then they ran to the abandoned bar station and poured themselves drinks. Eddie Saldivar was nowhere in sight.

My brother rubbed my neck. Mel asked a lady cop for a light. Tom's lips pulled tight as he watched the paramedics carry out Manny on a stretcher.

"So is Saldivar in custody?" I asked Tom.

"Julia, hundreds of people just saw him save the life of the mayor of New York."

"But the reason Manny went for the mayor is because he knew Saldivar killed Lee."

"And we know that because—?"

"Because Samuel Reid saw Saldivar do it."

"Right," he said, flipping through his pad, "and do you know what Reid told me? Let me find it. Here: Says he never set eyes on any of them. Not the Cohens, or Saldivar, or that hotel. Says he was kidnapped at knifepoint, doped up, and dropped in an alley." He slapped the spiral notebook shut and sighed. “What the hell am I supposed to do with that?”

“He’s lying, Tom.”

“Julia, I know. But until I catch him in the lie, we’re stuck.”

“The room must have his fingerprints.”

“Right. Once I can arrest the guy, I’ll fingerprint him and get right on that. And he’ll still say he was doped up and didn’t have any idea where he was. That way he won’t have to get his new boss or his boss’s assistant in trouble.” He waved to two policemen. “Fish rots from the head, Julia. This one stinks. And I don’t know what the hell to do about it.” He shoved the notebook in his pocket and joined the uniformed cops who were waiting for him by the table.

“You think Manny’s in danger?” asked Mel.

“Nah,” said Corky, “they can’t hurt him any more. They’ll just keep gaslighting him until he doesn’t know whether he’s crazy or not. . . . ”

“I can’t believe Sam won’t admit he was at that hotel,” I said. “I need to make a phone call.”

“You want my office?” asked Corky.

“No, thanks. Pay phone is fine.” His face fell. “I just don’t want all these people around, Corky. I’ll be right back.”

“I’m going to head out, okay?” said Mel. Corky offered to escort her to the cabstand.

I escaped to the bank of pay phones in the lobby. Isaac’s beeper number was on the scrap of paper I pulled out of my bag. Fifteen minutes passed while I stood by the phone, watching the stream of police who wove their way in and out of the clusters of disappointed party loyals who were discussing where to go for a nightcap. At last the phone rang.

“Isaac. Manny Cohen just tried to shoot the mayor at his victory party. Eddie Saldivar stopped him.”

Isaac whistled. I could hear the moan of a saxophone and people laughing in the background.

“And Samuel Reid has been offered a special deputy position by the mayor. In charge of African-American issues,” I said.

"My oh my. The cat does have nine lives."

"Sam told the police that he never knew the Cohens or ever saw the Miles Standish Hotel."

"How's that?" A woman cooed "Isaac, baby." He said "Hold on a minute," and I could hear the flat squeak of his palm pressing over the receiver. "Sorry about that. Please continue, Julia."

"We need to put our heads together. I don't know what we can do if Sam won't tell the truth."

"I'm ready whenever you are, Julia. You might say that my political duties have been temporarily suspended."

"Then let's talk soon. I'll call you tomorrow."

"Go safely, now. I'll let Elijah know that the 'brains behind the Baptist' has moved on."

I returned the phone to its cradle and rested my head against the cool metal of the telephone. When I turned to go, Corky was leaning against the pay phone next to me.

"I need to talk to you, Julia."

"I know you're upset, Corky."

"Yes, I am upset. Lee and now his father." He bit his lip and looked at the floor. "It's all too much. But give me a minute. I need to tell you what I've found out."

"I really don't have the energy right now. Why don't you call me tomorrow—"

"Goddamn it, Julia!" he shouted, punching the phone with his fist so hard that the change inside jangled. "Stop treating me like an idiot and listen to what I have to say. I know who killed Fitz. I know why. And it's not Lee or his father."

"Saldivar?" I whispered.

He nodded.

I looked around us to be sure that no one was listening. The evicted ballroom crowd had almost dispersed, but the lobby was still filled with people. Two older women with corsages growing on their shoulder lumbered past us and pushed through the swinging door into the ladies' room.

"I thought Manny killed Fitz," I said quietly.

"I don't think so. He knew about it. It may even have been his idea. But he didn't do it."

"Where can we go to talk? There are too many people around the second floor bar."

"We'll use the banquet sales office," he decided. I followed him down the hall and up a short staircase to a cul-de-sac of offices on the mezzanine level. He pulled a ring heavy with keys out of his pocket and opened one of the doors.

He flipped on a light and fit himself behind a small desk of imitation wood in a windowless room. I lifted heavy ringbound menu books off the guest chair and sat down. On the wall three posters showing swans and bears and skyscrapers carved of ice buckled beneath their cheap frames.

"This is where Fitz worked," he said. "He sat at this desk, helping people choose from the appetizer and entrée combos for their weddings and their benefits. You'd be surprised how seriously he took it. Always trying to cut someone a break on the shrimp platter."

"Should we go somewhere else?" I asked.

"Nah. It's the right place, actually. The most fitting." He loosened his tie and undid the top button of his shirt. "Today I called that teacher you gave Fitz's briefcase to. I wanted to get Fitz's stuff back, but I also wanted to talk to her."

"You talked to Sylvie Barr?"

"Yeah, I wrote down the number she left on your answering machine and called her. No big deal, you know?"

"I guess I should have tried harder to reach her today." I felt myself blush at my failure. "I only called her once."

"I told her you weren't feeling too good. She was fine about it." I nodded, unaccustomed to this Corky who was more diligent than his older sister. He continued, "I told her I thought there was more to the whole scandal thing than just the U-CAN stuff. The fake test results. It would be too easy for the mayor to distance himself from an outside group, even if he'd hired them. It would be like me with an outside vendor—if his ravioli were shit, I'd stop doing business with the vendor, you know?"

"Right, I know." Okay, Corky, pretty smart.

"So I knew there had to be someone on the inside who had a reason to keep U-CAN going. Like if one of the guys who worked for me kept renewing contracts for his brother's shitty ravioli, or ordered them so he'd get a break on something else, like the meats."

"Okay."

"Had to be someone high up who works for the mayor, but not the mayor himself. So get this: I remember that Lee once made fun of Fitz for going to take those extra courses—for public school certification. He said, 'I can get you a job in any high school in the city—except those fancy specialty high schools— without a college diploma, you dufus.' Fitz was furious."

"But was Lee telling the truth? Or was it just bravado?"

"Naw. He could do it. Said this Eddie Saldivar guy could get anyone white who can read and write a full teacher's job anytime. He did it too, for Bear Stokowsky. He'd failed out of college our junior year. Now he teaches history in Bensonhurst."

"Saldivar's just an assistant covering education in the mayor's office. I'm not sure he has that much clout."

"Yeah, but he was a pro at bypassing the red tape with the Board of Ed. And over the summer Fitz got furious about it. He kept stewing about the whole thing. How it was cheating the poorest students, who need good teachers more than anyone. You know Fitz. He hated it when people didn't respect the rules." He swallowed hard and took a pen out of an oversized ceramic mug on the desk that said "I'm Forty and I'm a Sexy Mama." He started tapping the pen against the palm of his hand.

"So what happened?" I prodded.

"Fitz told Lee he wanted to meet the guy after all. I remember they spoke on the phone a couple of times. They were supposed to hook up but I don't know if they ever met in person. Until Fitz died, of course."

"But I still don't get why you think Saldivar killed him."

He twirled the pen between his fingers like it was a little baton. "There was something inside the briefcase."

"You're kidding me." How many times had I stared at the contents of that briefcase? "What is it?"

"A tape. Fitz had taped his phone conversations with Saldivar."

"The only tape in that briefcase was a Muddy Waters cassette in the zippered pocket."

"That's what it said on the outside. Inside was one of those little tapes, like from an answering machine." He threw the pen on the desk and allowed himself a sad shadow of a smile. "Don't look so confused, Jule. I knew that Fitz hated Muddy Waters. Lee's the one who loves the blues. Loved, that is. Listen to this."

From his inner pocket Corky pulled the kind of small tape player tycoons use in the movies to dictate their thoughts. He pressed a button and stood the player on the table. The familiar, earnest voice spoke to us from the dead, the vowels tight in that peculiar twist of English known as Bronx Irish.

"Eddie, I just can't believe what you're telling me. Teaching is a vital profession. Students' lives hang in the balance," said Fitz. Static crackled.

"You stupid little prick," muttered Eddie Saldivar.

"How can you put untrained teachers in the worst schools in the city?"

"Were you born yesterday, man? No one wants these jobs. It is not teaching, it is zookeeping. For you, of course, I can find a position in a good school, nice middle-class children. No blacks. Maybe in Queens—lots of Asians."

"What you're doing is wrong. People need to know. The union, the taxpayers—"

"Don't threaten me, Irish Boy. Open your mouth and I will make sure you never open it again."

"Look here, Saldivar," protested Fitz.

Corky jerked his hand toward the machine and clicked it off. Tears slid down his face. "The same shithead destroyed my two best friends." I pulled a tissue from the flowered box that sat next to the computer and handed it to him. He blew his nose. "I'm sure he wanted to scare Lee. And me, in case I knew anything. That's why he put Fitz's body on ice for everyone to see."

"You don't know, Corky. Lee still could be the one who gave Fitz the overdose. He was connected to Eddie, even if he was afraid of him."

"Connected? You can say that again. Your friend Sylvie is going to check the appointments of a bunch of people who got jobs through Saldivar. Said it might take a little time but she has access to all the records. She bets that U-CAN tutors will be set up in the same schools where Saldivar places the teachers who don't know anything."

I took his hand and rubbed the scar of an old baker's burn on the pad of his thumb. "Have you told Tom Lynch any of this?"

"I've told him what I suspect. But I haven't given him the tape. Yet. He does work for the mayor, after all."

"Well, sort of. He hardly reports to him. Besides, he's a good man, I'm sure of it." I paused. "Where is the rest of the briefcase now?"

"In the safe in the general manager's office. I thought I should keep it there at least for tonight. Tomorrow Lynch will remember that he wants it."

"What you've done is really amazing, Corky. The police should at least be able to get Salidvar with what you give them. The mayor, that's another story."

He squeezed himself out from behind the desk. There wasn't enough room for him to back up the chair as far as he needed it to go, but he made it. I wrapped my arms around him. He still smelled like soap instead of scotch, which was something.

"See, you didn't need me to hold on to anything," I said, pulling away from him. "You're the one who saw what was there, in plain sight."

"I can see it now, Julia," he said. "But August feels like a lifetime ago."

"You can say that again." I closed my left eye so that the spots wouldn't start another wave.

"I'm going home to my own apartment tonight," he said. He looked around the shabby room, his eyes shining not with coke but with tears. "I wish I had helped Fitz when it still could have made a difference."

"How could you, Corky, if he didn't tell you the truth about what was going on? He should have taken some of those bricks out of his own bag."

"Yeah. I'm just getting my own load adjusted."

"Me too." I pressed his hand. "You're doing right by him now."

He turned off the light and we left Fitz's desk in the banquet sales office as we'd found it.

36

Corky and I stood behind the family and friends who gathered around Lee's grave on a cold September day a week later. Manny Cohen hung between his crutches like an old rug drying on the line. As the rabbi chanted in Hebrew the graveyard workers lowered the casket into the deep hole that was bordered with small mounds of freshly dug dirt. The wind blew the smell of earth toward us, then lifted the rabbi's words and Manny's wail above our heads and carried them away. Manny fought with his crutches to get closer to the grave.

The Cohen plot was crowded, and the hole dug for Lee sat snugly next to a pinkish marble headstone carved with a star of David and the words "Leopold David Cohen, Beloved Son, Brother, Patriot, 1923–1944." So Lee had been named for Manny's dead brother, the one who died in the Second World War. With a loud choking sob, Manny reached into his suit pocket and placed several small stones on his brother's grave. A slender gray-haired woman in a black silk suit moved toward him to take his arm, but he shook her away with a violent jerk. With the same fury he grabbed his left crutch like a spear and threw it into the hole that held Lee's casket. The second one followed and he fell to the ground. An empty wheelchair suddenly appeared, pushed by two men in black suits. They lifted Manny under the arms and placed him in the chair. The woman put her hand on his shoulder. Manny grabbed the hand and kissed it, quickly, before covering his eyes.

"Jews are supposed to bury the body as soon as possible," said Corky. "But they had to wait for the autopsy. It was the final blow." He wiped his eyes with the kind of white linen handkerchief our father used to carry in his suit pocket. I was touched by the formality of the accessory.

The early-autumn wind rushed again, sweeping around the black figures who had already begun to walk away from the grave. Several women reached for their hats and skittered forward as if the wind were pushing them off balance.

"I never thought I'd outlive either one of them. Fitz or Lee. I thought I was the one who lived on the edge," said my brother.

"Lee was reckless, Corky."

"But he always had his father protecting him. Or trying to. Lot of good that did him, in the end."

We stepped closer to the grave. Corky picked up a pebble that hid in the grass and put it on Uncle Leopold's headstone, next to Manny's.

"Do you want to go back to the house?" I asked him.

"Nah. I can't look at Manny and Pearl any more."

"Then come back to my office. Isaac and Roberta are supposed to join me for lunch."

One of the gravediggers lay on his stomach and used the retrieved crutch to lift out the other. Then he gave the nod to his coworker and they lifted their shovels to finish the job.

Kit was beside himself. I had reserved the small conference room without telling him why, and ordered the sandwiches from Mangia Tutti myself. As I paid the delivery man by the elevator, Henry Rawls appeared. His usually tidy silver hair fell across his forehead, and his bow tie was as crooked as if he had been attacked by the neighbor's dog.

"Julia, I must speak with you. Something terrible has happened."

I pushed two shopping bags onto my wrist and picked up the cellophane-covered platter. "Henry, can it wait until later? You can see I'm hosting a working lunch."

"But Samuel Reid has signed on to the Bellweather series. They're our main competitors! He can't sign on to our reading series and theirs. It's unethical. Not to mention a conflict of interest."

In his distress, Henry the Southern gentleman forgot to offer to help me. He simply followed me down the hall as I struggled to balance the bags and the platter. I reached the door to the conference room.

"Henry, I'm sorry. But the only interest Samuel Reid cares about is his own."

"I'll have to put our lawyers in touch with him. Oh, dear, Willis and McGee will be furious. These reading texts are their life's work. And they had to give the last installment of their advance to Reid."

"Good luck, Henry," I said, pushing open the door with my hip. "Let me know how it works out."

Corky took the tray from me and pulled sheets of cellophane off the bowls of salad. Once he had laid out the plastic cutlery and poured the sodas, we sat down. Roberta slid her chartreuse knit jacket onto the back of her chair and spooned some corkscrew pasta onto a paper plate. Isaac bit into a roast beef sandwich. Corky stabbed a slice of grilled eggplant with a plastic fork, examined it, and put it into his mouth.

I took a sip of sparkling water, and looked around the room. On the walls were blown-up jackets of the big books Beckham & Coates had published over the years. At the far right, behind my brother, was the original jacket for the hardcover of *A Native Son Bears Witness*. It was time to replace it, I thought.

Isaac caught me looking at the poster for Sam's book. "Not to worry, Julia. His time will come."

"Just not yet," I said. "I have to wait. Again."

"Girlfriend," said Roberta, touching the shadow of the bruise that my makeup still couldn't hide, "do not give up hope. It will be worth the wait."

"Julia and I went to Lee Cohen's funeral this morning," blurted Corky, as if he needed to keep the pain equally distributed around the room.

"So excuse us if we don't seem sufficiently outraged by the Cohens today," I added.

"Noted," said Isaac. "Why doesn't Roberta tell you what she confirmed about how the reading tests were switched? Might get you mad all over again."

"Here's the story," she said. "Manny had lobbied for Fly Express, a local delivery service, to get the Board of Ed contract. Then it was simple. In the targeted schools, the men who picked up the sealed test packages substituted them with ones they'd received from Lee. Because of U-CAN, Lee knew everything he needed to prepare the packages in advance—students' names, teachers' ID numbers. Later Lee paid the overnight delivery men in cash or drugs."

"I'd still love to know who actually filled out all those fake tests," said Corky. I remembered all those ladies with fat arms who worked for Manny at the Bronx Democratic Club and wondered what kept them busy at their tables in the slow time between campaigns. "Fitz would have gone berserk if he saw them," he said. His eyes filled, again.

"Maybe he did, brother," said Isaac. "Alas, we'll never know."

"Sylvie Barr couldn't join us today, because of a conference," I pressed on, "but she sent this report." I unfolded the many columns of her computer-generated four-color chart. "As she suspected, the U-CAN schools had the highest number of Saldivar-placed teachers. The two went hand in hand. But look at this: the six schools with the highest number of untrained teachers are also the ones up for takeover by Walker Communications."

"Ba-bing," said Corky.

Roberta slipped gold-framed reading glasses onto her nose and leaned forward on her elbows.

"That's what I was talking about last week. Remember, Jule?" said my brother. "The reason behind it all. Lee and Eddie, they were just pawns."

Isaac pulled the chart toward him. His face paled almost to yellow, as if his blood had stopped circulating above the neck. I looked at Roberta. The bow of her full mouth had pulled into a tight line.

"The horrible thing is, it's too late to stop the vote on the charter schools," I said. "With the fake tutors and the shitty teachers Saldivar hired, those parents must be desperate. Of course they'll vote for Walker to take over."

"So the mayor gets away with it?" asked Corky. "It's almost brilliant."

"Tom has enough to go after Saldivar. But I don't think anyone can touch the mayor. Even now." I folded and unfolded the corner of Sylvie's report, until a small triangle of the paper tore free.

"Wait," said Isaac. "Just wait. He hasn't gotten away with it yet." He closed his eyes, as if he was about to meditate.

"But it would take forever for the DA to build this case. How could you prove intent?" protested Roberta.

"Let's not focus on the mayor," he said, in a still voice that seemed to travel above his body. "Who really has the most to gain or lose?"

I stared at him. He opened his eyes.

"Follow the money," he said. "Follow the *money*."

"The money leads to Walker," I said.

"And money doesn't like trouble, does it Sister Julia?"

"But how could we touch him? He's a multimillionaire with an army of protectors."

Roberta drummed her perfect peach-colored nails on the table. Then she patted the wood-toned laminate in excitement. "I know. I know. Tell Walker you want him to write a book," she said. "You've gotten close to all sorts of hotshots that way, haven't you?"

"Yes, but usually—"

"You can do it," she cooed. As she rubbed my shoulder an inspiring whiff of coconut and mango lotion came my way. "We have faith in you."

Isaac smiled. "There you go."

37

"How do I look?" I asked, standing in Mel's doorway.

She spun around from her email. "Great. I like the jacket and pants combo. Brown is the new gray. Which was the new black."

"Then wish me luck. I'm meeting Walker in his office."

"Don't worry. You'll have him eating out of your hand. Remember—all these business gurus want to write a book. It's become the requisite middle-age act of self-creation. Like having a mistress used to be."

I waved and made my way to the ladies' room mirror, where I gave a final tug to the jacket of my suit and patted my nose with powder one last time. In the lobby Pat Muldoon stormed from the corridor that was home to Leigh Fleming and her junior fiction angels.

"Julia Moran," she acknowledged, lifting her voice at the end as if she were asking me a question.

"Pat. Great to see you." I smiled. "I'm on my way to talk to John Walker about doing a book."

"Of Walker Communications? Fantastic. Make sure he's willing to give up the dirt about that waitress in Atlanta. That's what people want to read."

I nodded, though I didn't have a clue what she was talking about. I pressed the elevator button. "By the way," I said, as she started to walk away. "Great news about Malefa Mfume, isn't it?"

"Great?" she asked, hesitating.

"She's been angling for senior VP over at Sugar Hill for so long. I'm glad they promoted her and finally gave her what she deserves. Aren't you?"

"Thrilled." She flashed the white teeth at me and changed course, heading for the hall where Mel and I sat. Oh well. If it was Mel's turn, she could handle it.

The reception area outside John Walker's office was designed like some kind of futuristic harem. In what used to be called a conversation pit, soft ultra-suede cushions surrounded a gleaming ebony table that held eight flashing television monitors, each set to a different channel. I struggled to keep from sinking into the pillows, but no matter how I positioned myself, my knees were higher than any other part of my body.

After about thirty minutes had passed, a male secretary in black cashmere announced that Mr. Walker was ready. As I followed him I shook my left foot, which had fallen asleep.

"Thanks for making time to see me, Mr. Walker," I said, admiring the floor-to-ceiling glass windows that formed an entire wall of his thirty-fifth-floor office at Rockefeller Center.

"Not at all, Miss Moran. It's my pleasure." He led me away from the brushed stainless steel desk and chairs to a leather sofa the color of eggnog, and positioned himself in a matching leather chair with his back to the door. It was the practiced, considerate choice, so that I wouldn't be forced to squint at him against the glare of the light from the windows. "I've always wanted to tell my story, my philosophy." He unbuttoned the jacket of his dark gray suit and crossed his legs. He had decided that he looked good in middle age, and he was right.

"I brought some catalogs to show you," I said, trying to ignore the four television screens that flashed mutely on the wall behind the desk. Monitors were clearly a key part of the decor at Walker Communications. I placed the booklets on the glass coffee table. "I want to tell you all about the benefits of an independent house like Beckham & Coates, how we'd get behind a major author like yourself. But first I thought we should get to know each other a bit. I'd love to hear about where you think you'll be taking Walker Communications next."

"It's been a remarkable ride," he said, stretching his arms on the back of his chair. "I never could have predicted I'd take my dad's local radio syndicate this far."

"That's right, you grew up in New York. You and the mayor were friends, right?"

"Yes. We went to grammar school together. St. Raymond's in Parkchester. When I transferred into the fourth grade, he was fighting to bring Little League to our parish. Ten years old, determined to break the sports monoply of the Catholic Youth Organization and those damn basketball teams." He chuckled at the memory. "He's always been a fighter. Me, I just got my father to sponsor the uniforms and the coach. We were in business."

"Well, he's put a lot on the line for your charter schools. The referendum comes up for vote on the general election day, doesn't it?" Not too fast, Julia, I thought to myself. Take your time casting this line.

"Trust me, Miss Moran. Privatization is the wave of the future. Break through all that Soviet-style red tape at the Board of Ed. Run the schools for results, and profit. I'd want that to be part of the book. The Walker philosophy. No red tape!"

"Of course. And you're taking the company public early in the new year, aren't you?"

"The exact timing of the IPO is still up in the air. It depends on several different factors. But I'd certainly be willing to include my editor among the 'friends and family' who get to buy shares at the offering price." He smiled with the easy grace of a man used to making presentations to investors who were not as smart as he was. "Not many IPOs worth much these days. But Walker Communications is top value, I can assure you."

"All sorts of nonfinancial issues affect an IPO, right?" I asked. "Say, good or bad publicity?"

To my surprise, he answered eagerly. He was so accustomed to holding forth that he didn't think twice about the actual question being put to him. "Sure, sure. A company can be in great shape financially and investors might pull out at the last minute if they smell something wrong. It's all very delicate."

I took a sip of water from the smooth crystal tumbler that sat on a black rubber coaster on the glass table in front of me. I spoke with deliberate nonchalance, not wanting to blow my chance. "Forgive me, Mr. Walker—I'm just so fascinated by all of this. I'd love to know more about the kinds of bad publicity that might get in the way of an IPO. Say, for example, there was financial impropriety? Someone cooking the books?"

"Of course, of course. But that's what the due diligence boys are for at the investment bank."

"What if you suddenly lost major talent to a competitor?"

"Wrong person leaves at the wrong time, could certainly look bad. That's why I work so hard to keep our people happy. Can't lose the war for talent." His cluck told me he knew the stock options weren't flowing at Beckham & Coates.

"And if it was reported in the news that you were associated with a very corrupt political figure? Would that hurt the IPO?"

He stroked the buttery leather of the cushion of his chair, as if it were the family pet. "It might. Might not. Depends on what you mean by 'associated.' "

"Say that this corrupt figure was the mayor of a major city, and he'd gone to great lengths to create an opportunity for you," I continued. "What would happen if he'd hired untrained teachers and allowed a fraudulent tutoring group into a handful of weak schools—all so that the parents in those districts would approve a charter allowing you to take them over? Would that be bad for your public offering?"

He fixed his eyes on me as if he'd just noticed that I was in the room. "If it were true, yes. Not if it were nonsense." He leaned forward and clasped his hands between his knees. "But tell me, Miss Moran—hypothetically speaking—why would I allow myself to be associated with any irregular practices? I've built an enormously successful business already."

"New York is a huge city. With a lucrative eleven-billion-dollar school system. A foot in the door could lead to lots of money down the line. But that's not the only reason. You'd love the chance to break through the red tape. Get a crack at doing it right."

He actually smiled. "Go on. I like the way you think."

"As for this hypothetical mayor—maybe he'd like to prove to his old friend that he can deliver something tangible and important. He can't deliver the uniforms, but he can deliver the playing field, the players. Or maybe he's just another one of those 'friends and family,' itching to get in on the stock. Politicians aren't well compensated in the war for talent." I almost hated pitting the mayor's lifetime of desperate and eager hard work against the easy machinations of his slick friend. But I could live with it.

Walker stood up and walked over to the window, his hands in his pockets. "The kind of story you describe might interfere withour public offering, yes. If it were true. Happily, in this case it's not."

"But if even a whiff of accusation hit the press, it would harm you, wouldn't it?"

He turned and faced the televisions. One played a financial channel charting the ups and downs of the day's stock prices in a colored band that ran in front of the face of a man reading from a TelePrompTer. Two others were set to the same program, where children sat at a table with a woman who was doing simple arithmetic using felt numbers on a board. Cartoon dogs dressed as letters of the alphabet flashed from the fourth. Blue "W" logos blinked in the bottom right corner of every screen.

"Bad press is always bad for business," he said. "It's not like Hollywood. Or books. What do you say? There's no such thing as bad publicity? In business, there is."

"You understand, Mr. Walker. I have to explore these possibilities because the value of your book goes up or down with the value of your image in the eye of the public."

"Of course."

I crossed my wrists in my lap and bounced my new expensive Italian loafers. Low heels.

Walker turned from the screens and rested on the edge of his desk, facing me. "Miss Moran. I don't think we have anything to worry about here. I don't think there will be anyone holding public office who can interfere with the IPO of Walker Communications."

"I like the way you think, Mr. Walker. Tell me more." I pinched my own arm so that my excitement wouldn't show.

"Suffice it to say that the hornet's nest of New York is not worth the trouble. Certainly not for me. And being mayor is an awful job. No one wants to do it for too long." He returned to the eggnog chair. "Now, why don't you tell me what Beckham & Coates would do for my book?"

As I'd done so many times before, I began my pitch for the marketing and sales strategies we'd use to build his book into a best-seller, from prepublication buzz with the accounts to key national media bookings after publication. Two hours later we were still there, and he was dictating ideas for the book outline into a small handheld computer that was outfitted with state-of-the-future voice recognition software.

38

The heavy crystal of the chandeliers glinted with the obvious prosperity of a hotel determined to remain every tourist's idea of "class."

"I've never loved the Plaza," said Tom. He looked more comfortable in his tuxedo than I had expected him to. In fact, the black jacket and tie suited him, throwing the red complexion into calm relief.

"Me neither," I said. "Except for a year in college when Trader Vic's was the only place in the city that would serve us drinks. Before my friends and I were legal."

"Trader Vic's? You gotta be kidding me. We just got fake IDs and went to Fiddler's Green on Fordham Road."

Together we moved through the crowd of well-dressed people who had gathered for the Hamilton Institute's annual Stuyvesent dinner. "I do appreciate your coming with me tonight, Tom."

"Happy to oblige."

"I just want to be clear that I'm not a right-winger, you know? I'm here for work," I insisted, unnerved by the genuinely happy look on his face. "There are always top police brass at this thing."

"Yes, I know." He smiled.

It was my brother's idea that I invite you anyway, I thought. So get that grin off your face.

The blotchy blond man who'd introduced the mayor at the primary party tapped me on the arm. "Excuse me. You're Julia Moran, right?"

I nodded. He winced as if it hurt him to talk to me. "The mayor would like a moment to speak with you in private, please."

"Here?" I twisted around. "Where is he?"

"In his suite upstairs."

I could hear my heart pound above the happy din of the crowd.

"Will you come with me?" I reached for Tom's wrist. "His office called me yesterday and I ignored them."

"Alone," said the blonde. "He specified alone."

"I'll stand outside in the hallway, then," said Tom. "Let's go."

The blond boy led us to a door on the fifteenth floor. He knocked and opened it with a key, gesturing with his hand for me to enter. The door closed behind me. I walked down the carpeted rose-colored hallway to the white and gold sitting room where the mayor stood by one of the small windows, looking out at Central Park. The room had the unfortunate air of a fancy women's powder room.

"One of my favorite views," he said, still facing the window. "Beautiful." He turned to me. "So we meet again, Miss Moran. Would you have a seat?"

"No thanks." I shifted my weight to the heel that wasn't caught on the carpet.

"No? Then I'll get to the point. You've been saying some very dangerous things to my associates. As has that troublemaker of Elijah's, Isaac Lord."

I waited.

"I'd like to persuade you to cease with these ugly accusations. What can I offer you? A cultural affairs slot in the administration? My book?"

"I'm afraid that a book by an ex-mayor isn't very valuable. Especially a crooked ex-mayor."

"I'm not crooked. And I have no intention of being an ex-mayor."

"Then you could always handle me the way you've handled other troublemakers. Like William Fitzgerald. Or Lee Cohen, for that matter."

"Miss Moran. I've never hurt anyone in my life. I'm—well, just ask John Walker. I was always the kid who didn't get picked for the team. Always the manager, never the pitcher. And certainly never the bully."

"So what if you get Eddie Saldivar to handle your dirty business. It's still your business."

"I can't control everything these ambitious young people do. Even Manny couldn't control his son. Jeez." He shook his head.

"You're wasting your time," I said, hoping that he couldn't hear the tremor I felt as I spoke. "It's way beyond me, don't you see? There's Manny, once he recovers—"

"Manny will be fine," he snorted.

"Isaac Lord. My brother. And of course, Sam."

"Reid works for me now."

"He does, for now. But that won't last. The minute he smells you're in trouble, he'll disappear. Trust me." I paused. "I know what he's like."

"Miss Moran, do you really think those kids would be worse off in a school run by John Walker's group?" he shouted. "Compared to those bored old union toadies who don't give a shit how they perform?"

The truth was, I wasn't sure they'd be worse off. But that didn't change things for Fitz. I said nothing.

"To withdraw from the ticket so late I would have to leave the state, or die. Or run for a higher office. It's not as easy as Walker thinks. He's so used to having his way," he said, as if to himself.

"Connecticut's not such a bad place."

"It's just that there are powerful people who'd be very angry if they thought I'd let things get out of control." He looked away from me toward the window. I noticed that the black color had drained out of nearly all the curls, which were now as gray as his sideburns. His shoulders sagged and the skin of his face hung as if he'd aged twenty years. The cocky man who'd pinched my arm at the Harvard Club had disappeared before my eyes, like a werewolf at dawn.

"There's always New Jersey," I said.

He let his weight fall forward, gripping the gilt wooden frame of the imitation French chair with his hands as if he were losing his balance. Suddenly I couldn't bear watching the change that was taking place before me. I almost felt sorry for him, and I didn't want to.

"I think we're done here, Miss Moran," he said, in the voice of an embarrassed old man who doesn't want to be seen using a bedpan.

I hurried down the pink hallway. Tom was waiting for me just outside the door, as promised.

In the elevator, the tight knot that had held everything together for so long started to come undone inside me, the threads pulling apart at last. I leaned into Tom.

"I think he's going to withdraw," I whispered.

"You're a brave woman, Julia," he said.

"Or a stupid one."

"No. Not that."

"Exhausted, then. And scared. What if it's not the right thing?"

I allowed myself to rest against his chest. Without thinking, I reached around his waist. His hands slipped beneath my beaded jacket and played up my rib cage to the curve of my breasts, where they stopped, waiting for permission to continue. Gently he touched his lips to mine. We rested there a second, before I opened my mouth and tasted the spearmint flick of his tongue. I stretched to my toes and let my hands roam over his lapel to his collar to the ruff of hair at the back of his neck. I felt his breath quicken. We kissed again. His hands slipped over my breasts and moved down my waist to the small of my back where they wrappped tight around me. I stayed in his arms, not wanting to move, for what seemed like an hour. I was still there when the elevator doors opened.

We walked into the crowd, dazed. I touched my own cheek. It was hot against my palm.

"I think I should go straighten up in the ladies' room."

"You look fine. And I'm not letting go of you now," he said.

I nodded, holding tight to his hand. "We'd better find our table, then," I said.

Like sleepwalkers at a carnival, we weaved our way through the crowd, our hands interlocked. Tom wouldn't even let go for the woman in pink silk with a cane who bellowed, "Excuse me" in an attempt to move between us. "I usually hate people who insist on holding hands in public, blocking other people's way," I said. Tom ignored me. As we approached our table, I heard someone call my name.

"Julia, I've said hello to you three times and you haven't answered," said Kit.

"Hey, Kit. You look great in a tux."

"Who doesn't?" His eyes popped when they took in who was at the other end of the hand that was wrapped around mine. "How you doing, Detective?"

"Pretty good," said Tom, still holding on. "Yourself?"

"Hey, lover, where have you been?" said a man with long blond hair who rushed toward Kit. He gave him a peck on the cheek before turning toward us.

"Gordon?" I said, raising my own eyebrow at Kit. "I had no idea—"

Kit grinned at me. I grinned back. We stood there for a second, pleased with ourselves and each other, and then found our seats at the table.

In his keynote address that night, the mayor announced that he would be withdrawing from the ticket for the election for reasons of life-threatening illness.

39

"So," said Mel, slipping a final mouthful of raspberry sorbet in her mouth, "Reverend Vaughn is the Democratic candidate for mayor after all?" She placed the long spoon in the stainless steel dish.

"Yes. Three days after the mayor withdrew from the election, the party committee voted unanimously to appoint Reverend Elijah Vaughn as their candidate," I said.

"And Sam is on the outs. Hah. Talk about putting your eggs in the wrong basket." She lifted a glass to her lips and glanced across the café where we'd been enjoying a Saturday afternoon rendezvous. "Too bad all he comes out of it with is a bruised ego."

"It's more than bruised. He's lost a lot of his support in the black community. It could get messy," I said, staring into the remaining sludge of a caffe latte.

"I'm sure you're right. Manny must have had something pretty awful on Sam to scare him into sitting in that hotel room for a week."

"It's definitely nasty. Enough to hurt his long-term prospects. Especially any shot at political office, or being president of a university." I still couldn't bring myself to admit to her how bad it had been. She would find out soon enough.

"Have they arrested Saldivar?"

"At the airport, about to board a flight to Costa Rica. Tom says the DA will probably give Manny immunity if he'll testify against Eddie."

"Tom? How is our favorite Irish detective?" she asked, without looking up from the leather bag in her lap. She placed several worn bills on the table and secured them with a glass. Streams of cranberry juice slid through the melting ice cubes.

"Great. He's been very good to Corky. And me."

"You're all becoming quite tight. How nice. Shall we?"

Together we scraped our iron chairs across the concrete. A breeze lifted my jacket out of my hands. It was one of those rare New York days when the air smells of the sea, and the caw of a seagull or two reminds you that the city bustles atop an ocean harbor. The golden light of Indian summer was abundant. But soon the sidewalk congregations that passed for outdoor cafés would disappear, the French-style sidewalk doors would be locked shut, and autumn would make its brief, brittle appearance before the gray slush of winter arrived.

Mel stopped on the corner of 18th Street and Eighth Avenue. "So are you done with Samuel now?" she asked.

"Yes. Yes, I can say that I am."

"Good. Then I would say that this whole adventure might even have been worth the trouble. Except for what happened to Fitz, of course. And Lee." She pulled me to her.

I rested at her neck, which smelled of citrus.

"Look, I have to run an errand up on Twenty-first Street. I'll talk to you later, okay?" she said.

Our lips met. Hers were soft and wet and tasted of berry.

"See you, kiddo." She winked. I watched her disappear into the sleek Chelsea crowd.

I turned down one of the blocks that had still not caught up with the brownstone boom to the west or the retail explosion to the east. It was a street filled with low concrete buildings that smelled of oil and metal and industry. Workshops for I don't know what. The light was fading and there was a feeling I did not associate with Manhattan. Of men in shirtsleeves leaning in doorways, weary and relieved that the end of the workday was here.

I thought of Fitz, and Lee, and my brother. I missed the easy hope of three college boys, drinking beer in the backyard, full of the promise their parents' labors had won for them. Rolling in the grass like puppies, before the realities of life hardened in their eyes. Before they became working men. The boys and their easy hope were gone. But at least my brother might persevere.

I too was weary and relieved, though I knew that difficult roads lay ahead. One final task still awaited me.

I sat in my usual place with the television muted. Its flickering light flashed silently onto the pages of the manuscript I had spread out before me. This was a piercing narrative of self-redemption that was also every woman's guide to financial independence. Author Marybeth Brown needed my help. I wrote my advice on pink Post-its and slapped them on the offending passages.

Finally the news flash came on. Reverend Elijah Vaughn had won the election, easily beating his Republican opponent. I dialed the beeper number that I now knew by heart. Isaac called me right back.

"Julia, baby. What are you doing home? This is a night to celebrate. Come on over."

"Sorry, Isaac, but I think I've had my fill of political parties in hotels," I laughed. "How's my brother doing?"

"Fine. Just fine. He seems to be smitten with a young woman from the reverend's original congregation. Never had a drop of liquor in her life, as far as I know. A Baptist through and through." The thump of a band pulsed behind him.

"Look, I don't want to keep you. We'll celebrate another time. I just wanted to hear it from the horse's mouth. We've won?"

"Yes, Julia, we've won. Believe it or not, Elijah Vaughn is the next mayor of New York."

"Then I'm going to proceed as we discussed."

"Name the day, Lady Julia."

"My meeting is scheduled for tomorrow. It will take at least a few days for things to develop. But the reverend should keep his distance. Now more than ever."

"Consider it done."

I shuffled the manuscript pages into a neat stack and secured it with a rubber band. Then I pulled the manila envelope from my briefcase. At first Tom hadn't wanted to give it to me. But Isaac had helped me persuade him that it was the right thing to do. The envelope and its files in exchange for everything Corky and I had turned over: Fitz's briefcase, with its tape and its tests and its lists, as well as Sylvie's careful reports. Not to mention Roberta's hard research. It was a fair trade.

Inside one folder were the photographs of Sam with other women that Tom had shown me when he first came to my office. Sam was laughing, hugging, kissing, squeezing. I stopped looking at the dates written in ballpoint in the bottom left corner of the backs of the photographs. If I started working out the calendar of deceit, my agony could still derail me.

The two other folders were thicker.

The first held the records of the case against Sam for rape the year before he went to college. A light-skinned black woman looked away from the camera as it recorded the bruises on her arms and abdomen and thighs. In the end she had refused to press charges. A note for the file from a social worker pointed out that such behavior was unusual from an overachiever like Samuel Reid, but he was young, troubled, working his way out of poverty. I didn't think he had been so poor as a kid, but maybe I hadn't remembered the story.

The second folder contained the paperwork from the sexual harassment suits. The earlier case occurred at the midwestern university where Sam had been teaching when he wrote his first book. The second case was from his last job, before he'd come to the City University. Tom had remembered it correctly. Fifteen female graduate students had banded together to file their complaint. I reread one of the transcripts:

> —And Miss Rotor, what did Professor Reid say when you told him you didn't want to sleep with him, as he was your dissertation advisor at the time?
> —He told me that if my reason for not sleeping with him was because he was my advisor, then I should get a new advisor. He said that I couldn't let a stupid thing like work get in the way of our obvious passion for one

> another. (Witness cries.) The whole reason I came here was to work with him! Who else would be my advisor?

I closed the folder.

I remembered a night years before. Dinner at an expensive Indian restaurant in midtown. The pink cloths hanging, the brass trays gleaming, the air shimmering with spices. A famous professor of African-American studies ordered a second bottle of wine. His new editor sat before him, thrilled at the opportunity to work with the great man.

"Julia Moran, I am in lust with you."

"Samuel, I cannot sleep with you. That would destroy our relationship as editor and author."

"Julia, if your reason for not sleeping with me is because you're my editor, you can forget it. I'll just ask your boss for another editor."

"You can't do that! Signing you up is my biggest coup so far."

"Then don't be silly and let something stupid like work get in the way of passion."

I slid the folders back into the manila envelope.

The truth was I had handed myself over to him. That I had loved his "can you believe I'm king of the world" laughter as we sat naked on my bed, fingers thick with Chinese food and each other. The dangerous thrill of knowing a public man's private habits. He was a thousand colors to me.

I balanced the large manila envelope on my knee. It probably weighed a few pounds. I placed it in my satchel next to the green envelope that contained duplicates of every document it contained. I could still change my mind. Take the high road. Transcend my pain.

A distracting floater drifted like an illuminated thread across my left eye, reflecting bright in the light of the TV. The doctor had said my eye might never be 100 percent. Debris in the vitreous humor.

I picked up the phone and dialed Nancy Meyers's voice mail at the *New York Times* to confirm our lunch meeting for the next day.

40

As soon as the stories began to break, mayor Elijah Vaughn issued a statement expressing his deep sorrow. How could a black leader fail to live by a higher standard of respect and love for women, and for all people, of every sex, race, and creed? The minister who had taken over the reverend's church in the Bronx offered to lead a prayer service for the redemption of Samuel's soul.

People say that Nancy might win a Pulitzer for her series, "The Invention of a Role Model." Her public hero/private monster theme was picked up by a host of magazine and television commentators when they discovered that Sam's story could be used as a mirror to reflect on every news story from racial violence in California to sexual harassment on Wall Street. I couldn't bring myself to watch the hour-long special, "Sam's Women Speak." But a whole new generation of scholars and critics are making their reputations commenting on the tragic paradox of Samuel Reid. In a decade or so there will be a movement to redeem him as a victim of stereotypes about black men and sex. But not now. Now there are too many facts. Too many sad stories. Too many women.

The first lectures to disappear were those at the black churches. Next, the black colleges started canceling, followed by the black professional organizations for engineers, journalists, nurses, and such. By the time Black History Month rolled along in February all the big universities had pulled out, too. The weekly syndicated column continued until Sam announced he was tired of defending himself. Word is that a beautiful French entrepreneur is pursuing him to be editor-in-chief of a new online magazine called *Noir Vingt-et-un*. And someone told me that he's slated to give the keynote address at the national disability studies convention next winter.

Isaac said that I shouldn't feel guilty about Sam's wife leaving him, as she's better off now that she's without the bastard. And, of course, Sam will always have tenure.

Tom believes that I've just forgotten about the bum, and he's almost right. He's thinking of starting a private investigation firm, now that he's got his twenty years. He says he'd prefer working outside the system. But I don't think he really means it. He loves the system.

Corky says, "good riddance." He wants me to start jogging every morning, just like he does. His new addiction is exercise. When he has to work late, his new girlfriend sits in his office in the second floor bar and reads her law casebooks. Then they use the weight machines in the hotel health club together. He says he wouldn't lose one minute of her company to a drink.

Mel just smiles.

I have to admit that sometimes the ache still visits me. Sits in my stomach and plucks at a nerve of pain. No matter how much I know, I can never know this: did I matter?

The other day I was in the R & B section of a midtown music store, searching for a recording I'd heard in a restaurant the night before. From the overhead speakers, Ella Fitzgerald crooned a song from the Ellington songbook. "In a Sentimental Mood." Something pressed on my heart. Around me stood men and women of every shade and size. All of us listened to the music together, swaying and humming and tapping our feet, carried by the melody to our own private places marked for desire, or hurt, or longing.

On the TV monitors overhead, Samuel Reid was talking to a female interviewer who looked like she was about sixteen. He had shaved his head and the iridescent sheen of his collarless silk jacket almost matched the shine of the interviewer's black Lycra shorts. No one could hear what they were saying. Ella sang. Sam laughed with his hostess.

I flipped through the Monk selections without remembering what I was looking for. The man standing next to me wore a familiar cologne that both alarmed and excited me. He spoke to the friend by his side.

"That brother on the TV got a raw deal, you know? My experience, white girls are hungry to do the nasty."

"I'm telling you, brother, no black man ever did himself any good messing with them. History of the race. I'll meet you up front."

I froze in place. The man who remained brushed against my side and rested there. From the corner of my eye, I caught the drape of a soft knit shirt in blue. I let my eyes travel up to the shoulders, then to the strong face. He cocked his head to the right and our eyes met in a smile. He wasn't as handsome or polished as Sam. But a gleam of laughter, of possibility against all odds, drew me to him. I almost reached out to touch the folds of his large brown hand. The hand with the gold band on the ring finger. I shook my head and walked away.

"No harm in trying, baby," he called after me.

When I left the store I untied my dog, Molly, from the parking meter where she waited, patted her red neck, and set out on the long walk home.

About the Author

Upon graduating from Harvard, Elizabeth Maguire entered the publishing world as an Editorial Assistant in the New York office of Cambridge University Press. Since then she has held various editorial positions that include Executive Editor at Oxford University Press, Editorial Director of the Free Press at Simon and Schuster, and Associate Publisher and Editorial Director of Basic Books. She lives and works in New York City. This is her first novel.

Acknowledgements

Though a first novel is a slight raft to carry a heavy burden of thanks, I owe gratitude to the many wonderful people who encouraged and supported my efforts: To Betsy Lerner, friend and agent, who believed in this editor's inner writer; to Herman Graf, who took a chance, and Philip Turner, for his insight and energy; to Arthur and Nina Maguire—especially Nina, who urged me not to wait; to my brother, the younger Arthur Maguire, for his invaluable information and inspiration; to Tim O'Mara, Mike Herron, Matt Fenton, Alison Field, and Dallas Murphy, who helped me get to the monkeys; to Marc Baum, for expecting nothing less; and finally, but most importantly, to Karen Wolny, who never doubted.